The War Ahead – Part II

Revised Edition 2010

Josh and Zeke's penchant for adventure, passion for love, and a monumental fear for their lives, have caused them to flee the family plantation in coastal South Carolina with no destination in mind, only a direction, to head west to live on the frontier in a land where no one knows who they are. Lacking experience in a wilderness life, and having little knowledge of dealing with and defending themselves from the highly experienced Indian warriors, they willingly leave their eastern civilization in hopes of finding a place so remote, they could finally be alone to allow their relationship to grow. Only the power of their love gives each man the strength, determination, and fortitude to endure all that the wilderness could fling in their faces. Their life and love inspire new friends, as they often use their skills learned in war to put their lives on the line to help total strangers survive as well.

They learn how to hunt wildlife for food, and track the ferocious Kaga Ozuye demon warriors to ensure the survival of their new friend Yuma. With the help of an old ally from their past, and John Bridger—brother of famed mountain man and explorer James Bridger, they battle renegade former confederate soldiers, and attacks by a vicious Sioux tribe. They sought paradise, but soon learn that finding a haven for love is a constant battle they must fight for, and they would do so, because they would let no man, beast, or wild Indian stop them. No matter how tough the fight, their love for each other still remained supremely more important than all that the world could throw at them.

Information on **The World Apart – Part I** is available at
www.ItsFiction.com

Books by TJ Johnson

The War Apart - Part I
(A Josh & Zeke Story)

The War Ahead - Part II Revised 2010
(A Josh & Zeke Story)

The Will
(A Brett & Chase Story)

Stranded
(An Austin & Ryan Story)

The Raceboys
(A Jack & Thad Story)

A Writer's Fantasy
(About His Favorite College Basketball Star)
(A Shane & TJ Story)

Gay Grifters
(An Eric & Tyler Story)

The Blackfeet Boys Part I
(A Kiyo & Windtalker Story)

Coming soon:

Crosshairs
(An Eric & Tyler Story)

The War Beyond - Part III
(A Josh & Zeke Story)

The Blackfeet Boys Part II
(A Kiyo & Windtalker Story)

Rock Solid Part III
(An Eric & Tyler Story)

Web Site and Release Information
Read A Chapter
View The Book Cover
Sign Up For Advance Release Notice
TJ's Blog
News
Details
Available at:

WWW.ItsFiction.com

The War Ahead

Part II

Revised Edition 2010

By
TJ Johnson

Dedication

This is booked is dedicated to my longtime friend Rick Wooley who has been there for me time and again. Every time we talk is like we just spoke the day before. His advice is well taken, even when he is right and I am wrong—increasing his value all the more. Good loyal friends like Rick are found only on the top shelf, and are well worth the reach.

Finally, to my fans who ask about my beagles: Huckie and Mickey. They are doing fine, getting older, gaining gray hairs, and always ready to meet a new friend. They love our new home, but not as much as they love their daily walks around the parks where they spend time making new markings and new friends.

Revised Edition Note

Many readers spotted a few errors in the type of this sequel, and I have written the rough draft for Part III of the war series called **The War Beyond**. This required a few changes to Part II to set up the new adventure. This revision gave my new editor a chance to work on the old story as well as the new additions. I hope you enjoy the story as much as I did in writing this revised edition.

ONE

Josh felt uneasy with the situation surrounding him so he hurriedly tied the final load of supplies as the second packhorse shook his head to discourage an annoying, pesky fly. Josh's twisted emotions flipped back and forth like the old black cook in the plantation's kitchen, flipping flapjacks from a hot, black iron pan. His brow wrinkled with worry because he felt a bit anxious to get out of Denver, a feeling that made the short hairs on the back of his neck rise like a cat hunched down in preparation for a pounce on a mouse.

He and Zeke had left Josh's home in Charleston at the end of the War Between the States almost three years ago. Their time together had flown by with daily adventures in hunting and fishing, finishing their cabin, barn, and smokehouse, and trying to grow crops in the rock-filled fertile soil. He often wished he had paid more attention to the plantation's crops, as they both learned everything about farming the hard way. Except for stops in the towns and cities along their journey to northern Colorado, and occasional trips to a mercantile in Denver for supplies, the couple remained in seclusion, but deliriously happy to take as much joy as possible from their daily escapades together. They savored every moment they could spend with the other—especially after their many years apart during the war. They still believed they needed no one else to make their lives complete, and Zeke, in particular, felt he had not yet caught up on all the days of making love they missed during the war. They could communicate in silence with a look, a wicked wink, a fretful frown, or even a sweet smile.

Josh walked around to his horse to put a few small items he purchased in his saddlebags before tying the leather straps. He placed ammunition in one bag, and loaded the other with a bag of hard candy, a shaving razor, a deck of cards, several books, including one on farming, and several out-of-date newspapers that still read new to him. Just as he was tying the straps, he noted a group of rough looking men riding slowly into the town. He casually moved around to the front of his horse, doing his best to remain hidden. As they rode past, he stood as still as a statue, while remaining between the boardwalk and the hitching rail, turning his face slightly from their view as they continued moving along. He looked towards the store as if looking for someone, while watching the riders in the reflections on the glass of the storefront windows.

He recognized their old, well-worn, dirty, grey uniforms, and spotted the big CS initials on their saddles, but they no longer looked like the honorable Confederate Soldiers they once were. He saw before him a hybrid of beaten soldier and poor cowboy. Each man's hat looked like the newest thing he owned, or more likely, the latest thing stolen. Josh read about ex-

1

soldiers becoming criminals, and he could almost understand it, knowing many were treated badly on the field of battle, or behind the tall walls of prison camps where former soldiers died daily in large numbers. It did not, however, give them the right to hurt others, he thought. He felt honor in being a soldier, even on the losing side, and these men instantly disturbed him. He wanted nothing to do with the renegade former soldiers, but old scouting habits from the war kicked in, and he counted the dusty riders as well as their weapons.

Becoming soldiers, for many of these men, had been a step up from the poor dirt floor farmhouse where many grew up. After years of free food in the army, it was hard to go back to working for your food. Stealing and pillaging became an easy habit, and killing a man was something they did almost every day during the war, and thought little of it. They had survived many weeklong battles where thousands of men died. They had seen the blood and guts of the worst of war and it changed them. They survived starvation by killing civilians over a chicken or even a single egg, and committed murder without raising their pulse. They no longer dreamed nightmares of the faces of those they murdered. They long ago lost their moral compass, and desperation became a mere direction in which to go. Josh looked cautiously over the neck of his horse, his face still hidden by the shadow of his hat pulled low to the top of his eyes. The gang caused a nervous itch to his scalp, and a damp spot in the middle of his back.

These were men who fought long and hard in battle, and grew used to never paying for food, ammunition, housing, horses, or clothing. In the war when supplies ran out, they ransacked houses, robbing the rich and poor alike, while caring little for their victims. He despised the men, without knowing a single one, but in his heart, he feared one of the dark brooding men might recognize him. His horse neighed at the smell of the group. He quickly rubbed the face of his horse to calm him down and perhaps avert their attention. Josh knew many months had passed since these men experienced a bath. He did not want any trouble, and promised Zeke not to look for any, but he watched them carefully while resting his hand on the pistol strapped to his right leg. Slowly, he removed the leather safety strap that kept the pistol from falling out while riding the steep hills to their hideaway ranch. He prayed he would not have to shoot to defend himself, or protect a citizen, but with a gang like this, it was best to error on the side of sensible caution.

Women and children, dogs and chickens, all scurried out of their way, as if a dark thunderstorm had descended from the mountains. Josh swore he felt a cold chill leave his body as the last of the men turned the street corner out of sight.

"Creepy looking bunch, don't you think?"

Josh looked around and found the owner of the mercantile standing nearby with a broom in his hand. He, too, watched the men carefully. Ed Leary, his wife Ruth, and their three children moved to Denver after a drought pushed away their dreams of owning a farm in eastern Missouri, but after moving to Denver, they returned to the store business. The latter brought renewed success, especially since the discovery of gold in the Rocky Mountains. Ed remained a good friend of Josh and Zeke's, offering advice and a quick wit. Their children adored both boys, but especially Josh. Every time he visited, he magically pulled the same silver dollar from each boy's ear, while producing a yellow flower for the little girl.

Josh smiled just slightly at his friend. "I think they are former soldiers with a big chip on their shoulder," he replied as he turned to grasp the hand of his friend. His smile grew a bit larger. "Mind you keep you and your family out of their sight. These men can no longer be trusted to be honorable and decent, if you get my meaning."

Ed shook his hand firmly, while returning the smile. "Thank you. I will take your advice with great care. You and Zeke need to watch your backs as well. The negotiations with the Indians are not going well. Last week, they burned two farms east of here to the ground, with most of the families killed and two children missing. I know white settlers and the government did the poor savages wrong, but their raiding parties and scalping is forcing the army into a fight the Indians can't possibly win."

"I'll see you when I see you," said Josh as he grabbed the reins of his horse and swung into the saddle.

"Ride safe, and you boys come for dinner when you can," replied Ed.

"We will and thank you. I'll bring you a deer roast."

Josh tipped his hat to Ed, pulled on the twisted rawhide leads of the two packhorses, and began his journey out of town. He had only passed a few stores when he heard a gunshot. Instantly, and without thinking, he drew his pistol, while prodding his horse with his spurs to keep moving. He looked in no particular direction, but rather allowed his peripheral vision to capture any movement. His reaction was the result of his raider work behind the enemy lines during the war, where a moment of hesitation could result in the loss of his life, or the lives of his friends. His brain ruled out all of the town's normal habits and routines, and zeroed in on one of the rough riders with a bottle of liquor in his left hand and a pistol in his right, as he stumbled down the steps to the saloon. Josh turned his head away as the man shot his pistol once again into the air.

"Just a drunk," he muttered to himself, and then kicked his horse to hurry out of town. "It's time for us to go home, old boy. Time to go back to our peaceful and quiet mountains," he repeated in a whisper. He holstered his pistol, and tied off the horse leads to his saddle horn as they left the streets of Denver.

He galloped his horse and the packhorses for over a mile before relaxing his palm on the handle of his pistol, and felt thankful to be heading back to their mountains. As he crested the ridge of the first mountain, he paused to study the trail to the town, checking for followers attempting to track his trail. He waited ten minutes to be sure, and then moved on after seeing nothing moving in his direction. He looked at the northwestern sky and saw a rain cloud. A few more days of rain, he thought. "Just what I need," he said to no one. He squeezed his strong inner thighs and the well-trained horse leaped forward. "Hee-yah!" he exclaimed.

On the ridge of a beautiful mountain a few miles east of their cabin, Zeke knelt in the middle of a group of bushes, trying his best to remain silent, still, and hidden. He wished the gnat swirling around his face would go away. He dared not move a single muscle to swat the irksome creature because one little sound, one glimpse of movement, and the doe would surely leap and scamper quickly out of his line of sight. Nervously, his finger twitched as he waited for just the right moment. He pulled the rifle tight to his shoulder, and exhaled as Josh had taught him at the military academy before the war. In the mountains, he learned how to hunt, a skill he had not learned as the son of a Maine fisherman. Finally, the moment came. He pulled the trigger. Boom! The crisp shot caused the birds to fly from the trees, while rabbits and squirrels darted into holes, and his horse neighed loudly.

Quickly he stood up, and watched the deer take but three steps before kneeling over and hitting the ground with a thud. He grinned, knowing it had been a good shot, and the deer would provide fresh meat for their winter stores. He walked back to his horse, put the rifle in the long pouch underneath his right stirrup, and swung into the saddle. Carefully, he maneuvered his way around the briar thicket he had hidden in, and meandered over to the fallen deer. He tied the reins for his horse to a tree limb, and checked to make sure the doe had expired. He threw the deer over the back of his horse, and tied it tightly to prepare for the up and down terrain on his journey home. The horse did not like having the freshly killed deer on his back, but with Zeke's thirty kills this season, the animal had reluctantly grown accustomed to it.

Zeke glanced up and saw rain clouds moving in. He hated riding his horse in the rain, but knew the rain was good for the earth. He grew up in the far north and could take the cold, but damp and cold felt miserable at best. If he left now, he could be home by dark, he thought, and perhaps beat the rain to the cabin. He turned his horse towards the trail leading over the mountain to the west, back towards their valley, and squeezed the horse with his legs to put her into a trot.

They had found their valley in the mountains at just the perfect time of the year. Fall had just begun, the leaves were golden, and yet the grass still green. The creek and rivers flowed with beautiful clear water, and they found the game plentiful. They had but sixty days to build a place to live before the first of many snows, store up supplies and meat, and create winter clothes to keep their lean bodies warm, and food for their horses. The winter arrived on the predicted "Farmers' Almanac" schedule, but was far worse than anything Zeke experienced in Maine as a child. The snow rose higher and faster, while the temperature descended rapidly. It did not return to light jacket weather until late April. The months preparing for winter raced by, but after the snow began falling, they were forced to slow down on the chores.

With two winters under their belts, they knew what to expect and how to prepare. They added a barn for the animals after the first winter, and a smokehouse for their venison. They used a cave as cold storage in the summer time, and later found gold there after a lucky cave-in. They became rich from their find, but told no one, and certainly never acted as if they had a lot of money. They loved their new way of life, and plotted carefully on how to preserve their paradise and their time together.

Near the top of the ridge, the ears of his horse suddenly rose, so he pulled her to a stop while trying to hear what she might have heard. "What is it girl?" he whispered.

He turned his head in each direction, and picked up the faraway sound of gunshots. The shots came from the east, but most likely on the plains, or the edge of their land. He did not mind settlers passing through, but he dreaded the day he had to tell a family they must move on when they thought they had found their new farmland. At least once or twice a month, they would ride to the high ridges and scan their land for any sign of settlers, hoping to alert the farmers before they began building a cabin.

He moved his horse to the crest of the mountain, and tied her off. He walked to the edge, and looked down into the valley. He spotted a stream of smoke. He hustled back to his saddlebags, retrieved a pair of binoculars he bought in Saint Louis on their way west, and returned to the ledge. He focused the lens until he had a clear view of the smoke. He followed it down until he could see a wagon on fire, and a party of Indians rifling through the boxes they pulled onto the ground. He moved the field glasses to his left, and immediately felt a pain of sadness. His eyes focused on two white men with arrows in their backs, lying face down in the dirt with their scalps missing. He saw a woman, stripped bare with nasty knife wounds across the pale skin of her back, lying dead near a wagon.

5

He wished he could do something, but knew he was not only late, but helpless to rewind the clock and prevent the attack by the Indians. His emotions remained mixed when it came to the Indians, as he knew the white men took their lands unfairly, and yet he knew from his history classes every civilization grew through difficult times of progress. His heart went out to the family, perhaps a father and son, and a dear mother now lying on the ground. He hoped they died as quickly as the deer on the back of his horse.

He moved the glasses once again until he spotted the leader of the group of Indians, a fierce warrior with black and white stripes beneath his eyes. The Indian held the bloody scalps in his hand as he shouted and yelped triumphantly to his warriors. Another brave lifted a spear in the air with chunks of white meat on the end. Zeke adjusted the glasses, and then gasped when he realized the spear held the woman's teats. It was a brutal death by a ferocious gang of murdering Indians. He felt there was no honor in killing poor city folks who only wanted a new start as settlers in the west, with dreams of a happy farming life for their families. Zeke returned to his horse and sadly turned for home. It would be a day he would not forget for a long, long time.

By late afternoon, with only a few hours to go, Zeke couldn't wait until he arrived at their mountain ranch, and get some hot food in their cabin. He cleared a ridge and followed an old deer trail along the top. The trees had grown over the path providing a natural canopy. Zeke thought the trail beautiful and loved to pass through it on his way east to hunt. Even with the rain beginning to fall, he could see the spectacular colors of the fall leaves. He was tired from the long day after leaving before dawn to begin his hunt, but just as he approached a narrow section of the trail, and began weaving in and around some big rocks, he saw the ears of his horse abruptly point upward again.

He said nothing, but slowly leaned back in the saddle indicating a stop command to his horse. She did stop, and then slowly turned her head around to see if Zeke planned to dismount. Zeke remained absolutely still while carefully listening. He thought he heard the soft exhale of a breath, but was it the breath of a human or animal, he wondered. His right hand fingered his pistol before slowly drawing it.

Suddenly, he heard a scream off to the rear of his left shoulder. Quickly he turned, and caught a glimpse of an Indian flying through the air at him. He brought his pistol around to fire, but only got off a quick wild shot before the Indian knocked him off his horse, and together, they rolled down the steep embankment. The warrior tried to smash his brains in with a big tomahawk as they tumbled over each other. Zeke lost his grip on his pistol when he hit the ground, but gave the Indian a hard kick to the groin at least once before he grabbed the brave's right hand, which held the tomahawk, and smashed his wrist down on a rock. He flinched at the sound of the brave's breaking bones, but the maneuver worked, and the tomahawk fell away. The Indian screamed at the pain, but defiantly pulled a knife from his waist with his left hand. He snarled at Zeke like a wolf. It scared Zeke, but he knew he had no time to be scared.

Zeke pulled his knife from his boot just as they landed on a small clearing about twenty feet below the trail. The Indian took a quick swipe, nicking Zeke in the upper left forearm. Zeke would have given anything for his military academy sword, as he could have easily finished the warrior with a quick stab. Desperately, he swung the blade of his eight-inch knife to put the warrior on the defensive, but it did little to deter the Indian. Nevertheless, the warrior made a crucial error in judgment by leaping in the air at Zeke. Once his feet left the ground, his opportunities for adjustment left him with no backup plan.

Zeke sidestepped quickly, as if in a sword fencing fight at the academy, ducked, and came up with his shoulder, catching the sailing Indian in the knees and flipping him in the air. As he came around, Zeke lunged and stabbed him directly in the heart as the man descended. The Indian instantly collapsed on top of Zeke. Zeke scurried to get out from under the Indian, not knowing if the man died or not. He saw no movement, lifted the man's head, and found his eyes in a permanent gaze.

He did not waste any time, fearing other Indians could be in the area. He needed to get back to his horse, and get the heck out of there. He looked up the hill and spotted his pistol just ten feet above him. In an attempt to hide the body, he rolled the Indian over the edge of the mountain, but did not watch him fall, nor did he wait for the inevitable bone crunching impact when the limp body hit the big boulders below.

He hustled to his gun. Just as he reached for his weapon, an arrow flew through the air, slightly grazing his hand. Zip! Cleverly, he did not look at who shot the arrow, but continued his determination to reach his pistol. He snatched it up, and rolled to his right just as a second arrow flew through the air where he crouched. He brought his pistol up and fired just as the second warrior let go of another arrow. The arrow pierced Zeke's left shoulder, going all the way through with the arrowhead sticking out on the backside. The powerful punch knocked him to the ground, but this time he held on to his gun.

He took aim for a second shot, but saw the bow fall from the hands of the warrior, and then slowly, his limp, lifeless body fell downwards towards Zeke. The body rolled and stopped at Zeke's feet. He pulled the man over, and

7

noted the stripes on his face. They were similar to the ones he had seen with the binoculars on the Indians attacking the wagon. He wondered what tribe they belonged to. His bullet had hit the man in his right eye, killing him instantly. Zeke knew it was a lucky shot. With his good right arm, he once again dragged and rolled the warrior over the side of the mountain. Normally, he would have kept their weapons to add to their stockpile in the cabin, but now wounded, he kicked their weapons over the cliff.

He waited briefly for another attack, but none came. Carefully, he made his way back up to the ridge with his pistol cocked and held in front of him ready to fire. Each step over the briars and rocks made his face grimace at the pain in his left shoulder, but the adrenaline raced through his veins, the result of his fear and his close brush with death, and forced him to keep climbing. When he reached the ridge, he searched around the area looking for other Indians. He stopped long enough to break off the arrow as it went into his shoulder, but he could not reach the arrowhead on the backside to pull it and the rest of the broken shaft out. Touching the shaft brought tears to his eyes as the pain shot through his body, almost causing him to blackout.

He gave up trying to push or pull it out, feeling he needed to get out of the area before someone missed the dead Indians. He also feared they heard his gunshot, and if so, more of their warriors were rushing to the ridge. He studied the footprints and realized they had been trailing him. He also saw drops of blood and followed them back to his horse. They must have seen or heard him shoot the deer, and easily followed his trail by the blood dripping from the wound to the deer.

He bent down and studied the footprints carefully. Only two pairs of moccasins, but he felt sure there must be more Indians nearby.

He broke off the limbs of several spruce trees and wiped the trail clean, including the area where they fought. He felt it would be bad enough if they captured him, but worse if they knew he had killed two of their tribe. He led his horse down the trail, then went back and wiped the new trail clean, and continued doing so for about two hundred yards. Painfully, he climbed into the saddle and nudged his horse forward. When he reached a creek, he turned away from the cabin by walking his horse up the stream, trying to avoid leaving any trail for the Indians to follow.

It was then he almost passed out from the loss of blood from the wound. He forced water from his canteen down his throat, hoping his body would make additional blood. He placed a rolled up rag over the wound in the front to slow the blood loss, but he couldn't do anything about the exit wound. The blood dried around the shaft protruding from his back, slowing the blood loss. He left the creek and made his way to the cabin. Several agonizing hours later, he slid off his horse, and led her into the barn, closed the door, and staggered as he struggled to make his way to the cabin. He opened the door hoping Josh had returned from Denver, but the cabin remained empty. He latched the door, laid his rifle on the table, and made his way to the stove. He moved a pot of water close to the fire so it could begin heating up, tossed some recently split firewood into the coals, and began pulling his jacket off.

The pain nearly made him faint, but he sighed, took a breath, and tried again. It then dawned on him he could not get the jacket off because the arrow had pierced it on the front and back. He looked around the cabin for a tool to pull the arrow out. He found nothing. He grabbed a mirror and held it high over his head so he could see the arrow. The stone point was bigger than he thought it might be, and it stuck out of his back about two inches.

He moved to the center of the room and turned slowly, looking for a solution, when an idea came to him. He returned to the door, pulled up the latch, and slowly opened it just a little. He moved his back to the door, and carefully centered the arrowhead in the slight crack of the frame and the door. He pushed into the door with his back squeezing the arrowhead. Bolts of pain shot up his back to his brain. He felt he had only one shot at getting the arrow out. Once he had the door closed, he pushed back his hips tightly until he could close the latch on the edge of the handmade door, tweaking it just a bit.

He took a deep breath and tried to fall forward. The arrow held for a second, suspending him briefly before his body abruptly fell forward, leaving the arrowhead in the door. The pain overwhelmed him. Zeke hit the floor face first, mercifully knocking him unconscious.

Josh had pushed his horses hard, making the six-hour trip in four hours. He would stop and rest the horses, give them some feed, and then move on. When he reached the ridge just south of the cabin, he let out a whistle. He expected to hear Zeke's whistle in reply, but heard nothing. It puzzled him, but he kept going assuming Zeke was out on a hunt.

When he reached the cabin, he felt something was wrong. It was just too quiet, though it was close to midnight. He pulled his coat back and away from his pistol, just in case he needed to draw it quickly. He opened the barn and led the horses in. He found Zeke's horse with the deer still on its back. It was an odd sight, as Zeke would never have left his horse saddled with game still tied on top. His heartbeat picked up speed.

Hurriedly, he untied his horses and closed the door. He drew his pistol and crept towards the cabin. When he reached the door, he stepped on something. He looked left and right, and then slowly bent down and picked up the pointed end of a broken arrow covered in blood. He pushed in on the door, but discovered it latched.

"Zeke? It's Josh, let me in," he said.

He heard nothing and tried again. He thought for a second and then retrieved his knife from his boot, and swiftly slipped it between the boards and pulled upwards. The door was tight, but on the second try, it came open. He pushed in a few inches, but the door stopped. He slid in through the small sliver of an opening, and discovered Zeke on his face on the floor with a dark blood stain on the back of his jacket, and a jagged torn hole in the upper shoulder.

"Zeke? What happened? Are you okay?" asked Josh as he quickly knelt down.

Zeke remained silent and cold. Josh latched the door, and then lifted Zeke and carried him to the bed. He gathered the pot with the warm water, and their medicine box, before returning to the bed. He began cleaning the arrow wound front and back. He managed to get Zeke out of his clothes, bathed the dried blood from his skin, stitched up the wound, and got him under the covers.

Then he began praying. He had no idea how much blood Zeke had lost, or how long he had been lying there, but it scared him. He sat at the edge of the bed all night, getting up just long enough to put another log or two on the fire, and make some coffee. Now and then, he would place his hand on Zeke's heart to feel the beat. Each time, he sighed slightly with a sweet smile of relief that it was indeed beating strong.

He kept his rifle propped against the bed, and wondered how far from home Zeke had run into Indians. This was the first attack on either one of them, though they both knew it was always a possibility. They had seen Indians on many hikes through the mountains, but felt the Indians had never seen them, as they always remained carefully hidden from view.

The occasional earthquake-like tremors, large geysers, and several small ones in the valley felt like a godsend to Josh and Zeke. The sudden exploding streams of steaming hot water terrified all the tribes. Zeke told him the tremors happened because deep beneath their land must be a dormant volcano. The hot molten earth heated spring water, causing it to boil until finally, it became too big for the cavity and spewed out the top like water out of a teakettle. There were numerous hot springs in the area as well, and the boys built the cabin just a few steps from a hot bubbling stream, creating an outdoor hot tub for them to bathe.

Several of the springs were too hot to get in for bathing, and constantly boiled like a pot of water on the fire. Many Indians believed the area the result of evil spirits, and did their best to stay away. Sometimes, the hunters would take a weeklong journey around the valley just to avoid it. For these reasons, he suspected Zeke had gone over the far ridge in the east to find game, but the sound of his rifle might have brought the Indians to him. He hoped they didn't follow his trail home.

While the valley and its bad spirits discouraged the Indians, it remained perfect for Zeke and Josh. There was plenty of wood to build a cabin, smokehouse, barn, and keep their fires going. The gold rush ended almost two years before their arrival, so many of the white men who came in the early wagon trains had long since moved farther west. They found evidence of their digging for gold, including some deep shafts into the side of the mountains as well as broken wagon wheels and tools. Denver just recently became the capital of the official United States Territory and thus, the town continued to grow. They could find all the supplies they needed at the mercantile while primarily living off the land for meat and vegetables.

Josh soothingly wiped the sweat drops from Zeke's forehead, and replaced it with a soft cool cloth. He spooned a few drops of water down his throat. He knew Zeke must have been suffering from a fever. His face was as white as snow, and his lips looked as if they were chapped. He leaned down and kissed his head tenderly. "Come on Zeke," he whispered. "You can beat this fever. You're going to get well. You have to."

Josh tried not to cry, but a single tear slipped from the corner of his eye to his cheek. He wiped it away, put on his jacket, grabbed his rifle, and went out the door to attend to the animals. He got the saddles off the riding horses, and the pack cradles off the packhorses. He removed all the bridles, fed and watered the horses, and hauled the supplies to the cabin. He dragged the deer Zeke shot outside to a nearby tree, tied a rope around its rear legs, and threw the other end of the rope over a high limb. He grunted and pulled until the deer hung a few feet off the ground to make dressing it much easier.

He started back to the barn to fetch his butchering knives when he caught a glimpse of the sun reflecting off something shiny across the valley to the east, on top of the ridge. He froze where he was and tried to spot the reflection once more. He feared it was the Indians that attacked Zeke, but he stared for several minutes and could not find it again. He quickly moved to the barn and retrieved Zeke's binoculars from his saddlebag hanging over the stall rail. He also grabbed his knives and returned to the deer. He started preparing the meat by removing the skin, and then faked a slight break in his work by moving around the other side of the tree. Quickly, he brought the binoculars to his face, and studied the surrounding mountains while hidden in the low limbs and leaves of the trees. Carefully, he moved panoramically from right to left, but found no sign of any movement anywhere. Relieved, he returned to his work.

He thought back to the first time he had seen a deer skinned and the meat removed. He was about seven and his dad had just returned from a hunt with one of his older slaves. He had two deer strapped across their packhorse. His father washed up outside the cookhouse before coming in and sitting down to begin a late lunch. He told his family about the hunt. Young Josh was fascinated at his dad's adventure, and wandered out of the cookhouse and down to the barn where two slaves pulled the deer into the air just as he had done.

The plantation owners killed deer so often they were wasteful of the hide, but here in the Rocky Mountains, almost everything might be useful. He pulled the hide off in one large piece and hung it over a limb to dry. He went back to the barn for salt and a clean hide, and laid them on the ground near the deer. He began carving up the meat, salting it, and then taking it to the smokehouse. He left his knives and rifle at the tree while making the short walk back and forth.

In the smokehouse, he snatched a section of a broken antler from a pile in the corner, and used it to hang the meat on one of the many cross poles near the ceiling where the smoke hung like a cloud. Just as he placed a big chunk on the rail, he heard a loud growl. Carefully, he stuck his head out the door, and looked at the cabin, but saw nothing. He crept out the door and moved to the corner of the smokehouse. At the tree was a small brown bear cub eating the spoils of the deer.

Relieved, he decided to try to scare the cub off, but just as he was about to leave his hidden spot, he spotted the much larger mother as she waddled into the clearing. She was at least four hundred pounds and brown in color. He thought she might be a grizzly, but so far, they had only spotted black bears in the nearby forest. She pushed through the bushes easily and joined her cub in feasting on the remains of the deer.

Josh scanned the area and could see his rifle leaning against the tree. He had not put his pistols on, leaving him with only his boot knife against an extremely large bear, who would most likely attack him in order to protect her cub. Thankfully, he had already cut away the best meat and put it in the smokehouse. He carefully relocked the smokehouse door, but knew if the bear got a scent of the meat, she could easily knock the door down. He hoped the smoke from the slow burning fire inside would warn the bear away.

He went into the barn, took the binoculars off his neck, and retrieved a big iron triangle he had purchased in Denver. He thought it might make it easier for them to signal each other. Josh taught Zeke how to whistle various types of tones, and even how to imitate various animals, including a turkey, an owl, and a hawk. In spite of the situation, he couldn't help but grin while recalling when his boyfriend from Maine said he was going to teach Josh how to whistle for fish. He was pretty sure Zeke was kidding him.

He moved back to the corner of the smokehouse, and cautiously leaned around to check on the bears. They were making quick work of the deer. Momma bear tore off a leg as easily as Josh could swat a gnat. He decided to wait a little longer, hoping if she was full of meat that she might be willing to leave.

Almost a half hour later, the bears seemed finished with their meal. He held the triangle in one hand and the clang tool in the other. He took a few steps out from the corner of the barn, and began slamming the clang tool down on the iron bar as hard as he could. It rang louder than he thought it might, making his ears ring. He kept walking towards the bears while continuing to ring the triangle. They immediately turned around in the direction of the noise and spotted Josh.

Terrified, the little cub took off for the woods, but momma bear was not scared as easily. She quickly stood up on her hind legs, and Josh gulped when he realized she was over six feet tall. She flailed her forearms in a warning at him. Her claws were huge, and easily capable of ripping through Josh's flesh like a knife through wet newspaper. She snarled a warning to him, and the effect froze Josh in his tracks, but he kept on clanging the triangle.

The noise must have irritated her, as she dropped her big paws to the ground, gave him one last large growl, a raspy snort, a swing of her right paw, and farted as she turned into the woods. Josh started moving forward again until he reached the deer. He lowered the remains of the deer and dragged the carcass into the woods. He knew various small animals would pick it clean in a day or two. He grabbed the hide, his knives, and his rifle, and went back to the barn, feeling relieved the bears had moved on.

He had made a mistake today, but he vowed he would not leave himself unarmed again. He knew if the bears had been the Indians who attacked and wounded Zeke, he would have most likely died, and they would have killed Zeke as well. He resolved to forever protect himself so he might also look after Zeke.

TWO

Zeke opened his exhausted eyes before dawn on the third day. Without moving his head, he let his eyes roam around the room. The only light in the cabin came from a low fire across the cabin. He looked to his left, and found Josh sound asleep in a most uncomfortable position in a homemade chair by the bed. Zeke smiled slightly while realizing Josh must have arrived and put him in bed. His mouth was dry, making it difficult for him to swallow, so he tried to lift his arm to wake Josh.

Josh had been dreaming about a fictional battle with the Indians earlier that evening, but as often happens, his mind moved to his past, and he found himself in the middle of trying to blow up the Yankee iron foundry in Pennsylvania. He saw his friend Skeeter die from a shot to the head while Josh tried to pull him over the wall. He hated his war dreams, and did his best to recall a better memory of a happier time, but his mind replayed what it wanted in spite of his wishes.

When Zeke touched him, Josh jolted awake as if suddenly bitten by rattlesnake, and quickly drew his pistol.

"Whoa," said Zeke alarmed at the gun pointed at him. "It's me!"

Josh blinked his eyes a time or two, and then half laughed as he put the pistol away, "How are you? I thought you were a grizzly!"

"I am thirsty. Can I have some water?"

"Of course, hang on." Josh filled a mug of water, and brought it to him. "Are you hungry?"

"I'm way beyond that. I'm starved. How long have I been out?"

"I think three days. What happened? How did you get shot with an arrow?"

Zeke took another long sip of water before replying. "I'm lucky, huh? I had been waiting in the briar thicket on the backside of Edger Mountain for several hours when suddenly a deer came into view. I sighted her carefully, waiting for just the right moment, and then dropped her with one shot. I put the doe on my horse and started home. As I rode slowly along the ridge, I thought I heard something take a breath. It was my fault. I should have immediately drawn my pistol and dropped off my horse, but I hesitated. A split second later, a huge Indian leaped across a big boulder, and knocked me off my horse, and together, we tumbled down the hill. He had a tomahawk, and though falling over each other down the hill, he kept trying to bash my head in with it."

Josh interrupted him, "That head of yours would have broken the tomahawk and scared him to death."

"Shut up, I'm telling you the story," shot back Zeke. He took another long draw of water and swallowed hard.

Josh smiled knowing Zeke was going to be all right as he still had his fight in him. "Okay, okay, go ahead."

"As I was saying, I broke his wrist over a rock while knocking the tomahawk away. He pulled a knife with his left hand so I pulled mine. We fought with knives and I killed him. I started back up the hill after my pistol, and an arrow suddenly grazed my hand. I snatched my pistol, spun, and shot. I killed the Indian just as he released a second arrow that caught me in the shoulder."

"Let me see if I have this straight. You killed not one, but two Indians?" asked Josh, while shaking his head in disbelief.

"I killed a deer, too. What did you do today or the other day?"

Josh laughed and thought a minute, "I chased a big bear and her cub away with a triangle."

Zeke gave him a confused puzzled look, "You did what? How could you do that? We don't even own a triangle."

Josh walked quickly to the kitchen table and lifted the black wrought iron triangle. "I had just bought it from Ed, so we would have a means of signaling each other. I did not know I would have to shoo the bear away with it."

"Why didn't you just shoot it with your rifle?"

Josh dropped his eyes and his face turned red, "Because I took the deer from your horse and began skinning it at the tree, I left my rifle against the tree when I took some of the meat to the smokehouse."

Zeke grinned. "And how many times have you told me not to go anywhere without my gun?"

"Yeah, I know. I take it you used the door to pull the arrow through? That was clever."

"Clever maybe, but it hurt like hell. I could not come up with any other options. What's for supper?"

Josh laughed. "You mean breakfast. It's almost daylight. I'll get you a plate. I'm glad you're awake. I missed talking to you."

"I can't say the same," teased Zeke. "I was unconscious." He paused a second for effect then added, "But you did look cute in my dreams."

While Zeke ate, Josh told him about the gang of rough riders in town. He warned him to avoid them no matter what he had to do. Zeke told him about the attack on the wagon train, and the killing of the three people. He told Josh he also saw scalps tied to the waist of one of the Indians that charged him.

15

"The black and white strips on their faces were the same as on the faces of the two Indians who attacked me. I have to tell you they scared me stupid. They snarled at me like a wild animal. I had no choice but to kill them. They never gave me a chance to say we're friendly."

"You and I both know our ancestors began doing the Indians wrong from the moment we set foot on their soil. While in town, Ed gave me several Denver newspapers, and a stack of newspapers from Saint Louis. They went back several years, and I read most of them while waiting for you to come around. I learned the gold rush was over in 1861, several years ago."

Zeke laughed. "Then how did we find gold?"

"Because we did not know the rush was over. I think we should continue to keep our find a secret, as those thousands of miners would come rushing right back to dig up our land. I doubt we can trust anyone with our secret. One slip of the tongue and our mountain paradise would become a nightmare."

"Do you think we should continue buying up land around here?" asked Zeke.

"Yes, but we'll have to continue to go slow to avoid suspicion. Anyhow, as I was saying, what I learned from the newspapers was during the war, they sent most of the army troops back east to fight. This left the plains of the western Kansas and Missouri, and eastern Colorado unprotected. The Ute in the Rockies, and the Cheyenne and Arapahoe from the plains, seized upon the lack of troops, and began attacking and burning out the settlers. All of this land used to be their hunting grounds, and the army took it without giving them a single dollar.

"I don't think the army left the brightest leaders behind because Colonel John M. Chivington decided to retaliate for these raids on the settlers. Oddly, this idiot used to be a clergyman. Like many folks, he used religion in ways that suited him, and not necessarily the teachings from the Bible.

"Governor John Evans wanted to open the plains as development land for more white settlers. He wanted to increase the population so Colorado could become a state."

Zeke added, "I guess being governor of a territory is not as much fun as governor of a state, huh?"

"You're probably right, at least when it comes to an ego. Evans increased the size of the Third Cavalry to run the Indians off their own land. Black Kettle was a chief of six hundred Cheyenne and Arapahos. He sought peace with the whites, and although they followed the buffalo for centuries along the Arkansas River, he moved his village to Fort Lyon to surrender, and made camp at Sand Creek."

"What happened?" asked Zeke intrigued and still hungry. "Can I have another biscuit?"

Josh smiled and got one from the stove. "I thought you hated my biscuits."

"Well, normally I do, but I am so hungry, right now these hard things taste wonderful. I might eat your boot next."

Josh laughed. "Well, anyhow, when Colonel Chivington arrived with the Third Cavalry of seven hundred men, the garrison at Fort Lyon explained Black Kettle had already surrendered. Disappointed, he replied no matter, and made his plans for attack on them anyhow."

"Didn't anyone try to stop him?" asked Zeke.

"I guess deep down, everyone was so afraid of the Indians they wanted the tribes pushed out of this area for good. Black Kettle was so proud of his peace agreement that he placed the American flag and a white flag of surrender on poles outside his tipi. Chivington and his troops, many of them drunk, arrived early in the morning on November 29. They hauled four howitzers with them. Chivington did not want any prisoners—only victory. With cannons firing, they charged the village.

"The terrified village of mostly women and children began running and scattering in all directions. The soldiers shot and killed almost everyone, but that was not good enough. They ripped open women's wombs, smashed the heads of children, stabbed old women with swords, and gunned down anything moving including animals. It was a bloody, gory slaughter."

"Did they arrest him?" asked Zeke.

"Not right away. At first he was considered a hero, and spoke on the stage of theaters in the area holding up a lanyard of over hundred scalps including the pubic flesh of women."

"That's disgusting!"

"Yep, but later Congress forced him to resign. In the inquiry, one of the soldiers said the reason they killed children was because they suspected they were spreading lice.

"Needless to say, the news of this massacre spread like a firestorm from village to village, and tribe to tribe. His shameful disgusting atrocities ignited a firestorm among the tribes. All of the Indians are on the war path, and you and I are sitting right in the middle of it."

"Jesus," said Zeke. "What do we do? Should we move?"

Josh dropped his head for a moment collecting his words, "While you were asleep I had some time to think about this. I doubt there is anywhere we could go where they would welcome two men who love each other. I also doubt we could find gold twice, as we were incredibly lucky to find it the first time. That money secures our independence forever. We also love this land. It

17

suits us. We especially love the beautiful mountains in the spring and the huge snowfalls in the winter. We hunt and fish all we want, and the game is plentiful. We have everything we need here."

"But what do we do about the Indians?"

Josh sighed, "Well, for one, they are afraid to come here. This is the land of the devil. They call the tremors and bubbling water evil spirits. They do not even hunt here. You were on the other side of the mountain when you shot that deer, and they must feel safe there. I say we stay, but we have to be more careful, and we must look for a way to make friends with the Indians."

Zeke started laughing, "I vote to stay, too, but how do you make friends with a guy that is trying to kill you?"

"Next time we'll stop them without killing them if we can. Then we'll give them gifts," stated Josh.

"Gifts? What have we got they would want?"

"I don't know, maybe a mirror, a blanket, a box of matches, anything as long as it appears to be a worthy gift."

"Right, and if you don't mind, I'll hold the rifle on them while you do the gift giving," added Zeke with a laugh.

"Do you have any ideas?" asked Josh.

"Okay, you've got me. I'll try it your way because I want to stay here, and I want to love you here forever. How about getting me one more biscuit?"

Josh laughed. "I guess you'll always love me as long as I keep feeding you, huh?"

"Yep!" replied Zeke between bites of his food.

"One more thing," began Josh as he tossed Zeke a biscuit, "I don't think we should go away from here by ourselves anymore. We should fear both the war veteran renegades I saw, and the Indians who want to kill white men. We should only go off our land together, and well prepared to do battle in hopes of not having to. Agreed?"

"Yep, but I'll need a few days until I can go hunting."

"You're right." He got up and grabbed his coat. "I'm going to check on the horses, and bring some meat in from the smokehouse. I'll be back in a few minutes. You finish eating and go back to sleep. The sooner you get well the better."

"Yes, mother dear," teased Zeke as Josh went out the door smiling and feeling greatly relieved his mate was going to be well again. He looked up at the fading stars as the sun began to rise far in the east and whispered thank you.

18

For the next four weeks as Zeke healed and regained his strength, they attempted to hunt while staying in their valley, but except for a few rabbits, they were pretty much unsuccessful. Apparently, the animals did not like living near the bubbling waters either. Early the following morning, they saddled up for a long hunt over the ridges. Josh placed gifts in each of their saddlebags in case they had an encounter with the Indians. They both strapped on two pistols, a long knife secured inside one of their boots, and placed their rifles in sleeves under their right stirrups. They were as armed as he was as a raider behind the Yankee enemy lines during the war.

One of the surprises Josh brought back from Denver was a high-powered hunting rifle, or as Ed explained, it was actually a Sharps buffalo rifle. It was a single-shot rifle designed by Christian Sharps in 1848. It featured a breechblock in a perpendicular fashion allowing the use of very large cartridges. Ed bragged the bullet would stop an elephant. Josh had laughed, though not sure what an elephant was. It also had an adjustable sight on top of the rifle allowing a very long kill shot with deadly accuracy. If fired from a distance, these guns could drop twenty or thirty buffalo before causing the herd to stampede in confusion. Zeke could not wait to see Josh put it to use on a big buck or a moose.

By midday, they climbed up the mountain out of their valley and into the same area where Zeke bagged the deer. They tried not to be nervous, but caught themselves looking around every rock and bush, anticipating another Indian attack. Nothing happened. They studied the ground for tracks both for humans and for horses. After a few hours, they began to relax, and fall back into their hunting mode, looking for four-legged movement ahead and below them.

They reached the knoll on the backside of the mountain. The view off to the east displayed the beauty of the mountains and valleys that made up the Colorado land they loved. The Spanish gave the territory its name "Colorado" meaning reddish color due to the terrain around the Colorado River to their southwest. However, to the north and east, the land was full of all kinds of life featuring animals, plants, trees, boulders, and high peaks creating a collage of many colors.

Zeke lifted his binoculars and began searching the area for deer. Josh used his eyesight and instinct as he had all his life. The hours ticked by, and not a single living thing crossed their path that they considered edible. Bored, Zeke swung his view around to the east where he spotted the wagon a month ago. He looked to his far right and then slowly began making his way to the north. He saw nothing.

"This is probably the most boring day I have ever experienced," whispered Zeke.

Josh smiled. "We're obviously very alone, should we have sex?"

Zeke grinned. "We're in the middle of a field of briars. I don't think I'm in the mood to get a thorn in my ass today."

"I was thinking of something much bigger sticking you in the …"

While looking through the binoculars, Zeke exclaimed, "Damn!"

"What? You found a naked Indian?"

"No, I see a group of Indians like the one that attacked the wagon I told you about. Here look." He handed Josh the glasses.

Josh scanned left and right until he found them. They were eight painted face warriors. He realized he had instantly counted the warriors just as he had done on his raids in the war. "Eight. They don't look too friendly."

Zeke teased him, "I'll stay here. You ride on over there and give them a blanket."

Josh replied while still looking through the glasses, "Very funny. I think these guys could use a few beers and to hell with a blanket. Wait a minute." Josh moved the glasses to his right. "They're waiting on something. Do you see that line of dust?"

Zeke took the binoculars back from him. Just as he lifted them to his eyes, a wagon appeared through the dust. "I see a wagon. No, there are two wagons. Don't they usually travel in larger groups like wagon trains?"

"You'd think so. Two wagons against those menacing eight Indians will be a slaughter. How far apart are they?" asked Josh.

"Six or seven miles I think. The wagon wheel dust gives them away. The Indians just have to wait for them to get there."

"Let's go," said Josh as he stood up and started back towards their horses.

"Go where?"

"We have to save them," stated Josh as he swung up on his horse.

"I thought we were going to try to be friends with the Indians," said Zeke as he swung up.

"Yeah, but not at the expense of the lives of those folks. Come on, we have to hurry." Josh kicked his horse.

Zeke knew he was right, but he could still feel the wound from the last time he tangled with these Indians, and he was not yet ready to face them again.

They knew the way down the mountain, as it was the same trail they used to find their valley a few years ago. Quickly, they rushed downward, crossed the river, and started up a hill on the other side. When they reached the top, Josh pulled his horse to a stop.

"We're too late, they're already attacking!" he exclaimed.

"What do we do?" asked Zeke.

"Let's test the Sharps rifle."

Josh swung off his horse and retrieved the prized rifle from the sleeve attached to his saddle. Zeke tied both horses to a tree limb, and pulled his binoculars from the saddlebag.

"They're swarming around in a circle around the wagons. The settlers are on the ground hiding and shooting from underneath. There is one white man down already. Josh, you'd better hurry."

Josh took the small leather satchel holding the cartridges and laid it on the big rock he was standing on as he knelt down. He lined the gun up, resting it on his left hand, and steadied by his elbow on the rock. He looked through the eyepiece. He could see the Indians, but they kept moving. He realized he was going to have to lead his shot a bit to allow for the movement like shooting a charging galloping buffalo.

"Josh, they just got another man with arrows. They are deadly with those things."

Suddenly, Josh pulled the trigger. The gun gave a hard kick, but he anticipated it by holding it tight to his shoulder. It was a long second, but the bullet missed the Indian he was aiming at, but hit his horse. It threw the Indian hard to the ground. One of the settlers shot him.

"Good Josh. Two white men, one Indian, and one horse down," said Zeke with a chuckle, as if calling the score of a game at the academy.

Josh learned a little from his previous shot. He knew with the hollering and yelling the Indians were doing, and the gunfire from the settlers, they had no idea someone from so far away was shooting at them. This gave him a little more confidence.

He lined up his next shot and was just about to pull the trigger when the leader reared his horse on his hind legs, letting out a big yelp. Josh rapidly adjusted his aim, and pulled the trigger, nearly taking the Indian's head off.

"Wow!" exclaimed Zeke. "What a shot. Way to go. You hit him like a watermelon on a fence post. Hurry Josh—do it again!"

Josh reloaded the single shot smoking weapon, and took aim again. Boom! He downed another Indian, and then another.

"Four Indians are down and four to go—yahoo! Wait a minute; they've given up and running away! Come on, let's ride."

Josh and Zeke saddled up, made their way down the mountain to the plains, and rode over to the wagons. The Indians, outgunned by the boys and the settlers, escaped quickly without seeing Josh and Zeke.

"Are you folks okay?" asked Zeke as he rode up quickly.

An older son crawled out from under the wagon, "Are they gone?"

"Yep, they've run off. Looks like we killed a few and you did, too. Anyone hurt?" asked Josh as he climbed off his horse.

21

A stout lady with teary red eyes slowly walked over to her husband lying face down in the dirt with three arrows in his back. She knelt down beside him, and started sobbing while rocking back and forth. Her two children came up beside her, knelt down, and tried to comfort their mother. Another lady under the other wagon trotted quickly to her husband. He died from a single arrow through his neck. Zeke surmised it must have cut his jugular vein and pierced his windpipe. There was blood everywhere, as he bled out like a butchered pig.

"You boys get some shovels so we can bury these men. We must hurry before the Indians come back with a lot more warriors. Hurry now!" ordered Josh, knowing the children were in shock. He felt it best to get them busy doing something as soon as possible. He had done the same with green recruits during the war.

Zeke knelt down to a boy of about ten. "Son, you walk up to the crest of that hill and watch for anything that moves. If you see anything, you holler out. Okay? Can you do it?"

"Yes, sir," replied the boy feebly.

"Where were you heading?" asked Josh to the oldest son.

"Fort Bridger. We were going to join a wagon train there on the Oregon Trail so we could go to the northwest."

"I'm sorry. That dream is over for now. You should not have been in this wild frontier with just the two wagons. You were easy pickings for the Indians. You must go back to Fort Collins and regroup. If you must go west, you can join a train there, or but if you go ahead as you are, you all will be slaughtered. I'm sorry for speaking harshly, but time is running short. Do you understand?"

"Yes, sir," they replied solemnly.

"Can you lead them back?" asked Zeke,

"Yes, sir, the trail was easy, at least until now. We saw Indians several times in Kansas and in Colorado, but they never hurt us. They mostly begged for food."

"That's the trouble. The white men have killed and diminished their main food source, the buffalo, so they will have to leave the plains, and then the white men can just take over their abandoned lands and sell them for farm profits. It is a difficult time. You must be better prepared next time, and travel only in a big group." Josh dragged the dead man into the hole.

Zeke pulled the other man to the shallow grave and began shoveling the dirt to cover the body as quickly as possible. Josh and Zeke helped them back to their wagon, tied the extra horses to the wagon, and loaded everybody up including the little boy from the hill.

"Sir, can you keep the cow?" asked the lady. "We can't travel as fast as we like with the cow tied to us. I want to get my family back to the safety of the fort."

Josh sighed. He wondered what was he going to do with a cow, but replied politely. "Yes ma'am. I can take care of the cow, and you're right. For the next few hours, I would ride the horses hard back towards the fort, but then slow down to a walk so the horses can rest. You don't want them to give out on you." He shook the lady's hand, and then the oldest son, placed his hand gently on the little girl's head, and patted the shoulder of the little boy. He walked to the back of the wagon and untied the cow.

"Let's go. Get moving. Turn them around in a tight circle and head back east," encouraged Zeke, as he slapped the wagon horses with his hand. "Hee-yah!"

The hunters stood there for a moment and watched them. "Let's hope the dust doesn't give them away again," said Zeke.

"Should I shoot the cow?" asked Josh.

"Hell no, you're talking milk, butter and cream. I'll drag her fat ass home!" replied Zeke picking up the rope, and tying it off to his saddle horn. He pulled on the cow that mooed a time or two in protest, and then started trotting after him.

Josh laughed. "Yeah, right, and I guess I will carry your fat ass home, too."

"My cute ass and you know it!" shot back Zeke over his shoulder.

Josh laughed hard, "Hee-yah! Let's get the hell out of here, but go southeast for a while just in case those Indians are watching us. We'll ford the stream and walk in it for a while, too. We don't want to show them where we live."

THREE

Zeke opened his exhausted eyes before dawn on the third day. Without moving his head, he let his eyes roam around the room. The only light in the cabin came from a low fire across the cabin. He looked to his left, and found Josh sound asleep in a most uncomfortable position in a homemade chair by the bed. Zeke smiled slightly while realizing Josh must have arrived and put him in bed. His mouth was dry, making it difficult for him to swallow, so he tried to lift his arm to wake Josh.

Josh had been dreaming about a fictional battle with the Indians earlier that evening, but as often happens, his mind moved to his past, and he found himself in the middle of trying to blow up the Yankee iron foundry in Pennsylvania. He saw his friend Skeeter die from a shot to the head while Josh tried to pull him over the wall. He hated his war dreams, and did his best to recall a better memory of a happier time, but his mind replayed what it wanted in spite of his wishes.

When Zeke touched him, Josh jolted awake as if suddenly bitten by rattlesnake, and quickly drew his pistol.

"Whoa," said Zeke alarmed at the gun pointed at him. "It's me!"

Josh blinked his eyes a time or two, and then half laughed as he put the pistol away, "How are you? I thought you were a grizzly!"

"I am thirsty. Can I have some water?"

"Of course, hang on." Josh filled a mug of water, and brought it to him. "Are you hungry?"

"I'm way beyond that. I'm starved. How long have I been out?"

"I think three days. What happened? How did you get shot with an arrow?"

Zeke took another long sip of water before replying. "I'm lucky, huh? I had been waiting in the briar thicket on the backside of Edger Mountain for several hours when suddenly a deer came into view. I sighted her carefully, waiting for just the right moment, and then dropped her with one shot. I put the doe on my horse and started home. As I rode slowly along the ridge, I thought I heard something take a breath. It was my fault. I should have immediately drawn my pistol and dropped off my horse, but I hesitated. A split second later, a huge Indian leaped across a big boulder, and knocked me off my horse, and together, we tumbled down the hill. He had a tomahawk, and though falling over each other down the hill, he kept trying to bash my head in with it."

Josh interrupted him, "That head of yours would have broken the tomahawk and scared him to death."

"Shut up, I'm telling you the story," shot back Zeke. He took another long draw of water and swallowed hard.

Josh smiled knowing Zeke was going to be all right as he still had his fight in him. "Okay, okay, go ahead."

"As I was saying, I broke his wrist over a rock while knocking the tomahawk away. He pulled a knife with his left hand so I pulled mine. We fought with knives and I killed him. I started back up the hill after my pistol, and an arrow suddenly grazed my hand. I snatched my pistol, spun, and shot. I killed the Indian just as he released a second arrow that caught me in the shoulder."

"Let me see if I have this straight. You killed not one, but two Indians?" asked Josh, while shaking his head in disbelief.

"I killed a deer, too. What did you do today or the other day?"

Josh laughed and thought a minute, "I chased a big bear and her cub away with a triangle."

Zeke gave him a confused puzzled look, "You did what? How could you do that? We don't even own a triangle."

Josh walked quickly to the kitchen table and lifted the black wrought iron triangle. "I had just bought it from Ed, so we would have a means of signaling each other. I did not know I would have to shoo the bear away with it."

"Why didn't you just shoot it with your rifle?"

Josh dropped his eyes and his face turned red, "Because I took the deer from your horse and began skinning it at the tree, I left my rifle against the tree when I took some of the meat to the smokehouse."

Zeke grinned. "And how many times have you told me not to go anywhere without my gun?"

"Yeah, I know. I take it you used the door to pull the arrow through? That was clever."

"Clever maybe, but it hurt like hell. I could not come up with any other options. What's for supper?"

Josh laughed. "You mean breakfast. It's almost daylight. I'll get you a plate. I'm glad you're awake. I missed talking to you."

"I can't say the same," teased Zeke. "I was unconscious." He paused a second for effect then added, "But you did look cute in my dreams."

While Zeke ate, Josh told him about the gang of rough riders in town. He warned him to avoid them no matter what he had to do. Zeke told him about the attack on the wagon train, and the killing of the three people. He told Josh he also saw scalps tied to the waist of one of the Indians that charged him.

"The black and white strips on their faces were the same as on the faces of the two Indians who attacked me. I have to tell you they scared me stupid. They snarled at me like a wild animal. I had no choice but to kill them. They never gave me a chance to say we're friendly."

"You and I both know our ancestors began doing the Indians wrong from the moment we set foot on their soil. While in town, Ed gave me several Denver newspapers, and a stack of newspapers from Saint Louis. They went back several years, and I read most of them while waiting for you to come around. I learned the gold rush was over in 1861, several years ago."

Zeke laughed. "Then how did we find gold?"

"Because we did not know the rush was over. I think we should continue to keep our find a secret, as those thousands of miners would come rushing right back to dig up our land. I doubt we can trust anyone with our secret. One slip of the tongue and our mountain paradise would become a nightmare."

"Do you think we should continue buying up land around here?" asked Zeke.

"Yes, but we'll have to continue to go slow to avoid suspicion. Anyhow, as I was saying, what I learned from the newspapers was during the war, they sent most of the army troops back east to fight. This left the plains of the western Kansas and Missouri, and eastern Colorado unprotected. The Ute in the Rockies, and the Cheyenne and Arapahoe from the plains, seized upon the lack of troops, and began attacking and burning out the settlers. All of this land used to be their hunting grounds, and the army took it without giving them a single dollar.

"I don't think the army left the brightest leaders behind because Colonel John M. Chivington decided to retaliate for these raids on the settlers. Oddly, this idiot used to be a clergyman. Like many folks, he used religion in ways that suited him, and not necessarily the teachings from the Bible.

"Governor John Evans wanted to open the plains as development land for more white settlers. He wanted to increase the population so Colorado could become a state."

Zeke added, "I guess being governor of a territory is not as much fun as governor of a state, huh?"

"You're probably right, at least when it comes to an ego. Evans increased the size of the Third Cavalry to run the Indians off their own land. Black Kettle was a chief of six hundred Cheyenne and Arapahos. He sought peace with the whites, and although they followed the buffalo for centuries along the Arkansas River, he moved his village to Fort Lyon to surrender, and made camp at Sand Creek."

"What happened?" asked Zeke intrigued and still hungry. "Can I have another biscuit?"

Josh smiled and got one from the stove. "I thought you hated my biscuits."

"Well, normally I do, but I am so hungry, right now these hard things taste wonderful. I might eat your boot next."

Josh laughed. "Well, anyhow, when Colonel Chivington arrived with the Third Cavalry of seven hundred men, the garrison at Fort Lyon explained Black Kettle had already surrendered. Disappointed, he replied no matter, and made his plans for attack on them anyhow."

"Didn't anyone try to stop him?" asked Zeke.

"I guess deep down, everyone was so afraid of the Indians they wanted the tribes pushed out of this area for good. Black Kettle was so proud of his peace agreement that he placed the American flag and a white flag of surrender on poles outside his tipi. Chivington and his troops, many of them drunk, arrived early in the morning on November 29. They hauled four howitzers with them. Chivington did not want any prisoners—only victory. With cannons firing, they charged the village.

"The terrified village of mostly women and children began running and scattering in all directions. The soldiers shot and killed almost everyone, but that was not good enough. They ripped open women's wombs, smashed the heads of children, stabbed old women with swords, and gunned down anything moving including animals. It was a bloody, gory slaughter."

"Did they arrest him?" asked Zeke.

"Not right away. At first he was considered a hero, and spoke on the stage of theaters in the area holding up a lanyard of over hundred scalps including the pubic flesh of women."

"That's disgusting!"

"Yep, but later Congress forced him to resign. In the inquiry, one of the soldiers said the reason they killed children was because they suspected they were spreading lice.

"Needless to say, the news of this massacre spread like a firestorm from village to village, and tribe to tribe. His shameful disgusting atrocities ignited a firestorm among the tribes. All of the Indians are on the war path, and you and I are sitting right in the middle of it."

"Jesus," said Zeke. "What do we do? Should we move?"

Josh dropped his head for a moment collecting his words, "While you were asleep I had some time to think about this. I doubt there is anywhere we could go where they would welcome two men who love each other. I also doubt we could find gold twice, as we were incredibly lucky to find it the first time. That money secures our independence forever. We also love this land. It suits us. We especially love the beautiful mountains in the spring and the huge snowfalls in the winter. We hunt and fish all we want, and the game is plentiful. We have everything we need here."

"But what do we do about the Indians?"

Josh sighed, "Well, for one, they are afraid to come here. This is the land of the devil. They call the tremors and bubbling water evil spirits. They do not even hunt here. You were on the other side of the mountain when you shot that deer, and they must feel safe there. I say we stay, but we have to be more careful, and we must look for a way to make friends with the Indians."

Zeke started laughing, "I vote to stay, too, but how do you make friends with a guy that is trying to kill you?"

"Next time we'll stop them without killing them if we can. Then we'll give them gifts," stated Josh.

"Gifts? What have we got they would want?"

"I don't know, maybe a mirror, a blanket, a box of matches, anything as long as it appears to be a worthy gift."

"Right, and if you don't mind, I'll hold the rifle on them while you do the gift giving," added Zeke with a laugh.

"Do you have any ideas?" asked Josh.

"Okay, you've got me. I'll try it your way because I want to stay here, and I want to love you here forever. How about getting me one more biscuit?"

Josh laughed. "I guess you'll always love me as long as I keep feeding you, huh?"

"Yep!" replied Zeke between bites of his food.

"One more thing," began Josh as he tossed Zeke a biscuit, "I don't think we should go away from here by ourselves anymore. We should fear both the war veteran renegades I saw, and the Indians who want to kill white men. We should only go off our land together, and well prepared to do battle in hopes of not having to. Agreed?"

"Yep, but I'll need a few days until I can go hunting."

"You're right." He got up and grabbed his coat. "I'm going to check on the horses, and bring some meat in from the smokehouse. I'll be back in a few minutes. You finish eating and go back to sleep. The sooner you get well the better."

"Yes, mother dear," teased Zeke as Josh went out the door smiling and feeling greatly relieved his mate was going to be well again. He looked up at the fading stars as the sun began to rise far in the east and whispered thank you.

For the next four weeks as Zeke healed and regained his strength, they attempted to hunt while staying in their valley, but except for a few rabbits, they were pretty much unsuccessful. Apparently, the animals did not like living near the bubbling waters either. Early the following morning, they saddled up for a long hunt over the ridges. Josh placed gifts in each of their saddlebags in case they had an encounter with the Indians. They both strapped on two pistols, a long knife secured inside one of their boots, and placed their rifles in sleeves under their right stirrups. They were as armed as he was as a raider behind the Yankee enemy lines during the war.

One of the surprises Josh brought back from Denver was a high-powered hunting rifle, or as Ed explained, it was actually a Sharps buffalo rifle. It was a single-shot rifle designed by Christian Sharps in 1848. It featured a breechblock in a perpendicular fashion allowing the use of very large cartridges. Ed bragged the bullet would stop an elephant. Josh had laughed, though not sure what an elephant was. It also had an adjustable sight on top of the rifle allowing a very long kill shot with deadly accuracy. If fired from a distance, these guns could drop twenty or thirty buffalo before causing the herd to stampede in confusion. Zeke could not wait to see Josh put it to use on a big buck or a moose.

By midday, they climbed up the mountain out of their valley and into the same area where Zeke bagged the deer. They tried not to be nervous, but caught themselves looking around every rock and bush, anticipating another Indian attack. Nothing happened. They studied the ground for tracks both for humans and for horses. After a few hours, they began to relax, and fall back into their hunting mode, looking for four-legged movement ahead and below them.

They reached the knoll on the backside of the mountain. The view off to the east displayed the beauty of the mountains and valleys that made up the Colorado land they loved. The Spanish gave the territory its name "Colorado" meaning reddish color due to the terrain around the Colorado River to their southwest. However, to the north and east, the land was full of all kinds of life featuring animals, plants, trees, boulders, and high peaks creating a collage of many colors.

Zeke lifted his binoculars and began searching the area for deer. Josh used his eyesight and instinct as he had all his life. The hours ticked by, and not a single living thing crossed their path that they considered edible. Bored, Zeke swung his view around to the east where he spotted the wagon a month ago. He looked to his far right and then slowly began making his way to the north. He saw nothing.

"This is probably the most boring day I have ever experienced," whispered Zeke.

Josh smiled. "We're obviously very alone, should we have sex?"

Zeke grinned. "We're in the middle of a field of briars. I don't think I'm in the mood to get a thorn in my ass today."

"I was thinking of something much bigger sticking you in the ..."

While looking through the binoculars, Zeke exclaimed, "Damn!"

"What? You found a naked Indian?"

"No, I see a group of Indians like the one that attacked the wagon I told you about. Here look." He handed Josh the glasses.

Josh scanned left and right until he found them. They were eight painted face warriors. He realized he had instantly counted the warriors just as he had done on his raids in the war. "Eight. They don't look too friendly."

Zeke teased him, "I'll stay here. You ride on over there and give them a blanket."

Josh replied while still looking through the glasses, "Very funny. I think these guys could use a few beers and to hell with a blanket. Wait a minute." Josh moved the glasses to his right. "They're waiting on something. Do you see that line of dust?"

Zeke took the binoculars back from him. Just as he lifted them to his eyes, a wagon appeared through the dust. "I see a wagon. No, there are two wagons. Don't they usually travel in larger groups like wagon trains?"

"You'd think so. Two wagons against those menacing eight Indians will be a slaughter. How far apart are they?" asked Josh.

"Six or seven miles I think. The wagon wheel dust gives them away. The Indians just have to wait for them to get there."

"Let's go," said Josh as he stood up and started back towards their horses.

"Go where?"

"We have to save them," stated Josh as he swung up on his horse.

"I thought we were going to try to be friends with the Indians," said Zeke as he swung up.

"Yeah, but not at the expense of the lives of those folks. Come on, we have to hurry." Josh kicked his horse.

Zeke knew he was right, but he could still feel the wound from the last time he tangled with these Indians, and he was not yet ready to face them again.

They knew the way down the mountain, as it was the same trail they used to find their valley a few years ago. Quickly, they rushed downward, crossed the river, and started up a hill on the other side. When they reached the top, Josh pulled his horse to a stop.

"We're too late, they're already attacking!" he exclaimed.

"What do we do?" asked Zeke.

"Let's test the Sharps rifle."

Josh swung off his horse and retrieved the prized rifle from the sleeve attached to his saddle. Zeke tied both horses to a tree limb, and pulled his binoculars from the saddlebag.

"They're swarming around in a circle around the wagons. The settlers are on the ground hiding and shooting from underneath. There is one white man down already. Josh, you'd better hurry."

Josh took the small leather satchel holding the cartridges and laid it on the big rock he was standing on as he knelt down. He lined the gun up, resting it on his left hand, and steadied by his elbow on the rock. He looked through the eyepiece. He could see the Indians, but they kept moving. He realized he was going to have to lead his shot a bit to allow for the movement like shooting a charging galloping buffalo.

"Josh, they just got another man with arrows. They are deadly with those things."

Suddenly, Josh pulled the trigger. The gun gave a hard kick, but he anticipated it by holding it tight to his shoulder. It was a long second, but the bullet missed the Indian he was aiming at, but hit his horse. It threw the Indian hard to the ground. One of the settlers shot him.

"Good Josh. Two white men, one Indian, and one horse down," said Zeke with a chuckle, as if calling the score of a game at the academy.

Josh learned a little from his previous shot. He knew with the hollering and yelling the Indians were doing, and the gunfire from the settlers, they had no idea someone from so far away was shooting at them. This gave him a little more confidence.

He lined up his next shot and was just about to pull the trigger when the leader reared his horse on his hind legs, letting out a big yelp. Josh rapidly adjusted his aim, and pulled the trigger, nearly taking the Indian's head off.

"Wow!" exclaimed Zeke. "What a shot. Way to go. You hit him like a watermelon on a fence post. Hurry Josh—do it again!"

Josh reloaded the single shot smoking weapon, and took aim again. Boom! He downed another Indian, and then another.

"Four Indians are down and four to go—yahoo! Wait a minute; they've given up and running away! Come on, let's ride."

Josh and Zeke saddled up, made their way down the mountain to the plains, and rode over to the wagons. The Indians, outgunned by the boys and the settlers, escaped quickly without seeing Josh and Zeke.

"Are you folks okay?" asked Zeke as he rode up quickly.

An older son crawled out from under the wagon, "Are they gone?"

"Yep, they've run off. Looks like we killed a few and you did, too. Anyone hurt?" asked Josh as he climbed off his horse.

A stout lady with teary red eyes slowly walked over to her husband lying face down in the dirt with three arrows in his back. She knelt down beside him, and started sobbing while rocking back and forth. Her two children came up beside her, knelt down, and tried to comfort their mother. Another lady under the other wagon trotted quickly to her husband. He died from a single arrow through his neck. Zeke surmised it must have cut his jugular vein and pierced his windpipe. There was blood everywhere, as he bled out like a butchered pig.

"You boys get some shovels so we can bury these men. We must hurry before the Indians come back with a lot more warriors. Hurry now!" ordered Josh, knowing the children were in shock. He felt it best to get them busy doing something as soon as possible. He had done the same with green recruits during the war.

Zeke knelt down to a boy of about ten. "Son, you walk up to the crest of that hill and watch for anything that moves. If you see anything, you holler out. Okay? Can you do it?"

"Yes, sir," replied the boy feebly.

"Where were you heading?" asked Josh to the oldest son.

"Fort Bridger. We were going to join a wagon train there on the Oregon Trail so we could go to the northwest."

"I'm sorry. That dream is over for now. You should not have been in this wild frontier with just the two wagons. You were easy pickings for the Indians. You must go back to Fort Collins and regroup. If you must go west, you can join a train there, or but if you go ahead as you are, you all will be slaughtered. I'm sorry for speaking harshly, but time is running short. Do you understand?"

"Yes, sir," they replied solemnly.

"Can you lead them back?" asked Zeke,

"Yes, sir, the trail was easy, at least until now. We saw Indians several times in Kansas and in Colorado, but they never hurt us. They mostly begged for food."

"That's the trouble. The white men have killed and diminished their main food source, the buffalo, so they will have to leave the plains, and then the white men can just take over their abandoned lands and sell them for farm profits. It is a difficult time. You must be better prepared next time, and travel only in a big group." Josh dragged the dead man into the hole.

Zeke pulled the other man to the shallow grave and began shoveling the dirt to cover the body as quickly as possible. Josh and Zeke helped them back to their wagon, tied the extra horses to the wagon, and loaded everybody up including the little boy from the hill.

"Sir, can you keep the cow?" asked the lady. "We can't travel as fast as we like with the cow tied to us. I want to get my family back to the safety of the fort."

Josh sighed. He wondered what was he going to do with a cow, but replied politely. "Yes ma'am. I can take care of the cow, and you're right. For the next few hours, I would ride the horses hard back towards the fort, but then slow down to a walk so the horses can rest. You don't want them to give out on you." He shook the lady's hand, and then the oldest son, placed his hand gently on the little girl's head, and patted the shoulder of the little boy. He walked to the back of the wagon and untied the cow.

"Let's go. Get moving. Turn them around in a tight circle and head back east," encouraged Zeke, as he slapped the wagon horses with his hand. "Hee-yah!"

The hunters stood there for a moment and watched them. "Let's hope the dust doesn't give them away again," said Zeke.

"Should I shoot the cow?" asked Josh.

"Hell no, you're talking milk, butter and cream. I'll drag her fat ass home!" replied Zeke picking up the rope, and tying it off to his saddle horn. He pulled on the cow that mooed a time or two in protest, and then started trotting after him.

Josh laughed. "Yeah, right, and I guess I will carry your fat ass home, too."

"My cute ass and you know it!" shot back Zeke over his shoulder.

Josh laughed hard, "Hee-yah! Let's get the hell out of here, but go southeast for a while just in case those Indians are watching us. We'll ford the stream and walk in it for a while, too. We don't want to show them where we live."

33

FOUR

Most wagon trains consisted of twenty-five or more wagons, several scouts, a wagon-master or captain, armed guards, a grub wagon, several wagons of goods and supplies for mercantile stores, a feed wagon for the horses, blacksmith and wheel repair wagon, and the rest filled with settlers. Many times, they carried bundles of mail, newspapers, or mail order goods from the east. Most of the settler wagons were comprised of one family or sometimes two families, and often the husbands were brothers. The families brought along their children, not realizing the journey would be treacherous at best. If they were lucky, a doctor and his family were traveling along, and sometime a parson, both of which came in handy. Each train carried about one hundred twenty-five people or more, and rarely did the entire group arrive at the planned destination alive. Many died of sickness, wounded by rabid animals, snakebites, or eaten by grizzly bears, mountain lions, or wolves. Some died instantly after their horses stepped in a prairie dog holes, flipping the horse while breaking the rider's neck, and too often deaths occurred after a settler tripped and fell under a rolling wagon or a team of runaway horses. Sun up to sun down, their lives were in constant danger.

Wolves often followed the trains digging the dead up from their shallow graves. Wolves, panthers, and mountain lions waited for a child to stray away from the train. Often they snatched a modest woman attempting to shield herself from the rest of the train to make a bowel movement. The fierce animals were silent and cunning, and when they struck a human, they went right for the throat. Most of the time they were successful by striking so quickly the victim rarely had a chance to scream. By the time the alarm went out about a person missing, the wagon train guards would only find pieces of torn clothing, or a dismembered foot in a boot and lots of blood.

Grizzlies, on the other hand, made a lot of noise prior to their attacks. The scouts said the bears rarely attacked humans unless they had been wounded or abused by humans, or desperate for food. If they growled loudly, it meant they were simply trying to scare humans away. Men with rifles reacted in fear by shooting wildly at the bear. One shot from a pistol or a Winchester would not kill the bear, and thus, in anger, the bear would attack violently, ripping the flesh from the body with its massive sharp claws. Few humans survived attacks by wild animals in the Rockies.

With the increasing attacks by the Indians, the soldiers built forts along the trails making it easier for squads to ride east and west to meet or escort the wagon trails along the way. However, the forts were far apart, and time schedules for travel did not exist. There were more forts in the east and far less in the west. The wagon-master had a goal of twenty or thirty miles per day, but situations changed his plans all the time. Delays due to sickness or even the birth of a baby on the trail happen too frequently, but daily, wheels broke, spokes cracked, axels snapped, and horses spooked or came up lame. Sometimes a passenger became delusional, got in a fight, or drank too much, and the entire train stopped to solve whatever problems occurred.

The cavalry would patrol the area north and south of the trails, and to the west looking for the Indians, and attacking where necessary. The Indians were on their turf, and knew the mountains and plains well. They had scouts in the high country with relay scouts on opposite sides. They used smoke from a small fire, or sun reflections off their sharpened knives to relay their signals. They planned attacks in steep passes, high cliffs, swamplands, or river crossings, all of which were difficult for the settlers to defend. Sometimes the attacks were coordinated with different bands in the same tribe, or various tribes attacking at the same time. They knew the cavalry soldiers were limited, especially during the war back east, and they often led the patrols away from the planned attacked by letting them chase a small group of warriors.

Since the Sand Creek Massacre, the Indians had a new reason to fight harshly and without mercy, as well as for revenge. The army generals knew that if they encouraged and permitted killing all the buffalo, the Indians would have to leave the plains, but they never anticipated that John Chivington's merciless attack on women and children at Sand Creek would make the tribes join together to fight an all out war against the soldiers and the settlers. The Indians were out-gunned, but the cavalry outmaneuvered and far less dedicated to the cause. They were in it for the money, a job, and perhaps adventure. The Indians fought to save their homelands, hunting grounds, and their way of life. The Indians had far more reasons to win.

Wagon-master Captain Wayne Moore was a widower and approaching fifty-nine years old. Ten years ago, after his wife died, he gave up his sea legs as the captain of a cargo ship, caught a train west as far as he could go, and then joined a wagon train heading to the northwest. Contrary to his previous occupation, he made no plans as to where he wanted to go, but rather intended to just stay busy. He kept his grief to himself, slept little, worried a lot, and possessed a gruff quality with a friendly fare that made most folks want to follow his direction. He hired on as an armed rider on his first trip to the west, which meant he did a little bit of everything. He started by protecting the right side of the long line of squeaking wagons, or as he called it the starboard side. Sometimes he rode his horse ahead of the train with the other guards to scout around and find the right site for the next campground. He discussed strategies for fighting the Indians with the captain of the train and as well the scouts. He wasn't too happy to discover there were little plans in place to help the greenhorns defend themselves. He had learned how to shoot rabbits as a boy, but spent most of his life on a ship sailing from port to port, requiring little use of a firearm. He knew how to manage his crew as well as his passengers, but he bit his lip and said nothing, hoping to just learn all he could about the western frontier. He found himself happy with working on the never ending trail, riding his horse, smelling the fresh air, taking in the mountain views, and it helped him greatly with his grief and loss of his wife.

When the wagon train reached its destination, Wayne took a long soak in a tub, ate a steak dinner at the saloon, rented a room and slept for two days before catching a smaller wagon train heading east. Several months later, they arrived safely in Kansas City. Once there, he wasted no time and immediately signed up for a return trip to Oregon, but on the morning of departure, the assigned captain fell sick with appendicitis. The wagon train organizer asked him to take over. Wayne surprised him by never giving it a second thought. He was man that could make quick decisions and enjoyed leading men. They gave him the keys to the cash box, and a list of the settlers and crew. He met with the scouts and the rest of the wagon workers, made some minor changes to their procedures and duties, spoke to the entire group of settlers as if he had been doing the trail for fifty years, and they left the noisy city early the next morning. Wayne was more than ready to get out of town and back on the trail.

Each night for the first week, he held a meeting warning and teaching his guests as to what they would experience when they reached Colorado. He told them about bears, wolves, lions, and panthers, and went into great detail on defending themselves against Indians. He also warned the settlers about robbers appearing to be traveling alone, when in fact over the next hill was a group of twenty men ready to kill for anything of value, or just for the sport of it. Because of his seafaring days, he called them pirates.

He used the same leadership skills he used all those years on his ship. He drilled his workers and his guests in procedures. If attacked by Indians, they quickly circled the wagons, not in one long slow line like most wagon trains, but breaking in the center with one group going left and the other right to create a circle faster. They practiced the maneuver and once in place, they rapidly dismounted from their horses and wagons alike, tying off the horses on the inside of the circle to keep them under control, and preventing the Indians from stealing the animals, and then with their rifles they slid under the wagon to make it more difficult for the Indians to shoot them.

They kept weapons and ammunition at hand at all times. His men also taught the women and children how to shoot and reload a gun. They knew what to do in case of a fire on their wagon. He warned them if someone shot a settler in the open, they must be left there until the battle is over, as the

Indians knew the settlers were tender and soft, and lacked courage and honor. They expected a woman to run to her falling husband, and then they would shoot her, too. His plans were tough, and some thought harsh, but they respected him, and soon would understand why.

He worked his scouts hard, too. William Teemer, a tall good-looking man who always had a two to four day beard, led them. He chewed constantly on an unlit cigar. His group consisted of two white scouts and two Indian scouts. The Indians dressed much like the white men with the addition of beads around their neck, or feathers in their hair. Somewhere in their past, they had made friends with the white men, and worked for wages and liquor, both of which Captain Wayne kept under strict control. He paid a little wage every Sunday for motivation, but held seventy percent of their pay until the entire train made it to their destination. These were rules he used at sea successfully for many years. It kept every man at his best, protecting the settlers and the train.

The journey would take four months give or take four or five weeks. Captain Wayne expected to lose ten to twenty percent of the settlers due to death, some of which would be natural, and the others violent.

"William!" yelled Captain Wayne as he rode his beautiful chestnut horse alongside the first wagon.

"Yeah, Captain," replied William as he turned his horse in a circle before darting back to see what he wanted. They rarely called him by his Christian name, but honored him by calling him simply by his title.

The captain pulled out his gold pocket watch and popped the lid to check the time. "We've got about two more hours of riding today. Send your men up ahead, survey the area, and find us a good campsite with water." He closed the lid before returning his watch to his pocket.

"Aye-aye," replied a grinning William. He knew the order well as the captain did the same thing every day. He kicked his horse into a trot and called to his men. The order was simple. The five of them would fan out looking for a good campsite as instructed, but also checking the area for any signs of Indians or other humans. They did not care much for either. They considered any white man alone suspicious, and any Indian would most likely kill you if given the chance.

They rode several miles ahead of the train with William in the center. Once he found the campsite he wanted, he sent the men further out in all directions. The scouts first looked where they were heading, and then they looked at the ground searching for horse or human tracks. If they found any, they would dismount and determine how old they were. Sometimes, they would find a burned out campfire, or feel the ashes. If cold, they figured humans recently sat there and moved on. If warm, the hair stood up on their neck.

If they found anything, they would make a whistle much like that of a hawk or sometimes an owl. They relayed the signal until it reached William. Usually, William would ride over to investigate. They would cover about a mile in all directions before returning to the campsite. If everything met William's approval, he would leave the men watching the area while he rode back to update the captain.

"Looking good just over that next hill and to the left, sir," yelled William.

"Very good, and the area is secure?" asked the captain knowing the answer.

"Secure."

"Excellent. William if you don't mind, please ride to the back of the train, and tell the rear guards the plan. Do your usual disappearing act for me," ordered the captain.

William grinned. "Yes sir, will do."

As William rode to the back, he nodded with a tip of his hat at the wagons of settlers. Many of the older girls maintained severe crushes on William, but he never came on to them. He reached the guards, circled around, and walked his horse up alongside. "We're camping just over that hill and to the left. I'm sure the captain will want you to drop back a bit while we set up camp. As usual you will take turns coming in for your grub."

"What's for supper?" asked one of the men with a grin.

"I believe the chef said stew and beans," William replied slyly.

"Chef? Hah, that's a laugh. He's barely a cook. Isn't that the same thing we had last night, and the night before that, and for the last ten nights?" asked the guard.

"If you know that, then why in the hell do you keep asking me?" He laughed, as did the rest of the men.

William rode a while longer and then said to his men, "I'll see you boys in a while." He broke away from the group as they went through a small thicket of trees and climbed off his horse to hide. They knew the plan and did their best to ignore him. They did not look where he went, but rather kept their eyes peeled ahead.

William rubbed his horse's head gently to keep him calm and quiet. He listened for any sound at all, but especially for horses or humans following the train. He knew that often Indians or robbers would follow a train all day, and then wait until the middle of the night to attack. He waited for an hour, heard nothing, and began his ride to the camp by steering his horse to the top of a hill for one last look to the east.

By the time he arrived and unsaddled his horse, the grub cook, Barney London, had supper almost ready. William filled a feeder bag with grain and placed it over his horse's head. He wiped his hands on his pants and headed to the fire to get the chill off his bones. Riding in the sun on top of his horse, he always felt warm in the fall, but once the sun went down and he dismounted, he loss two huge sources of heat, and swiftly chilled. He put his hands towards the fire palms down, warming his body. He took a sip of the hot coffee.

"Damn, Barn!" exclaimed William, "This coffee would choke a horse." The crew called Barney 'Barn' affectionately because he was about as wide as a barn at three hundred and fifty pounds. If he had to, he was not afraid to use his weight to his advantage. Rumors had it he knocked down six warriors by flinging himself into them. All but one escaped, but not before Barn caught him, and crushed the Indian after sitting on his chest.

"Good," shot back Barn. "At least the horses would appreciate my art!"

The captain, William, and some of the crew around the fire all laughed. Barn brought him a plate of stew, beans, and a biscuit.

"Thanks Barn, I was wondering what we were having for 'dinner' tonight," said William sarcastically.

Barn laughed as he sat down with a plate to join them. "How much farther to next town or fort?" asked Barn. "I'm going to need a few supplies when we get there."

"Oh, the next one is probably eight or ten days away, if the weather holds, and that is a big if. With no hard rains, I think we have been lucky with the weather so far, but our luck will run out sooner or later."

"We've been lucky with the Indians, too," added William.

"Yep, I just hope they don't hit us during a storm," replied the captain, as he watched a settler approaching their fire.

"Captain, if I could have a word," asked a young father of two who walked up to the group sitting around the fire.

"Sure, son, what is it?"

"My wife is sick. She's burning up with fever."

"Did she drink some bad water?"

"No, she drank the same water as the rest of us. I don't know what is wrong."

"Don't worry. I'm sure she'll be okay. Do you see that wagon with the letter "D" painted on the side?" asked the captain as he pointed with his spoon.

"Yes sir."

"Go there and ask for Doc. He'll take care of her."

"Thank you, sir," replied the settler as he hurried off.

Once out of earshot, "I bet she is pregnant," said the captain.

"If not, what kind of fever is the question," stated William.

"You're right," replied the captain, and then turning to one of the train workers, "Eddie, move their wagon to the very back tomorrow. If she is contagious or something, I dad-gum don't want it to spread through the whole train. You hear me?" he added, knowing Eddie heard him. Eddie nodded and that was the affirmation the captain wanted. It was his way of asking for the man's word without insulting his integrity.

"Keep a sharp eye tonight," ordered William, as he walked around the train to his men. Part of the guards and scouts slept while the others stood guard duty. Shift changes would be in four hours. For them, every night was long, and the dawn never came soon enough.

FIVE

It was after dark by the time Josh and Zeke reached their cabin with the Indian boy. Carefully, they unloaded the sleeping Indian and put him in the cabin on a pallet made from a stack of hides and fur after wrapping him in a blanket. Once they felt he was secure, they added a few logs to the fire, ate a late meal of beans and rice, and a few biscuits, along with several mugs of cold milk. They quickly did their chores by lantern light, milking the cow, feeding the animals, and then returned to the cabin to check on the Indian. Satisfied the boy continued snoozing, they winked at each other, and began stripping out of their clothes. Wrapped in blankets, they made their way to the nearby hot springs pool, dropped the blankets on a stack of wood, and jumped in. Soaking nightly in their outdoor natural hot tub was a ritual of theirs, but after a long day's ride from Denver, it never felt better. After washing each other, they settled back to enjoy the bubbling hot water.

"What if the Indian wants to leave?" asked Zeke.

"I guess we have to let him. I am done with slavery," replied Josh, "and besides, he is a kid of about sixteen or so. In this western world, he is old enough to make a man's decision. However, living all alone with winter coming would be foolish."

"But if his people were nearby, he could make his way to them," said Zeke.

"If they were nearby, don't you think he would have already gone to them? I bet he doesn't know this area at all. With those scars and bruises on his back, it appears he was running from something or someone, and not to them," added Josh. "I think he has been whipped many times, and harshly."

"Oh, I hadn't thought of that. I guess we'll play it by ear," said Zeke.

"Are we talking about the Indian or sex?" quizzed Josh with a very sly look on his face.

Zeke grinned. "Both!"

They met in the middle of the pool, kissed deeply while fondling each other. An hour later, they returned to the cabin with steam rising off their nude bodies. The Indian suddenly raised his head when they closed the door. He gave the nude white men a puzzled look, and then fell back asleep, caring little if they were nude or white.

Josh and Zeke made their way to their bed and soon fell fast asleep.

At dawn, they awoke to the sounds of pot lids falling to the floor, as well as things falling off the shelves. They both jumped up, while still naked, and grabbed their pistols.

"Stop!" yelled Josh.

The Indian slowly turned. They saw his face covered in flour and jam. He held a pot up as if it was a weapon.

"Hold on, Josh. I think he is scared," said Zeke, as he quickly pulled on a pair of long johns. He put his pistol in his holster on the chair, and began slowly walking over to the boy. "Friend—we are friends. We won't harm you. We want to help you." Slowly, he walked closer to the Indian. "Friend—we're friends. Please put the pot down."

The boy looked frightened. He stared at Josh with his pistol. Josh caught on, returned it to his holster, and started dressing. Then Josh had an idea, "Zeke, get him one of Ruth's cookies. He's a kid. He'll love them."

Zeke slowly moved to the cabinet where he put the new cookies last night. He removed one. Took a small bite to demonstrate it was good food, and then handed it out to the Indian boy. The boy reached for it, but Zeke shook his head no. "Give me the pot, and then you can have the cookie."

The Indian considered the gestures Zeke was making, though he thought the white man looked a bit stupid, but cautiously, he gave up the pot for the cookie. Zeke set the pot down while Josh got the boy some milk. The boy drank it quickly while still devouring the cookie. He licked the crumbs from his finger.

"I think he is still starving," said Zeke.

"He's not the only one. Let's cook a big breakfast today. Is that okay with you?" asked Josh.

"Fine with me—let's do it."

Slowly, they sat the Indian down at the table. Zeke poured some ground grits into a pot, added water, salt, and butter, hung it on a fire hook, and pushed it over the fire. Josh put the big black frying pan on the fire stand. He removed some fresh ham from the butcher paper Ed placed it in, and tossed it into the pan. It started sizzling. The Indian boy turned to watch. He was catching on as to what the crazy white men were doing. He had never seen men cook. In his village as a child, the squaws did all the cooking. Josh retrieved six of the eggs they brought home from Denver, broke them, and scrambled the insides with milk. Zeke removed the ham onto three plates, and then Josh poured the eggs into the frying pan. Zeke sliced some of the biscuits open, buttered them and then put them on a flat tin pan, and set them on a high grate over the fire. They were working as a team as they always did.

Ten minutes later, the plates were full of fried ham, eggs, grits, and toasted biscuits. Josh set small jars of butter, honey, and jam on the table. "This is a feast," he said.

"I'm starved, too. Coffee or milk?" asked Zeke.

"Milk, sit down, and I'll serve you," suggested Josh.

Josh brought Zeke's plate around and set it down. He then gave the next plate to the Indian. He took the last plate to his place and sat down.

The Indian boy watched them for a moment. Zeke put honey on a biscuit, while Josh put jam on his. They loaded a fork with a bite of eggs with a bite of grits, and then shoved it into their mouths and smiled. They drank some milk and did it again.

The Indian thought the entire affair was a waste of time, and he had grown tired of waiting. He leaned over and began lapping up the food like a dog to a plate or a pig to a trough. He ate all the eggs, then all the ham, then the grits, and then the biscuit. He finished it off with the milk. When his mug was empty, he held it out to Josh. For the first time, they saw a hint of a smile just below the big milk mustache.

Josh brought the pitcher over and filled the boy's mug. "I think we had better eat quickly, or he'll eat our plates, too," said Josh with a chuckle.

"I agree," replied Zeke, but he did fix the boy another biscuit with honey. "I think we'd better buy some chickens the next time we're in town. We're going to need a lot more eggs."

"The way he devoured the ham, we'd better buy a couple of hogs, too," laughed Josh.

Afterwards, they helped each other clean the table, and put the utensils away. Josh washed the dishes and pots in their homemade sink. Since they couldn't speak each other's language, they felt showing him by example might be a start. Afterwards, they sat back down to the table.

Josh used his thumb to his chest, "I'm Josh. Josh," he repeated. Then he pointed to Zeke, "Zeke. That is Zeke."

"What is your name?" asked Zeke as he and Josh together pointed to the boy.

The boy's face became an expression of confusion. They went through the routine again. This time the boy caught on, he smiled shyly, and said, "Yuma."

"Yuma," said Zeke. "His name is Yuma. That is a good name."

"I wonder what it means," added Josh.

Like in a classroom, they went around the table saying Josh's name and pointing to him, then Zeke, and then Yuma. Then the boy picked up his cup and pretended to drink.

"Cup," said Josh. They all repeated it.

"Milk," said Zeke as he poured from the pitcher.

The boy said milk, and then drank it all. They continued their teaching until they all grew tired. "I think we need to give him a bath, and get him some white man clothes. He'll freeze to death in that little piece of hide he is wearing."

"How are we going to get him to do that?" asked Josh.

"Let's strip down, grab towels, and walk to the hot springs."

"Aren't Indians afraid of hot pools?" asked Josh.

"You get in first and show him how wonderful it is."

"All right, smart guy. I bet we have to drag him into the pool."

Josh and Zeke stripped. To their surprise, the Indian boy got a very sad look on his face, and then took off his loincloth. Zeke grabbed towels, and Josh snatched up their wash bucket. They each grabbed a pistol, and walked out the door towards the pool with the boy between them. When they reached the water, Zeke set his pistol down, jumped in, and splashed around, went under the water, and came up spitting water into the air. He made a big deal about how much fun it was.

He then held out his hand for the Indian to join him. The boy went to the edge, felt the bubbling water, but appeared frightened. Slowly, he sat down, and slid into the warm water. Josh climbed in to, keeping their pistols close to the edge in case danger arrived.

Zeke started washing Josh's hair, and then Josh washed Zeke. They both cautiously scrubbed the boy's hair. Little by little, he relaxed and enjoyed their scrubbing, and though worried, he dipped his head beneath the water to rinse his hair.

Josh then washed Zeke's back and his chest. Zeke stood up and washed his genitals, and then sat down and stuck a foot up for washing by Josh. Josh copied him and soon Yuma was washing his dirty body as well. Zeke helped remove all the dirt from Yuma's legs and feet, as it was caked on.

Thankfully, a steady stream of hot water refreshed the pool, so when the washing was done, they sat around soaking for a while as the bubbles and dirt washed away.

"Time to dress and get busy with the chores, I guess we're not going hunting today," said Josh.

"Yeah, I think we should continue our training. The sooner he learns to speak English the better."

"Yeah, but it would be smart of us to learn to speak his language, too. Due to the white men's lies and broken treaties, I suspect we are going to run into more Indians next spring."

Dressing the boy made them all laugh. Since Zeke was a little smaller than Josh, he put a pair of long johns on the boy. Yuma thought that the flap in the back was very funny, as Zeke showed him how to unbutton it and sit down as if in the outhouse. The boy laughed. They kept working until they had him dressed, but he did not seem to like his boots. They were a little big, so Josh rolled up rag and stuffed it in the toe of each boot for a better fit.

Then they headed out the door showing Yuma about their life and chores. He helped feed the animals, and he liked stroking the horses and rubbing their ears. Yuma wanted to help so when he spotted the new deer hide over the railing, he showed the boys how the Indians prepare a deer skin for clothes and tipis. He used Zeke's knife to scrape the hide clean of any morsels of meat.

Later, they decided to see if he could ride a horse. They only had two saddles, but after bridling one of their packhorses, Yuma swung up and rode the horse easily bareback.

They practiced riding around the corral a while before heading for a ride to the stream. Everything they saw they would say the English word, and he would say the word in his language, and several times more in English. By evening, the boy was tired, but he looked better, appeared happier, and smelled a whole lot better.

Once Josh and Zeke realized they had not been alone the entire day, they tiptoed to their room, and snuggled in their bed and made out. As usual, one thing led to another until they were both sexually satisfied and settled into their favorite spooning position.

It took several days of practicing before Yuma could balance his food on a fork, but grinned when he accomplished the task. The boys instantly praised him. It did not take them long to realize that in his life as an Indian he had not received much praise. If Josh lifted the water bucket to fetch water, Yuma picked up the second bucket and followed him. If Zeke brought in an armload of firewood, then Yuma did the same. They continued teaching him at every opportunity, and he seemed eager to learn. They thought he was very smart, and marveled at how quickly he was speaking English words.

He learned their whistles and calls, and he knew their boot prints. He was an expert tracker when they went hunting. He would walk ahead of them, and upon finding game; he would stop, crouch down, and turn to the boys and motion for them to stop. He would point in the direction of the game. Zeke and Josh took turns shooting. In a few days, they added four turkeys, several geese, and a few rabbits to their smokehouse. Yuma took charge of skinning and tanning the hides.

At the beginning of their fifth week together, they spotted smoke rising far to the east. They did not think there was a settlement there, and feared a wagon train might be burning. However, when they let Yuma look through the binoculars, he became very excited, but then he did something amazing. He was staring at the smoke to the southeast of them when suddenly, he turned forty-five degrees to the northeast, and immediately found another stream of smoke.

He became very excited and pointed at the each of the locations of smoke. They could not understand him, but they knew he was not happy.

"Do you think it is some kind of smoke signal? Is that where his people are?" asked Zeke.

"I don't know, but he knew right where to find the second one. He's definitely clever."

Zeke tried to talk to him, "Yuma, is that your people, your tribe?" Zeke pointed at the two fires.

Yuma shook his head no, and then said, "Kaga Ozuye. Kaga Ozuye. Kaga Ozuye." He pointed anxiously as repeated the words, and then shook with fear.

Josh spoke up first, "I wish we knew more of his words, but I know he doesn't want to go where the smoke is coming from."

"Yeah, I agree, but he did teach us those fires were not accidents, or even a wagon train. He recognized the smoke patterns as signal fires. Next time we see one of those smoke signals we should turn in the opposite direction, and high tail it home."

"That's right," replied Josh.

Then suddenly Yuma did a very odd thing. He pointed at the northeastern smoke trail, then yanked his pants down and slapped his bare butt. He made a terrible scream sound, and then said, "Kaga Ozuye." When Josh and Zeke still did not understand, he pulled his shirt up off his back, placed his hand on his scars, and repeated Kaga Ozuye several times. Then as he put his shirt down, pulled his pants up, and he began to cry.

Zeke pulled him into his arms and hugged him tightly. "You're okay, lad. You're okay now. We're not going to make you go there. You're safe here."

Josh smiled. "I think whoever is at those fires treated him badly. Do you think he was a slave Indian?"

"Maybe he was captured from another tribe and made to work for these warriors. They must have beaten him badly."

"I think they mistreated him for sure," added Zeke solemnly.

Josh sighed while thinking. "Well, he'll never have to worry about them again. This would explain why we found him alone and without weapons. He must have escaped."

"Time to change the subject and the scenery—let's head home," suggested Zeke.

"Okay, but I'm going to soak in the hot spring after supper. My butt is sore." He winked at Zeke.

"Don't blame me, you were begging for it last night," Zeke shot back.

Just then, Josh put his finger to his lips for Yuma and Zeke to hush. Slowly, he pulled his rifle up and took a deliberate steady aim. Suddenly, the gun fired and Josh grinned.

Yuma jumped with joy, and quickly led his horse to where Josh had aimed.

"What did you hit?" asked Zeke.

"It is going to take more than my horse to get him home," laughed Josh.

Zeke and Josh arrived to find Yuma kneeling beside a big moose. Josh immediately wished he had used his buffalo gun, as the animal, though down and bleeding, was not yet dead. Yuma came back to Zeke and pointed at his knife on his belt. Zeke handed it to him.

Yuma went back to the moose, knelt down again, and began touching the tip of his third finger on his right hand into the palm of the left, and then he reversed the procedure starting with the left hand while chanting and looking up at the sky. Then he stopped, felt the chest of the moose like a doctor might when examining a patient, found the animal's heart, picked up the knife and thrust it in as far as it would go. The animal sighed heavily and died.

Yuma pulled the knife out, took some of the blood, and wiped it on his forehead. Josh and Zeke dismounted. Yuma came to them, and made the same stripe of blood on their foreheads, too.

"Never thought I would start playing Indian at my age," grinned Josh.

"I think they believe the animals are a gift of God, and he was giving his god praise for the animal's good life, and perhaps thanking him for the food provided," said Zeke.

"Aren't you the wise old bird," laughed Josh. "We'd better start carving this moose up, if we are going to get home by dark."

Yuma went to work quickly by expertly cutting the hide in large squares. Josh and Zeke removed empty canvas sacks from their saddlebags. Yuma cut the meat from the animal and placed it in the sacks. For a boy so young, he knew exactly what to do. Zeke and Josh followed his grunts and orders. When finished, Yuma rolled up the hides and tied them to his horse. He returned to the moose and grabbed a leg, stepped on the knee joint, and pulled as hard as he could until the lower leg bone popped out of the knee socket. He tore it loose from the animal with great determination. He then looked around and found a sharp rock. He grabbed the severed leg by the upper part and flung the hoof down on the rock until it broke off. He repeated the same procedure for each leg, then tied the bones with a piece of rawhide onto the back of Zeke's his horse. He then swung up on to his horse.

Josh began leading the way home. "What do you suppose he wanted with the leg bones?"

"Got me? I have never seen anyone do that before in my life. He was tenacious," said Zeke.

"He is also a bloody mess," added Josh.

"That he is," laughed Zeke.

When they reached the bottom of the mountain and started across the stream, Yuma stopped and gave the reins of his horse to Zeke. He then walked into the river, and though the water was very cold, he plunged in. He came up laughing and scrubbing the blood from his body and clothes.

"Well, at least he has good manners," laughed Josh.

"Yep, he washes up pretty good," laughed Zeke.

Yuma twisted most of the water out of his clothes, and then laid them over the back of his horse to dry. He swung on his horse broad naked.

"That's got to hurt," said Josh as they began their way home once more.

"My balls would be hurting. I think he is definitely tougher than we are."

After they took care of their horses, stored the new meat in the smokehouse, put away their weapons, Zeke and Josh removed their clothes, grabbed the wash bucket, and the three of them headed to the hot springs. They took turns washing each other's hair and bodies, and Yuma seemed determine to give the boys as much attention as they gave him. Once clean, they all settled down for a good long soak in the water.

"Do you think we should show affection for one another in front of Yuma?" asked Zeke.

Josh thought a moment. "This is our home that we've built with our own hands, as well as our sweat and blood. I think we are entitled to be ourselves in our own domain. The actual sexual acts might be best reserved for quiet time alone."

"That's going to be hard since we all live in the same cabin," replied Zeke.

"Perhaps we better think of a way to add a loft or a room so Yuma can have a space of his own."

"That is a good idea, but for now, I think I could stay in this hot water all night."

Zeke let his hand wander over to Josh and beneath the waters gave Josh's penis a squeeze. Josh turned to him, and pulled him into his arms. Yuma watched with great interest, but made no expression good or bad. They lay back in the water with an arm around the back of the other's head, and kicked their feet splashing Yuma. The boy grinned and splashed them back, and before long, the three were involved in a huge water fight.

Josh hung Yuma's clothes on an arrangement of sticks near the fire to dry. Yuma possessed no modesty, and walked around the cabin easily in the nude. Zeke gave him a long shirt to put on, and soon they all settled down to sleep. After they thought the boy was asleep, they began making love. Yuma watched them from out of the corner of his eye. They did not know it yet, but the band of demon warriors he called 'Kaga Ozuye' in his Lakota tongue often raped him and the other boys every night. This group murdered his family in an attack on their tribe while they were moving to their summer hunting ground. Then they transported him over three hundred miles away. He was only seven at the time, too old to be killed like his little brother and sister, but not too old to be a threat. In their eyes, he was the perfect slave.

They fed him little more than they did their dogs or horses, but they demanded a lot of him. He took care of his master's needs in every way. Getting food or water, or keeping him warm at night, packing up the camp, and hauling it to the next site were just a few of the things he did. Once he tried to run away, and they tied a rope to his feet, and hung him upside down from a tree limb. They whipped him with a thorny branch, and burned him by poking his flesh with hot sticks from the cook fire. He did not run away again until the boys found him. One day he would get even with Kaga Ozuye. One day, he thought.

SIX

The captain hoped to reach Fort Laramie in Wyoming without trouble from the warriors, but after a two days ride from Fort Bent in Colorado, they began spotting small gangs of Indians daily. At first, the braves remained far off, but now they were moving closer, observing the wagon train through the day. He knew they were looking for weak links to pounce upon, like wolves stalking a wounded buffalo. After they crossed the North Platte River, the Indian riders became greater in number. He assumed the Indian scouts sent for reinforcements with the smoke signals from the mountain peaks that he spotted.

"Do you see them on the ridge?" called William without pointing, thinking it better to let the Indians assume they were invisible.

"Afraid I do, damn heathens," replied the captain.

"Why haven't they attacked us?" asked Barn, between spits of his tobacco juice, which mostly ran down his chin to his well-stained shirt.

The captain thought for a moment. "I think they are waiting until we're too far from Fort Bent to go back, and not yet close enough to Fort Laramie for a patrol to help us. It could be snowing in Wyoming, and if so, the patrols have probably cut back, leaving a free range for the Indians to roam in —at least for the winter."

"So they are going to attack, the question is when and where," stated William.

"Yep, I think we must change our plans a bit," said the captain.

"What do you mean?" asked Barn after spitting again.

"We are closer to Fort Collins than we are to Fort Laramie. We could reach the fort before they attack us."

"How do we manage that?" asked William.

"We'll pretend to make camp, early I think. We'll put big piles of firewood near our campfires. After dark, we'll quickly pack up, and in secret head southwest. Once we are out of camp, the rear guards will throw the extra wood on the fires so they burn all night. The Indians will assume we are asleep by our fires."

"Aye, Captain. That sounds good, but we'll have to hurry once we are out of ear range, and we'll have to find a place to cross back over the North Platte River," stated William.

"I know a place, near Winston. It was a mining town, but a ghost town now. We can cross there, and hold for the night. It is a two-day ride from there to Fort Collins. If any wagon breaks a wheel, we must abandon it, and the passengers spread to other wagons. We'll keep the horses in case we need them, because if a horse becomes lame, we'll have to let him go."

"That the plan?" asked William to be sure.

"Yes," nodded the captain, "pass the word. Everyone should act normal, and do not look at the Indians directly. We must appear harmless and stupid. Once we're camped, I'll call a meeting and explain."

If the captain had not instilled discipline from their very first day on the trail, many of the settlers might have felt dishearten to an abrupt change in directions, but the captain warned them they had no choice. They could turn south with a chance to live, or continue northwest, and most certainly die in the next twenty-four hours. Therefore, the entire train faked setting up camp, fed and watered their horses, adjusted and tied down all their belongings, and then checked their weapons.

As soon as darkness arrived, William and his scouts slid out of camp, and made their way south, based on the direction the captain gave them. William looked up to the skies, and said a quick prayer of thankfulness for the cloudy skies, which would block the light of the moon. He left his men moving slowly forward, while he returned and gave the captain a thumbs-up sign. In the dark of the early night, they followed the wagon in front of them as William led them through the woods and southwest. Once all the wagons were away the rear guards began adding firewood to the fires until every stick of wood was burning. They crept out into the forest where they hid their horses, and rode quietly to catch up and protect the rear of the wagon train.

By daybreak, they had at least a ten-mile head start. William reported to the captain that so far, there were no signs of any Indians following. The captain knew better than to think they were out of hot water. By noon, he spotted puffs of smoke rising from the top of the ridge of the mountains to their west. Later, William saw another trail of smoke from a mountain far behind them. The captain kept pushing the wagons, only slowing down for water for the horses, and for passengers to run to the woods to pee. They set aside any modesty with children squatting down just a dozen feet from their wagon, and men urinating in plain view, while still holding their reins of their horse.

By nightfall, the captain called a halt to allow the animals to rest for a while. He posted sentries, and sent William and his team out into the darkness to find the North Platte River. Two hours later, William returned with good news that he had spotted the river in a valley, but they would have to wind their way to the west and go through a gorge to get there. He felt it would take them ten or twelve hours to get to the river.

The captain lost no time hurrying the settlers back to their wagons and getting the train on the road again. There was plenty of grumbling, but not a word within earshot of the captain. They had no choice but to trust his instinct and leadership on their behalf.

Two nights ago, Zeke gave Yuma one of his knives in a leather sheaf, which he immediately strapped to his waist with a leather cord. He had been taking shooting lessons with the rifle, but they had not yet given him a firearm to carry on his own. He was a pretty good shot and when he took aim, he possessed perfect posture, while remaining motionless, as he concentrated harder than any man Josh or Zeke had ever seen. Josh surmised it took a long time to make a spear, and even more time to make a dozen arrows for a hunt. In most cases, they could not afford a second shot. They learned every shot had to count, and recovered, or more work done. Yuma exhibited a deathly eye for his target. He would make a good hunter.

The trio left way before dawn as they had seen a herd of deer in the valley on the eastern side of Edger Mountain the day before. It would be at least a six-hour ride to get there. The sun hit their faces as they went along the ridge before descending downward. They were at an elevation of about eight thousand feet allowing a magnificent sunrise as the sunbeams sliced their way through a thin line of black clouds. The sun felt good to their skin, as they had ridden damp and cold all morning. As they started down, they were mostly sheltered under the extensive canopies of tall Ponderosa pines. As they rounded a rise, Yuma suddenly became very chatty while pointing to the northeast. He finally managed a single English word, "Smoke!"

"Where?" asked Josh as turned around to see which way Yuma was pointing?

Zeke retrieved his binoculars and turned the focus ring. "I think it is a signal fire."

"Wow, Yuma has great eyesight. I did not even notice the smoke," replied Josh.

Yuma pointed eastward.

Zeke turned his glasses to his far left, "Yep, there's another to the east. I wonder what is going on."

"How far from where we plan to hunt?" asked Josh.

"Probably still a pretty good ways, but let's don't plan to spend the night there," replied Zeke stowing away his binoculars. "Let's get moving. We need to make our kills and get back over the ridge."

"Still no sign of them?" asked the captain as William rode beside him.

"Nope, but I suspect we've still got a fight ahead of us."

"You're right. Out here, I'm confident we can circle quickly, and put up a pretty good fight if there aren't too many of them. Going through the gorge is another matter. If I did the planning for them, I would attack there. We'll have to be ready."

"How do we fight in such a narrow pass?" asked William.

"I've been thinking about it. As we start through the pass, we'll have the settlers extend their reins on their horses. The entire group should remain out of sight beneath the canopy of the wagon, and below the wooden sidewalls. They should also have their guns ready. We should push them to keep moving as fast as possible, but when the attack happens, they should move double time. That will keep our casualty numbers down. My biggest concern is if the Indians block the trail with a rockslide or a fallen tree. We would have to stop and move it under fire, as there will be no retreat and nowhere to turn around. Most likely the largest part of their force will attack from the rear."

William sighed before speaking, "Dang, this is going to be a huge fight. Why don't we put only men in the rear wagons, and move the women and children to the middle?"

"Good idea, William. Move a case of that dynamite in the supply wagon to the last wagon. I'll handle the rear. You'll stay in the front and keep them moving. Whatever you do—don't stop."

"Aye, Captain," replied William as he took off to give orders for the adjustments they discussed before returning to the front. They briefly stopped to move the women and children to the middle, and put more men with rifles in the rear wagons.

A few hours later, they entered the gorge. William thought the area appeared excessively still and quiet for his taste. He failed to see a single bird or squirrel. His scouts made it to the river and returned to push the wagons ahead.

Later in the day, Yuma silently tapped Josh on the shoulder and pointed to the far right. Josh smiled as he spotted what Yuma had seen, a huge buck. He nodded in appreciation, lined up the shot, and fired, killing the deer in one shot.

Zeke held his rifle up waiting to see if there was a reaction from perhaps a hidden herd. He saw movement far off to the right and sighted the target. His right index finger twitched as his muscles tightened on the trigger. Josh and Yuma held their breath for the shot.

Suddenly, Zeke dropped his rifle. "There's a man there," he whispered, "an Indian."

Yuma did not catch all the words, but he knew something was wrong. He ran to Zeke's saddlebag, brought him the binoculars, and held his rifle. Zeke scanned the ridge on the other side of the valley. He moved slowly to his left and found nothing. Quickly, he turned to the center and failed to spot the warrior. Then he turned to the right, and again found nothing. Had he been wrong? Did his eyes deceive him? At last, he saw the man again, attempting to hide behind a tree. He slowly paned the binoculars farther up to the ridge, and he saw more men. He moved the field glasses over to the right on the ridge and spotted even more.

"Shit!" said Zeke. "The ridge is full of Indian warriors, and they all have war paint on their faces."

Josh took the glasses and scanned the area. When finished, Yuma took the glasses, stared at the men, and said, "Sioux warriors, we must run or die."

Before they could saddle up, they heard gunfire mixed with whoops and screams, followed by more gunfire. Zeke grabbed the binoculars and stared across to the ridge. "They are not after us. They are firing down the ridge to the other side. What is on the other side of that mountain?"

Josh wrinkled his brow and the replied, "North Platte River."

"We crossed it early this morning but farther downstream. Why are they attacking there?" asked Zeke.

Josh replied, "It is narrow pass from the east to the west to cross the Platte River. But who is trying to make it across the Platte River?"

"It must be a wagon train. They are going to get slaughtered," stated Zeke.

"Yep, we have to go back up the steep part of this mountain to get around them and head home," said Josh as he pointed upwards.

"What about the wagon train? We can't just leave them."

Josh sighed, "Unfortunately, it is too late to warn them. I hope they are ready for them. There's only two of us, plus Yuma. What could we do?"

Zeke bit his lip, and Josh knew it meant he was thinking hard. "Let's hurry to the top, maybe we can pick off some of the Indians, and then we'll head down to the river to see if we can help."

"I knew you would say that. You realize you're getting us right in the middle of a battle. We rode all the way to Colorado to get away from war," complained Josh, as he led his horse quickly through the thicket.

"Yep, I know, but the trouble came to us. I guess we're just lucky."

Josh sighed. He wanted to be done with killing men, but his Southern way of life required honor as well as valor. He could not leave those city folks to the Indians. Reluctantly, he saddled up, and began leading them upward.

Yuma followed silently. If he understood or had a vote, he would have voted to make a run for it, but he followed the boys anyhow.

The captain heard the gunfire from the lead wagons followed by the war whoops from the Indians even before the last wagon turned into the pass. He knew their turn would come fast. He tied his horse to the next to last wagon and climbed aboard the last one. "Everyone ready?" he asked, He found his rifle and ammo stacked up waiting for him. "Keep the dynamite near the front. I don't want a stray bullet hitting that case, or we all be blown to smithereens. Stay low, and aim carefully. If you miss the Indian, then shoot his horse—anything to slow them down. They will not hesitate to kill you or your family. You must do the same. Don't think about killing—just do it!" he demanded.

William had his hands full upfront. The Indians started with a barrage of hundreds of arrows. The deflected arrows came through the canvas tops, and wounded many settlers. Unfortunately, so were several horses, most of which kept running because they were terrified. Two wagons crashed, spilling the occupants into the woods along the trail. Quickly, survivors jumped onto the approaching wagons. A deluge of arrows killed many running settlers. The Indians dropped burning piles of brush onto the trail ahead of them.

The horses reared at the sight of the fire. The wagon behind ran into the wagon ahead. William realized there would soon be a pile up of wagons. He drove his horse to the front, lassoed the biggest burning brush, and pulled it down the trail knocking the other bushes out of the way with it. As he did so, he had to duck low on his horse avoiding the flying arrows. The wagon horses quickly followed him. Once he had the trail clear, he doubled back just as two wagons came rolling by on fire. Apparently, the Indians managed to roll a few burning bushes right on top of the wagons. As the wagons began burning, the terrified horses turned sharply, flipping the wagons over, and spilling the settlers.

"Hurry up. We must get through!" he yelled. He twisted around, looked up the mountain, and turned pale. A swarm of over a fifty Indians began running down the sides of the mountain. He drew his pistol and began firing, trying to make every shot count while dodging arrows.

"Here they come! Wait until you have a good target and fire," ordered the captain.

They topped a hill and realized they were at least forty or more Indians chasing them on horseback. The men were scared, but the captain fired first, and the men quickly joined him with a torrent of fire. Their shots were good, and a dozen or so warriors fell in the first volley, but the fearless Indians just kept coming, while trampling the wounded warriors who had fallen with no mercy.

Josh reached the top of the hill, grabbed his Sharp buffalo rifle, and knelt down behind a rock. Zeke gave the reins of his horse to Yuma, pulled his Winchester from the saddle sleeve, and joined Josh.

"They are charging the wagons," said Josh.

"We're shooting downward and stationary, so we have the advantage. Try to take down the Indians from the right, and I will start on the left. If we are lucky, the wounded could cause others to stumble and fall, or perhaps think the cavalry is charging from this side of the pass," said Zeke.

Josh laughed. "Boy, you are an optimist. I think our plans of making friends just went out the window. We'll be lucky to keep our scalps."

"Well, that may be true with this bunch, but there are lots of Indian bands and tribes. There has to be some friendly ones. Fire!" yelled Zeke.

Josh caught a man charging down a steep hill, and hit him dead center of his chest. The buffalo rifle was so powerful the bullet went through the Indian, and hit the man behind him in the stomach. They both went down, tumbling as they fell, knocking other warriors down with them. Josh reloaded.

Zeke carefully sighted his Winchester using the boulder to steady his gun and fired. With the rifle's ability to ratchet another shell, he took down two men before Josh reloaded and fired the single shot Sharps. Together, they kept firing. Yuma tied off the horses and brought more ammo from the saddlebags. During the firing, Zeke noted the Indians did not wear the same black and white stripes on their faces that attacked him. They were dark red stripes.

Across the pass, the Indians were swarming down the hill. The settlers were fairing a bit better hidden behind the wagon walls and firing their rifles and pistols. However, the accuracy of the Indians amazed Josh. Almost every wagon loss one or two settlers, but each wagon took down eight to ten warriors. Josh did another double shot just as Zeke took out two Indians just a bit to the right of his targets. Together, the wounded warriors stumbled, knocking down another group of Indians. In just a few minutes, the Indians lost control of their charge down the hill, and became an avalanche of human legs and arms, as well as bows and arrows. They could not stop as the loose soil came down with them, and some fell in a pile right on the road. Many of their bows and arrows were broken and useless.

Just as they looked about for good weapons, the next wagon of horses ran right into them. They heard the screams over the gunfire as the horses trampled the Indians. The driver of the wagon was too terrified to even think of slowing down. He kept to his job, urging the horses forward, and keeping his head down. He did not see the Indians until the last second, but it was too late. He felt the bumps as the wheels rolled over the bodies snapping and crushing their bones. He would remember their horrifying screams for the rest of his life.

The next wagon continued running over the fallen Indians, and then the next. It instantly became a gruesome bloody sight. The event caused Josh to pause for a second before his instincts and training took over, and he began firing once again.

William and his scouts reached the river. They spread out, took cover, and began returning fire. The first wagon rushed to the river and began crossing. Williams yelled to them, "Keep going until you're well hidden by the trees. Go deep and leave room for the others."

The Indians managed to shoot the driver of the next wagon approaching the river. The out of control wagon had gone off the trail near the last turn of the river and crashed. The Indians pounced on the victims.

At the rear of the train, the captain and his group cut the size of the group of Indians behind them in half. In a narrow section of the pass, the captain deliberately shot the lead Indian horse. As he fell, he took out the horses around him, creating a logjam of confusion. It gave him a chance to turn and look ahead, and he did not like what he saw. Numerous wagons crashed off the trail. Most were on fire, and surrounded by a small group of warriors. They took scalps. It sickened him, but he began firing once more.

The Indians were beating the fallen settlers with tomahawks, and a few were chopping the settlers with huge axes the size and shape of which he had never seen. As a warrior raised his axe to strike again, the captain took quick aim, and shot him right between the eyes.

His wagon roared by before the other Indians could retaliate. As they came round another curve, the captain spotted another spilled wagon off the trail. A boy and his father managed to climb out. His father began shooting his pistol at the approaching Indians. They saw the captain's rolling wagon so the father and son started running to catch it.

"Grab them!" yelled the captain.

The father could have easily outrun his son, but he bravely kept turning and firing, giving his son time to catch the wagon.

"Run boy! Run!" the men in the wagon yelled.

The boy slightly tripped a step or two, but then gave the run one last effort. The captain snatched his left arm just as he was about to fall, and yanked him into a wagon like a fisherman bringing a big fish aboard his boat.

The father saw his son make it to safety. He turned to shoot one last time, but his gun did not fire. He was out of bullets. He threw the gun at the Indians chasing him, and then turned, concentrating on running and catching the wagons.

With his son yelling for him to run, the father would have caught the wagon, but in a flash, an arrow seared through his back, and the arrowhead stopped on the front side of his bleeding chest. The captain saw it, and knew the man was done for. The man stumbled and ran a few more steps before a second arrow got him in the leg. Before the white man destroyed their hunting lands in the plains, the archer spent most of his life taking down huge buffalo with similar techniques. A third arrow to the hip sent the severely wounded settler crashing to the ground. Before the dust could settle, a third Indian ran up and bashed his head with a twenty-four inch club with a large rock strapped to the top. The man's head split open like pumpkin. The captain quickly grabbed the boy, and turned his face away from the gruesome scene.

"I'm sorry son. He's dead. Now lay down so the arrows can't get you. Come on, do it now," urged the captain, as he pushed the sobbing and petrified boy to the floor near the front of the wagon.

The captain spotted the dynamite, and retrieved a stick, lit it quickly and threw it out the back. It blew up in the middle of about twelve warriors racing towards them. He quickly lit another.

"Time to move forward," said Josh as he ran to Yuma for the reins of his horse.

"How far to the river?" asked Zeke as he followed and swung up on his horse.

"Not far. Probably three hundred yards, but if we go down the ridge to the left, we can cross in an easy spot, and then come back upriver to provide cover fire for the wagons to cross. We must hurry!" yelled Josh.

"Hee-yah!" yelled Zeke.

"Hee…" yelled Yuma, not at all sure what he was yelling to his horse, but he had no time to wonder as Josh led them down a very steep ravine, through a small pass and into the river. Although the water was deep, the width was far less than where the wagons would cross.

"Yuma, hold on to your horse's mane, and don't let loose. You go where he goes. He'll swim, just hang on!" urged Josh as he showed Yuma what to do. Josh held his rifle above the water with his right hand. Zeke did the same.

"Go ahead of me," yelled Zeke.

Yuma did as told, though he only understood part of the words. He copied Josh and frantically his frighten horse swam to the other side. Zeke nearly fell off as his horse stumbled on a smooth river rock, but once on shore Josh led them up the bank into the woods where they quickly turned upstream.

Four wagons made it across until the Indians on the hills reached the river. William and his men began returning their fire with good results, but they would not be able to hold out for long. William gulped as he saw another thirty or more Indians charging down the hill towards them. He glanced back and realized the wagon train only had seven more wagons to go with the last wagon leading a swarm of Indians. He knew the captain would keep firing until his last breath, but the odds were against him.

Then suddenly, William took an arrow to his left thigh. He yelled out at the pain and fell back, but he knew he could not rest, or they would kill him. He pushed the arrow through, broke off the arrowhead, and then pulled the broken shaft out of his leg. He quickly took his neckband, tied it across the wound, snatched up his pistol, and began firing once again.

Two more wagons passed, but they were attempting to corner the remaining five from the hill and the rear. Then he heard gunfire behind him, and turned to see two white men firing across the river at the leaders of the hill charge. One of them held a larger bore buffalo gun, the sound of which he heard above all others. They began taking down one Indian after another.

"Cross over," yelled William to his men. "Hurry wagons! Hurry!"

Two of William's men made it across, but the Indians killed the rest. The scouts swiftly forded the river, moved their horses into the trees, dismounted, and ran back to the bank to continue shooting. They took up a position behind the rocks on the safe side of the river. Two more wagons crossed, but the horses with third wagon spooked, reared up, and the water quickly flooded and flipped the wagon, pinning and drowning the settlers.

William looked around as the surviving settlers ran back from their parked wagons to help, and in a few minutes, they had eighteen men firing at the Indians, and only two more wagons to go.

The captain glanced ahead and saw the river. "Come on boys, keep firing. We've got fifty yards to go!" The wagon ahead of him hit the water. The captain tossed another stick of dynamite out the back, and flinched at the explosion before returning fire.

Josh spotted a tall Indian yelling an order to his men. He sighted him quickly, and hit him dead center of the chest. The wagon crossing the river lurched passed him, and up the bank into the forest out of sight.

William saw an Indian reach for the reins on the horses pulling the captain's wagon in an effort to steer them off course. He fired twice before his gun failed. As he quickly began reloading his pistol from the bullets in his belt, he saw another Indian catch the horses on the other side, and this one managed to swing up on top of the horses. The captain was still firing to the rear, and did not see the danger in front.

"Josh!" yelled Zeke as he pointed at the last wagon.

Josh spun back to his right, and saw the horses, the wagon, and the Indians attacking it. He took quick aim and hit the Indian on top of the lead horse, spinning him backwards into a full flip before tumbling down and between the horses. The rapidly spinning wagon wheels instantly crushed him.

Josh quickly reloaded, but could not get a clear shot at the Indian pulling at the reins on the left, but all of a sudden the Indian leaped into the air to jump forward to the lead horse. Josh fired and caught the Indian in the chest in midair. He fell beneath the horses, which terrified the wide-eyed animals as they trampled him and charged into the water.

The captain and his men nearly fell out of the wagon as they clung on as the horses quickly dragged the wagon across the water and up the bank.

The Indians continued their charge towards the river, but the settlers, along with the scouts, plus Josh and Zeke, took them down one man at a time, until finally, the Indian's retreated. The scouts quickly caught some of the horses that broke free from the wrecked wagons, and followed the train across the river. The Indians captured, wounded, or killed many of the horses left behind across the shore.

Josh and Zeke looked around at the bloody and horrified travelers. The smell of gunfire and blood, the cries of pain, and lifeless bodies, reminded them of the war they thought they left behind. The battle had been brisk but deadly. They shook their heads in disbelief at the bloody carnage with the Indians taking the brunt of the losses. He counted over seventy dead on the far shore, and guessed at least that many on the hill and along the wagon route to the river. He had no idea of how many white settlers died.

SEVEN

Zeke pulled up his rifle and wiped the sweat from his brow. Steam rose from the barrel of his Winchester. He looked to his left, and smiled. "Josh? Are you all right?"

A trail of smoke rose from Josh's buffalo gun. He turned to face Zeke. He had black gunpowder streaks across his face created by his sweat, and the smoke and gun residue. He smiled. "Yep, and you? How's Yuma?"

Yuma grinned as he pulled the horses up to them. "Me, good," he said smiling.

"Yes you are," laughed Zeke as he gave him a hug.

Josh laughed. "Well, I know they suffered many casualties, but I hoped we saved some."

"More than some," began William as he approached with a limp from the arrow wound to his leg. "I can't thank you enough for your help. I'm William Teemer, the lead scout. Is that a buffalo gun?"

Josh looked up at the tall fellow and smiled. "I'm Josh Johnson, and yes it is a Sharps rifle. It is very deadly for three to four hundred yards, perhaps farther."

Zeke spoke up as he shook William's hand, "I'm Zeke Robertson, and this is our friend Yuma."

William shook Zeke's hand warmly, but suddenly realized Yuma was an Indian dressed in white man's clothes. "Is this Indian really a friend?" he asked apprehensively.

"Yes, a good friend. He helped spot the smoke signals as the warriors prepared to do battle with you. We would have been too late had it not been for him. Not all Indians are bad Indians," added Zeke.

"Just as not all white men are good men," added Josh.

William slowly nodded his head approvingly. "I'm afraid that is true. Very well, then, thank you again. I'm sure the captain will want to meet you," said William as he shook Yuma's hand and smiled. "And thank you, young man."

They all turned to follow the road to where the wagons pulled to a stop. At just about the point where they would lose sight of the river, an arrow suddenly whizzed by Josh's head, and planted itself dead center in a tree about head high. His military training took over. He spun without hesitation, and brought his rifle around to a firing position with the last cartridge already loaded and cocked.

A single Indian warrior refused to quit. He had forded the river and just as he reached their side of the riverbank, he knelt down on one knee and brought up his bow. As he began drawing back his second arrow, Josh pulled the trigger. The bullet raced right into the heart of the Indian knocking him into a back flip. As he spun in the air, he dropped his bow and quiver of arrows on shore. He crashed into the water about midway across, instantly dead.

"Damn!" exclaimed William. "What a shot!"

Yuma quickly gave Zeke the reins of the horses and began running towards the river.

Alarmed Zeke shouted at him, "Stop! Where are you going? You'll be killed!"

Josh quickly reloaded his weapon, and began scanning across the river. Zeke pulled his rifle up while cocking it and took aim.

Yuma reached down and gathered the arrows spilled from the quiver, grabbed the bow, and ran back to Zeke.

"You scared the crap out of me," exclaimed Zeke.

Josh laughed. "Your yelling probably scared him, too. I suspect he knows how to use a warrior's bow and arrows." Josh patted Yuma's shoulder. "Come on, let's get out of here."

Together, they continued towards the wagons.

The scout led them towards his boss. "Captain, these are the fellows who helped us," said William as he waved the captain over.

The captain immediately shook their hands. "I'm Wayne Moore. Thank you very much. I'm glad this Indian was on our side. We're trying to quickly bandage the wounded, repair the wagons and harnesses, grab some food, and then we'll quickly move on. I dare not stay and allow those bastards to attack us again."

"You're still two full days journey to Fort Collins, but they have patrols out almost every day," said Josh. "Maybe you'll run into one soon."

"William," began the captain, "go see the doc and let him fix your leg wound, then get some grub and ammunition, and feed your horse. Take another scout with you, and find one of those patrols. Get them to come escort us in."

"Yes sir," replied William who then turned to his new friends. "Thank you again. I hope we meet again someday."

"You're welcome. Ride safe," replied Zeke.

"Gentlemen, what are you doing in this wild Indian territory?" asked the captain as he led them to their grub wagon, and didn't give them an immediate chance to answer his question, as he barked orders to his men. "Barn, get these heroes something to eat and drink, if you don't mind."

"Yes, Captain," replied Barn who had been feeding the wagon train settlers and the scouts.

"Men, scatter out and stand watch. I don't want a single Indian to get within two hundred yards of us."

The men quickly finished their food, grabbed their rifles and horses, and made their way back towards the river. Josh, Zeke, and Yuma sat down on a log. Barn brought each of them a plate of his beans, rice, and a biscuit. He followed with a cup of coffee.

"We live in these mountains. This is our home. The Indians generally leave us alone, but we've experienced a couple of run-ins with a bad group that wears black and white stripes on their faces. However, the Indians that attacked you are not part of that bunch," said Josh. "They were Sioux."

Zeke spoke up, "The Indian tribes are banding together to fight the settlers. They have been pushed off their hunting grounds, which are the plains you crossed from Missouri, Kansas, Eastern Colorado, and Dakotas."

"According to the newspapers, some of the leadership in the government and army decided if they shot all the buffalo, the Indians would be forced off their land. This would allow the government to sell the land to the settlers with a one hundred percent profit. Put yourself in their shoes. They have been here for centuries, and the white man has been here for just four or five decades or so. Do you think they got a fair deal?" asked Josh.

The captain gave him a grunt, "I see your point, but they should bring their cases to a court and stop shooting people. None of these settlers did anything to them."

"They have no lawyers in their tribes, and they've already signed a dozen treaties offering concessions, but so far, the white man has broken every single one of them," said Zeke.

"I see, well, I think I'm going back to the ocean. I've had enough of these Indians. I'd rather fight pirates," said the captain with a laugh. "Again, I can't thank you enough. You're welcome to ride along with us if you like."

The boys quickly finished their food, "No thanks. Our home is in a different direction." Josh deliberately did not point to where they lived.

Zeke took up the hint. "I hope you don't run into any more trouble. You gave the Indians a pretty good whipping. I doubt they will bother you again. They tend to go after smaller groups where victory is certain."

"I hope so. It was nice to meet you lads. Thank you for saving us. Have a safe journey home," said the captain as he shook their hands once more. "Here take this horse and saddle as a gift of thanks. It belonged to one of my men that didn't make it." He handed the reins to Yuma with a tip of his hat, and then walked off to issue orders for everyone to load up.

"Let's get out of here," said Josh to Zeke and Yuma.

"I'm with you. Let's go."

63

Yuma tied Josh's rope around his packhorse, climbed on the new horse with the saddle, and tied off the rope to the saddle horn. Zeke quickly adjusted the stirrups for his shorter legs, helped him with the reins, and then smiled. "You look like a cowboy."

Yuma smiled, as Josh laughed as he swung up on his horse. They followed the same road to Fort Collins for about a mile, before cutting-cross country up and over the ridge, down a mountain, over another ridge, and into their valley. They led the horses into the barn, removed their saddles and bridles, and fed them. They had been forced to abandon their kill, but felt good they were able to help the settlers. It had been a long day that left Josh worrying as to how many battles they would have to fight to remain on their mountain. They ate quickly and made their way to the hot springs before turning in for the night exhausted.

Lieutenant Robert McCaffey enjoyed the life of a soldier more than any other man in his company. He looked like a typical Irishman in every feature: red hair, blue eyes, freckles on his face and hands, and a quick temper. He arrived in the west with his best friend after the war, fully believing his days of battles and wars were over. He and James Wilson wanted adventure without death, as they had seen more than their share in the march with Sherman near the end of the war. Many of their friends were getting out of the army, but Robert and James were promoted after showing interest of staying in, and after a bit of coaxing, they convinced their captain to recommend their transfer to the west. That was almost two years ago, and it began with long patrols with very few sightings of Indians. They mostly ate dust as they rode mile after mile, survived the heat during the summer, the cold during the winter, and still loved being in the army. Initially, Robert was sympathetic to the Indian cause, but that all changed just over four weeks ago when they were resting their horses after a long morning ride on patrol. James lifted his canteen to his lips. Robert heard the sound of a zip-thud. He turned to see where the sound came from and gasped at the scene before his eyes.

James still held the canteen to his lips, but an arrow hit him in the back of the neck, and now stood still sticking out the front side of his neck piercing his windpipe. The water and blood poured down the front of his blue uniform. Robert started to run to him while telling his men to take cover and fire at will.

Horrified, James dropped the canteen, and fell face first in the dirt, gasping for air as he continued bleeding. Robert carefully turned him over after breaking the arrow in the back of his neck. He pulled out the remaining front section of the arrow, and began to cry out.

Robert screamed, "No, no, no! James don't you die on me. I need you. Stay alive, damn it! Stay alive!" James went into shock with his left foot twitching rapidly until abruptly his heart stopped, his eyes locked, and he was gone.

Robert slowly lowered him to the ground, wiped the tears from his eyes, and looked up at his men. "Do you see anything?" he asked as he drew his pistol.

"No, sir," replied Andy, a corporal who had just arrived from Washington.

Robert scanned the area where he thought the shooter might be, and made a decision. "Damn bastards. They killed James, and for what reason I do not know. Okay Andy, take four men and make your way up that left slope. The rest of the men will follow me as we go up the right side. I want you to find that assassin and kill his ass. Do you understand me?"

Andy nodded, "Yes sir we do. I'm sorry about James. We'll find that Indian."

"Good. Okay men, let's do it."

Robert led his squad up the right side of a big ravine. He felt like the shot had to come from a knoll near the base of the mountain, as the top of the mountain was too far away for a bowshot. The Indian worked smartly by not waiting to watch the success of his shot. He dropped back, moved off to his left and waited. Andy and his squad jumped from rock to rock, trying to hide from an unknown and unseen shooter.

Zip! A second arrow flew taking out the man right behind Andy with a shot in the chest. Andy fired quickly at the rock, but once again, the warrior darted to a new position. They fanned out left and right to encircle the shooter, but he surprised them for the third time. Zip! Another man went down with a shot to his face, forcing him to drop his rifle, and fell to the ground screaming in pain before he died.

Robert heard the gunfire, making his squad more cautious, but still they tried to hurry their way up the hill.

Zip! With another of the squad shot and down, Andy became terrified. He told the remaining man to follow him, as they began to make their way back down the hill giving up the search.

The Indian saw their retreat and grinned. Boldly he stood up and fired taking out the other man leaving Andy alone. Andy turned just as the warrior threaded another arrow and began pulling back his bow. Andy froze in fear becoming an easy target.

Boom! Andy jumped at the sudden sound of the unanticipated gun. The Indian's shot went wide missing Andy. The big warrior fell over with most of the back of head missing. Robert climbed up on the rock he had fired from. He stared down at Andy.

Robert asked, "Are you all right?"

Andy's pants were soiled, "Yes, sir, but I'm the only one alive."

"Damn," replied Robert. "Okay men, scout out for others." Robert walked down and looked at the Indian. He did not believe in taking scalps, but he was so angry for the shooting of his men, as well as his best friend James, he wanted to cut the Indian into tiny pieces. However, his training took over so he regained his composure, and held his temper. He walked over and looked at each man shot by the Indian. Every day after today would be different, he thought, much different. They buried his men, gathered up their weapons, preventing the Indians from finding and using them, and left the Indian rotting on a rock in the sun. Wild birds were already circling overheard as they rode off.

Both Josh and Zeke had let their hair grow far longer than their days at the academy, but at least once a month they took turns trimming it a bit. After Yuma watched them do so, and laughed along with them as Josh and Zeke threaten to cut an ear off, or make jokes as to how ugly the other was, he decided to let them cut his long black hair. They asked him several times if he was sure, and he smiled and said yes.

Every day they continued his education. He was a quick learner and soaked up the praise they generously gave him like a dried sponge. They knew his life must have been a hard one with little rewards and lots of abuse. They no longer hid their love for each other, but rather showed him how affectionate they were with each other, and how much they loved each other. During his early life, he had to keep his attraction for males a secret fearing abandonment or death. With Josh and Zeke, he found hope that one day he might find a man to love him like they do.

On the level of a parent, they liberally gave Yuma hugs, tickled him, wrestled with him, gave him approving pats on the back, and showed they loved him. Josh and Zeke struggled to learn his Lakota language, but he enjoyed teaching the grownups as if he was a schoolteacher. In the beginning, his laugh was a small timid laugh, as if expecting to be slapped for doing so, but hanging around Josh and Zeke, he soon learned laughter was a key ingredient to their relationship, and the basis for many happy times.

With Yuma's help, they learned how to make heavier clothing out of the hides and fur they retrieved from the animals they killed for meat. Yuma taught them how to take bones from the animal, filing sharp slender bone pieces into needles, as well as how to take the tough fibrous tissue uniting a muscle to the bone called sinew, and cut it down so it would become the thread for the garments.

Zeke showed them how to make winter mittens out of the fur from rabbits, although Josh protested he could not fire his weapon with his mittens on. Zeke sewed a piece of long rawhide between the mittens and showed Josh how to sling one or both off and leave them dangling around his neck when he needed to use his fingers to fire his rifle. Zeke showed them how to quickly put his covered right hand under his left armpit. He tightened his left arm and easily pulled his right hand from the mitten. It took some practice, but soon they could quickly pull their warm hands out, and snatch up a pistol or rifle.

It took a full week, but they cut a hole through the wall with their axes, and built a room on to their cabin. They made a bed with four wooden posts, and rails, and then they took rope to create a lattice across the frame. They piled hides and furs on the bed, and Yuma finally had his own room. He had never slept in a bed, but rolled back and forth giggling as he checked it out.

The last big improvement they made was finding a place for a better outhouse. The cabin stood right in front of a large rock wall. They chose it initially because it prevented an Indian attack from the rear. In the mountain, they dug numerous caves most of which delivered not a single flake of gold. One had been successful, but they made it look like a dead end as well. It made them extremely wealthy, but came with a heavy load to keep their mouth shut to everyone. They liked things just as they were, using some funds to improve their settlement, and secure a peaceful future by buying up as much as land around them as they could. If word got out about their gold, their land would be crawling with thousands of gold diggers.

One of the caves became their new outhouse or in-house, as Zeke called it. On a previous dig, they failed to find gold, but discovered a natural pit. Carefully, they dropped pebbles down, and listen to how far it went. Then they tied a torch to a rope, and quickly learned they had to wet the rope to keep from setting it on fire. The pit was forty feet deep with no water at the bottom. Josh went down the rope into the pit looking for gold, but found nothing but sand.

They made a wooden box to cover the opening of the pit, with a round hole at the top to place their butt in. Josh drove a long nail into the dirt wall, and hung paper catalogs and old newspapers on it. They took turns showing Yuma how to make a bowel movement while sitting on the hole. The boy broke up laughing, but soon they coaxed him into doing so. Now and then, they would throw a shovel or two of dirt down the hole. They sewed two hides together to cover the entrance. To their surprise, the cave remained about fifty-four degrees year around, allowing them to go to the new in-house even when the outside temperatures were below zero. Fifty-four degrees in the cave felt cool in the summer, but nice and warm to their bare butts in the frigid winters.

They experienced two early snows, but continued working outside, knowing that soon the big snows would come. Yuma showed Zeke and Josh how to shoot the bigger bow and arrows he retrieved from the battle at the river, but neither was quite as good as Yuma. His patience and unshakable concentration won him many words of praise. He could be laughing uncontrollably one moment, pick up the bow, draw the arrow, and instantly became silent, still, and deadly.

Already dreading the effects of another long winter of cabin fever, even with the early snowfalls, they went hunting as often as possible. Last night about six inches of snow fell around the cabin, but the next morning they saddled up, rode over the crest of the mountain, down the next valley, and up to the top of Edger Mountain, enjoying partial blue skies once again. They checked the plains with the binoculars, found no signs of wagon trains or Indians, and hoped the winter would settle things down again creating peace for a while.

They went down the far side of Edger Mountain, and spread out in the valley below to search for wild game. Josh and his rifle went to the far left, with Zeke and his Winchester going to the far right, while leaving Yuma and his bow in the middle. Using stealth-like steps, they carefully and cautiously made their way through the forest. Once or twice, they spotted small game, but they held out for a moose or at least a deer.

The snow on this side of the mountain was much deeper than in their valley. They found places with a foot or more of beautiful white snow with occasional drifts of three feet. The leaves were down, and the sky overcast, with deep fluffy white clouds. The air felt crisp and clean, but they breathed very shallow to keep the fog of their breath to a minimum.

They tried to stay within sight of each other, but as the trees and wild brush became thicker, they occasionally lost sight of each other. Josh had just turned to look for Yuma, when he heard a limb creak not far to his left. He froze and slowly began turning while looking for the animal. At first, he saw nothing, but a minute or two later he saw a small rabbit scurrying about. The game was too small for his Sharps buffalo rifle, so he let his finger slide off the trigger and let out a breath.

At that moment, he heard another stick snap behind him. He quickly turned, and saw an Indian dressed in white fur, leap off a big rock with a knife in his hand, sailing towards him. He was too late to bring the rifle around, and had only enough time to catch the right arm of the hand holding the knife. His momentum pushed the arm with the knife away from his body, and sent them falling into a thicket of mountain laurel. Hundreds of tiny frozen limbs entangled them, but Josh held on to the Indian's arm. Somehow, he thrust a punch to the Indian's face, noting it was painted in black and white stripes. The white fur and the body paint, allowed him to camouflage himself in the falling snow. Josh realized he must have walked right past him. He cursed himself, as he should have sensed the man was there, or certainly smelled him, because as they struggled, he smelled the vile aroma of a man who lived totally off the land.

Repeatedly, the man tried to push the knife towards Josh's head, but the Indian was tough as he took a punch to his head, to his ribs and still held his arm with the knife. Josh's feet were tied up in the little limbs. Abruptly, he tripped backwards, and the Indian fell on top of him. Josh still held off the knife. The Indian snarled at him viciously, but Josh said nothing in reply, as his mind raced for solutions to kill the warrior.

Carefully, Josh reached for his pistol only to discover it was missing from his holster, knocked out by the thicket of stiff limbs. Slowly, he allowed his right hand to slide down his leg, and into his boot where he kept his knife. His fingers could not quite reach the handle of his knife. His right boot remained twisted in a limb. He felt his strength failing. The tip of the Indian's blade was no more than an inch from his bare face. Josh had to get his knife.

Unlike Josh, Zeke never heard the snap of a twig. A second Indian leaped off the rock and knocked him to the ground, while just missing his ear with a swipe of his knife. Maybe it was his previous experience or just plan luck, but Zeke rolled over in a summersault, instantly came to one knee, and drew his pistol all at the same time.

The Indian spun from his fall and turned to leap on Zeke to kill him. In a flash, Zeke shot him right in the face. The Indian fell to the snow covered ground like a dead bird from a tree. The snow quickly became red as the man bled out. Zeke searched left and right expecting another charge. Finding none, he grabbed his rifle and started running towards Yuma and Josh.

The Indian attacking Josh glanced away for just a split second at the sound of gunfire. Josh grunted as he managed to free his leg, grabbed his knife, and quickly brought it up and into the Indian's chest just beneath his heart, piercing the man's stomach. The man's eyes bulged as Josh angrily jerked the knife upward cutting deeply into the man's heart killing him.

Josh wasted no time getting to his feet, found his pistol, made his way back to his rifle, spun left and right, but saw no other Indians, and then began running towards Zeke and Yuma.

They met on the deer path. Zeke saw the blood on Josh's chest. "Are you all right?"

"Yep, a bad Indian tried to kill me. I had to kill him with my knife," replied Josh.

"Same for me, but this time I got off a shot and killed the bastard. Where's Yuma?"

"I don't see him," whispered Josh.

They searched the ground until they picked up his tracks, and followed them into the forest for only twenty yards until suddenly, two larger moccasin tracks appeared. They found Yuma's bow and arrows on the ground, and then only two tracks leading north.

"They've captured him!" whispered Zeke.

"They will kill him. Hurry, we must catch them," urged Josh, as he took off running, easily following the trail in the snow, but finding it tough to run in the foot or more snow drifts.

EIGHT

The warriors surprised Yuma by attacking from both sides. One of the warriors tapped Yuma hard with a club, knocking him unconscious. His body fell limp to the ground. The warrior wasted no time, as he hoisted the limp Yuma over his shoulder like a killed deer, and began their run to the north. The second Indian trailed the first while watching for the white men, his bow ready to fire.

They, too, were hunting when they spotted Josh, Zeke, and Yuma. Capturing Yuma would put them in good favor with their leader. They made quick plans, spread out, and waited for their prey to approach. They were cunning, patient, and fearless. They expected to kill the two white men, steal their horses and weapons, and haul the slave back to their camp, as they felt far superior to all men, especially the white men.

The warriors with Yuma made it down the hill quickly, but their horses were over the next ridge. They never paused for a breath. They slipped occasionally in the snow as they began their ascent. Their legs were bare with only moccasins on their feet, and legging on their lower legs, but they appeared immune to the cold.

Josh and Zeke tried to be cautious, but feared if they were too slow, they would lose Yuma forever. They were near the bottom, when they caught sight of the two carrying Yuma upwards on the other side.

"There they are," said Josh.

"Can you shoot them?" asked Zeke.

Josh swung his rifle around. "I can get one, but the other will hide or make it over the ridge before my second shot, and I have to be careful not to hit Yuma."

"Take out the man not carrying Yuma, and we'll continue the chase. He can't defend himself and carry Yuma at the same time."

Josh agreed but added, "You're right, but I fear he may kill Yuma and run. I guess we have no choice." Josh sighted carefully and fired.

Boom! The warrior was knocked flat to the ground as the big shell bore through his back and out his chest. The second Indian carrying Yuma glanced back and then kept running. Josh and Zeke started running as well in pursuit down the mountain while the warrior was already running up the other side. They wished they had their horses, but the terrain would have been too tough, and they would have lost time going back to their horses. They had to catch the Indian before he got out of sight.

The jostling of Yuma's body soon brought him awake. However, could not get his eyes to focus and his head throbbed. He heard the Sharps rifle and knew Josh was near. He quickly recalled the split second he saw the first warrior before being clubbed. He stared at the ground and after a minute or two he could finally bring the ground in to focus, though he was bouncing up and down with the warrior's rapid steps.

"Hurry, Josh. We must catch him!" exclaimed Zeke.

"We'll get him," replied Josh without missing a step or looking back as he placed another cartridge in his rifle without taking his eyes off Yuma.

They reached the top of the mountain breathing hard. "Do you see them?" asked Zeke.

"No," replied Josh. "Scan the area."

Zeke gazed left and right until he spotted movement off to the right. "I think I found them." He brought up his binoculars for a closer look "Dang, he's tying Yuma's hands and feet, and he has horses. He just swung up. Can you kill him?"

Josh quickly sighted in the direction Zeke pointed, but the rider was already moving, and he never had a clear shot through the trees. "We'll lose him now as we're on foot."

Zeke scouted the area. He pointed off to the north. "He'll have to go out that pass. Let's run the ridge, go down ahead of him, cut him off, and shoot him."

Josh took a quick look at where Zeke pointed and then took off, "Come on, let's hurry!"

They ran as fast as possible across the ridge, leaping over fallen trees, through brush, and up and over rocks. When the ridge started down they ran as fast as they could down the ravine, hoping they would not fall or lose their footing. It was more than three hundred feet down, but they kept moving though slowed up by thickets and briars.

"I think I saw movement off to the left," whispered Zeke. "They're coming!"

Josh did not answer, as he cocked his Sharp's buffalo rifle while still moving down the hill. After they reached the bottom, they had to jog along a stream to the pass. Exhausted from the run, they forced themselves to keep going. They found an animal path, which made the going a little easier.

"There they are," whispered Zeke as he pointed to the pass off to their right.

Josh knew he would only have time for one shot, or they would be through the pass, and gone in the valleys where his horses could easily outrun them. Quickly Josh stopped, took aim, but discovered a tree in his way. Zeke passed him and continued down the path. With no shot as Josh caught a glimpse of the warrior on his horse pulling Yuma. He moved again hoping to get a shot as they came around a big boulder, but as he moved his feet in the dried frozen grass, he stepped on an unseen large steel trap. Snap!

"Damn!" exclaimed Josh as it closed with the sharp sound of a metallic crack on his right ankle. He caught his breath, and though in excruciating pain, he turned once more to fire. Before he could take aim at the warrior, a large grizzly suddenly appeared to his left. Josh turned as the bear, standing over seven feet tall, growled fiercely at him, while taking big swipes with his paws in the air. Terrified, Josh turned the rifle to fire at the grizzly but he was too late. The big bear lunged, and his right claw knocked the rifle from Josh's hands, twisting several fingers in the process, and cutting into the flesh of his left arm.

Stunned, Josh reached for his pistol, and just pulled it out of the holster, when the bear leaped on top of him, knocking him to the ground, biting hard into his left shoulder. "Damn it! Zeke!" he yelled as he pushed the bear's nose with his right hand, trying to keep the bear's teeth from digging into him. He desperately punched at the bear's left eye with his right fist.

Zeke stopped running down the path and came back up. When he saw the bear, he brought his Winchester up and fired. The bear winced at the shot, but kept mauling Josh. Zeke ran closer and fired again, but the gun jammed. He snatched up his pistol and fired all six shots at the bear. The grizzly growled loudly, but did not slow down.

Zeke grabbed his knife, ran up the trail, and leaped off a rock onto the back of the bear. He stabbed him at least three times before the bear slung him off, ripping a claw across his chest. Zeke rolled into a heap, catching a boot between some rocks, which badly twisted his ankle. The pain shot quickly to his brain. He gritted his teeth, as he tried desperately to get up. He watched helplessly as the bear bit Josh once more.

Boom! Zeke heard the thunderous explosion of a big bore rifle, and thought it might be the Sharp's rifle, but he could see it on the ground not far from the fallen Josh. The bear froze and slowly stood. For just a glimpse, Zeke saw Josh's bloody face while looking through the bear's huge hind legs. Zeke saw a large stream of blood pouring from the bear's chest. Boom! A second round slammed right into the bear's upper chest. The bear stumbled backwards off Josh and towards the fallen Zeke.

Zeke started trying to drag himself out of the way, but his foot was still caught in the rocks. The bear gave out one last weak growl, and fell dead to the ground just inches from Zeke's foot. Zeke stopped screaming when the bear ceased moving. He tried to see Josh around the huge furry mound of the bear. He feared Josh was dead.

Though close to passing out, Zeke struggled to free his foot. Suddenly, he saw what appeared to be the feet of another big bear. He gasped in fear, but as he followed the feet upward, he soon caught sight of a white man with a big gray bushy beard, dressed in buckskins, and wearing the hide of a bear. His bright blue eyes gave Zeke a start. Off to his right, he held his immense rifle with the barrel still smoking. Zeke sighed greatly, and fell back unconscious.

The Indian warrior stopped when he reached the valley, untied Yuma, and removed him from lying across the top of the second horse. He set him up on the horse like a rider, and tied his hands around the horse's neck. He ran a second piece of rawhide cord from one ankle under the horse to the other. Yuma would not let the man see him cry, as he helplessly looked back up the mountain for any sign of Josh and Zeke. He saw movement, heard the gunshots, but saw no other sign of them. He hoped they survived the Indian attack, and if so, he hoped they would come for him.

The warrior swung aboard his horse, and began pulling Yuma's horse into a fast walk, and then into a gallop as they cut across the valley. After they started riding again, tears fell from Yuma's face to his shirt, but he had no time to sob. They would ride over fifteen miles that day, and ten more the next, before reaching their hidden camp in a deep valley far into the Rocky Mountains of Northern Colorado.

Zeke came to a day later in the warmth of a tipi. He gazed up the walls of the structure as the wind blew outside. The smoke from the small fire in the center drifted lazily to the vented top like a chimney. He closed his eyelids again, but soon opened his eyes as he stared into the face of an Indian woman. She must have thought he would be frightened so she said, "Peace. Peace. Peace." It was the first English word she learned, but rarely used. The tone of her voice made Zeke relax. She smiled slightly. Zeke sighed heavily. He thought he had been captured.

She turned to go outside, and came back with a white man about six feet tall and two hundred forty pounds or more. He wore buckskins for clothing, a broad leather hat, and with a head of gray hair that flowed right into his long gray beard. His eyes were bright blue, and he smiled at Zeke with mostly brown teeth. "Are you hungry?"

Zeke recognized the fur leggings on his lower legs, recalled the blue eyes like his own, and tried to smile back noting the man was missing a tooth, "Yes, I guess, but mostly thirsty."

"Good. That's a good sign," replied the man. He turned to the woman and said in her language to fetch water, and the rabbit stew on the fire. Zeke recognized the words Lakota words for water, rabbit, and fire.

"Where am I?" asked Zeke. "And who are you?"

"You're in our tipi in the Rocky Mountains about fifty miles, give or take ten or twenty miles or so, from Boulder. I'm John Bridger. This is my wife. She is a Siha Sapa of the Blackfoot tribe. She has a long Indian name, but I call her Liz, short for Elizabeth my first wife's name. My first wife died of smallpox." He paused for a second thinking fondly of his first wife before smiling and continuing. "Liz is a good woman, and she knows medicine, too. She believes she prevented a possible infection from the bear's claw to your chest. That old bear ripped you good. It must hurt like hell."

Zeke looked down at his bare chest with the strips of clean rawhide across his wounds. "It does," replied Zeke.

The woman knelt down, and helped him drink from a dried yellow gourd. After a few sips, she set it down, and picked up a small pottery bowl. She dipped a well-worn wooden spoon in, and lifted a bit of the rabbit stew to Zeke's lips. He quickly downed it feeling starved. After he finished the bowl, he asked, "Where's Josh? Did he make it?"

"Too soon to tell, he's over there," said John as he pointed behind him. "He's been unconscious since we brought him here. The bear bit him hard in the shoulder, and broke a tooth on one of your friend's bones. Here," he tossed the tooth to Zeke. It fell on the bear hide by his side. Slowly, he picked it up.

"It's huge," replied Zeke fingering it.

"The bear must have had a tooth problem for it to come out so easily. Maybe that's why he did not bite all the way down and rip the shoulder away from…"

"Josh," helped Zeke.

"Right—Josh. He was lucky. A full bite would have caused massive blood loss, and may have pierced his heart."

"What happen? We were chasing an Indian who had kidnapped our friend, when all of a sudden I heard Josh scream, and saw the bear on top of him."

"This was my fault. I'm sorry, so very sorry. Last summer, a bear killed our only child. I just could never let it go. I had never seen a woman cry like Liz did over losing our child. I held a grudge against that bear. Whenever I had some time, I hunted for that bear."

"How'd you know which bear is the right one?"

John laughed, reached back, and flung a bear's foot to Zeke. Zeke caught it, but held the smelly foot away from his face.

"That's his rear right foot. Do you see? He's missing a toe. I remembered that track when I found my dead son. I tracked only him. Here's what happened. That ravine you were in has a thicket near the back where the grizzly camped out if you will. When I discovered it, I knew he would be back, so I put a few bear traps in his path, so if he came home while I was away, I'd still catch him, and then I could kill the bastard.

"Unfortunately, your friend accidentally stepped into one of my traps. When he heard the bear, he turned to fire, but the bear knocked the gun away ripping flesh from his left arm. Then the bear fell on top of him, and began to maul him. The grizzly weighed almost three hundred pounds pinning Josh to the ground. I had just left the traps, and started home. When I heard the steel-trap snap, and then the growl of the grizzly, I thought I had him, and came rushing back. I had to quickly get closer before firing, so I could kill him.

"When I topped the ridge, I saw you fire your last pistol shot, and then you did something I have never seen anyone in my life do. You ran and jumped on top of the bear with only your knife in hand. You stabbed him about three times, but he slung you off, and swiped you with a claw.

John continued, "I shot the bear once, and he reared up off Josh, and then I shot him again. He fell back and landed just inches from you. He must have looked like a big tree falling towards you."

"I remember that," said Zeke. "Thank you for saving and taking care of us."

"My wife has treated all of Josh's wounds, and we forced some water and soup down his throat carefully to give him some nourishment while still unconscious. The fact that he is asleep will help because he is going to be pretty sore. It will hurt to move."

Though afraid to hear the answer Zeke asked, "What about the boy?"

"I spent most of today sorting things out. I followed tracks not far from the bear attack, where I found the trail of two riders, one heavier than the other, and their trail led out the pass to the valley and out of sight."

"That was probably the warrior and Yuma. We rescued the boy after finding him in the woods starved, and obviously abused and beaten. We taught him our language. He speaks pretty good English, and was apparently a slave of some bad Indians."

"Describe the warriors."

"Well, they all look fierce, and they wear two stripes of war paint on each cheek, one white and one black, with no feathers. We have seen them attack and kill settlers viciously."

"There are hundreds of bands in this area, many of which are some part of the Sioux tribes. Sioux is translated as 'sued by' as if someone stole or harmed you, you would sue them. Like us white folks, there are good Indians and they are bad ones. This group is partly Lakota. Word has it that a chief had twin sons, both of which wanted to become chief. Onc of the sons killed the other, and tried to make it look like a buffalo gored him, but after inspecting the body, they saw a knife wound under his left shoulder into his heart.

"The chief was greatly distraught with his son's treachery. He stripped and whipped his son, and banished him from the tribe. The son and about twenty of his friends left with him. They had no food stores or tipis, only their horses and weapons. Stealing from the white men was easy for them, but they enjoyed the killing. They are like a wolf that has tasted blood, and now cannot get enough of it. With no regular structure like a village, they are like a gang of thugs. They capture young boys and make them slaves to do all their dirty work. When the boy becomes old enough, he can choose to join them or they will kill him. Not much of a choice, huh?

"They capture women both Indian and whites alike, but they never last but a few weeks, because they all rape a new female captive repeatedly. They treat her like a slave, then rape her some more, and then beat her to death—especially when she tries to fight back. The white women are tortured to death by cutting off ears and teats, breaking toes, and running knives into their private areas. Usually they leave her with a slit to a leg vein, letting her bleed out while hanging from a tree limb. I've heard they often allow their dogs to feed on them while still alive. They are ruthless, and my wife and I do our best to stay out of their way. If you'll take my advice you boys should do the same."

"Bridger," said Zeke. "I think I've heard of you. Don't you have a fort named after you in Wyoming, and I believe Bridger Pass is also your discovery."

John laughed heartily, "I have to laugh for I'm not as famous as my brother James who did all the things you have heard of and more. I am the unknown younger brother, and I enjoy my privacy very well. We both came west from our home in Richmond."

"Virginia? I went to the academy near Petersburg. I know Richmond very well," added Zeke.

"I miss Virginia where the seasons are far more normal than here. Colorado gives you a very long winter season, beginning and ending with a short fall and spring. The summer is usually only about ten weeks in length, but we all live for the summer. James and I first worked for the fur traders, but after hearing the stories of the early hunters and mountain men, we gave up our jobs for a life of adventure. James went on great explorations. Did you know he was the first white man to see the Great Salt Lake of Utah? He also saw Yellowstone and discovered geysers and hot springs, but when he returned to civilization to tell of his adventurers, everyone laughed for my brother James was far better known as the greatest inventor of tall tales. For example, he said there was a valley in the Yellowstone that was so large you could yell hello before you went to bed and while fixing breakfast the next morning the echo would finally come back to you." John laughed again. "He's slowing down a little and lives in Wyoming."

Filled with curiosity Zeke asked, "Why didn't you go with him?"

"Love, young man, probably something you know nothing about, but love. I met Liz while trading with the Indians, and it was love at first sight. We would have no life traveling on explorations far out west, and on the other side of the Rockies. That country is much too hard on a man, and even harder on a woman, and we had a child back then. My son from my second wife died at the age of four—smallpox got him and most of her tribe. We moved away from the tribe, and I managed to survive, but his mother died of the pox, too.

"I'm a mountain man of the old variety. In the beginning, we hunted and killed all the beaver possible because back east, everyone thought it fashionable to wear a fur hat. With no regulation, the style and demand for fur changed, but at the same time, we hunters were too good, and killed just about every beaver west of the Mississippi. We also killed thousands of buffalo. This made for a good life. I would travel by myself all year, including the harsh winters, and hide my pelts in caves until July, when I would load up my packhorse, collect my hides, and head down the mountain to a rendezvous."

"A rendezvous for what?" asked Zeke.

John smiled as he pulled his pipe from his big coat pocket, open a small leather pouch, and retrieved a pinch of fresh tobacco. He packed it tightly in the pipe bowl with his brown stained thumb, removed a stick with a red ember on one end near the edge of the fire, and lit his tobacco while slowly drawing a little air through it. He softly blew out a puff of smoke from his lungs and smiled. "A rendezvous made trading the furs for money and supplies much easier. The fur companies would fill wagons full of all the supplies a mountain man would want: sugar, flour, coffee, blankets, clothes, lead, gunpowder, knives, and guns. In the beginning, you could get rich with fur pelts selling at nine dollars apiece. I often brought in a thousand hides so I'd make about nine thousand dollars.

"Sugar and coffee sold for just fifteen to twenty cents in Saint Louis. Therefore, a fellow could spend fifty dollars and go back to the mountains with all the supplies he needed and rolls of money in his saddlebags. It became dangerous to carry that much money because it turned a bad trapper into a good thief. If you only had a hundred pelts, and you watched another man trade in over a thousand, you became envious, jealous, and angry. Many a great mountain man was killed not by a big old grizzly bear, but by a fellow hunter in the middle of the night wanting his money.

"Greed also infected the fur companies. They started hauling in more liquor, and would throw grand parties including whores for several days before trading would begin. Then they sold the supplies with a huge markup. Sugar went from fifteen cents a pound to two dollars a pound. Everything went up, so the more you made, the more they charged you for the supplies. It was a quite a racket!

"However, it was also great fun. For a year, the mountain men like me traveled and hunted their own part of the mountains and did it all alone. They took the best nature could throw at them and won. They fought blizzards and floods, Indians and wolves, and as you know, an occasional grizzly, but they were a tough lot. Like the buffalo, it would take more than one bullet or a few arrows to put their chin in the dust.

"At the rendezvous there were wrestling events, knife and hatchet throwing contests, and of course rifle competitions. These were the best hunters and explorers on the continent so the alcohol flowed, the tall tales grew even harder to believe, and the fun began. Many friendly Indian tribes came, too, and traded their furs and enjoyed the festivities. They would wear their best skins, and thousands of feathers and beads. I met my wife there, and it was love at first sight. I mean, she had all her teeth, which was better than most of the women," he added with a straight face.

Zeke scrunched his face a bit, and smiled. "I suspect you love more than her teeth."

John laughed. "Indeed I do. She and I learned to sip just a little liquor, and fake being drunk. We would wheel and deal with the fur companies until we got the best price. We also argued over every supply item we bought. If the rendezvous ended on Sunday, we left the night before, and way after midnight when all but a few had fallen asleep with a gut full of alcohol. We doubled back often until we were sure we were not followed, and then rode quickly away to our mountains. We were never robbed, and we did well until the fur trade died. Now, we are in early retirement. Although I have treasures of cash buried all over the place, we prefer to live off the land, and keep moving, so no one can plan to either rob or burn us out. We stay away from towns and settlers, and away from the Indians. We'll let them fight it out, and perhaps we will not be in the middle. We have a good life.

"Well, I have been rattling on. You must get your rest. Why don't you sleep a while, and if Josh stirs, I will wake you. Don't worry. He looks tough. I am sure he'll make it," smiled John.

"Thank you," he said to John and then to Liz, "Le mita pila." He closed his eyes and drifted off to sleep easily.

John and Liz looked at each other and wondered how he learned to speak the Lakota language. These two boys were quite a mystery, but they would have to wait until they were well and strong before discovering answers to their questions.

NINE

Four days later, Josh finally opened his eyes. He could only speak in a whisper, too weak to move or talk very well. He managed a slight smile at Zeke, ate some soup, and promptly went back to sleep. Every hour or so, he would awake, eat, and go back to sleep. John said for Zeke not to worry, as it would take time for Josh's body to replace all the blood he lost.

Liz sewed a piece of fine buckskin into a new shirt for Zeke, as the bear and the blood messed up his old one. He admired her handiwork, her judge of his size, and the speed in which she could work with the hide. John told him she first scraped the hide until it was clean. She wet and stretched the leather, pounded it flat with a rock, and stretched it again. He felt it was as if he was wearing the skin of the animal, and yet, it was soft but durable.

The days were getting shorter and the nights colder. The dry fall season was over, and the long cold winter had begun. Snow fell almost daily, and Zeke feared they would be snowed in, unable to return to their cabin. He tried to walk farther each day building up his strength, and working the soreness out of his bruised body. He made short hikes back and forth across the campsite. He forced himself to stretch his arms and chest. The pain brought silent tears to his eyes, but he kept at it until the wound no longer impaired him. He hadn't felt this bad since being beat up in the Confederate prison in Andersonville when Sherman marched from Atlanta to Charleston, and where Josh finally found him.

John would hunt alone each day returning in the afternoon to build up the fire outside the tipi. Liz would welcome him home with a big hug and a kiss, which always made John blush in front of Zeke, and then he would hang up the game he had shot on a pole. He raised and lowered it based on the length of the animal, and how far Liz could reach, as she was only five feet tall. Zeke watched and tried to learn quickly from her. The Indian women did the dirty jobs, but she did it magnificently, and with the skill of a New York butcher. She carried two large leather pouches which carried the herbs she had dug up, dried, crushed in a stone bowl, and secured in early fall. She used handfuls of salt and her herbs to season and dry the meat. Her venison steaks, grilled carefully over the fire, were far better than any he enjoyed back home.

Yesterday, Zeke went hunting with John. He got lucky and killed an elk. After returning to camp, Zeke watched carefully as Liz removed the hide with a sharp serrated knife chipped from a hard black stone. She cut strips of the meat, and hung it over a pole to dry by the sun and wind. She removed some of the fat, threw it in a black cast iron pan John traded some skins for, and soon Zeke chewed on fresh grilled elk steaks.

He, John and Liz would sit around the cook fire until they had eaten well, and the cold caught up with them. John would tell stories of his adventures, but mostly Zeke wanted to know how a mountain man survived on just the supplies on his packhorse, and his own ability to hunt.

John told him the wintertime allowed only short days for checking traps and getting firewood. It was during this time of year that he and his wife worked on new clothes, cleaned their rifles, made bullets, carved out cooking tools including bowls as well as utensils. They made big sheets of rawhide for future tipis. Liz showed him the moccasins she made for him explaining they made their moccasins from old tipis because the sun and smoke dried the buckskin until it was strong. John showed him the leggings that Liz made from the tough neck area of a buffalo hide. No briar or snake teeth could penetrate the hide. In the early days, the Indians made shields with layers of the tough hide that would deflect arrows in battle.

She made gloves and hats from the hides, and then lined each with rabbit or fox fur for warmth. Zeke thought the amazing woman was capable of making anything. At night by the fire in the tipi, she would create intricate beadwork on a piece of buckskin, creating many beautiful and colorful designs. John told him she made the large beads from hollow bones from birds or small animals. She would cut the bones beads with her knife and leave them in sun so they would bleach white. She used berries and roots to make a dye and would soak handfuls of beads in the various color mixtures, and then once again dry the new colorful beads in the sun. The small ones were glass beads John secured at trading post as a present for her. The glass beads were blue, red, or yellow her favorite colors.

One day Zeke asked John how he killed a buffalo by himself. He said he and Josh had seen one in Denver in a corral, and it was about six feet tall, ten feet long, and was told it weighed just over two thousand pounds. Zeke thought it must take a cannon shot to drop the animal. John laughed heartily at the notion.

"The idea, my young friend, is to kill any animal with minimum shots, or the hide will be full of holes!" he laughed again as he said it. "I must say you almost ruined the grizzly hide by shooting it six times, and stabbing it three times. What were you thinking?" he asked before coughing due to his heavy laugher.

Zeke laughed as well, "I wasn't thinking, John, I was just trying to kill the bastard!"

"Next time shoot him in the heart, or at the worst in the eye, but please, don't try to tame him like a bronco horse. Grizzlies don't make a very good riding creature!" he laughed again making Zeke blush.

The laughter woke up Josh, so Liz grabbed a spoon and fed him another bowl of her special protein filled stew she kept warm by the smaller fire inside the tipi, and gave him water to drink.

John said gunpowder and lead were expensive for a mountain man. He used to make lead balls over the fire for his musket, but a few years ago, he learned how to make his bullets from a new mold, and remake his cartridges. He always picked up his shell casings after killing his prey, and retrieved the lead from the kill to melt and use again. It takes me a while to make one bullet, but can you imagine how long it takes an Indian to make just one arrowhead. Therefore they practice until they are very good archers, and steadfastly make sure every shot counts. Mountain men are also limited in the quantity of their supplies because of their packhorse. The animal has to be able to carry a load safely, and be able to escape other Indians, a wild buffalo or mountain lion, or even a grizzly by galloping away.

John explained that to the Indian and the mountain man, the buffalo is their main crop so to speak. One buffalo could feed several families for a month or more, and in the case of John and Liz—all winter. Almost every morsel from the big beast could be used to sustain life as well as improve it. The buffalo provided meat for sure, but the remaining carcass could become blankets, traditional Indian tipis, mattresses, clothing, medicine, condiments, and even knives and buttons. He had yet to kill a bison this fall, and intended to keep hunting until he did, or the snow became too deep.

John said bison, as the Indian called them, have a strong sense of smell. The hunter must arrive downwind. John said he often soaked dried buffalo meat in a bowl of his own urine the night before a hunt, and then would rub his face and hands in the mixture to hide the scent of a man.

"But wouldn't the human urine give you away?" asked a skeptical Zeke, beginning to think his story was the work of a tall tale which is brother Jim Bridger was famous for.

"The acid in the urine breaks down the meat. After I pour the urine off, I rub the meat on me. It works—you should try it," laughed John. "You smell almost as bad as that old bear you wrestled!"

He said that once he spotted a herd, he often rode for hours to get downwind. Then carefully he would lie over his saddle to hide his shape as he walked his horse inward to the herd as if the horse might be lost. He would slowly raise his rifle and fire. If he was lucky, he killed two or three before the herd stampeded. Unlike horses, which gallop on good pastureland, a bison would run at full speed over the worst terrain hoping to lose his prey. His stout hooves could handle gopher holes and rocks with ease. He would charge a man on a horse, so the shooter always remained on his horse ready to gallop away until the wounded beast hit the ground with a thunderous thud.

"Never get caught on your feet near the herd or a wounded buffalo. He'll charge like the old bulls in Spain. The only way to kill a buffalo with one shot is to shoot it between the breast and the shoulder. If you hit his heart, he'll crash to his knees and fall over dead. However, most of the time, it takes numerous shots to bring one down. He is angry with you, and will try to gore or stomp you until his last heartbeat. They are as ferocious as an African lion," added John with a snort.

"When I was younger, I was good at it. We did not have guns like your Sharps rifle that fires cartridges. I must tell you I admired your gun very much. Don't worry it is over there with the rest of your stuff. We fired our weapons from the back of our horses running at full speed. We fired, reloaded using our power horn, tapped the ball down by slamming it down on our saddle, and then fired again until the animal died.

"Liz will tell you the Indians hunt in packs like wolves. They use ten to twenty braves who shoot three or more arrows into one bison to bring him down to the ground. They are very skillful with a bow and arrows. Before the Spanish brought horses to this continent, the Indians were all on foot. They would drive the bison over cliffs, or into corrals, and the whole village participated in the kill.

"I tell you what, if you're feeling up to it, why don't I take you on a bison hunt, and show you what it is like?" asked John.

Zeke gleamed, "I'd like that very much, but I'm not sure I can ride fast just yet."

"Don't worry, lad, I'll do the hunting while you'll stay on the ridge with your binoculars, and watch an old fart do his job!" laughed John. "Now if you'll excuse me, I've got to go pee on some meat in a bowl to get ready," he said as he left the tipi laughing all the way.

Zeke gulped at the thought of the smell, but could not wait for the big adventure to begin. He checked on Josh, and then pulled the bear hide up to his neck to keep him warm. He returned to his own hide, covered himself carefully with another hide, and was asleep before John turned in for the night.

Yuma sat tied to a pole inside the tipi. His return to the village of 'Kaga Ozuye'—the demon warriors, broke his spirit. During the journey, he tried to escape from the horse, but the warrior had tied his wrists so tight the leather cord cut into his skin. He did not care how much it hurt; he still pulled as hard as he could. They rode far away from Zeke and Josh, a journey that took several days. His only rest was at night, so the warrior and the horses could rest. He had been slapped several times, and from experience, he knew better than to complain, cry, show weakness, or display anger. The warrior ate, gave Yuma a few morsels of food and water, and then promptly raped him before falling asleep. His face became void of emotion, but he could not help hoping that somewhere behind them, Josh and Zeke were tracking their movements. At every opportunity, he wrote his name in the sand where he lay for the night, or he spelled Yuma with small pebbles near a river, and broke tiny twigs so he could spell his name on a rock.

When they reached the warrior camp, he knew he would be beaten for escaping, but because he wore white man's clothes, they would treat him especially bad. When the warriors saw them ride into camp, they encircled his horse and began making jeers at him. They cut the rawhide rope and pulled him from the horse. They spit on him, ripped his shirt off, and then knocked him to the ground, and stripped off his pants. They kicked him in the ribs, his buttocks and delighted in kicking genitals. Yuma covered himself, kept a stone face, and prayed they would soon grow tired of him. If he begged them for mercy, he knew they would delight in creating more pain for him to endure.

Abruptly, a tall warrior pushed through the crowd, leaned down, grabbed a fistful of Yuma's hair, and yanked him to his feet. He yelled at the others to back off, while shaking his fist at them. They knew Yuma was his slave, and they all felt thankful they were not. The big Indian was by far the bravest and wildest of the lot, and none dared cross him. He was their chief and leader since his banishment from his tribe by his father. They have seen him ride out alone, snatch a hat from a settler, and then ride like the wind displaying his bravery or counting coup as they called it. When a cavalry squad ambushed his group, he ran straight at them firing one arrow after the other until all six where killed. Not one single bullet from their rifles touched him. He kept a tall pole outside his tipi, and from it hung a hundred and twenty-six scalps he personally collected along with an assortment of ears and noses. No one he had fought, lived to brag about winning. He fought hard, cheated often, delivered extreme ruthlessness, and terrified all. He always fought until his opponent died.

They called him 'Mila Hanska' which meant long knives because unlike the rest of the tribe that carried a single knife, Mila Hanska carried two knives much like a cowboy carried dual six guns. He could throw them rapidly with great accuracy to forty feet, but often used both in battle to carve up his victim before finally killing them. He liked to take his trophies while the settler, soldier, or warrior was still alive. The more they screamed, the more pleasure he took in the kill. He always took the scalp last before slitting their throats and watching them bleed out.

Yuma's feet barely touched the ground as Mila Hanska dragged him towards his tipi. When they reached it, he threw the boy inside. The warrior stepped in, and closed the flap over the entryway. Yuma crawled to the far side of the tent, pulling his bruised and battered body into a squat. The warrior spent several minutes screaming obscenities at him, while occasionally kicking him. Nevertheless, after a while the man stopped yelling, and sighed heavily, as if exhausted from the effort. He began barking orders to Yuma just as he had done for the past several years. He had captured Yuma after attacking his tribe when the boy was just six years old, making him his personal slave, to be abused and used in every way. Yuma, now almost eighteen years old, was fed little, so his body remained small.

Yuma quickly got to his feet and began undressing the warrior of his garments. He removed the moccasins, and then his knives, followed by his hide pants, and then his buckskin shirt. Gently he untied a thin rawhide string from around the man's waist that held a soft fur lined sack. Yuma carefully loosened the string at the top of the sack and then pulled it off the warrior's genitals.

Yuma placed a cloth in a gourd of water, rung out the water, and then slowly began washing the warrior from head to toe. He had been doing this for years, and he knew every square inch of his master's body, including his battle scars and his markings. The warrior spread his legs as Yuma washed his genitals and buttocks before finally cleaning his feet. The Indian then lay down on the fur hide of a grizzly he killed several years ago by himself.

He spoke new orders to the boy. Yuma sighed, but did as he was told. He wet the rag again and began washing his own body while the warrior watched him. He wiped away the spit from the warriors that had dried on his skin. He washed away the blood from the cuts and scrapes he received on the journey back to slavery. His body was soon covered in chill bumps, but they were not there because he was cold. They had arisen because he was frightened and terrified. In the warmer months, Mila rarely let Yuma or any if slaves wear any clothing, believing they would be less likely to run away.

The warrior ordered him to bring food to him. Yuma quickly filled a gourd with the stew simmering in a pot near the edge of the fire. The man ate quickly and asked for more. Yuma refilled his gourd and brought a bowl of water for him to drink. When satisfied, the man told him to eat. Yuma quickly filled the bowl and devoured the stew. He could have eaten more as he was starving, but he knew better than to ask. Quickly, he drank some water. He held the bowl of water to his lips, and felt the water tasted better than any he had ever encountered.

When finished, he slowly set the bowl down, and walked over to a disorganized pile of household items. When he found the power horn, he pulled the leather cap off the wide end, and stuck his index finger in to scoop up a little animal fat he stored there. He turned around to face the warrior, bent over slightly, and put his greased finger in and around his anus. He walked over to the Indian and lay down beside him.

Most of the rest of renegade clan treated their boys much worse than their horses. They battered the boys and cared little for them. When they captured a woman, they fought for turns to rape her, but usually the woman only lasted a few days in the camp. The women sometimes bled to death in the night. Yuma could remember one white lady who committed suicide after securing a knife while being mounted from the rear. She sliced her throat, but her death did not stop the warrior. He finished his orgasm on her dying body, and then bragged to the braves his member was so huge he had ruptured her heart.

Mila Hanska pulled the boy on top of him and began rubbing his hands up and down Yuma's backside. The boy rested the top of his head against the man's cheek hoping to satisfy his master, and avoid another whipping. After arousing, he ordered Yuma to suck him. The boy spun around, straddling the Indian as he had been taught, and immediately took him in. Sometimes the man blew cool air towards his anus to make him flinch. Other times he pushed a finger in and out of him. Tonight the warrior reached for a leather bag he kept next to his buffalo robe and removed a single eagle feather. He pushed Yuma's legs apart until he could see his gleaming greased anus. He began tickling the boy's private areas with the feather, while delighting in his twitching. Yuma knew better than to stop his work, but after a while, the man moved the feather away. He told Yuma to spin back around and mount him.

An hour later, the Indian slept while cuddling Yuma who had his back to him. The boy rested his head on the man's arm as tears silently slid down his cheeks to the buffalo hide. He closed his eyes and wished he were back in the cabin with Josh and Zeke. He hoped they would come for him, but felt conflicted because he knew if they did, most likely they would be killed. He knew if that happen, he would have to commit suicide like the white woman, for he could not live with the guilt of their deaths on his heart.

TEN

Albert Finney had been desperately working the streets of Fort Kearny all afternoon with little success. His nervous wife was four months pregnant with their first child, and they frantically wanted to get to Oregon before the baby's birth. His wife became even more apprehensive while staying in the noisy and wild frontier town of Fort Kearny. She feared the rough talking, unclean, drunken mountain men, as well as the supposedly friendly dirty Indians who roamed the streets begging for food. The smells from these people offended her, and she couldn't wait to get out of the disgusting town. Yesterday, a group of former Confederate soldiers robbed the bank killing anybody who got in their way. A marshal attempted to stop them, and they shot him in the street with a shotgun to the face, and then rode over his body with their horses. They also shot and killed a five-year-old boy holding a wooden pistol, who ran across the street as they were riding out. They continued on as if they had just swatted a mosquito from their line of sight.

Albert's wife grew panicky, and neither felt safe, but worst of all, they knew their money would run out if they stayed there for the winter. He asked every scout in town to lead them, but they all laughed and pushed him away. The blacksmith told him about an old mountain man by the name of Leroy Colbert. He said he would be their best bet. Albert found the man sleeping in a stall in the back of the barn. Albert's first impression of this old man was that the stench of his booze filled face was even worse than the shit in the horse stalls where he was sleeping off his last bottle of whiskey.

Albert swallowed his pride and made his pitch, "Sir, I beg your mercy. My wife is pregnant, and she is afraid to stay in this town. We don't have enough money to stay in town for long—only enough to get to Oregon. We need a guide. Will you take us?"

To Albert's surprise, the man suddenly smiled. "How much?"

"Fifty dollars is all I can pay," said Albert.

The scout burped with no apology. "We leave at dawn," replied the man without a second thought, "but I need a little advance to get supplies."

Albert looked from the drunk to the blacksmith who was busy shaking his head no. "I'm afraid that is not possible. I pay when you deliver us to Oregon, and not a cent until then. I have supplies already. My wife is a good cook. You'll eat well."

"Not even a dollar?" asked the disappointed Leroy.

"Not a cent," replied Albert stubbornly.

"All right, you win. I'm tired of this town anyhow. Meet me out back of the barn at dawn ready to go." Leroy fell back into the hay, and promptly fell back asleep.

Albert turned to leave when suddenly a boy swung down from the loft while hanging on to a rope and landing just in front of him. Albert jumped back a little thinking the young man was going to attack him. "Sir," began the boy of eighteen. "My name is Jeremy Gordon. You must take me with you. I'm a good worker, and I can ride and shoot," he lied, at least about being a shooter. "I can't find work in Fort Kearny. I'll starve to death if I stay here."

Albert thought for a second, thinking perhaps another man might be of help in keeping this drunken scout under control, so he made a quick decision. "You can go, but I can't pay you anything, but I'll feed you and your horse. We'll see you in the morning."

Jeremy grinned. "What is your name, sir?"

"Albert Finney, nice to meet you," he replied as he shook the boy's hand, and made his way out the door.

To everyone's surprise, Leroy saddled up and met the rest of the group behind the barn at sunrise as promised. He said little the first few days on the trail, and Albert assumed the large consumption of alcohol was still gradually leaving his body. Sarah was a good cook, and though pregnant, she fed the men as best she could. They particularly liked her biscuits, but she also made some oatmeal cookies. The men loved those cookies, and offered to help her in any way possible.

Around the campfire, Leroy began telling Albert and Jeremy what to do in case of an attack, be it from robbers or Indians. With the winter coming, he hoped there would be less chance of an attack, but expected it might happen eventually. Every day for the first week, Jeremy rode along with Leroy far ahead of the wagon. Leroy showed him how to scout left and right of the trail, while looking for any signs of shoeless horses. Jeremy possessed only a six-shooter pistol he picked up in Saint Louis for seven dollars and two boxes of shells. Leroy scoffed at the weapon. Albert stored a Winchester and new Parker shotgun in the wagon. He loaned Jeremy the Winchester, and kept the shotgun loaded and placed near the seat on the wagon.

Jeremy spent nearly eighteen years of his life on the streets of New York City. In all those years, he never went more than a mile from home, so he considered every view more spectacular than the last. He rode quickly over hills to see the next valley, while carefully scouting the ground for any sign of riders. When they reached the Upper Platte River in western Nebraska,

Jeremy spotted tracks for a dozen ponies. His heart began racing, but he followed the tracks to the ridge overlooking the river. There he found yet another group of tracks. Combined, he guessed there were twenty to thirty riders. He gulped at the thought of facing that many Indians.

Quickly, he rode back to Leroy who rode about fifty yards in front of the wagon to report what he had found. Leroy immediately swore, knowing his luck had just run out.

Leroy asked, "How old were the tracks?"

Jeremy had climbed off his horse, felt the ridge of the tracks, and they were soft and wet. "Not very old…they are still soft," he replied. "The horse droppings were covered in flies."

"That means at this time of the year they are less than a day or so old. If we continue on this course, we'll probably run right into them. I was hoping they would be settling down, and preparing for winter, which is what we should be doing. Indians never do what you want them to do. This trip may be the dumbest thing I've ever done, and believe me—I've done some really stupid stuff.

"We'll have to turn south into Colorado, and try to make Fort Morgan. From there, we can move on to Fort Collins, and if we're lucky, we can head to Fort Bridger, and get back on the Oregon Trail before the big snow falls.

"Come on, let's tell Albert the plan," said Leroy as he pulled his horse around, and together, they galloped to the wagon. After the hearing their plan, Albert asked, "Are you sure we have to go so far out of our way?"

"Sir, you hired me to get you there, and refused to pay me until I do. Jeremy saw the tracks of over twenty braves. We are only three against twenty. What chance would we have?"

"But we have rifles. They just have arrows," Albert protested.

"They are deadly with those arrows, so don't fool yourself. They have been raiding wagon trails for a few years now, and captured various rifles. The only problem they have with the rifles is they are short on a supply of bullets. This means they want to rob more wagon trains in hopes of pilfering more bullets. We're safer going from one fort to the next, and if we can talk the commanders into an escort, we'll be in good safe company."

Albert sighed. He knew Leroy spoke with the voice of experience. "Will the wagon hold up off the trail?"

"Once we cross the Platte River, we'll start climbing into the mountains. We'll be forced to follow a trail to the fort. Now I need for you to turn your wagon and head for that big tree. Jeremy and I are going to try and cover your tracks so if the Indians come along, perhaps they will miss seeing a single wagon leave the trail."

Albert did as requested, while Jeremy and Leroy rode over to a stand of small trees. They broke several limbs off and tied them together with rope in two bundles. They hooked the end of the rope to their saddle horns and began dragging the wagon trail to sweep the tracks. They rode a few hundred yards back to cover the wagon ruts, and then followed the wagon to the tree.

"Okay Albert, head for that big tree over there," pointed Leroy at another one.

Jeremy and Leroy followed once again dragging the tree limbs. They continued the cycle until they were about a mile from the Oregon Trail. Feeling a bit more secure, they untied the ropes from the tree limbs, and Leroy sent Jeremy ahead to scout for a place to cross the river. The hills were getting taller, the valleys lower, and often he rode out of sight of the wagon. When he came over the third hill, he spotted a wagon with the canvas top missing. He pulled his pistol and carefully rode up to it. Immediately, he noted arrows sticking out of the sides of the slightly burned wagon. Quickly, he turned his horse and galloped back to Leroy. "There's a burned wagon up ahead!" he called as he pulled his horse up to a quick stop.

"Damn! How long ago?" asked Leroy?

"It's been a while," replied Jeremy.

"Let's go take a look," said Leroy, as he turned and whistled to Albert, and pointed at him to head in the direction they were riding. Leroy rode his horse around the destroyed wagon and knew right away the Indians had won this fight. He and Jeremy moved away from the wagon, and they found the body of a man rotting in the ground. His scalp was missing, and three arrows protruded from his chest. Jeremy found two children with their throats cut and decaying. Finally, Leroy found the body of a woman, horribly cut all about her naked body.

"They did not die quickly," he said to Jeremy. "We must be on our guard. This could happen to us." Leroy stood in his saddle, so he could see the valley of the river below him. "Ride down to the river and test crossing it with your horse. If the water reaches your knees, it is too deep for the wagon. If you find a shallow spot, then ride up the opposite bank and look for a trail heading southwest to Fort Morgan. Watch for tracks and report back in thirty minutes." Leroy sighed, "Ride carefully, son. Keep your pistol ready."

Jeremy gulped, "Yes sir, I will." He turned his horse away from the burned wagon.

Leroy rode back towards their wagon, and waved at Albert to turn a bit more south. He intended for the Finney family to miss seeing the burned wagon, and the mutilated bodies on the ground. He wished he had time to bury them, but he knew he must not stop. He waved again for Albert to speed up.

Jeremy scouted the bank looking for a good crossing. He tried three spots, but they were too deep. He was checking a fourth spot when suddenly he heard a pistol shot from the direction of their wagon. Quickly, he checked the river and felt it might work, but he had no time to check the far bank as instructed. He rode up the bank after hearing another shot, and then the yelping of Indians.

Albert drove the wagon as hard as he could. He saw Jeremy and turned towards him. Leroy was riding along side while turning with his pistol, and firing back at a group of six Indians trailing them.

Leroy yelled at Albert, "Get across the river, and we'll make a stand. We can't out run them with the wagon. Hurry!"

Leroy spun his horse around, holstered his pistol, and pulled his rifle from his saddle scabbard. He took quick aim, and killed the leading Indian, but the rest kept coming. He turned his horse, and galloped to catch up with the wagon while leaning low on his horse as arrows whizzed by his head.

Jeremy pulled up the Winchester, and took aim, but hit nothing. He should have practiced with the weapon. He got lucky on his fifth shot by missing a warrior, but hitting the horse. Rider and horse tumbled in a horrifying somersault killing both.

"Get that wagon across the river!" yelled Leroy as he turned to fire, but missed.

The wagon horses were as frightened as Albert and Sarah. They leaped down the bank pulling the wagon and almost overturning it. Sarah fell against the sidewall as she tried to stay low and still. She screamed out in fear.

Jeremy fired again as Leroy pulled up beside him. Leroy shot another Indian in the throat. The brave flipped off the back of the horse holding his hands to his throat. Blood spewed into the air as he hit the dusty plain.

The three remaining warriors broke from their gallop by skidding to a halt. Quickly, they exchanged words and spread apart as they began advancing once again. Leroy looked back as the wagon horses charged into the water. The jolt threw Albert from his seat into the river. He clung to the reins as the horses pulled him and the wagon across the river. The rushing river pushed Albert's body towards the wagon. Desperately, he tried to get on his feet, but the swiftness of the river knocked him down and under the wagon. The rear wheel ran over his legs breaking the bones. Albert let go of the reins as the pain leaped through his body. He did not know how to swim, but he tried a few strokes before being swept under. His head slammed into a rock knocking him unconscious. He drowned as his body was tossed roughly down the riverbed, and soon out of sight.

The wagon horses reached the far bank, and frantically pulled the wagon way up the muddy banks. To their dismay, there was no trail on the other side, but they did not stop as they charged through the bushes. The front wagon wheels hit a fallen log causing the wagon to abruptly overturn and fling Sarah to the ground. Stunned from the fall, she managed to get to her feet, and started desperately screaming for Albert.

"Jeremy, get your ass across the river," ordered Leroy. "I'll cover you. Hurry!"

Jeremy hesitated, as he did not want to leave Leroy, but reluctantly, he swung into his saddle, charged down the bank, and into the water. Once safely on the other side, he rode up the bank and into the bushes for a few yards, then stopped, tied off his horse, retrieved the Winchester, and returned to the river to cover Leroy.

Nevertheless, he was too late. When he spotted Leroy, he saw an arrow sticking out of his shoulder as he continued firing and killing a charging Indian. He dropped the empty rifle, and tried to swing into his saddle as an Indian charged from behind, and hit him across the back of the head with a big war club with a large stone attached to the end. Jeremy flinched at the sickening sound as Leroy's skull cracked like a melon sending him sprawling to the ground. The Indian clubbed Leroy's limp and bloody body over and over, then dropped the tomahawk, retrieved his knife and cut off Leroy's scalp. He jumped to his feet, and began screaming triumphantly, shaking the limp bloody scalp over his head. Angry and terrified, Jeremy took aim using a tree branch to steady his gun. He fired and hit the Indian square in the back of his head. He knew it was a lucky shot. The warrior dropped the scalp and his knife as he fell face first to the ground.

Jeremy failed to notice that the last Indian brought his horse across the river about twenty-five yards upstream. The Indian saw his fellow warrior fall from the rifle shot. He kicked his horse hard, screamed as he charged down the river, and then up the bank directly at Jeremy.

Jeremy yanked his head around when he heard the warrior's war whoop. Quickly, he cocked his rifle and fired, but missed. The Indian carried a big club in his hand, and swung it back, ready to send it careening into Jeremy's skull. Frantically, Jeremy ratcheted another shell, and brought the rifle up once again to fire. The rider's horse was but six feet from him, approaching fiercely at full gallop. Jeremy fired, but he never saw the bullet hit the Indian, as the horse's front left shoulder caught him, and spun backwards into the bushes knocking the gun from his hands.

The bullet caught the Indian in the left eye spinning him backwards. He was flung violently face first towards the mud along the river, and before hitting the ground the right rear hoof of the horse caught the Indian in his face. Instantly, the powerful blow broke the man's jaw, nose, and split his skull. He fell as limp as a rag doll and slid down the bank to the river. The water quickly turned red from the man's blood. The wild terrified pony flew through the bushes and ran right over Sarah knocking her to the ground and trampling her. A hard hoof to her neck broke her windpipe and severed an artery. She bled to death in seconds. The unborn baby was crushed in her womb. Suddenly, everything around Jeremy was silent and still. They were all dead, except for the horses and Jeremy.

If there had been any more warriors, Jeremy would have been killed. He lay bruised and battered in the bushes, feeling dazed but alive. He coughed to get the air back into his lungs and rolled to his side. He found no bones broken and no wounds, only a few scratches from limbs and briars. He got to his feet, retrieved his pistol that had fallen to the ground, as well as the Winchester. Carefully, he walked back to the river. He spotted the Indian who had tried to kill him lying half in the water. Blood swirled all around him. Jeremy knew the man had to be dead. He scanned the far shore, but saw no other Indians. Thankfully, Leroy had killed an Indian just twenty yards away from the river.

Leroy's horse carefully approached the river cautiously. Jeremy stepped from the bushes, and whistled to get the horse's attention. The horse drank a bit of the water then lifted his head and began fording the river before walking up the bank to Jeremy.

Jeremy took the lead reins, and together, they moved into the bushes. He tied the horse up alongside his own, and went to find Sarah and the wagon. He had only to go ten yards before he found Sarah on her back and dead. Tears slid down his face, but he made no sound. He walked a bit farther and found the wagon. It had overturned on its side with the front axle broken. The team of horses had broken free of the wagon and stopped a hundred feet farther into the woods, as did the Indian's pony. He knew he must keep moving, as there could be more war parties in the area that heard their gunfire. He had to reach Fort Morgan and Leroy told him it was southwest of them. He had to just follow the river to get there. Slowly, he came to the realization he was alone. After reloading, he put his rifle in the sheath on his horse. He found the Parker shotgun near the wagon, filled a pillowcase of shotgun shells, and put the shells in Leroy's saddlebags. He reloaded the shotgun, and placed it in the sheath on Leroy's horse. Finally, he reloaded his pistol, and filled his saddlebags with bullets for his guns.

Then he gathered up some supplies from the wagon, loaded several sacks and tied them on Leroy's horse. He found Albert's fire making and cooking tools, and tied them to the horse as well. He took everything of value he could spot quickly. Fifteen minutes later, he cut a fifteen-foot piece of leather from the reins for the wagon horses and tied it to the lead of Leroy's horse. He cut the wagon horses free from the reins and removed their bridles.

He left them to roam free. As he swung up in his saddle, he tied the other end from the bridle of Leroy's horse to the horn of his saddle. He wiped his face of the tears and sweat, pulled his hat on a little tighter, and made his way through the bushes until he was on the small ridge above the river, and then turned south. He placed his hand on his pistol expecting an Indian to step out and shoot an arrow at him at any moment. Silently, he walked his horses, hoping to avoid the noise the wagon had created and the attention of any more Indians.

He thought over the battle. It had lasted less than thirty minutes. He went from traveling with three friends to being alone somewhere in Colorado Territory with little skills for traveling alone in the mountains of the western frontier. However, he would not stop, and he would not give up. He did not know how long a ride it was to Fort Morgan, but he resolved in his heart to get there, and he would not allow himself to back down.

ELEVEN

Liz woke him before dawn, forcing Zeke's mind to give up the dream of him and Josh sitting in the hot spring, and thrusting his weary bones back to reality as he lay on the smelly, but soft bear hide in the tipi he shared with John, Liz, and Josh. He smiled at Liz as she handed him a long strip of beef jerky, and a cup of hot coffee. He smiled again after sipping the coffee, and then leaned over to Josh. He felt his face with his bare hand, and though warm, he had no fever. He knew Liz would take good care of Josh, but he hated to leave him alone. He wanted to plant a kiss on his head, but felt afraid to show his love for Josh in front of his new friends. He needed her help with Josh's recovery, and feared upsetting Liz and John.

He downed the coffee, and stepped out of the tent into the cold wind. Immediately, his nostrils flared at the stench of John as he prepared his horse for the hunt. "Good lord, that stuff stinks!" Zeke held his nose as he walked over to his horse.

"You'll get used to it," laughed John. "Do you want to put some scent on?"

"No thanks, I plan to stay far upwind and far away from you. Good god, you won't need a rifle, as that smell ought to make a bison drop to his knees at fifty yards."

John laughed heartily. "I took the liberty of packing the Sharps buffalo rifle for you, and put it in your saddle sleeve just in case you get a chance to shoot. I didn't put a cartridge in. I'll let you do that."

"Thank you. I will remain in protective mode in case the herd turns on you," replied Zeke.

John swung himself into his saddle, "I hope we find a herd, but every year the pickings are slimmer, as the white man has either killed or run off most of the buffalo. While hunting my bear, I found a valley on the eastern side not far from the plains. A small group of buffalo often feed there during the fall. I am hoping we find a big fat one. Let's ride!"

With a bit of a wave and wink to his wife, John led off with Zeke remaining ten yards behind, hoping to avoid John's special scent. Zeke felt good to be out of the camp for a while, and though thankful his wounds healed quickly; he hoped Josh's wounds would hurry and heal, so they could head home. As they traveled the ridge that would lead them to the valley, Zeke asked if there were many mountain men in the Rockies.

"Not like the old days when my brother was so famous. When the demand for beaver declined, as did the bison, many of the men moved west to a new frontier, but others felt they had played around enough. They finally settled down by leading wagon trains, building cabins, and raising a family.

I've met a few after they were civilized with a haircut, a shave, a bath, and real clothes, and I walked right pass them without giving them a second thought. However, they would yell my name loudly, and immediately, I would turn, look into their eyes, and finally recognize my old friend. Their transformation to civilization was an amazing miracle.

"I like visiting their new farms, as they used their hunting skills to put good food on their tables. A smoked ham or turkey taste good to this old mountain man. It's a bit tough to smoke some game over our cooking fire."

Zeke almost told John about their smokehouse near the barn in their valley, but didn't want to brag and let it go. "Why haven't you and Liz settled down?" asked Zeke.

"Good question," replied John. "I guess we will eventually have to, especially if the Indian wars keep growing. Most of the Indians leave us alone, but it is not the Indians I fear, it is the white men. When you marry an Indian, the tribe treats you like one of their sons. They taught me how to hunt better, and how to use every bit of morsel of the kill. Many a time I came upon an entire herd of buffalo all dead and skinned by the white men. They took only the fur hides, and left the meat of over five hundred head to rot. That meat would have fed ten tribes for an entire winter. The poor Indians starved most of the winter, as there were no more buffalo to hunt. Many of the tribes will not eat fish or fowl, preferring to feast only on the lean meat of the buffalo. White men are wasteful and disrespectful of nature. If a mountain man does not appreciate what nature has created, he has no business being here."

"I know what you mean. I read a newspaper article about white hunters in Africa killing the big elephants, and taking only their tusks, leaving the rest to rot. White men can be pretty stupid sometimes," added Zeke.

"Yep, a good Indian shows great respect for nature. When they kill an animal, they stop and say a prayer, and thank their god for the sacrifice. They waste nothing. This year's buffalo coat becomes next year's patch on the tipi, and the following year it becomes a pair of moccasins. They can make a great stew out of a ground squirrel or a few rats. In bad times, they can make the oldest dog taste like stewed beef."

"A dog. I think I would pass on that," replied Zeke.

"Not if you were hungry enough." John laughed and added, "Just wait until you taste their roasted rattlesnake feast!"

"No thanks. I'll pass on that, too. Where are we?" asked Zeke as they began going down the mountain.

John added, "Just over that mountain to the south is Fort Morgan. I trade there from time to time. I can usually get sugar, coffee, and buckshot pretty cheap, costing me just a few pelts."

Zeke replied, "We missed Fort Morgan when we came west. We'll have to make a stop there one day. We go to Denver when we need supplies."

"Denver is too big a town for me," replied John. "I went there a few years back, and there were nearly a hundred and fifty people just standing around pointing at me. They made fun of my natural good looks," added John with a sly smile. "I ain't going back there."

Zeke grinned. "I know what you mean, but if you ever need help, go to the mercantile and ask for Ed Leary. He is the owner and a friend of ours. He's fair, honest, and a good friend. Tell him I sent you."

"I'll store that in my brain for a maybe-I'll-do-that-one-day," teased John, "thank you".

They rode most of the day and camped out near the bottom of the mountain near a small creek covered with patches of ice. John said they would be riding way before dawn, and they should stay packed and ready to go. He also said they should leave camp as quietly as possible, as he felt the herd was nearby. He showed Zeke the lower sections of various trees a buffalo had rubbed hard against trying to stop an itch. The big animal's hide took the bark right off the trunk. Zeke slept little, and when he did he dreamed of Josh, but mostly he kept a bandana over his face to keep from smelling John. His awful hunting odor drove him and the horses crazy. Zeke was pretty sure that even the wild mice stayed deep in their holes to avoid John's stench.

They began walking their horses before dawn. Zeke was very cold, but his pride kept him from complaining to John. After an hour of steady climbing to the ridge, a small cloud of steam began rising from the neck and back of his horse as the valley began to slowly warm up on the eastern side of the mountain. Zeke chewed on some beef jerky, and a hard cracker to keep his stomach from growling.

John's horse started to limp, so he pulled the animal to a stop, and climbed off to check his hoof. Zeke remained in the saddle, removed his binoculars from his saddlebag, and began scanning the valley up ahead.

"Just a stick," replied John as he took his big Bowie knife and used the point to dig out the stick. The horse neighed a time or two, but remained still while trusting John to help him. "There you go boy," replied John as he let the hoof go, and rubbed the nose of his horse. "Good as new, well, plus about ten years," he grinned.

"John?" asked Zeke while still looking through the lens. "I think I see movement in that stand of trees off to the right." Zeke handed him the binoculars while pointing towards the trees.

"It is has been a long time since I looked through a pair of these. They sure help an old mountain man's eyesight. Let's see if I can see them, too." He scanned the area carefully, and at first, he saw nothing. He thought his green recruit was seeing things, but then he saw them—two, three, six, ten, and maybe more. The herd was moving out to the plains to graze for the day. He became very excited. "Way to go, Zeke. You found them."

John began scanning the landscape left and right of the herd until he found what he was looking for. "Zeke, do you see that knoll to the south? You walk your horse there very slowly. When you get within two hundred yards, get off your horse, and stay on the far side of your horse from the herd. They can see pretty darn well, and I don't want you to spook them before I'm ready. Tie your horse off on the down slope away from the herd, and pull out your Sharps rifle in case I need help."

He pointed north as he handed Zeke the binoculars. "I'll head up that way, and come all the way around from the east. That'll put the sunrise at my back, which will blind their eyes a bit. The air is still with little to no wind, and that's good. You ready?" asked John with a grin and a pat to Zeke's shoulder.

"Yes sir, I'll be waiting for you. Please be careful," added Zeke, as he turned south.

"Not to worry, as I've done this about a thousand times. One more is a piece of cake," replied John.

The herd nibbled at the grass and the branches of the small bushes, but now and then, a head would rise and an ear would flutter, as if they were shaking the cobwebs from their ear canals. A big bull buffalo would smell the air and snort occasionally, just to remind the others he was on watch for danger. A few baby bison followed the herd, never straying far from their mother.

Zeke reached the knoll and lay on his stomach behind some tall grass as instructed. He laid the rifle beside him after loading a cartridge in the chamber, picked up his binoculars, and began studying the mighty beasts. He tried to imagine what life must of have been like when Lewis and Clark explored the area decades ago. The Indians must have felt rich back then with so much beef just hanging around for the slaughter when they needed food. John told him the tribes used to live almost exclusively on bison. He said it was a good lean meat, and far better tasting than an old Texas steer. Zeke looked forward to trying it.

He moved the field glasses a bit higher until he spotted John slowly moving his horse towards the herd a few steps at a time. Zeke became alarmed when he saw John lean forward in the saddle resting his chin on his horse's neck. He focused the glasses and immediately caught on that John was hiding on his horse, as the bison would not be afraid of a single wild horse. Slowly, John dismounted away from view of the herd.

He saw John keep his rifle on the southern side of his horse, most likely cocked and ready to go. Zeke estimated John's position to be about two hundred yards away from the small herd. John gently lifted his rifle up a little closer to his waist in anticipation. Zeke knew John would not attack until he was fifty yards from the nearest bull, and he hoped the bull would look at him before he fired, so he would have a chance to shoot the animal in between the neck and the shoulder, while going for a single shot in the heart. He would reload quickly, and fire again, and if need be, he would reload and fire until he killed only one bison. He did not wish to kill anymore, hoping the rest of the herd would simply run away from the sound of his rifle.

After the kill, John would have to watch out for other bison to retaliate by charging him. He felt his pistol, knowing it was loaded and ready. If he had to, he would fire it into the air to scare off the rest of the herd. Forty more yards to go, he thought.

Zeke picked up the binoculars once more and moved left and right, looking for John when suddenly, he caught sight of movement about two hundred yards south of the herd. Quickly, he turned to face the area, and adjust the focus ring. He waited for a long minute finding nothing. Suddenly, a single rider on a horse came out of the line of trees pulling a packhorse. He studied the rider, but saw no weapons pulled up to fire, so he did not think it was another hunter. He was relieved the man did not appear to be an Indian, as he was dressed like a white man, and he sat on a store bought saddle. Zeke did not want to miss the kill, so he turned back to watch John.

John concentrated on every action he was about to execute. He never saw the rider to the south, but instead carefully watched a big bull buffalo on John's side of the herd. Ten more yards to go, he thought. His trigger finger itched, but he did not move it.

The bull raised his head and smelled the air looking north. Then something caught his large, dark eyes, and he turned a bit east, snorted, and kicked the earth with a playful hoof.

"That's it. Turn just a little more," whispered John to himself.

Zeke turned back to the herd and immediately, saw John now in the open range. The bull turned again. John suddenly swung his rifle over the saddle, took careful aim, exhaled slowly. The bull stared at him, squinting into the sun. Suddenly, his nostrils flared, picking up the scent of old John in spite of the nasty beef juice he rubbed on his face that morning.

John pulled the trigger. It was a deadly powerful shot. The bull stepped back a few steps in shock from the pain. The hot metal slug tore through his hide down to his fleshy parts, and in to his breastplate, chipping fragments as it soared by. In a flash, it entered and exited his heart, and lodged in his left shoulder joint with a hard thud. He snorted at John, stammered, and took a few steps as if ready to charge, but instead fell to his knees, and then plopped down harshly on his side to the ground scattering dust. John quickly reloaded his rifle.

The herd instantly lifted their heads as the sound of the gun echoed off their horns. They began moving quickly to the north, and then after sensing death, they picked up speed and began to gallop. Zeke could see clods of mud and grass flying from their hoofs into the air.

John waited for them to move out of sight, and then began walking his horse up slowly to the bleeding bull on the ground. He looked back for the herd once more, but after seeing the way clear, he waved at Zeke to come down.

Zeke smiled, momentarily forgetting about the single rider, and stood up, waving at John. He put the cord of the binoculars over his neck, and just as he leaned down to pick up his rifle from the grass, something to the north caught his eye. Quickly, he picked up the field glasses.

"Oh no!" he said as he saw not one, but two huge bison bulls sprinting south directly towards John. They were just over the ridge and out of John's line of sight.

"John, look out!" he yelled, but John did not hear him, as he knelt down, unpacking his knives and tools to prepare to dress the meat. Zeke yelled again, but time was quickly running out. He was too far away for John to hear him. He started to swing up into his saddle, but sensed he had only seconds before the animals attacked.

Zeke fell to the ground, removed the field glasses from his neck, picked up the Sharps Rifle, and took careful aim. He hadn't fired the Sharps in a long time, as Josh usually carried the big gun. He tried to recall everything Josh had taught him. If the animal is on the run, aim the rifle at the heart, and then begin moving forward until you can gauge the speed of the animal. Move ahead of the animal just enough to allow the animal to actually run into the bullet. He sighed slowly, letting the air gently flow from his lungs, and squeezed the trigger. Boom!

John's head shot up quickly as he heard the rifle. He turned towards Zeke, and instantly realized the gun was pointing to his north. He turned as he saw the first bull fall and roll in a somersault before stopping in a thud to the ground on his side of the crest. Zeke thought the big bull looked like what Josh had described when his men blew up a railroad trestle during the war, and the engine crashed down into the gorge. John dropped his knives, and quickly ran to his horse, mounted, and yanked the horse to the south. He kicked it hard in an attempt to gallop away, but the second bison came over the hill at top speed, and charged with his head down towards John.

Zeke quickly ejected the spent cartridge and placed another in the gun, preparing to take down the second animal. He took aim, but suddenly, his heart sank.

While attempting to stay away from the bull's sharp horns, John made a wild zigzag run back and forth while turning towards Zeke, hoping to reach safety in the tree line, but this change of course put John in Zeke's line of sight on the bull. He could not yet fire, but he kept following John's weaving hoping for a clear shot. The bull charged on, determined to gore the hunter. John's terrified horse ran as quickly as he could, but the bull still had the downhill momentum.

Just as the bull was about to ram the horse in the side, a rifle shot caught the bison in the left shoulder. It did not kill him, but it slowed him down a step. Now angrier, he grunted loudly before picking up his speed once more. John remained forty yards from the safety of the trees. Another shot fired hitting the animal broadside, but it must have felt like a bee sting, barely slowing the fuming bison down.

Zeke heard the rifle shots, but kept his eye glued to the bull, while sighting carefully, hoping the buffalo would turn away. The ferocious beast finally made a mistake. He lifted his head just as he missed a slight turn in John's wild ride, and instantly, Zeke pulled the trigger. Boom!

He hit the big bull right in the left eye after the bullet sailed past John's shoulder by mere inches. The animal went down hard, driving its scruffy bearded chin deep into the ground, kicking up the dirt creating a small cloud of dust, as dirt clops flew into the air from his hoofs.

Zeke stood up, saw that John was safe, and immediately felt overjoyed, but his heart sank yet again when he saw the lone rider with a rifle in his hand galloping towards John. "John!" he yelled to warn him, but old John was tuckered out, and thrilled to be alive. He sighed hard, and just waved back.

Zeke thrust the Sharps in the sleeve, saddled up, and began galloping down the hill, but the lone rider he spotted earlier would reach John before he could. Oblivious to the pain in his still healing chest, Zeke burst through the tree line at full gallop as the rider pulled up to a stop. He saw the man lower the rifle and swing off his horse.

Zeke pulled his horse up smartly while pulling his pistol. "Hold it right there," he yelled.

The man gave him a hard look, but continued pushing his rifle into his saddle sleeve with his back to John.

"Hang on Zeke. This man also saved my life. He hit him twice with that Winchester, but that old bull just kept coming. I'm sure glad you hit him with the Sharps rifle. Now you know why they call it a buffalo gun, and it sure did the trick. That was a great shot, and a little close I might add. I heard and felt the lead whiz by my ear," laughed old John.

Zeke put his pistol back in the holster and swung off his horse.

John walked over to the stranger just as the man was turning around. "I'm sure glad you came to help, and I hope you want some beef, as we now have two buffalos too many. I'm John Bridger," began John as he stuck out his big hand. As the man turned to face him, he suddenly realized the man was a boy, or perhaps a young man, but he shook his hand warmly.

"I'm Jeremy Gordon," said the stranger. "Glad I could help."

"Me, too," replied John, "this is my friend Zeke Robertson." John motioned at Zeke, as he came up to shake the stranger's hand.

Zeke gave the boy's face a careful study, but could not place where he had seen him before. Then a cold chill went up his back, as he feared the boy might have known him from the war. He prayed not.

"That was some good shooting," said Zeke as he shook his hand.

"I couldn't stop him, but you sure did," replied Jeremy with a grin.

"What the hell are you doing out here all by yourself?" asked John.

"In a word—Indians. I was part of a one wagon train, and the Indian warriors attacked us. I'm the only one that lived. I took what supplies I could, and I'm trying to make it to Fort Morgan."

"It's over that mountain to the southwest," pointed John, "but why not ride along with us. If you'll help, we'll give you some good dried beef to help you, and maybe teach you a thing or two about living alone in the mountains."

"I'd like that. I have pretty much been scared shitless out here."

Zeke slowly smiled. "I did not catch the name and face at first. You've grown. I guess we all do. Are you from New York?"

Jeremy smiled. "Yes, how did you know?"

"My friend and I met you in New York, uh, after we caught you stealing from us. I was about to thrash your brains out, but my partner made you a deal. Do you remember the deal?" asked Zeke.

Jeremy's face lit up, "I do remember you. Your friend, uh, his name was Josh, uh, Johnson. Josh Johnson, that's it," he said.

"You're right," Zeke shook his hand again.

"And the deal was he gave me a silver dollar and made me promise to quit stealing, get a job, and I would be required to repay him one day. Is he with you?"

"He and I were attacked by Indians, too, and then a bear," began Zeke.

"A bear. They have bears out here, too?" asked Jeremy naively.

"Big ones, called grizzlies," laughed John as he held his hand over his head indicating the grizzlies were taller than he was. Jeremy's jaw dropped as they began hiking back to the first kill.

"Oh," sighed Jeremy, thinking it was bad enough to have mean Indians.

"Come on boys, we're wasting daylight. Zeke head to those trees and cut us down several eighteen-foot poles. We're going to need three sets of two apiece to build travois to pull behind the horses. Come on Jeremy, let's carve up some meat."

"I have never carved up an animal before," stated Jeremy solemnly.

"Neither have I," deadpanned John for a long second before bellowing a big laugh. "Everybody has to have a first time. Mine was about forty years ago. You'll do fine—after you throw up a time or to." John laughed again as Jeremy's face turned pale.

It took a few hours with all three men cutting up the three bulls. Together, they stretched the large animal out on its stomach where John would cut the hide down to the ground, and then cut out the good meat. Zeke and Jeremy stood there amazed at how quickly John sliced through the carcass. They threw sections of hides over the poles after tying the poles to their saddles to drag the meat home. They tied a three-foot long limb between the dragging ends to keep the poles apart. They would drag the entire load of meat home to Liz. John placed big chunks of meat inside smaller sections of the hides, and then Zeke tied them off tightly. John also cut the horns off the animals, and grinned as he cut the tongues off, explaining the Indians consider the tongues a great delicacy. Zeke nearly threw up at the thought.

John ran back and forth between the bulls as Zeke and Jeremy began their own cutting process. He threw out what he called the bad parts and kept the good ones. John pulled a small sack of gunpowder from the leather sack he wore over his shoulder. He then cut out the liver and sliced it into three parts. He sprinkled the meat with a pinch of the gunpowder and a bit of salt, and then ate it raw. Blood squirted out the corners of his mouth, but he made it sound as if he had just eaten the best morsel of food on the entire planet.

Slowly, Zeke tasted the liver, then Jeremy, and before long they were devouring the rest of it. When all the meat had been stored, John pulled out the intestines that stretched a long way. He rolled it up, put it in a sack, and told them that boiled intestines made a good broth for just about anything. He took a gourd, and held it against the still warm heart. He cut a slice into the organ, allowing the blood to fill the gourd. He then drank it, saving a few sips for the boys. Jeremy gagged, and Zeke laughed, but together, they swallowed a few ounces.

He said they did not have time, but normally he would take the massive thighbones, as they used the thighs to crack the other bones to get at the marrow. He said the Indians used the skin of the neck to make shields or briar legging like his, as it was thicker and tougher than the rest of the hide. With darkness rapidly approaching, John wanted to get back over the ridge to home. He stored big sections of fat in other hides, and explained his wife would cut the meat into thin strips and dry it in the sun so it would last for many months. Liz would pulverize the meat and put it in dried bags with the fat, preserving the delicacy. He laughed at himself and patted his stomach, "However, with my appetite, it usually just lasts until spring.

"Her favorite dish," began John, "is to take wild berries and cook them with the meat into a stew. It is wonderful!" He laughed at the look on the faces of the boys. "Okay, everything is tied off tightly. Let's saddle up and I'll lead the way, as we need to get over the ridge before we stop. I do not want to be found on the plains by a group of warriors. They would love to have all this meat. If we are lucky the wolves, coyotes, and perhaps a mountain lion will eat anything we left behind, thus hiding any evidence of the kill by white men. What they don't eat, the vultures will pick clean tomorrow. Let's go," he ordered.

TWELVE

The horses were sweating from the hard work, even though the cool fall air began enveloping the hunting party as they steadily climbed the mountain. Zeke and Jeremy felt thankful for the light from the moon, while John cursed their bad luck, fearing that without the leaves, a war party might easily spot them. After they reached the summit, he led them along the ridge before stopping between several huge boulders. Zeke surmised the spot secured their location from discovery from either side of the ridge, and the rocks would make it difficult for anyone to sneak up close in the dark.

John swung off his saddle and turned to the boys. "We'll tie the horses on a rope line over there. They've had water, but they are tired, so it will not take long for them to settle down."

"They are not the only ones who are tired. It's been a long day," replied Zeke as he rubbed his sore butt. "I thought my ass was glued to the saddle. I guess my body became soft while recuperating."

The three of them laughed at him as they followed John's directions. "We'll each sleep with one of the big rocks at our back. Never sleep together if you suspect Indians might be about. They could easily shoot all three of us at once if we did. I'll take the first watch," he said as he pulled his rifle from his saddle sleeve, drank some water from his canteen, and sat down on his bedroll. "Zeke, I'll wake you in three hours."

"Okay," replied Zeke, as he rolled out his blanket over a pile of pine needles he had gathered, curled up, and instantly fell asleep.

Jeremy had to pee, so he walked to the edge of the ridge, and began to urinate while his eyes roamed the valleys below. He spotted a light far off in the distance. He wondered who it was—settlers or Indians. Suddenly, the light became much brighter. "John," he whispered while waving his hand for John to come over.

"What is it lad?" asked John as he walked over.

"Do you see that bright light across the valley to the south?" asked Jeremy.

"Yes, I think that is probably Fort Morgan. I can tell for sure in the morning when I can see the mountains in the distance there."

"When I first got here the light was pretty small, but just a moment ago it began to grow. See! It is still growing," added Jeremy.

"Damn!" replied John. "I think either a settler farm is on fire, or perhaps the fort. I bet Indians attacked them. This isn't good, because they attacked after dark, which is most unusual for them. They normally fight as if they were on a hunt in the daytime. Worst yet, they will most likely return to the north through the same valley we must cross over in the morning."

105

Jeremy sighed, "What do we do? Is there another way?"

"Not without going all the way around the top half of Colorado. Do you have a few months to kill?"

Jeremy fell silent, deep in thought, and filling with worry. In his short life, he had already seen enough bloodshed. He did not want any more trouble.

"The fort is about twenty miles from here. I suspect the warriors are still attacking, which is good for us. When the battle is over, and if they won, they will wait until morning so they can see what goods they can steal. They'll be looking for rifles and gunpowder. We have about five miles to go on the ridge in the morning before going down into the valley to cross the stream and head back up the other side. We should beat them. "However, if they end the battle soon or lose, they could start home tonight, trying to put some distance between the soldiers and the trail home. It would be better for us if the fire continues to burn, and the battle goes on." He sighed heavily, "That's a sorry thing to wish for, huh?" John patted Jeremy on the shoulder. "Better get some shut eye. We'll be leaving very early in the morning."

Jeremy took a last look, and then returned to his bedroll to sleep. John watched the fire during his entire shift. Before he woke Zeke, he disappeared around the back of the rocks, walking silently, and then stopping to listen intently for any movement or noise. Hearing nothing, he returned, woke Zeke, and explained the fire. He asked Zeke to check his pocket watch, and to wake him in three hours. They would leave long before dawn.

Lieutenant McCaffey had just taken his shirt off to prepare to fall into his bunk when he heard the distant gunshot. He rapidly buttoned his shirt back up, holstered his pistol to his waist, grabbed his hat and his rifle, and went out the door of his cabin. "Henry, which direction did the shots come from?"

Henry, an old-timer, way beyond retirement age, but loved the army and stayed in anyhow, was in the guard tower near the gate. He yelled down, "I think it came from the Finkles."

"Damn!" Then he turned to yell for his men. "Saddle up boys!" he yelled. "The Indians are close."

Soldiers came running from all directions and in a few minutes, they saddled up and began checking their weapons. Henry climbed down from the tower and opened the gate. Eight men rode out with McCaffey. They felt vulnerable riding out into the night, as the big gate slowly closed behind them, but they knew it was their duty to protect the settlers.

They galloped quickly as the farm was just three miles from the fort, but as they approached, they could see the flames through the bare limbs of the trees and the flashes of the fire. They also heard rifle shots from time to time. The last hundred yards they dismounted, pulled their rifles from the sleeves, and began fanning out. They got lucky as they arrived behind the Indians.

The Lieutenant counted about ten braves, most with just bows and arrows, but the leader was firing a rifle into the farmhouse. Thankfully, he saw gunfire coming from at least two closed windows. The barn was on fire. He scanned the area making sure all the Indians were at the front of the cabin. He was wrong. Just as he turned to give orders to his men, a young private pointed at the roof of the cabin. McCaffey turned around, and saw an Indian crossing the roof with a torch in his right hand. He held a small barrel in his left hand. It took Robert an extra second to realize he carried a small gunpowder barrel, and intended to drop it down the chimney along with the torch, which would explode in the cabin killing everyone.

Quickly, he brought his rifle up, took aim, and fired, hitting the Indian in the back. The warrior fell off the roof dropping the barrel in the process. The Indian and the torch hit the ground first. A second later, the barrel hit the ground hard knocking the wood plug out, spilling some of the gunpowder. Hearing the gunshot, the Indians turned to see who killed the brave on the roof just as the lieutenant yelled charge. Before the Indians could run, the gunpowder exploded, creating a large fireball and a blast of hot air, knocking some of the Indians to the ground. The soldiers quickly shot most of the attackers.

The rest of the warriors took flight, but Robert and his men killed two more. Three or four escaped. His men saddled up and gave chase, but in the dark, it was hard to see them.

"Come on out, you're safe!" yelled Robert to the cabin.

Slowly, the door creaked open and Lar Fickle, his wife, and two kids came out with the look of terror on their tear filled faces.

"I think you'd better come with us to the fort. You never know if those bastards will return or not. You're not safe out here alone. Get your stuff together, and we'll help load your wagon with your valuables and supplies, and lead you back. Hurry along now. You're safe with us."

Unable to find the fleeting Indians the squad returned with most of the men spreading out to watch for Indians, and the rest helping the family load up. It was too late to save the barn. Soon the roof caved in, creating a suddenly larger fire that burned quickly. By the time they set off for the fort, the fire was down to just a foot tall or so.

Zeke woke John and Jeremy about four. Together, they climbed aboard their horses, and with John leading the way they cautiously followed the ridge until time to start down the mountain. Half way down the sun crested the ridge behind them starting a new day. They said nothing and took slow steady steps with the horses. Everyone was listening for any sound of horses and Indians. John was also trying to smell them. Jeremy kept repeating silently what he was supposed to do if the Indians attacked them. His plan was to draw his pistol, get off his horse, look for something to hide behind, and if possible, take his rifle with him. When they reached the bottom, John pulled his horse to a stop, and gave the reins to Zeke. He slid off the saddle, pulled his rifle from the sleeve, and cautiously made his way to the stream and the trail that ran along it.

He first scanned the area in all directions, but after seeing nothing, he began searching the soft mud for tracks. His heart sank when he counted at least ten ponies all heading south. He wished the tracks where heading north, and the warriors at home in their tipis, leaving John and his friends free to cross in safety. He stared south knowing that somewhere downstream the Indians were there. He lifted his nostrils and tried to smell the air, but did not pick up the scent of humans or horses. He returned to Zeke and Jeremy.

"The Indians were here and they were heading south. I'm sure they had something to do with the fire we saw last night. They could be coming back this way at any time. We must hurry across, cover our tracks, and get the hell up the mountain on the other side. Check your weapons."

John led the way with Jeremy right behind him. They all took a long breath as they began crossing the open area to the stream. John crossed safely, so Jeremy tried it. The water was very shallow, but as they both went up the bank on the other side, Zeke could see the long ruts the travois poles were putting in the mud. They might as well have built a sign pointing the direction they were going. He sighed heavily and started through the water. He stopped halfway, thinking he heard something. He waited a few seconds, and then made his way up the bank and into the woods to safety.

Quickly, he climbed off his horse, retrieved a rope from his saddlebag and tied it to the bridle of the horse, and gave the other end to Jeremy. He pulled his Sharps rifle from the sleeve and turned to John. "Start up the mountain. I'm going back to sweep out those ruts. They easily point the way for the Indians. I'll be fine. Go on."

John sighed, "You do it quick and then get the hell out of there. Come on Jeremy. We've got to move out of here quickly."

Zeke ran back to the bank and scanned the area with his eyes while listening for any sound with his ears. Finding nothing, he propped the rifle against a tree, retrieved his knife, and cut off several scrub limbs to cover the tracks. He dragged his boots over the ruts smoothing out the soil. He worked on both sides of the river, and then began sweeping it with the limbs.

In his mind, his project was taking forever to accomplish, but once finished on the far bank, he crossed back over and began working on the other bank. Suddenly, he heard the hoofs of horses. He had ten feet to go and his rifle was another five feet beyond that. Frantically, he swung the limbs back and forth across the last of the tracks.

He heard a horse neigh—they were close. He climbed up and over the bank, while tossing the limbs behind a bush. He dove for his rifle. He snatched it, rolled quickly behind the tree, and snuggled down in the leaves.

The first Indian pulled to a stop in the stream just fifteen feet from him. He let his horse drink. Zeke's tried to breathe as silently as possible. His heart was pounding in his chest. A moment later, two more Indians rode up and stopped. They began speaking rapidly as if arguing. Zeke picked up a few words, but they were speaking too fast for him.

Abruptly, they stopped talking, allowing their eyes to scan the forest. One of the men sat straight up and smelled the air. Zeke thought surely he might smell him, but thought it might be old John and his urine-treated meat he smelled.

The Indian smelled the buffalo meat and it puzzled him as they were far from the plains. The one closest to him lifted his loincloth and began urinating on the bank without even leaving his horse. Once finished, he kicked his horse, and continued traveling down the trail along the river with the others following him.

Zeke breathed hard for the first time in about five minutes. Carefully, he began running towards John. He found them beyond a big rock at the base of the mountain.

"We just missed them," he whispered.

"Did they see the tracks?" asked John.

"Nope, but I think they got a whiff of you," teased Zeke.

"Me?" asked John, as he smelled his armpit.

"Yeah, to that Indian you smelled like a buffalo in heat!" They all laughed, but not too loud, as Zeke saddled up. Then they once again began following the trail up the mountain.

Liz came running from the cook fire the moment she heard John's owl call announcing his arrival. Zeke smiled as the big old tough mountain man quickly swung out of the saddle in time for her to leap into his arms. He swung her around and planted a big kiss on her lips like a scene from a ten-cent romance novel. John surprised Zeke and Jeremy as they noted his eyes had watered, and his cheek flushed to a shade of pink. Big John was a romantic and sentimentalist after all. He also surmised she loved old John in spite of the awful smell on his face.

As they tied off their horses, Liz immediately took charge. Before the hunt, John had setup several long poles parallel to the ground about ten feet off the ground. Liz used a bone with a small hole drilled in the dull end with a leather cord pulled through the hole. She pushed the sharp end through one of the big chunks of meat, and then tied the cord off to secure the meat. On the end of the cord, she tied a stick with a natural hook. Using another pole, she lifted the hook to the high pole to let the sun and wind begin drying out the meat to preserve it. Zeke felt amazed at her preparations, as she had created a pile of these hooks for the rest of the meat.

She picked out a big roast, took her long knife, and pushed it through the center of the meat. She took a five-foot long one-inch thick green stick, and pushed it through the chunk. Then she took a leather pouch from her waist, removed her own blend of flavoring, and patted it on the meat. John explained the stuff contain powdered herbs, wild dried onions and berry skins. He helped put the meat over the fire, and though working hard on the rest of the kill, she stopped every five minutes or so to turn the chunk of meat a quarter turn. She also ordered John to the stream to clean up. He protested, but after she said something in her language to him, he smiled and hurried to the stream. Zeke wasn't sure what she said, but he suspected she knew exactly what buttons to pull to get to John.

After securing all the meat, which took several hours, she went to work on the hides stretching them on the ground. She unrolled a pile of knives and meat scrapers, each one carefully sharpened until they could easily slice a single sheet of paper. She worked feverishly, and with great skill as she carved away every morsel of food, throwing little scraps to their dog, which John named Bear. The dog sat on his haunches as he waited patiently for her to throw another piece. The dog looked to be part wolf, and remained shy to strangers, but Liz and John talked to him like a human, and the animal responded to every word. John said he could not take the dog hunting, as the dog would try to protect him, and attack any animal John was trying to shoot. It made him feel a bit better to leave Bear protecting Liz when he was gone.

By suppertime, Liz and John stretched the new hides on a frame off the ground to allow the sun to dry them. Every day they would pull the four corners tighter, so they could stretch the hide until it was thin enough to use on the tipi or make clothes from it, but with winter coming, they planned on using the buffalo hide with the fur attached as warm blankets. They made their beds with piles of pine needles over which they would place a thick hide for comfort. As the temperature dropped, they would pull one to three of the hides on top of them. John explained the Indians slept in the nude to increase the warmth to all their body parts.

Zeke spent part of the afternoon with Josh. He recovered enough to finally sit up, and with Zeke's help, he made it out of the tipi to a log near the fire. It made him feel good to be in the fresh air and off the ground. Zeke retrieved a gourd of hot coffee while Liz gave him some root bread. She made the bread from the white bulbs of a Camas flower or a form of wild lilies. John explained the Shoshone called the staple root 'pasigoo' and is found most often on the prairie. He said Liz kept a basket of the stuff in the tipi for winter cooking. It tasted sweet to Josh, and he ate even the crumbs, licking his fingers.

John and Jeremy had walked the horses to the stream where they allowed them to drink freely. Once satisfied, John began going over the hide of the horses very carefully looking for ticks, burrs, sharp weed stickers, thorns or anything that might have stuck on the horses on their ride through the mountains. He told Jeremy over the years he had learned that a good horse was crucial to their survival. In the early years, wild horses were everywhere, but with massive killing of the bison by the white men, the horses fled the plains searching for quiet valleys away from the men and their loud guns.

He explained that Indians respect their horses and treat them like gods. They make friends with a new wild horse before they ever begin to ride it. They don't throw a saddle on it like the white man and force the horse to ride easy. Often the horses are not tied up and allowed to follow the Indian all around the camp, and would receive kernels of wild corn or slices of apples throughout the day. Indian boys or young warriors would sleep outside the tipi in the summer with the horse lying down beside him like a pet dog. There was a strong bond between an Indian and his horse.

When it was time for the horse to prepare for riders, the Indian would simply lie across the horse on his stomach like a saddle, and allow the horse to walk around with him lying there. If the horse were stubborn, they would lead him to a deep stream and then attempt to sit on him. A bucking horse in the water will soon tire, calm down, and then easily ridden. Once the horse was comfortable, the Indian would sit on the horse, and using only his legs he would squeeze inward and the horse would walk. When he wanted to stop, he would sit back on the horse. To turn, he would squeeze in with the opposite leg, and the horse would turn away from that leg in the correct direction. Indians trained all of John's horses, but he still felt better in a saddle with a bridle and reins. Many Indians ride with no reins at all, but rather they hang on by clinching the horse's mane. When hunting or attacking, they use their bow with both hands while remaining perfectly still on the back of the galloping horse. They practice over and over hitting targets while on a full run on their horses. He told Jeremy the Indians always amazed him with the skill of the horsemanship. He considered Indians the best riders in the world.

Jeremy helped with the inspection of the other horses until they freed the animal's hide of all foreign objects, while giving them a good rub in the process. They returned to the camp while letting the horses roam free to feed on nearby grass. John pointed out the advantages of selecting a good campsite. He had running water in the stream, a grassy area for the horses, and soft flat ground for their tipi. If possible, he said he always backed the tipi against a rock wall, or a strong thicket so his enemies would have to approach from the front so he could shoot them from within the tipi if he had to.

He walked Jeremy through a forest of underbrush until they reached another section of the mountain. Abruptly, John reached towards what appeared to be a wall of rock, and pulled a frame of dried bushes away revealing a cave. "This the campsite where we stay for the winter. If enemies are seen coming, we can hide in this cave. We keep extra supplies and blankets in the cave, and two more rifles. You can fight and win against two or three enemies, but not a gang of them. Enemies are not only bad Indians like the Blackfeet, Crow, Shoshone, or renegade Indians, but also there are gangs of riders who used to be mountain men, soldiers, or settlers, but took up a life of crime. They no longer hunt game—they hunt people. Some of them collect Indian scalps, and trade the bloody things for food and supplies at the forts. I never had much interest in taking a warrior's scalp. If given the chance, most Indians will avoid trouble. I only kill when I have to."

John turned to face the boy directly. "Jeremy, I want you to listen to this piece of advice very carefully. Never trust anyone when you just meet. I will give you an example: my partner and I were hunting beaver when we spotted a wagon broken down ahead. As we approached, we saw a woman laying on the ground moaning, and around her were other bodies with blood on their backs. My partner swung out of his saddle and walked over to help the lady. I stayed on my horse with my rifle cocked along with my pistol in my belt.

"Just as my friend leaned over to check the woman, she spun around and shot him with a pistol right in the face. Alarmed, I shot her with my rifle, and spun my horse around as the other men on the ground leaped up, and began firing at me. I managed to get away with one shot piercing the flesh of my left arm going clean through. I lost my friend and our packhorses of pelts and supplies, but I also learned a lesson. Things are not always, as they seem, so you be careful. You can be friendly later, but be safe when you first meet someone."

He replaced the frame of brush over the cave as they started back to the camp. "It was easy for me to trust you as you tried to save my life, but you should not have trusted me at first. I realize because you knew Zeke and Josh, you could most likely trust me, but always be careful. Make friends, but let them earn your trust over time. Can you shoot a bow or throw a spear?"

Jeremy grinned. "We didn't have many of those in my borough in New York City. A knife or a broken bottle was the only weapon I was familiar with throwing. I just got a pistol a month ago, and I know I need practice. Can I show you something?"

"Sure," replied John as Jeremy led him over to his saddle he had set on the ground near the tipi.

Jeremy pulled the Parker shotgun from the hidden sleeve stuffed with a few rags. "This is a Parker. It belonged to the man driving the wagon. He died in the attack. I grabbed it along with all the supplies I could quickly pack. The extra horse belonged to our guide. We didn't have many days together, but he tried to teach me all he could. I mostly learned to track game and Indians. His name was Leroy something."

John quickly asked, "Leroy Colbert?"

"Yes, that's it."

John scratched his head, "That's too bad. For many years, he was legendary in these parts. No one could hunt better or kill as many Indians as Leroy. Unfortunately, when the pelt business died in favor of silk hats from China, Leroy went broke, began drinking, and hanging around the towns. That's too bad," added John as Jeremy handed him the shotgun. "This is a beauty. I've never fired one, but I suspect they would blow a hole in most anything."

Jeremy smiled. "I hope I don't need it, but Leroy told me it was good for about fifty feet up to about a hundred feet, but very deadly. He said at close range it could cut a man in half."

"Whew," sighed John, "You keep it loaded and ready at all times, you hear? This thing could save your life. When you get a chance, you need to buy a hunting rifle like Zeke's buffalo gun. Let's go eat," he added as he handed the gun back to Jeremy, "I'm starved."

They found Josh sitting on the log with Zeke at his side. They had already started eating. Jeremy and John sat down across from them as Liz brought bowls of the sliced beef roast along with her stew.

John took a bite and chewed loudly, "Ah, yes, there's nothing like fresh buffalo beef. Liz, this is good," he said with a smile as he winked at her. She smiled as she filled another bowl for herself and sat down beside him. Jeremy timidly tasted the stew and smiled, and then took a bite of the roast. It was tender and tasty, and soon he was chewing his second and third bite.

Zeke swallowed a chunk of meat he had been chewing, lifted the gourd for water before speaking, "Josh, this is our new friend. He helped save old John when two bison bulls charged him. He shot one of the bulls twice with his Winchester, but the big beast would not go down."

"Then how did you stop the bulls?" asked Josh as he ate smaller bites, but yet determined to eat it all.

"I used your Sharps rifle and killed the first one. I killed the second one just yards from old John. He just about wet his pants," he teased.

John laughed. "Yeah, I was wondering what was taking you so long."

Zeke smiled back, and then said to Josh, "Take a look at this new friend and see if you recognize him."

"What?" asked Josh as he looked up from his bowl? Zeke did not answer, but waited for Josh to look across the fire at Jeremy. Josh studied him carefully, afraid he was in the Confederacy, a prisoner, a cadet at the academy, or from Charleston. Jeremy stopped eating, and looked up at Josh while slowing creating a huge smile on his face.

"Well, I'll be," said Josh suddenly. "You're that kid in New York we caught stealing. What the heck is you doing way out here?"

Zeke laughed. "I knew you would recognize him. He's all grown up, and eighteen years old. This is Jeremy Gordon."

"I never thought I would see you again. Are you traveling with your family? Is your mother okay?" asked Josh.

"No, the smallpox got her in Ohio as we were traveling. She wanted to create a new life in the west for us. After she died, my sister wanted to return to live with my aunt in New York, but I never wanted to go back. I loved the fresh air, the rolling hills, and especially the mountains. I made my way from town to town, and then joined up with the Finney family to travel west."

Zeke broke in, "Everyone with the wagon was killed by Indians except Jeremy."

"I'm sorry to hear that, and especially about your mother. I thought she was a fine lady," said Josh sadly.

Jeremy sat his bowl down and stood, "Yes, she was. She thought you and Zeke were gentlemen."

"Ha! That's a hoot," kidded John. "They're not gentlemen—they are famous bear wrestlers!" They all laughed.

"I think my bear wrestling days or over," grinned Josh. Jeremy unbuttoned a pocket on his shirt and reached inside with his fingers as he walked over to Josh. He stuck his hand out to Josh. As he opened his hand with palm upward, Josh saw two silver dollars.

Jeremy looked earnestly into Josh's eyes, "You gave me a silver dollar and told me to quit stealing. Then you got me a job so I would not be tempted to do so. In a few months, I made enough money to move us into better quarters, and we began to eat regularly. I learned to read and write, and earned promotions. I did all this because of your trust and compassion, and a silver dollar. I would like to return your investment as promised, and the second one represents how thankful I am to you for your help. I've been carrying them for a long time." Jeremy placed the coins in Josh's pale hand.

Josh smiled. "I want you to know I'm not Johnny Appleseed. I don't usually go around picking out vagrants and turning them into respectable citizens. As a leader in the war, I learned to judge men's character quickly. I must have started with my friend Zeke. Lord knows he is quite a character!"

Zeke gave him a playful but gentle elbow to the ribs. "Yeah, and I know a crazy person when I see them. I just felt sorry for this southern nut," he shot back.

Josh continued, "Jeremy, I was angry enough at your stealing from me to punch your lights out, but when I calmed down and looked in your face, I felt confident you could do better. I guess I was right. Thanks for the coins," he added as he shook Jeremy's hand strongly. "Best investment I've ever made."

"The pleasure is all mine," replied Jeremy.

"Liz, the stew is excellent," said Zeke as Jeremy returned to his seat and his bowl, which Bear had been eyeing, but stayed put, waiting for leftovers.

She smiled and said thank you, and John gave a kiss to her cheek.

Josh spoke, "I can't thank you both enough for taking care of us. I would probably have died trying to make it back to our cabin, plus with Zeke's injury, I doubt we would have made it."

"You're welcome, and you're looking stronger," replied John.

Zeke asked, "How long before the big snows come?"

John looked up the sky and thought for a moment, "I reckon about a couple of weeks. The snow is actually a little late this year. One year it came at the beginning of October, but usually towards the end of the month. We'll get some small three or four inch snows, and then suddenly it will snow nonstop for four or five days, and then we're talking several feet of snow. The high country gets ten or twelve feet of snow, but here on the edge of the mountains, not far from the plains, we usually do a little better. If you noticed, we're in a small valley, keeping our tipi out of the strong northwest winds that can drop the temperature to thirty below and freeze a man solid while trying to walk a hundred yards. To survive, mountain men and Indians alike all find a place to stay out of the winds. Most tribes move south where it is somewhat warmer, and the winter a bit shorter, before returning in the spring."

Josh finished his bowl, but Liz quickly refilled it, and then Zeke's bowl. Josh smiled. "Boy, she sure can spoil you. I think if I try to walk all I can for about four or five days, I should be strong enough to get home. It looks like Zeke is more than strong enough."

"I am and I agree. We need to make it to the cabin before the big snow falls. Our place in the mountains is probably a few thousand feet higher than here. We have plenty of wood cut and ready, as well as stored meat and vegetables."

"I think it will take more than a few days for you to get your strength. You've been on that buffalo hide for a long time," replied John.

Zeke spoke up, "I think we can make it if Jeremy helps us. Is that all right with you?" he asked Josh.

"Sure. He would be better off with us. I would hate for him to have to see old John's naked butt climbing into bed at night!" teased Josh.

John turned left and right trying to see his butt, "What the hell is wrong with my butt?"

Zeke laughed and said, "John, there's an old saying that if a man has an ugly face, his butt is at least three times uglier. From the looks of your face, you must have a very hideous butt!" They all laughed as John threw a piece of meat at Zeke. It missed Zeke's head, but not Bear's eyes. He quickly scooped it up.

John asked, "How about this? You boys stay about four or five more days, and I'll spend all my time teaching you everything I know about living in the mountains. I'd feel better if you knew how to fight Indians better, and how to hunt like an Indian as well. In exchange, you can help me stack up some firewood for the winter."

"That's a deal," replied Zeke, and then to Jeremy, "What do you say Jeremy? Will you come with us?"

"Yes," he replied softly, touched by the generous offer. "I'll help you," he added with a bit of pride, knowing he was getting the better part of the bargain.

THIRTEEN

Each day, Josh would walk back and forth across the campsite several times in hopes of building his strength. Then he would exercise as he had done at the military academy. He was slow and stiff at first, but he became better with more practice. When tired of walking, he would practice drawing his pistol, but when he tried to hold his rifle up to aim, his shoulder would throb with pain. During the war, Josh worked through pain, but now he did his best to hide it by repeating the movements over and over again. By the third day, he could climb onto his horse and took to walking the horse several times a day. His appetite grew quickly, and the bison beef made him stronger.

John showed the three young men how to identify the tracks of all the animals in the Rockies. He drew each animal's track in the dirt with a stick, and would point at it in random sequence until the boys could name each one perfectly. They spent hours learning to shoot a bow, as well as how to make their own arrows. The arrowheads often took a full day of chipping just to make one. Everyone shot fairly well except Josh. This made him angry, due to his misfortune of the bear mauling him, but pulling the string hurt his shoulder. He discovered if he just pulled the string a few inches and let it go, and then did it again, it would exercise and strengthen the muscles in his shoulder. Therefore, he forgot about shooting and concentrated on building strength, by pulling the bow over and over again with first the left hand and then the right.

John helped them make tomahawks and clubs. He rubbed black mud on their faces to cover the white skin to make it harder for the animals or Indians to spot them at night. He urged the fellows to practice walking at night until they could walk comfortably in the darkness. He said their senses would increase at night, especially their ears. He told them what Blackfoot Indians smelled like, as well as various Lakota tribes. They learned there were at least three bands of Blackfeet Indians with each speaking the same language but with a slightly different accent. He said he could sometimes smell an Indian over a mile away. However, they drew the line to trying his urine soaked meat and rubbing it on their skin to go hunting. He just laughed at them and said that one day they would.

Liz taught them how to prepare the hides so they would not rot. She did the same for seasoning and drying the meat. She gave them each a leather pouch of thin strips of buffalo meat old John called jerky. He said he sometimes chewed the same piece all day. She helped them make moccasins and legging, and showed them John's shirt and pants she had made all from dried deerskins. John told the boys that moccasins don't leave as much of a footprint like the tracks from their boots, and they don't rub blisters. However,

117

they do wear out quickly so they must carry several pairs in their saddlebags. She showed the boys what berries they could eat and what roots to dig up. They found herbs and plants they had never paid attention to before, but learned how to chop them up into tiny pieces to season their food. She dug out the marrow from a big bone from a bison, put the marrow in a pot of water on the fire, and let it simmer all day. By evening, they learned her marrow soup tasted delicious, along with another chunk of roast.

On the fifth day, they woke up to discover it was snowing. They ate quickly, and began packing their horses. Liz heated her soup for breakfast, along with a chunk of her root bread. The boys liked dipping the bread in the soup before devouring it.

They dressed in all of their clothes along with the new coats Liz made from the buffalo hides. They each gave John and Liz big hugs, and thanked them over and over again for all their help and hospitality. They promised to return in the spring to see how they were doing. Josh winked at Zeke before speaking, "John, we've kept our cabin and valley a secret fearing the bad guys would come for a visit. We live in the valley of the hot springs. Do you know it?"

"Yes, I have seen the springs. The churning bubbling water scares the daylights out of the Indians," he stated.

"Precisely, so far, no one has ventured in, but if you're ever in the neighborhood, please come see us. You are trusted friend, and we would take great pleasure in feeding you and Liz for a change. Thank you for saving our lives." Josh shook his hand firmly before putting on his new deer skin gloves.

Zeke and Jeremy shook his hand as well. Sadly, John and Liz stood by their cooking fire, and watched the boys lead their horses out of the camp and up the mountain. They wished them well and would sort of miss them, but once they were sure they were out of sight and gone, they headed into the tipi, quickly stripped out of their clothes, fell on a buffalo hide, threw another hide over them, and began making love as fast as they could.

The climbing in the snow was difficult with the trail covered by snow. Josh's horse seemed to find a trail better than Zeke's so he took the lead. Drifts of snow reached the belly of the horses, making their steps awkward, so the boys wisely didn't push the horses, but rather allowed them to move at their own pace. After a few hours, they realized there was no way they were going to make it home before nightfall. Late in the afternoon, they found a large rock ledge, and decided to hole up for the night under it. They tied off the horses, gathered up firewood, and soon downed a couple cups of hot coffee. They laid a buffalo robe on the ground against the back of the rock wall, covered up with another, and the three huddled together to sleep with their rifles ready at their side, and pistols drawn beneath their blankets. John had taught them to sleep apart, but it was so cold, they were almost positive the Indians would not be running about. As the snow continued to fall, they easily fell asleep, but got up before dawn to heat some more coffee, and begin chewing on some jerky, wishing they had some of Liz's flat bread. They packed up, and once again began following the ridge. Zeke pointed out their mountain on this side of their valley to Jeremy, while Josh rubbed his sore shoulder, feeling anxious to get home to their cabin.

They followed the ridge for most of the morning before finally beginning their descent towards their valley. Thankfully, they saw no sign of Indians along their journey, but they did see several elk and deer, and longed to go hunting, but for now, getting home remained their priority. From time to time, Jeremy began to see bubbling pools of water, and marveled at the steam rising from the hot water. He had never seen anything like it. Josh and Zeke could not wait to enter their own private hot pool near the cabin. A few hours later, they left the edge of the forest, and stopped on a knoll to gaze at their snow covered cabin and barn. They saw no tracks left by man or beasts. The cow was not in their small pasture, so they hoped and assumed she was in the barn along with their other horses. Slowly, they crept up to the cabin expecting trouble, but found none.

Zeke helped Josh out of the saddle. He felt weak and weary from the long journey, and longed to lie down and sleep. Zeke opened the cabin door and except for entryway cobwebs, and tracks of a few field mice, all looked well. He helped Josh to their bed, and returned to build a fire in the fireplace to heat up the cabin. He added more wood than normal to hurry the heating as Josh was shivering.

He returned to Jeremy and the horses. They unloaded some of their supplies and belongings to the cabin as well as their weapons, and then led the exhausted horses to the barn. Cautiously, Zeke opened the big front door and peered in. The cow immediately mooed at them. Zeke smiled. "Hey, girl, did you miss us?" He walked over to her where she began rubbing her head into his chest. "Horny, huh? Well, maybe Jeremy here can help you with that?" They both laughed. Jeremy glanced out the open back door of the barn and loved the view. He could not believe how lucky he was to find Josh and Zeke again. The horses left on the ranch came in the barn hoping for some fresh grain.

Zeke shooed them back outside for a bit longer. "Let's get these saddles and bridles off, and feed them. I'd better check the spring to be sure they are getting water, too," suggested Zeke as he closed the barn door. "We'll still leave the back door open so they can go out, get water, and return to feed and get out of the snow if they want to."

Jeremy was too tired to make much conversation, but began untying the straps on his saddle, threw it over a stall rail, and then walked his horse out. He returned to undo their packhorses, while Zeke took care of the other two horses. The horses moved slowly, though thankful to have the weight of the men and the saddles off their backs. Once they were out of the way, Zeke climbed into the loft and using a pitchfork, he pushed some stored hay down to the ground as well as some dried corn stalks.

He climbed back down and went over to a barrel, lifted a bucket and scooped out several bucket loads of dried corn. The milk cow watched him pour the bucket into the trough. She began eating immediately. Zeke noted how skinny she was, but he felt confident he could restore her to good health. He gave her ears a good rub, and she responded by wagging her tail, but she kept eating non-stop. They fed the horses, and then went out to check the spring to make sure the water was flowing so the animals could drink.

"We have two springs they drink from. In warmer months, we dug a trench to feed water from the creek just outside the fence to a pit I dug near the corner of the barn. On the other side of the corral was a small natural hot spring. I enlarged the pool so it could hold more water. The larger pool also allows the water to cool, as they don't like to drink it hot. I then dug a little ditch or spillway from that pool to a second one. The water flows down through it, and as it tumbles over the rocks, it cools in the air, but keeps everything from freezing. The second pool has no bubbles to frighten the animals."

"How did you learn to do all this?" asked Jeremy as he whistled for his horse to come to him, and then led him over to the lower, warm water pool.

"I grew up in Maine right on the ocean. We fought freezing water almost seven months of the year. It's a long story, but I bought an abandoned hot tub, and figured out how to heat the water by running brass piping through my fireplace, and made a windblown pump."

"A hot tub? Big enough to sit down in?" asked Jeremy.

"Big enough for me and Josh to sit down in, and it was heavenly. Here in the mountains we have an outdoor hot pool here just for us."

"You get in the tub with winter this cold?" asked a disbelieving Jeremy as he rubbed his cold red hands.

"Yep, and it is fantastic. You'll see, but not tonight. Let's get some supper and hit the sack. I'm pooped."

"Me, too, thanks for letting me come."

"No, we thank you. You were a big help to us, and besides, I couldn't leave you with John. He would have turned you into an Indian!" They both laughed as they made their way back to the cabin.

Zeke let Jeremy take over Yuma's bedroom space, but it saddened him. With their bear injuries and the arrival of winter, they could not go after him. He wasn't sure what Josh was thinking, but he planned to find Yuma in the spring.

Zeke stoked the fire to be sure it remained burning for the rest of the night. He locked the cabin door, and propped his rifle against the wall ready for use if needed. Josh was still lying where he left him. He knelt down and took off Josh's boots, then removed his pants, his coats and shirts, his long johns, and finally his hat. He pulled the covers back on their bed, and rolled him in and covered him up. He then stripped down and climbed in the bed from the other side. It was the first time in many weeks they had been able to cuddle up and sleep together. Though asleep, Josh instinctively moved into Zeke, and soon they were both warm and sound asleep.

A few weeks had passed since his forced return to his master, but his days were always the same with chores to do, and his nights belonging to the will and whim of the big Indian. Yuma sighed when Mila Hanska rolled off him leaving his butt slightly sore and wet, and then pulled Yuma into his arms to sleep. The warrior fell asleep in seconds, but not Yuma. He closed his eyes and dreamed of being free with Josh and Zeke. He had hoped they would find him before the snow began falling, but with more than a few feet on the ground, he knew he would suffer another long winter with Mila Hanska. He did his best to be a good slave, and avoid any beatings, but sometimes Mila Hanska was angry when an enemy killed one of his men, and took it out on Yuma. The boy did not know how old he was, but he knew he was approaching the age of manhood or about eighteen, when an Indian boy became a hunter or a warrior, but Mila would never allow him to carry weapons, or go out on a hunt. He guessed this age because his stopped growing tall, and his pubic hair no longer spread. He tried to look like a young boy, fearing Mila would think Yuma was now too old and kill him. He plucked any hairs that grew on his face, or in his armpits, and shaved away most of his pubic hair. He talked softly, in a high pitch, making his master think he was younger than he was.

Yuma was small and childlike for his age, and the squaws considered him good looking. If he was still with his tribe, he would be learning how to hunt and kill prey, but in this wild warrior village, he was his master's squaw in every way. He did all the hide cleaning, sewing, cooking, feeding the horses, washing his master, and satisfying his sexual needs when no woman was available. His master could have any squaw he wanted, but he treated his women horribly, and when he became unsatisfied, he would get angry and kill them. No one challenged his authority, and the women were all afraid to stand up to him. To show them he was their chief, he would sometimes take one of his warrior's wives to his bed. After he had his way with her, he would release her so she could go running back to her husband.

There was a part of Yuma that wanted to die, but having tasted the freedom of a better life away from here, he knew he must do all he can to make his master want to keep him, and not trade him in for a younger boy. He had seen many older abused boys become angry warriors, but some who were not suited for warriors had their throats cut, and died where they fell. Two of his friends failed in their training, and Mila Hanska would not allow him to bury his friends in the traditional way. He allowed his dogs and the vultures to feed on their bodies.

When feeling low and sad, Yuma closed his eyes and instantly, he could see the smiles on the faces of Zeke and Josh. He loved the way they playfully teased one another. He longed to hear them laugh. He had known from an early age that he was different from the other Indian boys. As a child, he ran around naked most of the time, and when an older friend's member began growing, he became envious and infatuated. He had kept his desires secret from all except the boy who taught him how to make love, and feel loved. He could still feel the touch of his friend in his dreams. After a while, his silent tears dried on his cheeks and he drifted off to sleep.

They all slept late, with Jeremy rising first and making his way to the fire. He put more firewood on the dwindling red coals, and watched the flames flicker up until the new wood caught on fire. He turned and saw Josh and Zeke still asleep in the same bed. It puzzled him a little, but he was hungry. He began going through his pack until he found some hard tack and jerky to chew on.

Zeke soon stirred, spotted Jeremy, and climbed out of the bed naked. "We sleep like the Indians—in the nude," he said quickly. "Your body heat keeps your toes warm," he added with a smile. He dressed and went over to the fire to get warm. "We need some coffee. Do you want some?" he asked Jeremy.

"Yes, of course," smiled Jeremy.

"Me, too," said Josh as he made his way out of the bed.

Jeremy noted he was nude, too, but his eyes fell on the huge scars in his shoulder where the bear had bitten him.

"Jeremy, there's the water bucket. There's a hot spring just behind the cabin. Will you fetch us some water, and I'll get us some breakfast together."

"Sure," the boy replied as he headed out the door. The snow was falling rapidly, but he hurried around the cabin, and found the hot pool as the steam was rising from it into the five-degree air. He rushed back to the cabin quickly, shutting and locking the door behind him. "It's snowing and very cold." He set the bucket down on the cabinet.

Zeke took a scoop and filled the coffee pot, and took it to the fire to heat up. He stoked the fire, and added a little more wood to continue to heat up the cabin. Josh managed to dress himself with some difficulty. He asked Jeremy to pull his shirt up over his shoulder. Zeke threw some thin slices of buffalo meat into a black iron frying pan and put it on the fire. He retrieved a tall pottery pot with a lid on it. He was pleased the mice could not get into the jar, and made a mental note to catch the pesky little creatures, and remove them from their cabin. He placed about six scoops of finely ground corn meal in a pot. He added water to the pot, added some salt, put a lid on it, and placed it over the fire on a cooking rod.

The meat started frying, and the boys grew hungrier as the smell of the frying meat hit their nostrils. About fifteen minutes later, Zeke placed the frying pan and the pot in the center of their little bench table, and before he could return with the steaming coffee pot, Josh and Jeremy were chewing on the hot meat, and spooning up the corn meal mush.

"This is good," said Jeremy with a mouthful.

"The chef thanks you for your compliments, but you still get to do the dishes," he replied with a smile, as he poured them cups of coffee, and then sat down beside Josh to begin eating as well.

"Yep, very good, I was starved," added Josh.

"How's your shoulder?" asked Zeke before forking another piece of meat into his mouth.

"It is as sore as hell, did you drop me off my horse?" he asked with sly grin.

"Nope, but you're going to have to keep exercising it until you get stronger. You recovered from worse during the war, and you'll do it again," said Zeke. "More coffee?" he asked them. They nodded yes without stopping their chewing.

"I wasn't eaten by a bear during the war," laughed Josh. Josh and Jeremy both picked up their cups at the same time, and held them for Zeke to pour. Deciding to change the subject Zeke asked, "What do you think we ought to do today?"

Josh sipped some coffee and replied, "Well, as much as I hate to, I'll get the cabin cleaned up and put away the supplies. How bad was the barn?"

"Not bad, but I suspect we're going to run out of hay and corn this winter. We'll have to plant more in the spring, and maybe fence in a larger pasture, so they can eat new grass half the year and dried grass the second half."

"Back home we would put our animals in one pasture for a few weeks, and then move them to the other. This allowed the grass to grow faster and taller before they started chewing and stomping on it," said Josh, after finishing his last piece of meat.

"Jeremy and I will put the bison meat in the smokehouse, and make a fire in there as well. We'll clean out the barns and check the animals. We'll return near lunch, and I think we should clean our guns and prepare ammunition in case we're attacked," stated Zeke.

Jeremy gulped as he finished his coffee. "Do you think they will come here during the winter?"

Josh smiled. "No, I doubt that. They would not want to be so far from home if a blizzard came. We've never seen any Indians on our land, as they are afraid of the bubbling waters. They think this place belongs to evil gods, or the place the white men might call hell."

Zeke laughed. "But we call it heaven, and I propose we hurry so before dark we can introduce Jeremy to the art of soaking in a hot spring!"

"Yes, I think I would like that, too," added Josh. "Let's get to it."

Zeke showed Jeremy around their land, including the privy cave. He did not show him the cave where they found the gold. Together, they cleared the barn and smokehouse of cobwebs, built a fire in the smokehouse, cut down a green tree, chopped it up, and placed it on the hot coals in the smokehouse fireplace. "This wood will burn slower and create more smoke," said Zeke. "You're going to love the taste of this meat. There should be enough here to get us through the winter."

Zeke investigated the small hot spring on a rise of ground behind their cabin. After telling Jeremy about his hot tub in Maine, and the pipe to and from the fire, he had an idea his engineering mind thought of. He realized the level of the water in the pool was several feet higher than the window of the cabin. He walked off paces to the back wall of the cabin and counted ten feet. He went inside and paced from that wall to the cupboard corner. Josh watched him with some amusement, but said nothing. He had seen Zeke deep in what he called mechanical thought like this before.

Zeke sat down at the table and drew a diagram, and then looked up at the bewildered Jeremy and Josh and smiled. "I think I can engineer running hot water into the cabin. Then we'll have water to cook and wash even if it snows ten feet."

"And how do you propose to do that?" asked a skeptical Josh.

"Well, if I had iron pipe like I did while working on the boats in Washington it would be easy, but there is no pipe out here. So we'll have to make some natural pipes."

"Natural pipes?" quizzed Jeremy.

"Yes, we have a hand drill and bit we used for the pegs for the logs to build the cabin, and to construct the door and window frames. We'll cut straight limbs from a tree with a soft center. We'll cut them in one-foot lengths, drill as far as we can from each end, and drive a spike through the center to carve it out cleanly. Then we'll make the receiver end a little bigger by cutting out much of the interior wall, and the opposite end smaller by carving down the outside wall. Then the small end of this wood pipe will fit into the larger end of the next pipe. We'll seal the joints with clay."

Josh and Jeremy sat there with their mouths open. "If you say so," said Josh.

Zeke grinned. "You'll see. Let's get those guns cleaned, and head to the hot pool."

"Now you're talking," laughed Josh.

They taught Jeremy how to take care of his pistol, rifle, and the Parker shotgun. Josh had fired one of these in the war, and knew it to be powerful with a hard kick. He explained to Jeremy not to fire it unless he pulled it tight into his shoulder, or it would knock him down.

Late in the afternoon, Josh and Zeke began taking off all their clothes including their socks. Jeremy felt a bit uneasy, but finally took his clothes off, too. They put their boots back on without socks, and laughed at how stupid they looked.

Zeke went to the door, "On the count of three. One, two, three!"

He snatched the door open. Jeremy went out hastily, followed by Josh. Zeke pulled the door to and locked the latch, and together, the shivering threesome quickly walked the snow-covered path to the pool. Josh kicked off his boots as did Zeke, and they jumped in. This time Jeremy did not hesitate as his butt was freezing in the wind. He jumped in making a big splash.

When he came up, he had a huge grin on his face. Josh and Zeke laughed at him.

"I told you it was heavenly," said Zeke.

"More than that, it is amazing. It stays this hot year around?" he asked.

Josh grinned. "Yes it does. My engineering partner could tell you the heated water comes from deep down in the earth, warmed by volcanic materials. Heated water has to expand, like in a tea kettle, so it goes up and out to the surface."

Zeke began washing Josh's hair for him while Jeremy laid back and enjoyed the bubbles of hot water floating all around his body. Josh washed Zeke's hair, and Jeremy looked a bit envious. Therefore, without announcement, Zeke pulled Jeremy over to them, and spun him around so Josh and Zeke could wash his hair, too.

"Thank you. This is so much fun!" exclaimed Jeremy with a grin. "How do we get back to the cabin without freezing to death now that we're wet?"

Josh and Zeke looked at each other, smiled, and replied in unison, "You run like hell!"

They laughed and soaked for an hour, but as darkness began to fall, they once again counted to three, jumped out of the water, put on their boots with wet feet and made a run for the cabin. Then they ran to the fire to once again warm and dry their wet bodies before dressing.

They talked for a while after dinner, but soon grew sleepy and made their way to their beds. Josh and Zeke waited a while hoping Jeremy had fallen asleep before beginning a much delayed love making session. The bed creaked a little from Zeke's thrusting, but quietly and slowly, he continued his work. Then using his mouth, he helped Josh ejaculate and finally, after several long wet kisses, they fell asleep in each other's arms.

FOURTEEN

"What's wrong?" asked Josh as he pulled the barn door behind him and began walking over to a stall where Zeke and Jeremy stood dejectedly.

"She won't give us any milk," replied Zeke.

Josh smiled thinking they were making it easy on him, "Perhaps you're not handsome enough." He laughed aloud. Jeremy smiled but Zeke kept a sour face.

"Very funny, I've pulled on her teats for so long they should be dragging the ground!" exclaimed Zeke.

"It's probably either the lack of good feed, or the fact that we left her alone for a few weeks, and she's pissed at us. I should know this as we had a number of cows on the plantation, but I never paid much attention to raising them. I did milk a few when I was a kid," added Josh.

"Give it a try," urged Zeke.

"Okay, but first you two step out of the stall so you're not frightening her. She probably saw your big bony hands and panicked. Come on, get out of there," grinned Josh.

Reluctantly, Jeremy and Zeke moved out of the stall. Josh reached into the corn barrel and grabbed a handful of corn. He walked in the stall and went around so the cow could see him face to face. He began talking to her softly while scratching her ears and head, and then laid his face against her cheek so she could feel him. He then showed her the corn in his hand and fed it to her. She chewed loudly, but did not drop a single kernel. Josh then began to sing to her, "Oh Jenny with the light brown hair..."

"What the hell is that?" asked Zeke.

Josh gave him a shut up look and whispered, "It's a Stephen Foster song, and he wrote it during the Civil War after his wife and child left him because he drank too much. Shut up now," he warned.

Josh continued singing as he rubbed his way around the cow before slowly he sat down on the stool, and began rubbing his hands together to get them warm, but it was so cold he did not think it was working fast enough. He unbuttoned his coat and put his hands under the opposite armpits. Zeke almost started laughing, but Josh once again gave him the 'don't even think it' look.

After a few minutes of singing, he removed his hands, placed them immediately on the cow's teats, and started pulling. Suddenly, the cow mooed loudly, and Josh grinned as he heard the first ping of a steaming stream of milk hitting the bottom of the cold empty bucket. He kept on singing and soon she was squirting milk as fast as Josh could pull. In minutes, the pail was full.

Josh stopped singing and winked at the boys as he handed Zeke the pail of milk. He walked around the cow, rubbed her head some more, and said

127

to her, "Jenny will be your name from now on, you did great. Thank you old girl—sorry we've neglected you for so long. We'll do better from now on. Try to be nice to these two young farts when they try to get milk from you. Make them sing if they want some milk, okay?" He gave her a kiss and led her out of the barn so she could get some warm water.

"Anything else I can do for you boys?" asked Josh with a sly grin on his face.

"How about making us some lunch?" asked Zeke. "Be sure and wash your hands first. We'll finish feeding the animals and come on in. The sky is clear so no snow today. I think I'll start my trench work. Jeremy volunteered to help," he added slyly.

"No, I didn't," replied Jeremy.

"Now you did," said Zeke as he flipped Jeremy's hat off and quickly climbed the ladder to the loft.

They had been home a few weeks and thankfully, the heavy snow forced them to rest and recover. Zeke was back to fine form because he and Jeremy took turns doing pull-ups in the barn each morning like he did at the academy. Josh kept working on building his strength, too. He pulled on the bow for about twenty minutes several times a day until he could finally hold the bow for a count of five while fully extended. He felt a great deal of satisfaction, but also felt a new drive to really learn to shoot a bow with dependable accuracy. He had learned a little from Yuma and little more from John, but it would be up to him to make it a skill as certain as he was with his rifle.

One night they took stock of their weapons and ammunition. Between them, they owned eight rifles and a dozen pistols. They counted every single bullet, and sorted them as to which gun they belonged to. They made small leather bags, put the shells in the bag according to the gun, laced a leather cord through the top, and tied it off. They had enough ammunition to hold off an Indian attack, and maybe a little more, if they didn't waste too much.

Zeke showed Jeremy where the extra pistols and rifles were hidden all around their place. They kept a pistol on the ledge above the door in a shadow of a knot in a log. They placed a rifle in the barn near the back door, and hung the ammunition bag for it on a nail above it. They kept two rifles and the Sharps Buffalo rifle in the cabin loaded at all times and placed by Josh's side of the bed. They both kept a pistol on their side of the bed under the edge of a bear hide. In a cave where they did not find any gold, they kept the remaining four rifles, along with some canned food, knives, an axe, and some rope. They also rolled up a few hides and kept them tightly bound, hoping to keep the bugs out. They stacked up dried wood in case they needed a fire. Zeke put a flint in a leather bag, and hung it on a stick of the stacked wood.

If they were burned out of their cabin by natural means or Indians, they kept enough stuff in the cave to start over. Jeremy did not know it, but they also kept bags of gold hidden in various locations. Josh kept saying to Zeke, "We don't have to be heroes to survive. I'm done with being a hero. I fought their war for nothing. I killed men and watched my own men die. From now on, I will do all I can to live because you give me a reason to live," he paused as he swallowed hard before finishing, "and to love."

Josh said to Jeremy as he moved a hide rug from the center of the floor. "This section has a trap door. If they set us on fire or overwhelm us, we'll go down in the cellar we dug. There's a tunnel to the back that comes out in the brush. We'll quickly make our way to the cave and rearm, and hope they go away thinking we're dead. Don't hesitate if either one of us tells you to head to the cave. Just do it when we ask, okay?"

Jeremy gulped and said, "Okay, I will. I promise."

Josh winked at him as he covered the trap door and returned to the bench. "I think we should spend a little ammunition teaching Jeremy how to shoot his rifle, shotgun, and pistol. I'll also teach him how to use the knife."

"Maybe I should teach how to use a sword," grinned Zeke as he retrieved Josh's sword from a long skinny felt bag in the corner. The blade was still in good shape, so he made a few good fencing moves impressing Jeremy.

"Yeah, that looks cool," said Jeremy.

Josh laughed. "Yeah that'll scare the pants off those Indians, but okay we'll teach you everything we know and have learned on how to survive out here in case you decide to move on in the spring or stay with us."

Jeremy did not know what to say. He had thought he might be intruding, but did not really want to leave. He felt good and comfortable with the boys. In a small way, Josh opened the door of possibility in case he wanted to stay. He smiled and nodded approvingly to Josh. Zeke gave him a wink.

"One last thing," began Josh, "I think we must learn to fight like our enemy. Don't get me wrong, I don't believe all Indians are bad, but we sure seem to attract the bad ones. We have made friends with two Indians so far. John's wife Liz saved my life, and Yuma became like a son to us after we saved him. He helped save a wagon train, but his enemies, a wild mean renegade tribe of warriors, recaptured him. He is a slave for them. I'm going to think all winter of how I'm going to get him back."

Zeke spoke quickly, "You mean how we are going to get him back."

Josh continued, "Well, anyhow, John showed us a little bit about a bow, tomahawk, and Indian fighting. When we can, we'll set up a straw dummy, and practice shooting with our new bows. We should use our many days of being snowed in making more arrowheads for additional arrows. We will throw the tomahawk until we can do it as good as they can."

"Why not just use our ammunition and shoot the bastards?" asked Jeremy.

"Many reasons, one of which is we never know how long winter is going to last. We can't get back to Denver to buy more ammunition until the spring thaw. However, honestly, it'll teach us how they fight, so we can learn how to defeat them," stated Josh.

Zeke jumped in, "At the academy we learned about stealth fighting like assassins in the night, or Oriental warriors. Bullets make a big noise and create smoke that would show the enemy where we are hiding. If we are outnumbered, which is easily done, as there are only three of us, we shoot and move before they spot our new location. Bows and arrows are silent allowing us to shoot many times from a hidden position. During the war, Josh did not fight in a regular army. He was part of a team of scouts that worked behind enemy lines. Many times, they had to sneak into a town and kill with only their knives. They learned to eat on the run, and to survive no matter what the odds."

Josh chewed his lip while thinking. "By making our own arrows, they will be confused as to who is killing them. When we can, we'll retrieve our arrows from the dead bodies to compound the mystery. Indians believe in mystics, ghosts, and evil spirits. They call our springs a devil ground, and they are afraid of it. We'll make them terrified of us. They'll lose confidence, weaken, and maybe make mistakes. We'll take advantage."

Zeke smiled and said slowly, "So you want us to learn to fight like them, and shoot like them so they'll think another tribe of Indians is after them?"

"Now you're getting the picture. Don't you see? There are many reasons for us to learn to fight like they do, so we can kill the bad ones, and hopefully get Yuma back."

After they ate, Josh stayed in the cabin to begin chipping away at a box of stones they hoped to create arrowheads from. He used one of John's arrows as a model, but it still took the rest of the afternoon to make one.

Meanwhile, Zeke cajoled Jeremy into helping him dig. They started around the side of the cabin, punched a hole through the dried clay between the logs, and pushed one of Zeke's homemade pipes through. He stuck a simple wooden ball cock valve off an old whisky barrel in the end of the wooden pipe. They packed clay tightly around the pipe to seal the wind and rain out of the cabin. They had to dig along the side of the cabin as it went up a slight hill. After ten feet or so, Zeke would push the joints of the pipe together with some clay until he created a long pipe, and then buried it with dirt and then snow.

It took the rest of the day for them to reach the small nearby hot spring. The water was much hotter here than the pool they bathed in. They buried the remaining pipe saving the last section for when they broke through the dirt to the pool. Zeke looked back and realized they were about four feet above the cabin creating some water pressure as the water fell.

He took a strong stake and used the back of the axe to drive it through the mud wall of the natural pool. Quickly he pushed the last piece of wood pipe through the wall, pushed it back into the last joint, buried it, and repaired the wall of the pool. He looked into the pool and the pipe was about six inches from the edge and about eight inches down. Excellent, he thought.

"That should do it. Let's head inside and see if it works," said Zeke as he grabbed his tools, and led Jeremy back around the cabin.

"Did you do it?" asked Josh as he looked up from the bench near the fire where he had been chipping the arrowhead.

"Come on over and see."

Zeke had cut the whiskey barrel in half with their log saw, and placed one of the halves under the spigot. He turned the handle and for a long second or two nothing happen.

Josh laughed. "You're crazy! It doesn't w…"

Before he could finish teasing Zeke, water came flowing out of the pipe into the barrel and the steam rose from it.

"Well, I'll—you did it!" exclaimed Josh.

"Hot running water, master," Zeke said mockingly.

"I'm impressed," laughed Josh, "but what happens when the bucket fills up."

Zeke thought for a moment, "I'll guess I had better work on a drain tomorrow. For now, just turn off the valve, and throw the water out the door." Zeke turned to Josh. "What did you do that was productive today?"

Josh held up his arrowhead proudly, "I made an arrowhead."

Zeke took it from him and lifted it up in the quickly fading light of the short winter days. "It looks a little lumpy don't you think?"

Josh snatched it from him, "It's a hell of a lot harder than making running water!"

Jeremy started laughing, as Zeke and Josh started arguing playfully. Finally, he had heard enough of their banter, and suddenly started stripping out of all his clothes. They kept talking and teasing until finally they noticed a beautiful good-looking young man standing nude in front of them.

Jeremy stepped back into his boots barefooted and looked up at them, "Last one in stinks like a skunk!"

No one moved for a second, but then suddenly Josh and Zeke caught on, and started pulling their clothes off. Jeremy laughed at them and headed for the door, trotted to the pool, kicked off his boots and jumped into the hot spring they used for bathing. Thirty seconds later, Zeke and Josh came running pulling and tugging at each other until they literally fell into the pool at the same time.

"Well, did I win?" asked Zeke as he came up spitting water.

"No, I did," stated Josh as he splashed Zeke.

"You tied, and you both smell like skunks!" laughed Jeremy.

Josh and Zeke looked at each other intensely as if speaking without talking, something they often did. Suddenly, they dropped beneath water, grabbed Jeremy's legs, and flung him out of the water into the nearby snow.

"Ouch!" he screamed as he felt the cold stuff on his hot skin. Quickly, he scampered back to the pool where they splashed and played until well after dark. When things quieted down, Josh showed him a flat rock near the edge of the pool. He removed the rock and recovered an oil soaked bag. In the bag were two loaded pistols.

"They're here just in case, okay?"

"Yes, I know, but I have to tell you, I've never felt safer in all my life than with the two of you."

Zeke patted his shoulder, "Yes, but history tells us the greatest armies make their biggest mistakes when they become comfortable and lazy. They make blunders that usually end with death. We must always be on our toes. We must come up with a plan in case Indians or bad men attack our settlement. We'll keep hiding more guns and ammunition in and around the cabin and barn as well as in the nearby forest."

Josh nodded approvingly and said, "We'll need an alarm so we all know trouble is about, but something no one else would understand."

Jeremy said, "How about the owl whistle? We all do it the best. We could whistle three times."

"That's a good idea," replied Zeke. "But if something extremely urgent happens we'll use the iron triangle, as the sound of it will go a lot farther."

Josh added, "If we fight like the Indians, we must learn to listen like them. Liz showed me how to make the sound of a crow or the shrill of a hawk. We'll use them for signals just as they do. We must be able to smell the Indians, hear the Indians, and when we have to—kill them."

Zeke argued in his reply, "Yes, but when we find good Indians, we must still try to make friends, or we'll be fighting forever."

Josh nodded silently, as they continued floating in the hot water.

They felt like Christmas came and went, but no one knew for sure what day it was, nor absolutely sure it was December or January, so finally Zeke just announced that tomorrow they were going to celebrate Christmas and they did. They each made a present for the other. Josh and Zeke received a new larger leather sack to hold their stuff when riding or hunting with a twisted rawhide cord to go over their shoulder. Jeremy did the stitching for the bags like Liz had shown him, then carved a reverse of their initials in a block of wood and hammered the new stamp into the leather. Josh liked his 'JJ' initials and Zeke his 'ZR' initials stamped into the leather.

Josh and Zeke actually cheated as they had been working for weeks on a present for Jeremy, and simply used Christmas as an excuse to give it to him. They made him close his eyes until they could open the sea chest they had bought last year in Denver for their clothes to help keep the moths and mice out. When he opened his eyes, he discovered a complete buckskin outfit including pants, leggings, shirt, and a jacket with three strips of fringe along the sleeves from elbow to wrist. Liz had taught them how to sew buckskin when she made a new jacket for John. She said he always needed a new one each year as he would rip a strip of the fringe off, and use it to fix his leggings, tie up a sack, or clean his rifle. Their last gift to Jeremy was a new leather wide brimmed hat with a rawhide cord to place under his chin when riding fast.

Jeremy almost cried at their generosity, but settled for a big hug from the boys. They continued their celebration with a feast because Josh had retrieved a turkey from the smokehouse, and managed to create a pot of corn bread dressing. It came out a little dry for his first attempt, but the gravy he made helped it along. Zeke roasted a few sweet potatoes, and Jeremy helped him churn fresh butter to put on them. They kept teaching Jeremy at every opportunity how to hunt, fish, care for his horse and his weapons, and how to cook so he could sustain his life. He made the biscuits and took a bit of ribbing when they crumbled. Josh added butter on top of his biscuits with some honey they found in a hollow log. Zeke loved the gravy and poured it over his biscuits. Jeremy fixed one biscuit with butter and honey, and the other with gravy. Nothing could ever fill up the boy's growing appetite.

Just as they were about to dig into the hot food, Zeke stopped them. "I think we should say a prayer of thanks." They bowed their heads as Zeke began. "For Josh and me, we left at the end of the war to find peace in a new land and live in paradise. We believe we found it in our home in these mountains. We are thankful for all our blessings. We also pray for Yuma. Please keep him safe and let him know we are coming for him. This year we have even more to be thankful for because Jeremy has joined us. He has brought great pleasure to us, and has become a grand friend."

133

Josh broke in, "That is so true, thank you God for caring and providing for us. Now let's eat—I'm starving!"

They all laughed and began eating. They ate until there was nothing left to chew on. Jeremy tried on his new clothes, but soon they ended their celebration with a naked run in three feet of snow to the hot spring to soak under the stars. That night became one of their favorite Christmases, and a memory they would cherish forever.

The snow fell at least four days a week and now reached the bottom of their cabin roof. Because of their daily treks to the barn, smokehouse, and hot spring, they kept a snow path packed down. Last night Josh slipped on the way to the hot spring pool and skinned his butt on a slick spot. They teased him for the rest of the night as he limped around wounded. Zeke massaged Josh's sore butt, and made it feel better after they went to bed. Josh felt better by morning and pronounced Zeke a miracle worker.

They did their chores by caring for the animals early in the morning, and spending the rest of the day inside the cabin making shafts for the arrows, and chipping arrowheads. The patience required to make just one arrow earned the Indians high praise from the boys. They used short turkey feathers to complete the task. They had made about twenty arrows so far and three tomahawks. Josh made three long skinny leather bags sort of like a rifle sleeve with a long pocket for their bows, a short fatter one for their arrows, and a strap to go over their chest so they could ride or run without holding it. They felt it best to keep their Indian weapons a secret from any strangers they met.

About once every week or so the weather would lift for a day or two with bright sunshine and though the temperature remained close to zero, they would bundle up, build a snowman and shoot their arrows at it. Week by week, they helped each other improve, so once satisfied, they would back up about five yards and start firing again.

Zeke would take a charred stick from the fire and draw an eight-inch circle for a head. They would take turns firing, while refusing to quit until they each hit the head at least ten times. The next chance for practice they would back up again and fire. It took several months, but they were pretty good at hitting the body of the man at a hundred yards, and deadly at seventy yards. Jeremy loved the bow, and sometimes he could hit the head at a hundred twenty-five yards, blowing Josh and Zeke away. They soon learned how to judge the wind to allow the breeze to bring their arrows in for the kill. On their longer shots they learned how to arc the shot upward a bit to allow for the drop. This technique took a lot more practice, but soon they were once again hitting the target correctly.

Josh became the best tomahawk thrower, but Zeke still insisted he could beat them both with his sword. They laughed and teased each other, but their skills continued to develop. On the days they were stuck in the cabin, they would wrestle with fake wooden knives. Josh taught them how to sneak up from behind, and then silence an enemy with a quick slice to the throat. A second stab to the chest area finished the job after a jerk upwards into the heart. They fought face to face with the knives, and sometimes, gave each other a big bruise but gradually they improved.

At night, they talked strategy for getting Yuma back. They made small tipis from hides, bushes with twigs, and made wood nuggets for Indians. Zeke excelled at battle strategy, but with only three fighters, they could not put together a frontal attack. Josh told them stories of his escapades behind the enemy lines, and instilled in them the absolute importance of sneaking into the camp in silent stealth, killing brutally, releasing the enemy's horses to prevent chase, and then preparing to fake a trail to throw off the inevitable attempt to track them.

They designed traps and hazards to kill the warriors and slow down the tribe. They also decided to do their best to trust their warrior instinct. They each had suggestions, but they decided to do two things to humiliate the enemy, and create a bit of a mystery, which they hoped would develop into fear. They would carve an inverted V on the dead man's chest and expose their genitals. It sounded harsh, but they reminded themselves of how many people they had already seen these warriors kill. They killed men, women, and children without mercy. They tortured their victims, cut off body parts, and paraded such items on sticks while yelling their war whoops. They could not think of anything they could do that would provide justice, but in the end, their ultimate goal was the rescue of Yuma.

Josh had learned from his war duties behind the enemy lines that pulling off freeing Yuma might be possible, but getting away would be very difficult. The Indians with the black and white stripes on their faces were fierce warriors, and stealing one of their slaves would be considered a huge insult—a loss of face that they would die trying to make right. He knew they would be chased hard, long, fast, and without end. If they could not get away clean, then more than likely they would have to kill every warrior who joined in the chase.

Josh began to dream of the attacks he planned in his head over and over again, and sometimes would wake up sweating because he saw himself kill a man with his knife. It bothered him, but never as much as the thought of what the warriors were doing to poor Yuma.

FIFTEEN

Gradually, the light of the day grew longer, and the snowfalls diminished, followed by days and days of rain that washed the winter ice away, while leaving everything damp and muddy. The long winters, with temperatures remaining well below freezing, and many times below zero, made the ground expand from the ice, so that when it melted, the mud became at least a foot deep. Everywhere they stepped made a squishing sound, resulting in an occasional socked foot pulling loose from a cemented boot in the thick mucky stuff. There was laughter from the other boys, and curse words from the victim. Once well-packed paths to the barn, privy, and hot spring, were now a boggy gauntlet, where they would likely become stuck, slip, or fall. Flowers began to bloom, and the buds awoke in the limbs of the trees. Josh noted the birds were flying north, and he knew they once again made it through another Colorado Rocky Mountain winter—something not every would-be mountain man could do. Many starved, while others were discovered frozen where they sat, clutching their prized rifles.

The boys quickly put their winter made plans into action. They rode their horses around the pasture to build up their stamina, and the strength of their own legs, especially their inner thighs. When not riding, they would run up and down the trails around the mountain. They pushed and chased each other, and their bodies became lean and strong, as did their determination. Their winter fat fell away leaving defined abdomens, arms, chests, and leg muscles. They did chin-ups in the barn, and pushups in the cabin. The Indian bow made Josh's shoulder and arm muscles powerful, and by doing so, his confidence once again rose. He could now do what he had been planning to do all winter—go after Yuma.

They rose early today, saddled their horses, secured their rifles and pistols, and left their land, as the sun began to peak over the mountain to the east. They each pulled an empty packhorse. Josh and Zeke carried secret bags of gold dust, hidden in their saddlebags, to pay for their intended supplies, and to bring home some currency for possible emergency needs. They would also make a secret purchase of more land.

Thankful to be alive, and to be living well in their minds, they also engaged their banker to arrange to send money to both of their families. They did this about twice a year, but this year they added a third name to their list— Jeremy's sister. Under the pretense of in case something happen, Jeremy gave Zeke his sister's address, but they never told him they sent money to her.

They warned Jeremy about Denver and the bad people hanging around near the saloons. He was told he would see stranded travelers begging for money, others fighting over money or a woman, and bad men that would kill him for just glancing in their direction. He was told to keep his eyes straight ahead, but using his peripheral vision, he should take note of every person he saw, their location, and whether he thought they were armed or not. He was to alert Zeke or Josh of danger with only a soft whistle, but to remain calm and in control. Their goal was to avoid any engagement while appearing poor and harmless.

When they reached the mercantile, Josh retrieved his saddle bags containing the gold placed in old flour sacks, and went into a small bank. Zeke and Jeremy watched Josh until he entered the bank safely, while pretending to adjust their saddles. They tied up the horses, and just as they stepped on the boardwalk, a gun fired down the street to their right. They both turned in the direction of the sound while putting a right hand on the handle of their pistols. It turned out to be just a drunk firing his gun in the air. The streets were filled with people, providing a measure of paranoia to the three loners, who lived in voluntary isolation in the high mountains. Once again, they tried to relax as they stepped into the store.

"Ed!" called Ruth from the back of the store. "Look who is here?"

Ed came down the ladder as Ruth made her way to Zeke and gave him a big hug. "Oh my goodness you are a handsome man," she said. "You must be eating well, too. Who is this with you?" she asked as she smiled at Jeremy.

Ed bear hugged Zeke before he could speak, "I was worried about you. That was a long winter. How did you fair?"

"Well, thank you," said Zeke. "I would like to introduce a new friend of mine. This is Jeremy Gordon."

Ed shook his hand warmly as Ruth smiled at him. "We're pleased to meet you Jeremy. Are you traveling through?"

"I was, but my settler group was attacked by the Indians, and I'm the only one that lived. Josh and Zeke rescued me, so I'm staying with them."

"Oh my goodness, more Indian trouble—we hear something bad just about every week," said Ruth.

Ed added, "Yes, you must be careful. The tribes are angry with the government, and taking it out on the settlers. Homes are burned, and like you, many of the wagon trains lose half their people on their way to Oregon. We feel safe in the town, but the whole thing worries us."

"Honey, they're probably tired and hungry after the long ride. I've got some ham in the kitchen so come join us for lunch," urged Ruth.

"Yes, you must eat with us. Where's Josh? Is he okay?" asked Ed, half afraid to hear bad news.

"He's fine now, but you can ask him about the grizzly he and I had to wrestle to the ground," replied Zeke with a grin. "He'll be here in a moment." Zeke pulled three pages of paper from his pocket. "Ed, these are the supplies we need to buy. Josh will bring the money. I hope you have everything."

"Whew, that's quite a list," replied Ed as he scanned the pages. "I think we can handle this. We've been getting supplies in just about every week now that the weather has lifted. The newspaper says that one day the railroad will make it to us, and then we'll have weekly supply deliveries. Nevertheless, come on let's eat. I know you're starved."

Josh came in the door, and they waved him on back. Ruth gave him a hug, while Ed sighed and smiled. He was glad to see Josh as well, as he vigorously shook his hand.

After catching up on Josh and Zeke's adventures, Ed began to tell them about the news in Colorado. "They're planning on building a courthouse soon and we sure need one. The sheriff's jail is always full. Most of the men in jail are there for being drunk, and many of them are former mountain men, soldiers, or settlers who lost their entire family on their journey west. There were at least fourteen shot and killed during the winter, so the sheriff has hired two deputies to help him. An old Indian tried to rob the bank with nothing but a knife. They shot him in the streets while holding a bag of coins."

"My goodness, it sounds like we're safer in the mountains fighting grizzlies," said Zeke.

"We would be safe in the mountains if you could learn to cook as well as Ruth," teased Josh, as he took the last bite of potato salad on his plate.

"Okay, pick on my cooking and see if I feed you anymore," replied Zeke, as they all laughed. "Thanks to you," began Zeke as he nodded to Ruth, "they love my biscuits. And our cow gives us milk, cream, and butter."

Josh laughed. "Yeah, you should see these boys trying to get milk out of that cow. I taught them how to sing to her." The entire table laughed heartily before Josh continued after wiping his mouth with a red checkered napkin, "Ruth, the lunch was perfect as usual. Thank you so much for your hospitality," began Josh as he stood. "We missed your cooking very much." He turned to Zeke and said, "I think we'd better get started on our supplies if we're going to get home by dark."

Ruth asked, "You're not staying overnight?"

"No ma'am. Not this time. We have a lot of work to do, and now that the weather has improved, we need to get started. Thank you so much for lunch."

Zeke felt they had plenty of time, but noted the serious look to Josh's eyes and agreed, "Yes, we've got a long list, and Ruth, could you help Jeremy select some clothes while we work on the other stuff?"

"Yes, dear, of course, just show me what you need," said Ruth as she stood to lead Jeremy back to the store.

"Make sure he gets several pairs of long johns. I'm tired of loaning him mine," said Zeke.

"And socks, too," added Josh, as he secretly handed Zeke a cashier's check he obtained from the bank. Zeke slipped out the door, and made his way to the land office to purchase the additional section of land.

Jeremy blushed as they all laughed. It took almost an hour to pull the supplies from the shelves. "You're getting a lot of ammo this time. You planning on going to war?" asked Ed.

"No, I don't want to fight in any more wars, but Zeke and I have been attacked by the Indians several times now, and we've seen what they do to the settlers on the wagon trains. We plan to keep our place safe and stay alive," replied Josh. "What's this? Are you stocking dynamite now?"

Ed turned from his ladder and saw Josh looking at the boxes on the bottom shelf marked danger. "Yep, we get requests for it from time to time. The miners use it. The stuff scares me to death. Do you know anything about dynamite?" asked Ed.

"I recall from a newspaper article it was invented by Alfred Nobel from Sweden. Apparently, it can blow up just about anything. We had to make homemade bombs during the war." He lied a bit, not wanting to tell Ed that he used it to blow up a train and a foundry during the war.

Ed came down the ladder and carefully pulled a box from the shelf and set it on the counter. Then he brought a second smaller box and set it beside it. "The instructions say you take a fuse from the box and carefully push it into one of the sticks. Then you light it and run like hell!" laughed Ed. "I have never seen one set off, but it'll kill you if you're not careful."

"We'll take a case and give it a try. Maybe I can blow up a few stumps so we can plant more hay for the horses," added Josh trying to give the impression he wanted it for non-violent reasons.

"Josh, don't forget that stack of newspapers in the corner," he said as he pointed towards the rear of the store. "I saved them for you."

Josh leaned down and picked up the stack. "Thanks, Ed. You know as a boy I never read the paper, but after riding on a train and having nothing else to do, I began reading the newspaper. It has become a habit I enjoy. It helps continue my education. You're very kind to save them for me."

Ed laughed. "You're welcome. There are worse habits to have."

Josh looked out the window, and immediately spotted the same gang of men he had seen on his way out of the bank in the fall. He frowned as a worry line wrinkled his forehead. He had hoped they had moved on. "Jeremy, how about guiding our horses around back, and we'll pack up there. The street out front looks a little crowded." He didn't want anyone to see all the supplies they were loading, as that might encourage someone to attempt to rob them on the trail as they left town.

Ed started to disagree, but when he looked into the street where Josh's eyes remained, he said nothing. He saw those men at least two or three times a month. They always got in fights with the locals, broke jaws and laws in the process, and destroyed the property of the town's citizens.

Zeke returned just as quietly as he had left, and helped carry another load of supplies to the packhorses.

It took another thirty minutes to pack everything carefully on the horses, and then they said their goodbyes to the Leary family. They left town cautiously along the back streets at a slow but steady pace, hoping to avert any attention. Once out of town, Zeke spoke up, "Why were you in such a hurry to get out of Denver?"

"When I came out of the bank, I saw the gang of former war soldiers sitting on the boardwalk across the street. I did not look directly at them, but I could feel their eyes on my face. I think they would kill us, and take our horses and supplies without hesitation. Let's go downstream about fifty yards before crossing," added Josh as he turned his horse south instead of north to their home.

"You're trying to throw off our trail to anyone following us, huh?" quizzed Zeke.

"Yep," Josh lightly squeezed his horse into a trot.

They walked their horses in the river for just under a mile before coming out on the opposite bank in pine thicket. He led them up and around a knoll in the forest. Once they reached the top, Josh stopped. "Zeke take your binoculars out, and see if you can spot anyone on the trail," suggested Josh.

Zeke retrieved the field glasses from his saddlebag, climbed off his horse while giving the reins to Josh, and walked to the edge of the hill to peer through the limbs of the trees filled with new foliage. It did not take long for him to spot them. "Two riders are pulled up where we normally cross the river. They're crossing over and checking the ground for our tracks."

Josh reached down, pulled out his Sharps buffalo rifle, and climbed off his horse. Jeremy grinned. "Can I try it?" he asked.

Josh started to say no, but agreed it would be good practice for him. "Ok, but I'm not trying to kill them. Just scare them off, okay?" In their winter rifle practice, Jeremy proved to be a deadly shot.

He handed the rifle to Jeremy along with a cartridge, and together, the three of them stood at the edge of the cliff still hidden by the trees. One of the men got off his horse, and bent down to the study the tracks in the mud near the river.

140

"He can see our tracks coming to Denver, but not our tracks leaving in that direction," said Zeke as he continued looking through his binoculars. "By now, our inbound tracks are mixed with many others."

The man stood back up, said something to his partner, and then lifted his canteen off the saddle horn. Jeremy took aim, while Zeke watched through the field glasses. "Hit the canteen, Jeremy," he said stoically.

Jeremy steadied himself pulling the gun tightly into his shoulder as he had practiced. "Easy boy, take your time. They're not moving, so no lead is required, and there's very little wind. Fire when you are ready," encouraged Josh.

The man pulled the cork stopper from the canteen and lifted it to take a swig. Boom! In a flash, the big shell went through the canteen ripping it from the man's hands. Josh handed him another cartridge. "Reload," he ordered.

"Great shot," added Zeke.

Jeremy grinned, as they waited to see what the men would do. The man went over, picked up the canteen, and showed his partner the big hole in it.

"Why aren't they leaving?" asked Jeremy.

"Most thieves and robbers are stubborn as hell," added Josh. "They also might be slightly drunk and stupid. Let's see you hit that canteen again. Your first shot might have just been lucky," he teased.

"Lucky? Naw, I can do it again. You just watch," bragged Jeremy.

Josh and Zeke winked at each other. Boom! The canteen flew from the attempted robber's hands a second time, and bounced off the neck of his horse. The man ran to his startled horse, started trying to get on, but the horse kept frantically circling trying to gallop away. The man cursed the horse. His partner crossed the river and took off at full gallop towards town without him. Once the other man got in the saddle, he, too, crossed the river and sped off to Denver.

The boys laughed. "All right, Jeremy! Great shooting, I believe you're a natural. Let's go home," urged Josh, as he reloaded the Sharps, pushed the big rifle into the sleeve, and swung into his saddle.

"Wow, that was fun!" exclaimed Jeremy, as he swung up on his horse.

"It'll be much harder when you have to do it under fire. Killing a man should never be easy. I did it in war too many times. Remember, you must not hesitate when the time comes. Hesitation could kill us all. Let's ride!" Josh kicked his horse, and they began the journey home.

They always liked the ride through the mountain passage into the Colorado Rockies leading to their land. The views were especially nice now that spring arrived. The sky was blue, the sun bright, and the days longer. When they reached the last ridge, Zeke pointed the boundaries of their land to Jeremy. He marveled at how much land they owned.

Josh stated, "We own a little more now. Zeke bought that land over there all the way up to the ridge today. He went to the land office while we were loading supplies. It was about five hundred acres."

Zeke smiled. "That'll help keep our little paradise even more private." Jeremy wondered where they got all the money, but knew it was none of his business. He just assumed they were rich, and he was lucky they were his friends.

With three riders and packhorses they made good time, but it was dark by the time they unpacked all the supplies from the horses and stowed them away. Ruth packed them a supper, so after feeding and watering the horses and taking care of the cow, they settled at the table to eat.

"What are you going to do with that dynamite?" asked Jeremy.

"I think we should test it tomorrow," replied Josh before stuffing his mouth with a biscuit. "Oh my, her biscuits are the best."

"Yeah, let's blow something up!" exclaimed Jeremy with a grin. "That'll be fun!"

Zeke laughed. "You better be careful with that stuff. I heard about it near the end of the war. What are you going to blow up?"

"I was thinking of blowing up some rocks to block the old trail into our land to the northeast of us. It would make it harder for anyone to stray in here from the plains, and may discourage any curious souls or settlers," replied Josh. Obviously, he had been giving the idea some thought while riding home from town.

"My butt is sore from riding. I guess we got soft over the winter. Let's head to the hot springs," stated Zeke as he pushed away his empty plate, stood up from the table, and started stripping.

Jeremy quickly forked his last bite of the ham into his mouth, and began taking his clothes off while chewing. Josh packed away the leftover food, and soon the three naked boys were jogging to the hot spring to bathe and soak.

"We have to tell him," whispered Josh as he remained in Zeke's arms after their lovemaking later that night.

Zeke sighed, "At least the weather is warm, and he has a choice now. He can stay or he can go. What do you think he'll do?"

"Well, our experience so far since falling in love at the academy is just about everyone we've met hates homosexuals. The odds are, he will leave us, but we moved here to be free. This is our land, our home, and we should be able to do what we want. We've given him the skills to make his own way in this world. That's the best we can do."

Zeke kissed Josh's neck. "I know you're right. I miss kissing you when I feel like it and pinching your butt. I'm surprised we haven't been caught. We'll tell him at breakfast, so he has plenty of daylight if he wants to leave, but I hope he doesn't."

"Okay, now let's get some sleep. My butt is sore."

Zeke smiled and whispered, "My penis is sore, too."

After eating breakfast, Josh told Jeremy, they wanted to talk to him. He served them all a second round of coffee, as the spring mornings were still a bit chilly.

"What did I do?" asked Jeremy, suddenly feeling guilty and about to be scolded by his parents.

Zeke grinned. "You did not do anything wrong…" he paused and added, "that we know of."

Jeremy smiled back, as he waited to hear what they had to say. Slowly, he returned to the table and sat down.

Josh took a sip of coffee allowing him just a few more seconds to get his thoughts in gear. "Jeremy, you're a great friend, and we both appreciate all you have done for us. We've tried to teach you all we can about living on your own and being your own man. That is why we live way out here. Back home, we would be following the rules of our parents and society. Here we live as we wish.

"Before we can ask you to risk your life for a boy you don't even know, we feel we must be completely open and honest with you."

"You lied to me?" asked Jeremy.

Zeke smiled slyly, "Not exactly—we just did not tell the whole truth."

"You're bank robbers aren't you? That explains all the money you have for supplies and land. You're going to use the dynamite to blow up a safe. How long have you been bank robbers?"

Josh and Zeke laughed heartily before Josh continued, "No, we're not bank robbers although I did blow up a train load of gold the Yankees were shipping during the war. I guess there is not an easy way to say this, so I'm going to give it to you straight. Zeke and I are homosexuals." He waited for Jeremy's reaction.

Jeremy's smile left his face, and you could see by the wrinkle on his forehead he was thinking very hard. "Okay, so what is that? Are you going to die? Is that a disease?"

Zeke looked at him earnestly, "No, though some people think it might be a disease. Most folks are attracted to the opposite sex like our parents, but God made us a little bit different, as we are attracted to each other."

Josh broke in, "We love each other and are committed to each other like a couple."

Jeremy replied somberly in a singular word, "Oh."

No one said anything for a long minute before Jeremy added, "Oh, you're queers. I saw queers in New York City." Then he paused again while thinking, "You don't expect me to be queer, too, do you?"

"No, of course not," replied Zeke. "We just want to let you choose whether you want to stay with us now that you know why we live way out here."

"You think I would leave because you're homosexuals?" asked Jeremy.

Josh replied, "Most folks would." "We are happy for you to stay, but it is your choice to stay or go."

Zeke added, "If you decide to stay, let me warn you, we are no longer going to hide our affection for each other. You won't see us having sex, but you might see us kiss."

"Now that would be funny," laughed Jeremy.

"Perhaps," smiled Josh, "but that is what people in love do even if they are two men."

"Boy, you two guys sure know how to start a day with a bang, don't you? Well, to tell you the truth, I clued in early on that you were different. Oh sure, I saw the way you looked at each other, and I felt the vibrations late at night. My friend Jimmy and I spied on two men having sex when I was little, so I knew what you were doing.

"Josh gave me a silver dollar and a job, and told me to make something of myself when I grow up. Well, I was never quite sure how I was going to do that, but I worked hard, so I could take better care of my family. Now that I've headed west, I really had no idea where I was going or what I was going to do.

"I like my life here. Unlike New York, the air is clean and smells fresh. Every day is an adventure and on some days even more so. I like hunting and shooting my guns and arrows. I like riding a horse. I almost like your cooking," teased Jeremy with a smile. "But most of all, I like being here with the both of you. I realize I might be in your way, and I try to go to bed early to give you some private time. I don't want to leave. I don't care if you're queers. I feel like you're the older brothers I never had, or maybe even the father I don't remember. I'm happy here, and if you want me to stay, I'll stay." Tears filled his eyes and his lips quivered a bit.

"We want you to stay, too," said Zeke as he swung an arm around Jeremy.

"Whew, I'm glad that is over," said Josh with a smile.

Zeke added, "Me, too."

"Okay, let's get it over with," stated Jeremy. "Go ahead and kiss. I want to see you."

Josh and Zeke gave him a puzzled look, and then slowly, they leaned in to each other and kissed once softly, and then deeper. After they stopped, they turned to see Jeremy's reaction.

He said nothing for almost fifteen seconds before suddenly laughing, "I can handle that just fine."

They all laughed before Josh added, "And rescuing Yuma?"

"I'm in. I'm sure he feels just like I do about you. In addition, you must feel the same towards him to risk your lives. He must be special. I'm going with you to help. I can't wait to meet a real Indian that ain't shooting arrows at my butt."

"Very good," said Zeke as he stuck out his hand for Jeremy to shake like a grownup.

"Let's get our chores done," spoke Josh as he, too, shook Jeremy's hand. "We have much to do today."

SIXTEEN

They had been on the trail for two weeks, heading north over the mountains enjoying the scenery and hunting for their supper. They brought along just one packhorse so they could travel rapidly if necessary. They had not seen a single Indian or another human being the entire time. They camped along a small stream filled with crystal clear water, meandering and tumbling over the rocks, allowing the boys to sleep easily. Since day one, they took turns standing watch at night, knowing they could be attacked at any time. They followed John's advice by sleeping apart with their backs against big rocks, and their pistols and rifles at their side. Earlier that day, they made a detour to see John and Liz, but they found their winter campground empty, and they had no idea where John and Liz would go for their summer camp. They hoped they were doing well, and would try again to find them in the fall.

After breakfast, Jeremy excused himself to head to the woods for a bowel movement. He was squatting when he heard a low moan off to his right. Quickly, he pulled up his pants, picked up his rifle, and cautiously crept in the direction of the sound. He could feel his heart pounding in his chest. He eyes scanned left and right, anticipating the sound of quick steps if he was about to be attacked by man or beast. He remembered to smell the air, but detected nothing but the fragrance of the wild spring flowers, especially the new blooming honeysuckle.

He went over a hill and stopped. He knew he should not go far without warning Josh and Zeke. He heard the moan again near the stream at the bottom of the hill. He turned back towards their camp where Josh and Zeke were packing away their gear. He whistled the sound of an owl to them.

Without hesitation, Josh immediately drew his pistol. Zeke snatched up his rifle, as they both looked towards the location of the whistle. Slowly, they turned in a full circle, but did not find any movement anywhere. Jeremy whistled again to assure them he was okay, and what direction he was. He then moved guardedly down the hill.

Josh nodded at Zeke. "Spread out so we make a more difficult target. Stay low," whispered Josh, as he secured his pistol in his holster while quickly pulling his Winchester from his saddle sleeve. Slowly, he cocked the rifle trying to make as little noise as possible.

Carefully, they moved towards Jeremy, trying to be ready for any sudden movement. Their nostrils picked up the direction of Jeremy's shit, but they moved on watching the ground for his tracks. They could see where he stopped at the top of the hill overlooking the stream. A vulture suddenly flushed in a nearby tree. Zeke spun quickly and nearly fired, but pulled up his rifle. Taking a breath, they once again continued to move down the hill.

When they reached the bottom, they carefully moved through the thick underbrush until they saw Jeremy on his knees.

Jeremy turned when he heard them and whispered, "Don't move."

Josh and Zeke realized Jeremy was kneeling beside a gray full-grown wolf. It puzzled them as to why the wolf was laying down instead of fiercely attacking Jeremy. Slowly, their eyes caught sight of a black steel trap tightly closed on the animal's rear leg.

"Careful," warned Josh. "He could take your hand off."

Jeremy heard him, but softly he talked to the poor animal that probably had lain in the trap for more than a day, weakened by the pain and blood loss. "Hold still boy. I'll get you out," he said softly as he gripped the trap in one hand and placed the tip of his long knife in between the steel jaws, and began to force it apart. Once open, he carefully pulled the wounded leg out, and then slowly let the jaws close. He set down his knife, snatched up the closed trap, and threw it away. He retrieved a rag from the leather sack he wore with a cord over his shoulder. He cleaned the wound, and then wrapped it with the rag while Josh and Zeke stood guard. Gently he tied it off, so it would stay on the wound for a few days. The poor wolf lay just twelve inches from water, but could not pull close enough to drink because of the trap. Jeremy scooped up water with both hands, and cautiously brought it to the wolf's parched tongue. The animal quickly drank the water. He brought the cool liquid to the long pink tongue a few more times, and the poor animal drank and licked every drop from Jeremy's hands.

Jeremy retrieved a strip of beef jerky from his pack along with a biscuit, and fed it to the wolf. He then got another handful of water, followed by yet another, and the starved wolf ate and drank all. Jeremy stroked his head, scratched his ears, and talked to him soothingly like talking to a family pet.

Slowly, the animal got to his feet and smelled the rag around his wound. He took a step to the stream and drank more before turning back to Jeremy. He nuzzled his face and licked him as if saying thanks. Jeremy stroked his head before gathering his stuff.

"We'd better go," urged Josh.

Jeremy did not reply, but nodded yes. He stood as the wolf walked with a limp off into the woods, turning briefly for a last look at Jeremy, as if to say thanks once more, and disappeared over the hill. Jeremy came up the hill to Josh and Zeke with a big grin on his face. "Pretty cool, huh?"

"You're lucky he didn't think you were the trapper and attack you," said Josh.

Zeke grinned. "Heck, he probably smelled the crap you left back there, and wanted no part of tasting you."

147

Josh added again, "Or he saw how skinny and ugly you are, and thought he might wait for a better meal!"

Jeremy laughed at them as they walked back to camp. The city boy beamed from the exciting encounter with a wild wolf. They were saddling up when Josh paid him a compliment. "You did the right thing in using the owl whistle twice. We knew it was you, and the second one told us which direction to find you. Still, we must be careful. The Indians will not fight fair."

"I know. I kept my guard up, but the wolf's moan told me something was wrong. I felt safe."

"All right then, time to get moving," added Josh as he swung up into his saddle. "Let's ride."

Later that day, they went along a ridge where they could easily see the valley and plains to the east. John had told Josh he thought the Kaga Ozuye warriors were most likely hiding in that section of the Colorado Rockies allowing them half day journeys to the plains to hunt for both bison and white settlers, before returning to the safety of their village hidden deep in the forest. His war training kicked in, and he began looking for rivers, streams and creeks because like soldiers during wartime he knew the village must be near fresh water. He knew all humans must have water to survive, so he surmised their village might be hidden from most folks, but not from the need for a good fresh supply of water.

Josh scouted the terrain with his eyes until he could pick out a good defensive campsite using the knowledge John taught him. After they set up their secret camp, including a place for a campfire carefully hidden from view in all directions by the boulders, they agreed to only have a fire at night so their smoke would rise undetected. It was less likely the smell of the smoke would be picked up, as rarely did the Indians hunt at night. John told the boys most Indians spend their day foraging for food via a hunt for meat or a scavenging for roots and berries. Their largest meal of the day was always just before sunset. He told them he suspected the Kaga Ozuye chief probably split up his camp, sending his best warriors to find, kill, and rob settlers and wagon trains. The rest of his men would hunt like the old days of their ancestors. John feared the warriors had become spoiled, sending out fewer hunters for game, and more warriors for blood and free supplies.

Zeke retrieved his binoculars and climbed the highest rock to scan the valley below. He found no movement anywhere other than a small herd of deer. They took turns standing guard, and looking for trouble for three days, but spotted no one. Josh announced he was going alone to scout farther north and would be back before dark. He planned to follow a stream north hoping to find unshod hoof tracks. He knew the Indians would do the same with their horses as they did, by not carrying water to the horse, but rather leading the horse to the water. He knew hoof prints were far harder to hide than moccasin prints. Zeke was reluctant for him to go alone, but in his heart, he knew Josh could take care of himself. He had grown used to being with Josh everyday throughout the winter season, but knew he would be careful, and he had to let him go.

Josh sat down, removed his boots, and put on the moccasins and leggings Liz had made for him. He knew his boots would not only make noise in the forest, but they created an easy trail for Indians to track, and they would know he was a white man. If tracked, the moccasins would make them feel other Indians were in the area and less likely to follow him. He took his Winchester instead of the Sharps, feeling his rapid firing rifle would be more important on a scouting trip. He did not intend to take on the Indians by himself, but sought to find them without being seen. He also slipped the leather bag holding his bow and arrows over his shoulder, and adjusted it to his back, slightly askew of a vertical line. This allowed him to walk or run easily, but still be able to retrieve it quickly when needed. He gave Jeremy a hug, then Zeke and added a quick kiss to his lips.

Jeremy smiled at him. "What? No kiss for me?"

The three of them laughed heartily as Josh playfully pulled Jeremy's hat down over his eyes and poked his ribs with his finger.

"I'll be back soon. Look after each other. Keep up the watch on the rocks as well as for any movement here on the mountain. I'll hawk whistle before approaching so don't shoot me," he warned with a grin. "Scout the area around our camp for any sign of life, as well as find some escape routes should we be forced to leave in a hurry."

The farther Josh walked, the more cautious he became. He made his way down the mountain to the valley and a stream. He watched the open areas for tracks, but seeing none, he began making his way upstream. He had only gone a few miles before suddenly hearing a horse neigh. He immediately stopped while surveying the terrain ahead. Carefully, he moved up the hill away from the stream, wanting the advantage of looking down on the enemy. He moved as silently as possible from tree to tree until he spotted a group of horses moving through the valley.

He counted fifteen horses and Indians. He studied them carefully, realizing they were not Kaga Ozuye warriors, as they did not have the stripes on their faces. He thought they might be Blackfeet, as John had described the fierce tribe who hated all white men. They seemed to be arguing amongst themselves while watering their horses. A lone Indian climbed down from his horse, and walked up the hill almost directly towards Josh. Afraid he might have been spotted, Josh lay still, allowing his body to be hidden by the brush, and yet he could see every step the man took. The Indian stopped just twenty yards from Josh, pulled down his pants, and squatted down. The poor man had diarrhea and grunted sadly. It took him at least a long five minutes before satisfied. He pulled up his pants and walked rapidly back down to his horse. Once he flung himself on his horse, the Indian party moved towards the north and out of sight.

He waited until they were out of earshot before continuing to scout the area, but by late afternoon, he was convinced they were the only Indians in the immediate area, and not the ones he was looking for. He began making his way back to the camp, taking a different route and memorizing landmarks like big boulders or fallen trees. He walked a few miles before realizing the campsite was just over the next crest of the mountain. His eyes suddenly caught sight of movement at the top of the hill overlooking their camp. Instantly, he knelt down and stopped. He saw the limb of a bush move, but he continued waiting. Finally, he saw the back of an Indian with a bow in his hand threaded with an arrow. He feared he might shoot Zeke or Jeremy. He did not want to use his rifle, so he laid it down, and quickly retrieved his bow and arrows from the bag over his shoulder.

Silently, he moved from tree to tree until just forty yards from the Indian. Abruptly, the Indian stood up from his hiding place and began taking aim at Jeremy. Josh quickly stepped to the right of the tree he had hidden behind, pulled back on the string, took quick sight, and fired. Zip! The warrior's left eye detected movement away from his target, and for a half second, he hesitated. Josh's arrow went through the man's back and out his chest. The critically wounded Indian dropped his bow wildly, and fell to the ground. Josh loaded his bow once more and waited.

Jeremy heard the Indian fall. He whistled to Zeke up on the big rock, and slowly cocked his rifle, while kneeling down behind an old fallen tree. He had just settled down when an arrow whizzed through the air landing in the trunk of the tree near his head. A second arrow struck the side of the tree near Josh's head, causing the feathers to just graze his neck. He turned to his right just in time to see the attacker retrieving another arrow from his quiver. Josh shot him with his bow, but just as soon as he did, a third Indian charged across their camp leaping over the tree with a long handle hatchet drawn back to strike Jeremy.

Jeremy had but a split second to fire his rifle but just missed the Indian's head. He lifted his rifle and fended off the swing of the tomahawk, as it struck his rifle knocking both he and the Indian down the hill on the backside of the tree. Josh snatched up his rifle and began running towards the campsite. Zeke quickly climbed off the big rock with rifle in hand.

Jeremy flung the man over him, and then rapidly turned and got to his feet, just as he had done in wrestling Josh and Zeke at home during the winter. The Indian said something to him as he came to his feet, but immediately charged Jeremy once again. Jeremy took a step backward, but his boot caught an exposed root causing him to lose his balance, and he fell back. Seeing opportunity, the Indian leaped through the air while swinging the brutal looking tomahawk with all his might.

Josh saw him and dropped his bow while drawing his pistol to fire. Before he could snap off the shot, Zeke fired his Winchester, hitting the man in the face just below his left eye knocking his aim with the tomahawk off to the right of Jeremy. The Indian fell limp on top of Jeremy.

Josh ran up, as did Zeke. "Get him off me!" exclaimed a terrified Jeremy, as he squirmed to get out from under the dead weight of the Indian.

Josh grabbed the Indian by the back of his rawhide shirt and pulled him off. Jeremy quickly got to his feet wiping blotches of the Indian's blood from his cheek.

"Are you okay?" asked Josh seeing the blood.

"Yes, this is his blood," replied Jeremy.

"Good shot," said Josh to Zeke. "Keep an eye out. We must pack and leave this place immediately."

"You think there are more than these three about?" asked Zeke.

"If there was a fourth, he would have already attacked, but their fellow braves will come looking for them, and we need to be gone from here. They might have heard the gunshots. I spotted fifteen Blackfeet warriors earlier today. Hurry," ordered Josh. He knew they would have to find a better campsite far away from this one.

Jeremy kept the man's brass hatchet head tomahawk, while Josh trotted back and retrieved his arrows from the other two dead Indians, and took their bows and arrows. Once packed up, they went back to the Indians, and cut away their clothes, leaving them naked where they fell. Josh took his knife and stuck it in the bullet wound of the dead Indian's face. He then twisted it around and around, leaving a much larger hole than the small bullet entry. He had no time to dig into the man's skull for the lead. He took a nearby stick and jammed it into the eye socket, and left it there. He hoped to disguise the fact that white men killed their friends. Zeke retrieved his brass spent shell casing. They used their knives, and carved a big inverted V across their chest. It would be a mark they hoped the Indians would fear along with the humiliation of their foe stripping the bodies in total defeat. It wasn't the same as taking a scalp, but they hoped it would throw a bit of fear and mystery into the Indians.

Zeke and Jeremy felt a bit squeamish about the ritual, but Josh assured them they needed every possible advantage to defeat these brutal warriors. They knew he was right about that fact as they swung up into their saddles. Josh led them down the mountain. He assumed the warriors were excellent trackers so in an attempt to lose the Indians, they led their horses in the stream for a mile before coming out on stretch of flat river rocks.

They camped without fire for two nights until they found an area of big boulders that appeared to have been dropped from the sky like a bag of marbles. While Zeke and Jeremy stood watch, Josh carefully searched the area along the mountain until he found a big cave at the beginning of a steep cliff. He knew they could defend themselves well behind these rocks, but would have no means of escape, but it would do for now, he thought.

They set up camp inside the mouth of the cave. They hid part of their supplies there, hoping to make this a base camp they could use while searching for Yuma. After two days of eating cold food, the pot of rabbit stew over the fire tasted wonderful. Each boy scraped up every morsel, and together, they laughed as Jeremy licked his plate clean.

Josh said, "I think we should ride east tomorrow morning to the ridge, and scout the beginning of the plains, looking for the warriors with the stripes on their faces. I think it will take too long to try to find their camp in the huge hills and lush valleys of these mountains. If we can spot them in the open terrain of the plains, we can follow their trail to the village."

He paused before adding somberly, "I think we will have to kill almost every one of them to secure Yuma. I hope you can live with that, because I can. These men are killers of white men and Indians alike. They not only deserve to die, we'll have no choice, but to kill them all, or they will surely hunt us down. I doubt they will take losing to a white man very well. They'll want revenge and will not stop until they get it. We have to kill them all."

He paused again to let his harsh words sink in before continuing, "Once we can find their camp, then we can plan a way to take Yuma away from them. We'll only have one chance and must plan carefully. If we fail and get away, they'll kill him for sure. If we're captured, they'll kill us. When you're a scout behind enemy lines, you cannot hesitate to kill. You must strike with quick speed, always assuming there is always one more we must kill. So strike, duck down, and reload," added Josh. "Always be ready to kill and kill again. Don't shoot to wound. Shoot to kill, and hopefully with one shot, because you may not get a second chance to put the attacker down. We practiced with all our weapons for head and heart shots. I call those kill shots. We must do so every time to survive, and our survival depends on the speed of our kills.

"You kill the first man, and instantly take aim for a second. Don't watch the result of your kill. Never pause, think, debate, rest, or wonder. You must assume there will always be another warrior ready to kill you. Hesitation from one of us could easily cause the death of us all."

Jeremy noted the coldness with which Josh spoke. It scared him some, but Josh had told them by the fire in the cabin how he and his men were trained to act fast and with great fury. Jeremy asked, "How many of them do you think we'll find?"

"I think at least a hundred or so. I think all the tribes are fed up with our government negotiations, treaties and threats, and laurels of lies. Sometimes I feel ashamed to be a white man. I think it will become far worse before it gets better. Our goal is to save Yuma, get back to our land, and defend it. We're not the army, and we're not some arrogant general like Custer. I've been reading about him in the stack of newspapers Ed gave me. Let's face it—the Indians have been treated badly. I am hoping a full- time war doesn't break out, as the Indians will lose against our weapons and knowledge of war. There has to be a better way. But the Indians we seek are a lot like those Confederate renegade soldiers, riding with no honor or purpose, but instead with a constant thirst for blood."

Jeremy sighed, "A hundred."

Josh smiled. "Don't worry we'll kill them one at a time—I hope."

Zeke sighed, "So we ride out at first light in the morning?"

"Yes, and we must cover our tracks to and from this place, or they will track us down. They are probably better at tracking that we are, as they have been doing it all their lives, and they learned from their ancestors. We must have a place where we can safely rest and regroup, and if necessary recover." Josh knew they were likely to be injured in their quest for Yuma's escape, but he didn't elaborate any further.

They continued their practice of taking turns standing watch. They wished they could burn the fire all night to keep the mountain chill off, as well as provide some hot coffee to make the start of the next day a little easier. They knew the Indians could mostly likely smell the smoke, even if they didn't see it. They followed the stream down the mountain until they drew close to the plains. They climbed a small hill to set up an outpost. They never stepped out into the open, fearing Indian hunters might see them. Zeke climbed to the highest point with his binoculars, and began scanning the ground below. He sat there most of the morning before seeing a dust cloud in the east.

"I think there is a wagon train coming," he called down.

Josh and Jeremy quickly joined him, and took turns looking through the field glasses. Just as Josh was about to pull the glasses from his face, he noted movement to the north. "We've got company," he said as he handed the binoculars to Zeke. "Off to the north. Do you see them?" he asked as he pointed.

"Yes, one, two, three…sixteen Indians, and Josh, they have the stripes on their faces," he added. "How do we warn the wagon train?"

"The Sharps," replied Josh as he rushed down the hill to his horse, retrieved his rifle, and returned. "Do you see anything I can shoot that will warn them?"

Zeke carefully looked through the lens at the train as it came into view. "How about shooting a big black cast iron frying pan hanging on a cord on the second wagon?"

Josh laughed. "You must think I'm a miracle shooter."

Jeremy laughed. "I can do it. Let me try."

Josh gave him one of his my-turn looks, and began scanning the train, but could not find another good target. He thought of shooting a dog or a horse, and if he had to he would, but reluctantly he sighted in on the frying pan. Boom! He fired and waited for the long second it would take the bullet to reach the pan. Ping!

The whole wagon shook as they heard the ping. The wagon behind them saw the frying pan leap in the air though tethered to the wagon. They had no idea what had happen.

"They are still rolling," stated Zeke. He turned to check on the Indians. "The Indians are looking towards us."

"They may not know where the shot came from, but if I shoot again they will spot us," said Josh.

"Yeah, but if you don't, the settlers could all die," countered Zeke.

"You're right," replied Josh in a whisper as he took aim again. This time, he spotted a shotgun barrel propped next to a driver with the butt stock sticking up to make it easy for the driver to pull it up and fire. Boom! The shell hit the wood stock splintering it as it flipped the shotgun up and out of the wagon. The man screamed, and the wagon master immediately swung his hat around in the air indicating the wagons must circle. The group split into two lines, and in just a few minutes, they were circled and climbing out of the wagons.

Zeke stared through the glasses, "They're circling!"

"How about the Indians?" asked Josh expecting bad news?

Zeke moved the glasses to where he had found them before, but there was no one there. "They're gone. No, wait a minute," he stated as he began panning left to his right. "Damn! They are heading at full gallop straight for the wagon train!"

"Come on, let's ride!" ordered Josh, as they all climbed down the hill. "We're going to find a stand of trees behind the Indians, and we'll pick them off. We do not want an open range fight. We're scouts, so keep your heads down."

They rode quickly down the hill and galloped across the open terrain of the plains. Josh kept his eyes scanning ahead of them searching for the right spot. His ears could hear the gunfire from the settlers, and the whoops and yells from warriors. They topped the hill and saw the Indians rapidly circling the wagons, firing their arrows while dodging the bad shooting from the settlers. Only the wagon master and his scout were successful at killing a few of the Indians.

"Over there!" exclaimed Josh as he pointed to a stand of trees on a slight hill over the battle area.

Quickly, they rode to the backside of the stand of trees, carefully walked their horses inside, and tied them off. Josh pulled both his Winchester and his Sharps rifle, and ran to the front of the trees. Zeke and Jeremy pulled their Winchesters, and Jeremy snatched up his Parker shotgun. Together, they laid down a few feet back from the edge of the plains in a stand of bushes, completely hidden from the Indians and the settlers.

"They're riding pretty fast, so lead your shot just a little, and they'll ride into your bullet. Aim for their chest or back if they are riding away. Make sure your shots are left and right of the wagon train, so we don't accidentally shoot the settlers. Okay, fire!"

Josh put a cartridge in his Sharps and laid it on the ground beside him, then picked up his Winchester, chambered a bullet with the cock of the handle, and fired, hitting an Indian in the chest blowing him backwards in a somersault off his horse, and directly into the legs of the horse behind him. This caused the frighten horse to rear up spilling his passenger. Just as the second Indian got to his feet, Zeke nailed him dead center of his chest.

Twice Jeremy felt he had a shot, but failed to fire. He had never killed a man. His heart was pounding so hard he could feel his pulse in his temples near his ears. Josh fired again taking out another. Zeke fired and missed, but fired again hitting his man on the second attempt. Josh realized Jeremy was not firing.

He spoke quickly to him, "Jeremy, they are the enemy. They are going to kill women and children if we don't stop them. They want to kill us! Don't think so much. Aim and fire like you were trained to do!" he ordered by lowering his voice.

Jeremy nodded, sighted his gun, and pulled the trigger. He hit the man in the shoulder, knocking him from his horse. Jeremy ratcheted his rifle and fired again, hitting the man in the chest.

"Good shot!" exclaimed Josh as he took aim and fired.

The wagon master knew he had only about twenty boys and men in the group. Several had been killed on the initial attack. He was taking aim at an Indian that suddenly took a shot and fell off the back of his horse. From the angle, he knew it was not one of his settlers. He looked to the trees and saw the flash of a rifle shot and then another. He knew then he had help, and wondered if the cavalry had arrived. An arrow suddenly screamed by his ear, and he quickly turned and fired at an Indian rapidly galloping straight for him. He missed the Indian as the man dismounted, and ran as fast as he could towards the captain. He leaped over the terrified horses, and tackled the wagon master before he could cock his rifle, knocking him to the ground.

The Indian dropped his bow, retrieved his knife, and charged the wagon master who brought his rifle up, aimed it at him, and pulled the trigger, but nothing happened. He had no time to cock his gun, so he used it to slightly fend off a thrust by the Indian with the knife. The warrior's blade dug in the meat of his upper right arm causing him to drop the rifle. He struggled to pull his pistol from the holster, but the Indian wasted no time, and charged him again. The wagon master would not be able to pull his pistol fast enough.

Boom! He saw the Indian lifted off his feet with a shot to his face, spinning the warrior in the air, and rolling him backwards like a limp doll. He crashed face down into the trail dust. The wagon master sighed with relief, and glanced back at the trees, knowing someone there had just saved his life. He picked up his rifle and began feeding it bullets so he could return fire.

"Great shot!" exclaimed Zeke as Josh lowered the Sharps rifle and loaded another cartridge.

"Thanks, I was lucky. We're reducing their numbers. Keep firing," yelled Josh.

Jeremy took aim on his fourth kill. All the months of practice were paying off as he finally relaxed, sighted the man in, exhaled, held the gun perfectly still, and squeezed the trigger as Josh had taught him. Bing! He hit the man right in the heart, spilling him off his terrified pony.

With just three warriors left, the leader pulled up while catching sight of a shot from the trees. Quickly, he turned away from the wagons, and steered his horse at full gallop straight towards the boys. Josh and Zeke had not seen him turn, as they sighted in on the other two men riding off to the right. With thirty yards to go, Jeremy turned and pulled the trigger, but his Winchester was empty. At first, he thought something was wrong with the gun, but when he ratcheted the handle and saw the chamber empty, he quickly dropped the gun and snatched up the Parker.

The Indian saw the boy and pulled back his arm with a spear ready to thrust it at just fifteen yards away. Jeremy never hesitated, and fired both barrels of the shotgun simultaneously. Josh and Zeke jumped at the sudden boom, and saw the shots take the Indian's head completely off, but they all dove out of the way as his mount ran straight through the bushes, and galloped out the other side without his rider.

"Dang, you saved us!" exclaimed Zeke.

"Way to go, Jeremy!" laughed Josh.

Zeke and Josh quickly returned to their targets, and fired killing the last of the Indians.

Suddenly, all fell silent. Josh and Zeke had taken out the remaining two Indians, while Jeremy had blown away the leader. The wagon master slowly stood up, as did his scout. The boys saddled up. Josh called out to them, "Don't shoot! We're white men. We're coming out!"

The wagon master told the group to hold their fire, as they watched just two men and a boy ride out from their hiding place. "Well, I'll be," said the leader. "I thought it was the cavalry."

They pulled up their horses just outside the circle. "Are you folks all right?" asked Josh.

"Yes, thanks to you. Thank you for saving us."

"No problem, but you better tend to your wounded, load your dead in a wagon and bury them tonight, and immediately head south to Fort Morgan. I doubt you'll be attacked today, so the more distance you put between this site and the fort the better. The Indians will want revenge for the killing of their warriors."

"Did you fire a warning shot at us?" asked the scout.

"Yes, I hit the frying pan on your second wagon with my Sharps buffalo gun from that hill over there, but you didn't take my hint. My second shot hit the stock of a shotgun in the same wagon."

The scout whistled as he turned from their position to the rise where Josh had fired, "That's some shot. That's about five hundred yards."

"Yep, it is quite a gun. It's pretty accurate up to about six hundred yards or so. We could see them waiting to ambush over there. It was the only way we could get your attention."

"Well, thank you sir," said the scout as he reached up to shake Josh's hand.

"Yes, thank all of you," said the captain.

"You're welcome, but time to get going. We'll take care of the Indian dead."

"Thanks again, and we will," replied the wagon master. He turned and began yelling orders to all the wagons. He assumed the three boys were going to bury the dead warriors, but he was wrong.

Josh dismounted and allowed their horses to eat some green grass from the plains. They had not seen fresh grass since last fall. The animals ate quickly. As the boys watched the line of wagons begin rolling up a hill, they took the chance to eat a hard biscuit, along with a piece of beef jerky, and drank from their canteens. They reloaded all their weapons, and stowed them away as they watched the last wagon disappear over the rise.

"Same as before?" asked Zeke knowing the answer.

"Yep, we must shake their confidence. We want them to fear the unknown. No one knows who we are, or how many men in our troop," said Josh.

"Troop?" laughed Jeremy. "We're hardly enough for a gang!"

Nevertheless, his laughter stopped as they set about the gruesome duty of cutting away the warrior's clothes, and making a V on the chest of each Indian with their knives. Josh studied the tracks of the ponies, but there was nothing unique about them. Jeremy dragged the Indian he had killed with the Parker down the hill and alongside his fellow warriors, hoping to divert the Indians that found the bodies away from their tracks. Josh grabbed the leader's severed head, dug a hole to bury it, and then carefully raked the ground to hide the location. He hoped the loss of the leader's head would shake the nerves of these warriors. He guessed there were about a hundred men in his village, and if so, they were down to about eighty-four. Not a bad day, he thought.

They gathered the extra bows and arrows, as well as tomahawks and knives, tied them to the back of their saddles, and then left quickly. They did not want to be spotted by anyone. Their first attempt had been successful, but they learned another important lesson—they must count their shots. Josh had forgotten to tell Zeke and Jeremy how they always counted their shots on his scout patrols during the war. Jeremy was skeptical he could count his shots while trying to sight in another kill, but they all agreed to try. He said they must know at all times, exactly how many bullets were left in their rifles and pistols. A mistake could kill one or all of them. They searched the ground where they had fired their guns, and picked up every shell casing. They saddled up, and rode out the back of the stand of trees away from the battlefield. They took a long winding path to the cave, and arrived just before dark.

Josh felt great relief that the packhorse they left behind that morning apparently remained quiet and did not give away their hiding place. They found no sign of any visitors. Josh was also grateful they survived two skirmishes successfully by killing three Indians of an unknown tribe, and sixteen of the Kaga Ozuye. He sighed with great relief for their luck.

SEVENTEEN

Yuma sensed something big had happened, as he heard the men arguing outside his tipi with his master, Mila Hanska. A group of his men had not returned from their attack on the approaching settlers. Earlier that day, Mila Hanska sent out a search party to find them. The men found some of the horses belonging to the group that had attacked the wagon train. The horses were grazing on green grass a half mile from the battle scene. The warriors tracked the horses until they saw their men lying dead on the ground. Vultures were eating the eyes of their men, and licking the blood from their wounds. They rode in quickly while whooping and yelling loudly, scattering the birds into the air.

Uneasily, they rode up to each body and stared in amazement that each man had been shot with a bullet and killed. They were shocked to see their bodies mutilated, and they had no idea what the inverted V symbol meant. They knew of no white men that would strip the braves naked, leaving their genitals exposed to the birds of prey. Overnight, the wolves ate away most of the meat from two of the bodies. When they found the leader with the missing head, it took them a full minute to realize who it was. They wondered what kind of gun could take a man's head off.

They scouted the area, but could not find his head. They assumed the victors put the head on stick outside their lodge. They also saw only the tracks of the ponies or the wagon horses. They left the horrific site, feeling afraid to be among the dead. They rode quickly, leading the Indian ponies back to their camp.

Hidden in the trees atop the ridge Zeke watched the group carefully. He pulled down his binoculars. "You were right. They did send a group out to see what happened to their men. They're riding northwest," he said. "Are you sure we shouldn't attack this group?"

"Yes, it would be much harder than it was to take out a squad with the deception and distraction of the trees and wagon train. I think we should try to follow the group from the ridge and see where they are going. If we have upset them, and it appears we have, they are most likely to head directly back to their camp to report. Saddle up, but remember the farther we ride north the more likely we are going to run into Indians. We'll take some of their arrows with us to confuse them. If we can fire without being seen, we'll use their arrows. Let them think the enemy is among them."

Jeremy handed Zeke and Josh about six arrows each, and then they saddled up and headed out. As usual, they went in an opposite direction covering their tracks before turning north. They reached the next ridge in time to see the group leave the plains and turn towards the mountains. After his previous scouting trip, Josh tried to guess where they were going, and rode silently to the top of another mountain. They lost sight of the group for almost an hour before spotting them again. They climbed off their horses to stretch their legs for a bit while they studied the Indians. Josh knew the Indians must be frightened, because they failed to scout the trail ahead, or look up to the ridges for sightings of an enemy. The warriors drove the ponies as quickly as possible back to the village, leaving a huge visible trail.

Just as they started to saddle up, Zeke spotted movement on the backside of the mountain they were on. Quickly, they tried to hide themselves amongst the brush, hoping they were not discovered. They spotted two Indians, and immediately realized their faces were void of the stripes of the other tribe. The second group walked their horses through the forest as if hunting elk or deer. Silently, they crept along, watching the ground for tracks.

The boys had no choice but to remain where they were, though they knew the Kaga Ozuye warriors were riding out of sight to the north. They stayed put for several hours, watching the hunters disappear over the opposite ridge, before the boys finally turned towards their cave. They rode in silence, carefully watching for any signs of movement, but by the end of the day, they reached the cave safely. After securing their animals, Jeremy decided he wanted a better supper so he took his bow and arrows and went out to hunt. Zeke built up the fire in the cave and fed the animals. Josh took watch for both Indians and Jeremy's safety.

Jeremy spotted a rabbit down the hill near the river. Silently, he crept closer and closer, until finally, he could fire his bow with certain accuracy. The rabbit hopped just as he let go, and he missed, but the arrow whizzed by the prey and flew down the mountain without making a sound. He loaded a second arrow and took aim. He anticipated movement and quickly fired. It was an excellent kill. He returned to their camp, and the boys grinned at him. Tonight, they would have roasted rabbit instead of more dried jerky. It was the end of another good day. They let the fire die out during the night, so by dawn there would be no chance of anyone seeing or smelling smoke. They planned to return to the trail to track the warriors at dawn.

However, during the night, a thunderstorm moved in with loud electrical cracks and booms that shook them awake before the clouds opened up with a drenching powerful rain. The water in the stream rose quickly until it came over the banks and onto the trail. The tracks from the ponies were easily washed away.

Disappointed they wouldn't have an easy trail to follow they began once again searching farther north for tracks. Josh hoped their actions after the last attack on the wagon train would bring the Kaga Ozuye warriors out in a mass to retaliate, but as the days went by, they could not find a trace of the warriors. In fact, it had been ten days since they last saw any Indians at all, and the first sighting was not the tribe they hunted. Josh led the group in hikes in every direction to scout the terrain around them. They hiked up to ten miles away before getting back to the cave before dark. They checked the tracks at every watering hole and stream, but found nothing. Josh knew their empty searches would weaken their alertness, and he feared the day when a sudden attack would arise because they were losing their rapid response to almost invisible signs.

Sometimes, they separated almost out of sight, communicating only by hand signals and occasional animal calls. Josh heard Zeke make the sound of an owl, and at first thought, he was just playing, but holding very still and silent, he noted a slight nervous temper to the call. Quickly, he scanned the terrain, but discovered nothing. Still on alert, he walked silently in his moccasins to the top of the ridge where he found Zeke. Jeremy arrived a few seconds later.

"Over there," whispered Zeke, "down in the valley. Do you see the smoke?"

Josh took the field glasses from Zeke, and sighted carefully down into the valley. He thought perhaps Zeke spotted the signal fires from the Indians, but this smoke was coming from something much larger, and burning rapidly, as he saw live embers floating upwards in the heat.

"What do you think?" asked Josh.

"I think it is a settler farm," replied Zeke.

"This far north—maybe a wagon on fire," stated Josh. "We've had no luck here for days, let's check it out. If we're lucky it will be the warriors we're after."

Zeke and Jeremy agreed, as they were bored with the lack of activity on the mountain. They rushed back to the cave, saddled their horses, rode quickly down to the river, and followed it towards the valley and the fire. They rode over the rough terrain, stayed off the natural trails, but never let up on their speed.

Finally, Josh put his hand up for the squad to halt much like his army days. They could hear occasional gunshots as well as smell the smoke of the fire. They walked their horses through the forest in silence, slowing down when they heard voices. They tied off the horses, pulled their rifles, and walked quietly but closer until finally they could see.

In a clearing, they saw the remains of two burning wagons, counted four dead settlers all men, and spotted three women, and four children including a girl and three boys. The children were very young between four and seven. They clung tightly to their mother's dress as they all remained under the last wagon with rifles aiming outward.

Across from the settlers were the riders Josh spotted in town. They were all former Confederate soldiers, and he knew they were cold-blooded killers. They would in time kill the children, rape the girl, and most certainly rape the women before slitting their throats. They cared for no one. Their taunts at the women were filthy as they laughed at the victims, and passed bottles of liquor around. Several of the men were going through the settler's possessions, tossed out of the wagons before setting them on fire, and loading anything they thought valuable.

"What should we do?" whispered Zeke.

"We can't let them do this," added Jeremy.

Josh hesitated, as he knew the odds were against them. They had close to thirty men, and his group numbered three. Quickly, he made a plan, and knelt down close to the ground to talk.

"We'll go back to our horses and get our Indian weapons. Zeke, you start way over there, and Jeremy you go about half as far as Zeke to the right. I'll go to the left. When I give the hawk call, pick a target, and nail him with one arrow. Now listen carefully, do not wait to see your arrow hit the target. Immediately move to your left about six paces and fire again. Keep moving immediately after you shoot. We must give the appearance this section of woods is full of Indians. We must make them panic. Do not use your guns unless you have, too. Got it?" he asked while waiting for Zeke and Jeremy to nod yes.

Just as Zeke reached the farther point, they each threaded their bows with the arrows they had collected from the Kaga Ozuye killed at the wagon train. Josh gave the call. Instantly the air began filling with arrows. Zip! Zip! Zip! Then a slight pause and zip, zip, zip! In fifteen seconds, they had killed six of the men.

The soldiers were so drunk it took the second barrage of arrows before they reacted. They fell to the ground and searched the forest for targets. A few fired wildly, but the boys remained hidden behind the trees, and fired again before moving to the left. Three more men fell.

All of sudden the lazy drunken ex-soldiers panicked, and ran for their horses. Their leader, a man wearing a captain uniform, screamed at them to stay put, but it was of no use. Nothing would bring them back. Reluctantly, he began running to his horse. When he realized he was their leader, Josh fired but missed him. Josh quickly reloaded as the man swung onto his horse and fired. Zip! He caught the renegade hard in the left rump with his arrow. The man screamed and cursed at the pain. His horse suddenly went wild, and it was all the captain could do to hang on, as the terrified horse took off in a full gallop bringing about immense pain to the wounded captain as his bleeding butt bounced off the well worn saddle.

Jeremy and Zeke ran up to Josh. "We did it!" exclaimed Zeke.

"Yes, but they are sly enough to come back. We must be prepared and alert," reminded Josh as he led them out of the woods to the wagon.

"We mean you no harm," began Zeke in a soothing voice.

Slowly the ladies came out from under the wagon. "They thought you were Indians," said one of the ladies.

"We wanted them to think there was a band of Indians firing at them. There are only three of us so we had to fool them, but we must get you moving quickly, as they may come back," stated Josh.

Jeremy knelt down and let the children come up to him. "How are they going to get to Fort Collins?"

Josh frowned. He realized they had no choice but to escort them. "Load up the last wagon quickly. We must leave now. Zeke you drive. Jeremy and I will scout. Everyone must climb aboard quickly," he ordered.

As the tears slid down her cheeks the woman asked, "What about my dead husband?"

"I'm sorry, ma'am," began Josh, "there is no time if we are going save you, your family and your friends. We must go now. There are real Indians nearby, and we don't know where these rough riders are. We must move quickly, and put some distance from them. The Indians could have heard their shots or seen the smoke just as we did. Let's go!" he yelled.

He lifted the children in the wagon as well as the ladies, and checked the reins on the horses. Zeke climbed up aboard, stowing his rifle beside him, and pulled his hat down a little tighter to block the sun from his eyes. Jeremy brought up their horses so he tied Zeke's horse to the back of the wagon. They retrieved all the usable arrows from the dead men, and prepared their guns. Jeremy and Josh dug in their heels springing their horses forward as Zeke slapped the wagon horses with the reins. The nervous horses responded by immediately following Josh and Jeremy down the road. Zeke heard the woman behind him sobbing as she stared out the back of the wagon until her husband's body was out of sight.

They rode until dark, stopping briefly at a stream to allow the horses to drink water, and their passengers to pee. Soon Josh ordered them forward, and they kept moving until the moon went behind a large cloud, and he could no longer see the trail. He stopped and allowed all to rest for a few hours until he could see again.

Not long after dawn, he noted the thumping sound of numerous hoofs rapidly riding towards them. With his recent experience with Indians and their ponies, he thought he could tell the difference in sound between a white man's shoed horse and the shoeless Indian ponies, but to be safe he and Jeremy pulled off the road and drew their rifles. Zeke pulled up the wagon and cocked his rifle. He told the women and children to stay down, and remain quiet. Nervously, they all waited to see what fate awaited them.

Jeremy rose slightly on his horse and then turned to Josh, "I see a small flag—no it is a banner."

Josh grinned. "It's the cavalry!"

They lowered their rifles and made their way back on the road. A few seconds later, a cavalry squad of ten riders pulled to a halt in front of them.

"We spotted the fire, but taking the trail around the mountain just took too long. How many Indians attacked you?" asked the lieutenant in charge. He was a descendant from Sweden with fair skin, blond hair, and rich blue eyes. He looked a bit out of place in the frontier.

"None," replied Josh. "They were rough riders."

"They're just dang Confederate bastards! They are just no good white trash!" he exclaimed.

Josh winced while Zeke and Jeremy smiled at each other. Josh said, "I've seen them twice in Denver. You boys need to catch them. They shot their men folk, burned two wagons and were ready to…" he paused to make sure he was out of earshot of the ladies, "to rape, maim and kill these poor women and children. Can you escort them to safety?"

"Yeah, sure—which way did they go?"

"Southwest," replied Josh.

"How in the hell did the three of you scare off their group which I hear numbers near thirty?" asked a skeptical lieutenant.

"We made them believe we were Indians with a much larger force. They never actually saw us. We killed six of their men with our bows and arrows."

"Bows and arrows? Why not your guns?"

"They are afraid of Indians and don't want to lose their scalps. They would not have been afraid of three white men with rifles. We're going to head home, and thank you for helping these folks." Josh felt an urgent need to end the discussion and exit their audience.

"Home?" he asked. "You live out here?"

Josh sighed knowing he had already said one word too many. "We live in the high mountains off to the north. I bid you a safe trip," replied Josh with a tip of his hat. Too many questions murmured Josh as he rode back to the wagon. He spoke briefly to the ladies to assure them the cavalry would take good care of them. Zeke grabbed his rifle and climbed down from the wagon. The boys nodded their hats at the settlers, and galloped away.

"I don't think I liked that lieutenant," stated Jeremy once out of sight.

Zeke grinned. "I thought he was cute. Did you see those blue eyes?"

Josh and Jeremy both gave him a funny look before they all laughed and decided to cut cross-country to the ridge to begin the journey back to their cave. By late afternoon, they pulled up to a halt as they saw a flock of birds suddenly fly up ahead. They stood still listening, while trying desperately to hear what sound or movement might have disturbed the birds. They walked their horses slowly along the ridge. As they topped the hill, Josh's horse neighed loudly. Josh drew his pistol and cocked it. He breathed in with his nostrils and caught scent of the Indians.

"Blackfeet," he whispered. They all immediately dismounted.

Zip! The first arrow scratched Josh's shoulder before bouncing off the rock behind him. The Indians did not wait to fire another shot. They burst from hiding spots under the brush to the left and right of them. Zeke and Josh turned to their left and fired, shooting a man as he swung a tomahawk at them. Jeremy did not get his pistol out in time. The Indian after him swung hard, but wild as Jeremy stepped back. The Indian drew back again, but Jeremy managed to get his pistol out of the holster. The brave saw it, hesitated, and then screamed loudly attempting to terrify his prey. The warrior took a quick breath and charged. Jeremy fired shooting the man in his left eye, spinning him around like a top, with blood and brains ejecting from the damaged socket. He fell hard down the mountain.

Another Indian attacked before Josh could turn back to his right. Thankfully, his horse was in the way, but the Indian tried to swing over the horse, but Josh ducked down. The Indian swung to the left and missed again. Finally, Josh faked coming up to the right. As the man stepped that way, Josh ducked down quickly and shot the man in the groin. The warrior dropped the tomahawk instantly, and grabbed his bleeding crotch while letting out a loud painful scream. Josh knelt down and shot upward hitting the man in the face, sending him spiraling down the mountainside.

Zeke had spun to check on Jeremy just as the boy fired. He turned back to see an Indian warrior flying through the air at him after leaping out of the tree. He knocked Zeke to the ground. Josh came around the front of his horse, and saw the Indian with the bow. He fired at him and missed. The Indian quickly let go his arrow and missed. Josh left his horse and charged forward. The Indian dropped his bow, retrieved his hatchet from his belt, let out a scream, and charged at him. Josh did not bat an eye, but simply and smoothly brought up his pistol quickly, and shot him twice in the heart.

Josh dropped to his knee expecting another attack but saw no movement. He spun around and spotted Jeremy coming up the trail seemingly okay, but he could not see Zeke. He started running down the hill and saw the Indian on top of Zeke trying to push his knife into his chest. Desperately, Zeke

165

pushed back. Sweat was pouring of his face, but the knife slowly moved closer and closer to his skin.

Josh was afraid to shoot the Indian since he was so close to Zeke. He holstered his pistol, quickly grabbed the feet of the Indian, and pulled hard sending him careening over Zeke's head. The warrior rolled over in a somersault, but quickly came back to his feet. Jeremy shot him twice with his pistol before the Indian had a chance to do anything with the knife. He fell to the ground right beside Zeke's head.

"Yeow!!" screamed Zeke as he quickly rolled away.

Josh almost laughed, but spun back around to check for targets. He found none.

"Dang, he almost killed me," complained Zeke as he got to his feet.

"Why didn't you shoot him?" asked Josh slyly.

"I was trying to, but he leaped out of the tree and was on me before I could bring my gun up."

Josh asked, "Well then, what did you learn?"

Zeke thought a second before reply honestly, "I should have already had my gun up and ready."

"Good answer. Well, apparently we all did fine. Jeremy shot two. Way to go, boy," added Josh.

Jeremy smiled. "I did what I had to do," he paused, and then grinned as he continued, "but it was tempting to let him kill Zeke. Then I wouldn't have to smell his old socks anymore!"

They all laughed, but Josh quickly asked them, "Okay, what's the first thing we do after we have secured the fight and neutralized our enemy?"

Zeke held back letting Jeremy think, "We reload our weapons as a second charge could come at anytime."

"Good boy. Let's reload, then we'll strip the bodies and make our mark. And then we'd better get the heck out of here," added Josh. "Our gunshots were probably heard for miles."

They kept the Blackfeet weapons, cut clothes away from the dead Indians, and quickly made the inverted V on their chests. Even though they were not the intended targeted tribe, they still hoped to instill fear in any Indian that attacked them. They saddled up and began riding away, hoping to get back to the cave after dark. The last quarter mile they took huge detours and turns covering their tracks. They sneaked into the cave carefully just in case any braves were trailing them. When they came out of the brush, Zeke pulled Josh's horse along with his, followed by Jeremy.

Josh stayed in the brush hidden from sight for almost two hours until he was absolutely sure they were not followed. He came into camp in time for supper. Jeremy took the first watch while Zeke and Josh lay down exhausted and instantly fell asleep.

EIGHTEEN

Mila Hanska had not forgotten about the attack on his warriors in the plains, but after two failed search parties and no sign of the enemy, he turned his attention to Wyoming and Fort Laramie. He felt angered his fellow tribes allowed the white man to build the fort in the heart of their homelands. In 1865, his band helped the Sioux attack the fort many times, in what became known as the Bloody Year on the Plains. For a while, the battles calmed down, and the white men began entering Montana over the Bozeman Trail in search of the gold fields there.

The search for the elusive gold in America began in the east with the first big find in Dahlonega, Georgia. Groups dug mines as they looked for a prosperous gold vein. Individual prospectors spent every day panning the river, and gold was indeed found. The government created America's first mint in the little north Georgia town making millions of gold coins, but mines were quickly bought up allowing the wealthy to control the digging and the price. Prospectors soon heard of gold in Colorado and migrated west faster than the settlers. When easy gold became once again scarce, a drunken mountain man in a Denver saloon spilled the beans on seeing gold on the Bozeman Trail, and in a matter of days, they began riding north to attempt to find it. Denver's population dropped from twelve hundred to three hundred almost overnight.

The Indians considered the Powder River country their sacred burial sites on the high grassy ridges facing the eastern rising sun, and the river gorge below where the gold was found in the middle of their primary hunting grounds. With the War Between The States over, the Union troops began returning in force to Fort Laramie, allowing an expansion by creating Forts Reno and Phil Kearny in Northeastern Wyoming, and C.F. Smith in Montana. Over the winter, Mila Hanska and his men fought and killed Captain William Fetterman, and eighty-one soldiers in a battle near Fort Phil Kearny.

The Sioux leaders did not trust Mila Hanska, nor did they approve of or find honor in his tactics or tribal life. However, they knew his men to be the fiercest warriors of all the tribes. They were trained in the use of all weapons, and could ride a horse at full gallop, while firing their bows or flinging their spears with great accuracy. However, their greatest weapon was their ability to establish fear in the eyes of their enemies. They wore the unique highly contrasting black and white stripes on their faces, and in battle, they quickly mutilated their victims, holding up cut off body parts to terrify and demoralize those still alive. They never accepted a truce, and killed all white flag attempts by the soldiers or settlers. Mila Hanska and his warriors never stopped an attack until there was no one left alive.

If they captured a white baby, they would hold the baby up for the enemy to see, and then begin tearing the baby's limbs off like they might do with a roasted rabbit. They would strip a white woman naked, and then hang her from a limb. The men would take turns ramming their fists into her vagina to make sure no more white babies could be born. They cut her hair from her head, and many times, they would cut her teats leaving her bleeding to death. At Fort Phil Kearny, Mila Hanska had done all this and more, but the white soldiers and settlers continued to fight. In desperation, he hung another woman from a limb, then tied individual long ropes to each ankle, and gave the end to two of his men on their horses. When Mila Hanska gave the order, they dug in their heels, and galloped in opposite directions tearing the legs from the woman. She bled to death in seconds, but no one there ever forgot her terrifying screams. He did the same to several teenage boys. He hung captured white men from trees, and began cutting off fingers and toes, peeling back their skin like taking the hide off a deer, stabbing their eyes with their knives, and cutting off their ears and genitals. On others, they made cuts with their sharp knives across their lower abdomen allowing their intestines to spill out to the ground. The victims screamed with great horror, but no one came to their rescue. They skewered body parts on their arrows, and shot them over the wall of the fort, creating as much horror and terror as possible. The battle ended only after he killed and mutilated everyone.

He planned attacks on cavalry squads just one mile from their fort so the remaining soldiers could hear the gunfire and screams. By the time reinforcements rushed to the scene, they found all of their men dead and horribly mutilated. Such atrocities resulted through centuries of revengeful wars among the tribes. They felt an enemy should be powerfully punished even after death. With every treaty broken by the United States government, along with the white man's total disrespect of their Indian homelands, hunting grounds, and sacred areas, the Indians hoped to punish the dead so the living would leave their lands forever. Bodies were stripped bare and scalps taken. Ears and noses were cut off and left on top of the corpses. Eyes were gouged out, tongues removed, genitals stomped, and a few had their penis filleted open like a Japanese fan. The Indians knew all men feared having their sexual organs destroyed, even more than losing their lives. Toes and fingers were cut off, and stood upright in a victim's mouth like carrot sticks. Some had the skin of their legs peeled off like taking the skin off an orange. Others were gutted with a long sharp knife, and their intestines stretched out from their bodies and looped over tree limbs. It was a horrible, gut-wrenching scene, causing even the seasoned soldiers to taste the bile of their worrisome stomachs.

Though the soldiers searched the forests, they failed to spot a laughing Mila and his men as they watched from a high ridge. They took great

169

pride in their ruthlessness, and considered their warriors better than all the other tribes. Their actions demanded fearful respect from all.

The tribal warriors had been riding for days to the north where they joined up with bands of Sioux, and planned their attack for the next morning on Fort C.F. Smith. Mila's men would lead the charge at dawn. Defiantly, his men snatched squaws from the Sioux and raped them. The Sioux warriors held their tongues and weapons for now, while moving their women and children back to the east away from the Kaga Ozuye warriors.

Captain Will Leland listened to the reports from his scouts. He knew the Indians were growing in numbers, so he sent riders to Fort Laramie, begging for the cavalry to save them. They spent the night strengthening the walls of the fort, while preparing all weapons and ammunition for the impending battle. He wrote a farewell note to his wife who thankfully remained safely in Saint Louis. He knew he and his men would not last more than a day without help.

Twilight came just after six the next morning. Mila Hanska fired the first shot from his bow. It was a long shot, and though he had aimed for the lookouts head, his arrow went through the man's neck rendering him speechless. In horror and pain at being shot, he fell forward off the platform on to a squad of resting men. The alarm went out immediately, leaving the convulsing wounded soldier to die in the dirt. The entire force of Indians launched their attack with bloodthirsty screams, and spine chilling shrills and whoops.

The soldiers fired from behind the protection of the fort's wall, while the Indians rode their horses up quickly and galloped around the fort firing their arrows over and over again. At first, the soldiers were successful killing warrior after warrior, but Mila Hanska's men were great shots, hitting a soldier most often in the face, as they were taking aim with their rifles. He knew a wounded soldier with a face wound felt too much pain to continue firing back at the Indians.

On his command, his men tied ropes to the bottom of the gates, and pulled with their horses until the gates popped off their hinges. With a whoop of a war yell, and the waving of his long handle hatchet, Mila Hanska led his men in a huge swarm inside the fort. The warriors used clubs with various ends of a thick rock, sharp stone, and some with two knife blades strapped tight on the end. A few carried captured big handle axes commonly used by the white men to build the forts or log cabins. They were vicious, sadistic weapons taking limbs, heads, and life away in a quick swoosh sound that often covered the attacker in bright red blood. They liked clubbing their enemy to death, inflicting as much pain and punishment as possible before smashing their heads open with a final blow. The siege lasted only twenty minutes. Every soldier was killed. No one survived. They stole their clothes, weapons, horses, and all their supplies. He then ordered them to burn the fort. By the time the troops arrived from Fort Laramie, the fort had burned to the ground.

Mila Hanska and his men waited for the reinforcements and quickly drove them back with massive attacks from both sides of the road leading to the fort. After losing forty men in just a few minutes, the cavalry was forced to retreat. The Sioux and the Kaga Ozuye warriors celebrated their overwhelming defeat of the white men by dancing to the tribal drums all night long.

The next day the Kaga Ozuye warriors began heading south to home. A few days later, his scouts spotted a small wagon train approaching on the plains. The temptation was too great to ignore. Mila and his men attacked at dawn. Though circled for safety, the settlers were caught off guard, and the Indians easily breached their fortress, killing all the men in minutes. His men lined up the women in one line and the children in another. Mila Hanska sat on a log by the fire, tasting the white man's food. One by one, the women were pushed towards him. The first two women were deemed too ugly, and he gave the sign of death to his warriors by pulling a flat hand with his fingers extended across his throat like a knife. The women were pulled out of line and immediately the warriors slit their throats.

The next lady was but twenty years old and so terrified, she said nothing, not even a scream. He liked her and motioned for them to bring her to him. He set his hatchet down and pulled her dress up and felt her vagina, then pulled her top down and played with her breasts. Satisfied, he told her to sit down behind him and remain still. She sat down as she quickly tried to repair her dress.

He selected four women, and murdered the rest. He began the same selection process with the children. All children under eight were killed. Boys over fourteen were killed, as they could quickly become a threat. He chose two boys about eleven and thirteen years old, a girl about fourteen, and gave the other children and women to his men. They would all becomes his slaves —some for work, and some for pleasure.

They took all the riding horses, loaded the supplies onto the wagon horses, and tied their captives two at a time on horseback as well. They burned the wagons and began once again their journey home.

Josh, Zeke, and Jeremy had made a decision to relocate while eating supper. By dawn, they packed up their horses and supplies, and rolled up three bundles of seventy-five captured arrows in a thin hide and tied it to the back of their horses. They hid the rest of the captured weapons. After yesterday's

171

attack, they knew the Blackfeet warriors would swarm the area looking for them, and besides, they had not seen Kaga Ozuye warriors in weeks. They hid their tracks, as they left the cave, and made their way to the stream and turned north. They traveled along the stream as the sun came up for several miles before moving back to higher ground. By nightfall, they had ridden almost fifteen miles through several passes and over the top of a ridge into the high country where picked a place to camp. Jeremy and Zeke made camp while Josh watched for anyone tracking them. After an hour, he sat down by his saddle feeling confident no one was looking for them.

The area they chose to camp gave them an eerie feeling. Zeke said lightning most likely struck the decayed dry mulch, creating a forest fire with the flames spreading, and quickly wiping away the brush and ground cover, and killing the trees. They found an area where they could hide behind some big rocks, but they could easily see anyone approaching over the barren land. They made no fire, as there was little wood around, so they ate a cold supper of jerky and water. It had been a long day with Zeke taking the first watch, followed by Josh, and then Jeremy in the hours before dawn. The night sky was clear and the air cool as Josh stared off to the north looking for any sign of an Indian fire. He found nothing, but he felt in his heart the farther they moved north, the more likely they would find the Kaga Ozuye warriors or other bands of the Sioux.

They left an hour before dawn so they would be hidden by the lack of light as they crossed the barren land and back into the forest before the sun came up. They looked for streams to hide their hoof tracks, and often walked for hours in the stream, brushing the soil where they made their exit to prevent anyone from following them. They also stopped periodically as they topped a hill or a ridge waiting for any sign of movement behind them. They kept their guns ready, as well as their tomahawks on a leather cord hanging from their saddle horn. They knew if they had to fire their weapons to stop an attacker, the sound of the gun would travel for miles, alerting all Indians in the area of their whereabouts.

Three days later, they spotted burning wagons at the edge of the plains. They were high in the mountains, which afforded a great view of the plains, and they knew immediately the train was too far away for them to save anyone. Zeke scanned the horizon several times until he spotted movement several miles away to the northeast of their position.

"I see them!" he exclaimed. "Off that way," he pointed with his left hand while still holding the glasses to his eyes.

Josh and Jeremy squinted into the sun until they saw the riders. "How many Indians are riding?"

"A lot, I would say fifty or more," replied Zeke.

Josh noted the direction in which they were galloping and then turned to look at the terrain ahead of them. "I think if we move down that valley and up to the next ridge, we might intersect them. We must get close enough to attack, but not so close we can be detected. We must find a new hiding place as well. Let's ride," added Josh.

It took another full day to make the journey through the rough and steep mountain terrain and a half-day to find a natural hiding place. They found it quite by accident because Jeremy was stalking a deer for meat. The deer bounced along a stream right up to a waterfall. He thought he had the deer trapped, but suddenly the deer went behind the waterfall, and came out the other side completely dry. Intrigued, he cautiously followed the deer's tracks until hidden by a wall of water. He then noticed a big cavern behind the rushing water. He rushed back and showed the place to Josh and Zeke. There was plenty of room for them and their horses, but before they agreed it was the right spot, Josh went back outside and looked left and right, and realized they could always make their way to and from by going through the water hiding their tracks with ease. It was indeed a good hiding place.

They set up camp, enjoying their first hot meal in days though they had to settle for rabbit instead of deer. They organized their weapons and rested. They stored up firewood and fed their animals. They scouted the area in all directions, learning possible escape routes, while agreeing no one should ever return directly to the cave, but rather stopping and listening for a tracker. They always changed directions numerous times to throw off the enemy from their camp.

After a few days, they felt they were ready. They moved out on foot early the next morning before dawn to ensure safety. They stayed out of sight just below the ridges, scouting left and right of the mountains for movement. They walked several miles every day wearing their moccasins and except for their pistols, they carried the weapons of their enemy: tomahawks, knives, bows, and arrows.

They spotted two single Indians they thought might be Crows tracking a bear in the valley below them to the west. They watched carefully, but did their best to remain hidden. They did not want the double jeopardy of another tribe searching for them while they were searching for the Kaga Ozuye warriors and Yuma.

Mila Hanska led his men back to their village. He immediately ordered Yuma to prepare him a meal as well as warm water for his bath. Yuma set about his orders quickly, but to his surprise, his master pushed the two white boys and the teenage girl captured on the plains into his tipi. He told Yuma to feed them as well. Mila Hanska gave the other slaves to his men.

173

Soon screams could be heard throughout the village as his braves began raping the captured women, the warriors' reward for a great victory against the white settlers. Yuma had heard these terrifying screams before, and knew many of the women would only live a few more days, while the children might make it a few years.

Mila Hanska made his way to the woods to relieve himself before returning to his tipi. Yuma quickly handed him a bowl of hot venison stew, a gourd of water, and pieces of flatbread he made on a hot flat rock at the edge of the fire. The food had been the first hot meal Mila had eaten in over a week of hunting on the warpath. He ate it quickly, licking his fingers, and sticking his bowl out for Yuma to dip him more of the stew and hand him more bread. Once satisfied, he ordered Yuma to feed his new slaves. The boy gave each of the children gourds of stew and pieces of flat bread. They were starving and ate quickly. Yuma managed to feed himself at the same time and ate rapidly.

Mila Hanska then ordered Yuma to bathe him. Yuma stood and removed the warrior's feathers, armbands, beaded breastplate, his waist knife, his moccasins and leggings, and finally his clothes until he stood naked before his slaves. Terrified, the children stared at him with bright soulful eyes, having no idea of what future they might have.

Yuma dipped a strip of hand woven cloth in the pot of warm water heating near the fire, and began washing his master's skin as he had done so many times before. After finishing, Mila Hanska dried himself near the fire, and then lay down on a big bearskin hide. Yuma hoped he was tired from his journey, and would perhaps go right to sleep, but he was wrong. The chief had other things on his mind rather than resting.

He ordered Yuma to strip his slaves. Yuma was tempted to tell the children in English what to do and to comfort them, but he did not want to use his new English words in front of his master. He went to sleep each night by silently repeating every English word he could remember. The words gave him hope of returning to Josh and Zeke. He spoke to the children softly and soothingly in his native tongue. Slowly, he removed the clothes of the younger boy, then the other boy, and finally the girl. Tears fell silently from the girl's eyes, as she stood naked for the first time in her life in front of a man.

Mila ordered him to take their clothes to the cooking fires and burn them. Yuma picked up the clothes, including their shoes, and left the tipi. He felt the pockets, and found only a pocketknife in the front pocket of the older boy's pants. He hid it under a rock, and then put the clothes on the fire as instructed and returned to the tent. With no clothes or shoes to runaway, Mila knew he could humiliate them into submitting to his every command.

Mila Hanska gave Yuma an order to come to him and suck him. Without hesitation, Yuma knelt down in front of him, but his master pulled him to his side so the children could watch Yuma's performance. After a few minutes, with an erection achieved, he told Yuma to bring the girl to him. Yuma pushed her down to her knees in the same spot where he knelt seconds ago. Mila Hanska spoke harshly to her warning her not to bite him in his native tongue. She had no idea what he said, but trembled with fear. Yuma leaned down once again showing her what to do. He then pushed two of his fingers in her mouth pulling them in and out while squeezing her cheeks with his other hand. Gradually, she began to suck his fingers like a new born calf.

Mila ordered him to teach the boys as well, so he went on the other side of the tipi pulling the children's hands with him. Yuma removed his loincloth, and pulled the children onto the buffalo hide. Mila Hanska allowed the girl to perform her new chore while his hands began roaming her naked body. He soon pulled her on top of him, began rubbing her small breasts, and then running his hands up and down her backside. Yuma had not seen his master perform sex with a woman in a long time, though he knew he did it with captives from time to time. He taught the girl how to kiss him, and suck his tongue. He made her clean his ears with her wet tongue. Her shaking gradually diminished, so he wrapped his big muscled arms around her and pulled her to him tightly. He pulled her legs apart and only slightly entered her with his erection. He was surprisingly patient with this virgin white girl enjoying the sex immensely. He placed his hands on her hips, and began just slightly rocking her forward and back. He felt her moisten and continued the rhythm. Moments later, he thrust deeply into her, and she screamed as her hymen broke, allowing him in where no other man had gone. He continued his thrusts as she quieted her voice, and responded with a new feeling, leaving him greatly satisfied as he exploded deep inside her.

Yuma tried to turn the boys' eyes from the girl, and he dreaded what he was about to do. Only his fear of being killed by his master gave him the courage to continue. He taught the boys how to suck without biting and reluctantly, he trained them how to loosen their butts for sex. Yuma felt back a strong urge to vomit while committing these awful crimes on these teenagers.

By nightfall, the girl had been raped numerous times, and now slept in the warrior's arms beneath a bear hide. Yuma slept on the other side of the tent under a hide with the boys on each side of him cuddling him tightly. He felt their homesick, lonesome tears on his skin until they fell asleep. He knew their days ahead would be hard as they adjusted from a life where their parents praised and comforted them, to a life of drudgery as their master would order and beat them severely if they disobeyed his commands. Yuma knew that many times he was slapped hard across the face for no reason at all, thus inflicting the most emotional damage of all. He wondered how many days he had left before his master would tire and dispose of him. None of the children could cook or provide for Mila Hanska, so for now, his job and his life would be spared. He was perhaps the only male slave in the camp that actually liked male sex, but because he hated Mila, having sex with him was a paradox of joy and revulsion. Maybe Mila knew this, but what he did know was Yuma was the first slave he had owned that performed all the sex acts on him with great skill and tenderness, so he allowed him to live longer than he usually did. It was now late spring, and Yuma hoped Josh and Zeke were coming for him. He spent part of his days scanning the horizons in a hopeful watch for their smiling faces. In his dreams, he saw freedom and love so he tried to fall asleep quickly, so he could quickly feel the peace and comfort he so desired.

Josh, Zeke, and Jeremy had been there a week before spotting another Kaga Ozuye war party leaving the valley off to the northeast mountain range. They watched them carefully from the ridge using the binoculars, while being mindful to avoid the sun reflecting off the glass and alerting the Indians to their position. They counted six men. Josh studied the terrain and pointed out five separate valleys to the north where they might be camping. Zeke scanned the area, but found no movement to the north. He felt if they went up the next ridge, they might be able to see down into the valley. Josh had another idea.

"I think we should take out these six men on their return. That would further reduce their numbers and shake them up a bit. They would probably send out more men, which we could kill as well."

"Wouldn't this tell them we are close by?" asked Jeremy.

"Yes, it would, if we left the bodies here. We'll strip and scar the bodies as usual, but tie them to their ponies and send them home to momma," replied Josh.

"We'll have to be careful to cover our tracks," suggested Zeke. "They'll probably assume his men were killed on the plains after losing a battle."

"You're right. We'll use no horses, but go down this hill on foot, and we'll kill them with bows, arrows, and rope," said Josh.

Jeremy gave him a puzzled look and asked, "Rope?"

"Yes, you see we can't shoot six men at once, and they could come in riding fast, or perhaps one might escape. We'll pull a rope across the trail, and bury it under some leaves. When they gallop down the trail to return to their village, we'll spring the rope just before they cross it, and that'll knock them off their horses. We'll either shoot the fallen warriors, or kill them with our tomahawks. Let's go. We have no time to lose."

Zeke began to see what Josh's life was really like during the war. Josh had become the natural leader, which was fine with him, as well as an extraordinary strategic planner. He was completely willing to give orders, and in battle, an unsympathetic but necessary killer. He marveled at his amazing skills, and he knew with Josh taking charge, one way or another, they were going to get Yuma back. He understood his partner and loved him even more.

It took Yuma a full day, but soon he had enough rawhide stitched together to provide some summer clothing for the girl. She smiled at him as he showed her how to tie on the loincloth, and then he put her head through a narrow piece that folded over the front and back. He tied a leather cord around her waist to hold the flap to her skin. Using an antler tip as an awl, he then punched a hole in the edge of the hide under her arms about half way to her waist, and inserted another cord and tied it. He did the same on the other side and stood back to look at her. She turned so he could see the hide now covered her breasts and private parts, and yet he knew Mila could get to her with ease. If he had not made sure of that, his master would have cut the garment to shreds. She smelled the hide and pinched her nose, but felt greatly relieved to have her body covered. She said thank you to him. He smiled and nodded silently, as he didn't know whether she could keep his English ability a secret.

Like many of the boy slaves, the new white boys had no clothes. It was the warrior's way of preventing them from running off and dying of exposure. After a few days, being naked no longer bothered the boys, but in the next few days, Yuma hoped to scrounge up some thin deer hides to make small loin clothes for them. He showed them where to pee and potty, and instructed all the children how to wash their butts after a bowel movement. He knew from experience that Mila would give a child with a dirty, stinky butt a terrifying beating. He didn't trust the children to remember, so if Mila was out for the day, Yuma would take charge and make the children wash themselves late in the afternoon.

They followed him everywhere. He took them down to the river to wash their hair. He showed them how to carry water to the camp. He put the girl and older boy to work scraping the fur from a deer hide. He showed the little boy how to carve out the inside of a new gourd for eating or drinking. He kept them busy all day, so they had no time to feel sorry for themselves, and entertain any thoughts of their past. He knew their parents, friends, brothers, and sisters were probably all dead and sadly, he knew in little time, they would most likely die as well. Yesterday, they all walked in the woods around the edge of the camp and helped him dig for herbs, roots, and wild turnips. They also picked more sassafras leaves to make tea.

About an hour before dark, he took the children to the woods, and made them potty and pee. He pulled leaves to wipe them, and then took them to the river and made them squat while scrubbing their bottoms once again. He could not take the chance that one might bring about a beating to all. They returned to the fire to dry. The children were hungry, but Yuma knew better than to feed them first. Mila Hanska spent the day hunting for deer. He had been gone all day, when suddenly, he came into the village with a deer slung over his horse. Yuma ran quickly to take his horse and weapons. The hunter walked to the river to wash the animal's blood and the mud from his skin.

Yuma tied up the horse, looped a rawhide rope around the deer's rear hoofs, threw the other end of the rope over a tree limb, and with the help of the older boy, they hauled the deer into the air with his head just a foot off the ground. He then sent the older boy to walk the horse to the river to allow him to drink. Yuma retrieved his knives from the edge of the cook fire. He quickly carved away the head of the deer with each pull of the knife going deeper. He motioned for the girl to help him. He made her pull the head backwards. He took his largest knife and cut the jugular vein. Blood spewed out covering his bare feet. He continued cutting until the head fell loose. Terrified, the girl immediately let it fall to the ground.

He made a cut from the between the deer's rear legs to his chest, and pulled back the hide by sawing and carefully cutting away the flesh. He cut and removed a big roast, skewered it on a long green stick, and put the stick on the v sticks over the fire. He dug his hand into a gourd of grease and smeared it over the roast. From a leather bag, he removed small bags of herbs he crushed and chopped. He spread them over the meat, patting to make the seasoning stick in the grease.

He returned to the deer. The girl gagged and threw up when Yuma cut out the heart and handed it to her. He ran his knife through the heart and pulled a leather cord through it, and motioned for her to hang it on the drying pole next to the tipi. When she returned he had another chunk of meat carved out, and repeated the process until there were no longer any chunks left. He then continued with removing the hide, and managed to get it off in one large piece. He tied four pieces of rawhide cord to the four corners and stretched the hide by staking it out at the bottom and tying it to a limb at the top. He left the girl with a knife scraping away the remaining meat from the inside of the hide. She put the morsels in a jar of water that would become a stew.

He gave the little boy a small piece of hide containing a pile of unusable innards. He motioned for the boy to go to the next tipi, and feed the dogs. Terrified, the boy walked to the dogs, but stopped short, and began throwing the food to the dogs. The dogs ate it in gulps. The little boy became the dogs' new best friend, and Yuma made sure only the little boy fed them.

He did this to prevent the dogs from attacking the small boy and eating him alive.

Yuma had become an exceptionally good multitasking cook and caretaker. He turned the meat allowing it to cook slowly. He took care of the hides, and then returned to season the meat hanging on the poles. He broke off the antlers with a rock, and saved the pointed spikes for utensils. He carved up meat and put it in a pot, added wild onions, sliced apples, berries, and small potatoes to make a stew. He added herbs from his bag, and soon the stew smelled wonderful.

He made flat bread on a hot rock next to the fire, and then once again turned the meat. He boiled a pot of water adding sassafras leaves to create a wild tea. From a jar, he dipped several fingers full of honey to add to the tea. After bringing it back to a boil, he removed it from the fire to allow it to cool. He spooned out the leaves. He had another jar full of water warming near the fire reserved for Mila Hanska.

Mila Hanska returned from the river, warmed his skin by the fire, and then walked through the village to see how his men were doing, and to hear the reports from his scouts. Earlier that morning, a scout spotted a small wagon train in the plains, and he sent out a war party. He kept scouts on various hilltops on the eastern side of the mountains watching for any and all white men. He also posted scouts to the north watching for the cavalry. He also had sentries watching their camp from all four corners, making sure no one attacked them.

He listened intently and wondered why his men had not yet returned from their attack on the wagon train. Nightfall would soon arrive, and so he thought they might have stolen a large cache of supplies, forcing a slower ride, and thus made camp to finish the journey tomorrow. Satisfied with his probable solution, he turned to walk home to his tipi.

NINETEEN

The boys climbed down the mountain, and selected an area with high banks on each side of the trail and thick underbrush to hide in. It would become the scene of their first planned attack on the Kaga Ozuye warriors. They tied one end of the rope to a tree trunk on the far side of the trail about the height they thought a rider might be. They covered the trail with leaves to hide the rope, and threaded it through a low limb on their side. They tied a short stick to the end of the rope for additional control. Josh put Jeremy in charge of the rope, showed him how to quickly pull it tight, then run around the tree one time, and then lean back holding the handles. With his weight while using the tree trunk for leverage, Jeremy would be able to fling two or three men off their horses.

Josh told Jeremy he should first shoot his bow at the last man, and then yank the rope to snare the leaders. Meanwhile, Zeke and Josh would kill the fourth and fifth man. Once the front men had fallen, Jeremy must quickly pick up his bow once again, and kill at least one of the fallen men or more if he could, while Josh and Zeke would be responsible for shooting the other two.

Josh and Zeke selected positions about ten yards apart on the same side of the hill overlooking the trail. They had a big tree between them and the trail to keep their position hidden. From the spot behind the trunk of the tree, they had a right angle cleared to shoot the men in the rear, and quick swing to the left to kill some of the men in the front. He warned them that if the attack went badly, they were to scatter quickly, covering their trail, and gradually making their way back to the cave. He warned they must do everything they can to avoid capture.

Silently, they waited for the war party to return. They felt a tinge of guilt since they were not able to kill the warriors before they went after the wagon train.

Josh looked to the west watching the sun slowly set while worrying darkness would soon arrive, making their ability to sight in their targets much harder. He also felt that if they came soon, the long shadows would help hide the rope as well as themselves, making it easier for them to escape. Moments later, they heard the clop-clop sound of shoeless horses crossing the muddy trail. Josh motioned to Zeke and Jeremy to get ready. They each had about a dozen arrows lying on the ground beside them, so they could quickly reload and fire again. Jeremy had the longest shot, but Josh and Zeke knew he could hit the target easily, and just hoped he remembered to lead the rider a little.

Jeremy was to hit the last rider as he came around a bend, so that his fall would be out of the eyesight of the other riders. Zeke would take the next from the rear and Josh the next. They all drew their bows.

Jeremy's heart rate picked up, but he remembered his training. He counted off four men, and slowly exhaled. There was the fifth man. He waited patiently. Finally, he saw the last man. The bend approached. Zip! He let the arrow fly. Zip! Zip! Josh and Zeke fired. All three arrows hit their mark, hitting their men dead center of the chest. One of the horses reared spilling the slumping dead Indian. One of the three remaining men saw him, and let out a whoop. All three riders kicked their horses into a gallop.

Jeremy dropped his bow, grabbed the stick, and began rapidly running with the rope, pulling the slack out, and then quickly started around the tree. Josh glanced back and hoped he would be able to tighten the rope in time. Zeke sighted in the next man and fired, hitting him broadside under his left arm. The arrow went all the way to his heart. Jeremy flung himself the last four feet, and yanked back hard on the rope. It went taut.

Josh fired, but his man just reached down to adjust his grip on his tomahawk, and the arrow missed. Josh reloaded. Zeke caught Josh's man from the rear. The remaining man kicked his horse hard, and hit the rope at full speed at his neck. The fleeting weight of the man's body nearly flung Jeremy into the air, but the rope held fast. The man sprung, flipped backwards, and spun two complete flips before hitting the ground hard, smashing his face down on a rock. The rope had broken his neck, and he died seconds later.

Josh gave them a thumbs-up sign. Quickly, they scooped up their arrows, and returned them to their quivers. Jeremy untied the stick and threw the rope down the trail. They scrambled down the hill.

"Jeremy, gather up their horses. Zeke, you know what to do," ordered Josh.

Josh went to the man flung by the rope, spun him over, and checked to make sure he was dead. He cut the man's clothing away. Carved the inverted V, then cut strips from the man's clothes, and tied his hands and feet. He quickly moved to the next man who was still alive. Without hesitation, Josh rammed his knife upwards through the rib cage piercing his heart. He yanked out the knife and wiped it on the man's shirt before cutting it away. Zeke started from the rear forward following the same procedure. Once completed, Jeremy held one of the horses still while Zeke and Josh lifted a warrior's limp body over the horse. They ran another strip of clothing under the horse tying it to the man's bound hands and feet so he would not fall off. Jeremy tied the horse to a limb, and moved back for the next man, until they were all secured on their horses in a similar fashion.

Zeke ran up the hill and untied the rope. He also cut branches to cover their tracks. Josh was already swinging a limb back and forth, and threw dirt over some of the blood splatters. Jeremy untied the horses, and slapped them hard to send them galloping to the village. He joined the others in covering their tracks all the way up the hill until they could disappear in a thicket. Quickly, they began making their way back to the waterfall and home. It would be dark in less than hour, their mission a resounding success.

Yuma cut another chunk of the hot meat from the deer roast over the fire and brought it to Mila Hanska. The man had been eating for thirty minutes, devouring the stew, the beef, and then downing it with the tea mixture Yuma made. It was one of the best meals he had enjoyed, but he never let on to Yuma. Suddenly, he heard a whoop from one of the scouts on the perimeter of the village. Quickly, he jumped up grabbing both his tomahawk and his spear, and ran towards the sound.

Yuma looked to see what was going on, saw nothing, and rapidly began feeding the children. They ate quickly, chewing as fast as they could. Yuma ate, too.

Just as Mila Hanska came around the last tipi near the trailhead, the ponies galloped into the clearing. Quickly, his men surrounded and stopped the frighten horses. The dead warriors were cut from the horses and laid down on the ground. Mila Hanska looked at each one. They were naked with the same mark on their chests. He wondered what the mark meant. He then studied the wounds. Each man had been killed with an arrow and not a gun. What tribe dared attack his men, he wondered.

Mila pulled his knife from the sheath tied to his waist and dug into the wound of the first man until he could pull out the arrowhead. He studied it carefully. It looked like one of theirs. He flipped the next man over, and found the broken remains of the arrow that had caught in the man's spine. He lifted the feathered end of the arrow so he could see it better in the twilight. It was indeed one of their arrows. What could this mean?

He ordered his men to retrieve all the arrowheads. On the last man, they found yet another arrow and feathers. This one was different. It was bound with a similar but different wrapping. He kept the broken stick in his hand as he looked at the faces of his men. He gave them orders to prepare the men for burial in the traditional way and returned to his tipi.

Yuma sensed something was wrong so he moved the children from the fire and off to the side. Mila Hanska strode quickly to the tipi and went in. He called for Yuma. The boy turned to the children and told them to stay put. He entered the tipi carrying a pot of warm water. His master ordered him to bathe him. Yuma set about undressing the Indian while noting the arrow in his hand. He said nothing, but stole many glances at it. He soon caught on it was an arrow he had made while staying with Josh and Zeke. An arrow he had used to teach them how to make arrows. How did it get here, he wondered.

Mila Hanska lay down on the bearskin hide and called for the girl. Yuma went out and called the children in. He took the girl to his master. He quickly untied the rawhide holding her clothing on, and lifted it over her head. He undid the waist cord and pulled off the bottom. She knelt down silently, and began servicing her master. Yuma turned away not wishing to watch. He took the boys to bed with him, hoping they would not be needed tonight.

He fell asleep dreaming about making the arrow in Josh and Zeke's cabin. Near midnight, he suddenly woke with a start. Mila Hanska had kicked his feet. He spoke his orders quickly. Yuma woke the older boy, and then pulled him up. Mila Hanska grabbed the white boy and yanked him roughly to his bear hide. He returned with the exhausted girl. Yuma saw a patch of blood between her legs. Mila no longer wanted her tonight. Yuma grabbed a piece of cloth, cleaned her up, and pressed the rag inside her. He then pulled her down to his bear hide, flung the top hide over her. She twisted until she was facing him, and then hugged him tightly. He felt her tears on his neck. She did not mind his erection rising between them. They fell asleep cuddling and quiet.

The boy was not as lucky, though he tried to remember what to do. He expected to be raped so he flexed and tighten, but Mila Hanska was not in a hurry. The master wanted to break his spirit through humiliation. He taught the boy his word for lick by having the boy lick his hand. Once accomplished, he made the boy lick his ears clean, as well as his nostrils, legs, and finally the bottoms of his feet. His ultimate humiliation came when he required the boy to lick his backside. Mila Hanska loved the boy's tender wet tongue, and decided he might just keep him alive a while longer.

Yuma had almost fallen asleep when he heard the older boy's muffled yelp, as his master entered him for the first time. Yuma had lost count as to how many times it had happened to him. He drifted off once again, thinking about the arrow, and wondering if Josh or Zeke had fired it.

The doctor in Denver did not much care for the man lying on his surgeon's table. He was a rough talker and smelled bad. The man removed his pistols and knives from his pants, took his boots off, though in great pain, and followed by pushing his pants and long johns to his ankles. He lay down on the table face down. The doctor inspected the bloody buttock, expecting to find a gunshot wound, but quickly realized an Indian had shot him. He took a stick of wood about a half inch in diameter, and told the man to place it between his teeth, and to bite it hard. He took his scalpel and cut into the man, without offering anything more for pain. Once satisfied that he had located the

183

arrowhead, the doctor picked up a large pair of tweezers, and pushed them into the bleeding wound until he could feel the shaft of the arrow. He tugged at it, as the man groaned loudly, slamming his fists into the legs of the table before gripping those legs as tightly as he could. The doctor paused only briefly, sighed, and then pulled hard. The tissue had already started healing itself around the stone. He pulled much harder, the man groaned again, and screamed, but finally it came loose, and he pulled it out. The man sighed greatly and passed out.

The doctor cleaned the wound and felt the man was lucky not to have experienced any gangrene. He then began sewing the damaged flesh together with ten stitches. He had just cut off the stout string of the last stitch when the man came to.

"Are you okay?" asked the doctor.

"No!" grumbled the man. "Did you get it out?"

"Yes, I did."

"Let me see it."

The doctor lifted a small tray and brought it around the table so the man could see it. "Damn!" cursed the man. "That's about ten times the size of a bullet. No wonder it hurt like hell. I think I would rather have been shot."

"I've put ten stitches in to keep the wound closed, so it will heal properly. Try not to break any of the stitches loose, or I may have to sew you up again. Keep the wound clean to avoid infection," warned the doctor. "After about ten days you can cut the stitches free. Try not to ride your horse. You'd be better off resting."

The man struggled off the table, pulled his pants up, stepped into his boots, and then reattached his weapons. He said with some weariness in his voice, "I hear alcohol, if consumed by large quantities, will stave off infection."

"No doubt," grinned the doctor, "but at the least it will numb the pain, and hopefully you will sleep a great deal."

The man grumbled, handed the doctors three silver dollars, and made his way out of the office. The doctor was glad he was gone, and went to work on cleaning up the mess from the surgery.

"Captain," called one of his men from the porch where he had been waiting. "Are you all right?"

"Fine, but it hurts like hell. Where are the men?" he asked.

"They are camped outside of town."

"Good, ride out and tell them to stay there, and I'll join them tomorrow," he ordered. "I can't ride a horse tonight."

The man quickly retreated to his horse and swung up in the saddle. The captain walked across the street with a painful limp. He made it to the bar and ordered a whisky. He drank at least three shots before noting an army lieutenant sipping on his beer to his right.

"You walk with a limp," stated the lieutenant.

The captain gave him a hard stare, soured the look on his face, and replied, "I was shot in the ass. The doctor just finished sewing me up. It hurts like hell."

The lieutenant laughed. "I'm sorry. Shot by a white man or an Indian?"

The captain rolled his eyes while wondering if this man would ever go away. He downed another shot pouring it with a steady hand. "It was an arrowhead. Have you ever seen the size of those things?"

"Big, huh? No wonder you're limping. I bet you can't sit down for a week."

The lieutenant thought for a second before speaking again. "One of the officers at the fort told me about three white men that rescued some women and children attacked by a gang of former soldiers."

"Well, it wasn't me. I'm a gang of one," he lied. "And besides, I wasn't shot by three white men, but by Indians."

The lieutenant grinned. "But that's the point. The three white men pretended to be Indians, and drove the gang off with arrows so they would think they were being attacked by a swarm of Indians. Bloody ingenious if you ask me, three men with bows and arrows driving off a gang of twenty or more."

The captain quickly surmised his men had been duped. He downed another shot and said nothing more to the lieutenant. He asked the bartender for a room, then gave him a silver dollar, and took the bottle and glass to his room. He drank the rest of the bottle, and then fell face first onto the bed and passed out.

Long before dawn, Josh, Zeke, and Jeremy took up their scouting positions high on the ridge. They never stood in the open, but remained always hidden by the brush, but they found spots where they could see to the north, as well as to the trail below, where they attacked yesterday. They could not see the plains, so they hoped another squad would leave the village to investigate the killing of their warriors.

About an hour after dawn, they felt lucky when they spotted a war party of twelve men, twice as many as before. They watched the men ride slowly along the trail looking for any sign of tracks along the beaten path, but they found none. Josh thought the warriors were either foolish or over

185

confident, as they never scanned the area for enemies. They rode as if they owned the path and the right to do as they wished. They moved to the east out of sight towards the plains and perhaps hit another wagon train. However, just as they reached the burned out wagons from the previous attack, they spotted the cavalry galloping towards them. Quickly, they darted back into the forest where they watched the lieutenant and his men inspect the wagon train. The soldiers began digging shallow holes, and hurriedly buried the dead. The lieutenant circled the area until he distinguished six riders on shoeless horses. He knew the attackers were Indians, the settlers must have killed some, but he would need far more men to pursue them into the mountains. Soon his men saddled up, and headed back south to their fort. The twelve hidden warriors realized they would not be pursued, so they began making their way back to camp with no explanation as to what tribe killed their men.

The next day as the sun began appearing to their east, the boys carefully and cautiously began moving farther north. They had to find the Indian village, but they sensed that each step north put them in a greater chance of discovery and danger. They were vigilant, moving quickly and quietly from tree to tree. They watched far ahead for any movement before moving again.

In the afternoon, they finally spotted a single Indian. At first, they thought he might be hunting, but though he walked around from time to time, he always returned to the same spot. Using his field glasses, Zeke surmised the warrior was in the perfect location to see the ridge and the valley below. He thought he might be a lookout.

Josh whispered, "He is probably on some kind of shift, which means another man will take his place at some point. We can't kill him or they will come looking for him. This would put them on alert that we are close to their village. At some point, we may need to watch him for a full day to find out when his replacement arrives. They don't have watches so I bet it has something to do with the sun. Let's move around him in the river to the west."

Zeke and Jeremy nodded in agreement, but Zeke added, "I bet they have more than one lookout. Unless their encampment is backed up to a large rock wall, I wager they have a minimum of four creating a square."

Josh nodded affirmatively. "We'll have to be guardedly slow. They could also have hunters looking for a kill to feed the tribe, and we mustn't stumble into them and become their prey."

They made their way down the hill and then moved silently along the stream until they were two hundred yards north of the lookout. Josh taught them most people would walk down the middle of the stream to avoid the spider webs, mosquitoes, and other varmints. The tree limbs and bushes hanging over the water provided additional cover, but Josh told them if they spotted someone, it was far easier and quieter to exit the stream if you were already next to the bank. He also said it was dangerous to be discovered in the middle of the stream because you cannot move quickly to find protection behind a tree. They hiked back up the ridge and walked another two hundred yards north until they spotted a second man. They sat down behind thick bushes and studied him.

"He's lookout number two. Do you think the village is close?" asked Zeke as he pulled down the field glasses. Josh nodded at him again as Zeke continued, "He can see the ridge and valley below, too. What does that tell us mister academy man?"

Josh was drawing the terrain in the dirt between them with a short stick. He marked the location of the two scouts, drew in the stream, the area the first scout had been spotted, and then slowly drew the inverted V symbols for tipis.

They each studied his drawing for a few seconds before slowly turning and looking off into the valley where they now felt the village must surely be. They scanned back and forth until finally Jeremy saw a single stream of smoke rising from a campfire. He pointed in that direction without saying a word. They all nodded, Josh wiped out his dirt map, and smiled. Then they began carefully making their way down the northeastern side with their hearts beating faster. They had found the village.

Yuma placed a log on the fire after securing another piece of venison over the fire for tonight's meal. He also cut numerous long strips of the dried beef to create a bag of jerky for the days when no game could be found. He looked across the campground at a group of men sitting around Mila Hanska. He listened to all their suggestions, but in the end, the deaths of his men remained a big puzzle. His war party returned with only the news that the cavalry found the burned wagon train.

Yuma found the feathered tip of his arrow in the tipi where his master had flung it in the night. He studied it carefully, and hid it under the edge of his bear hide on the floor of the tipi. He was afraid to get excited as the arrow could mean they were close by, or it could mean they were attacked and killed, and their enemies took his arrows.

He was afraid to get animated because he knew Mila would sense something was up, and because he knew if he found out Josh and Zeke were dead, then it would only be a matter of time until he was dead as well. He wanted to hope, but made himself push such thoughts deep inside him.

He moved the knife he had taken from the boy's pants, hid it inside the tipi in a small shallow hole, and lightly covered it with unpacked dirt to be retrieved if needed to escape in a hurry.

After reaching the bottom, the boys began making their way upstream very carefully. They had gone but a hundred yards when they saw the top of a tipi through the trees. Josh motioned for Zeke and Jeremy to stay put while he scouted the area very carefully, and picked a thorny thicket just over the hill from the village for them to hide in. He assumed no one in his right mind would wander into the massive briars. Crawling to avoid detection, the boys made it to the thicket. Silently, they ate jerky and drank water from their canteens. They remained alert and ready to fight, and agreed on a meeting spot should they be attacked at this location.

Near dark, they watched as two men walked out of the village carrying a deer hide over the shoulder and a gourd jug hung by a piece of rawhide from their neck. They also carried their weapons. Once they crossed the river, they split up, one heading to the northwest and the other to the southeast. The boys huddled down carefully as the Indian on their side of the mountain walked within twenty paces of them.

They realized it was the changing of the guards with the night shift heading out. They now assumed they stood guard about twelve hours a day. Zeke took out his pocket watch to time how long it took the men to get in position, and the other men to return the village. It might be something they could use to their advantage. Forty minutes later, the tired but hungry watchers came down the hill to the tipi and supper. They stopped briefly to report to Mila Hanska they had seen nothing all day. Relieved, he made his way back to his tipi. Although he kept four lookouts posted at all times, over the past few years no one had ever attempted to attack them, as they were known as the most dangerous warriors of all. Even the Lakota, the Crows, and the Blackfeet hated and feared them.

Yuma had supper ready when Mila Hanska returned to his tipi. He devoured strips of the beef, plus two bowls of stew, several clumps of flat bread, and then drank the tea. Satisfied, he left the group and walked to the woods to relieve his bladder.

Josh decided it was too dangerous for all three of them to scout the village, so reluctantly they agreed to let him go by himself. He crept back to the river and retrieved handfuls of mud, covered his tracks, and returned to the group. Zeke helped him cover his white skin by putting mud on his face. Taking only his knife, he crept upstream, until he lay across the stream from the village. From this point, he could see the entire campground. His old scout training from the Civil War took over. He forced everything and everyone from his brain, as he would have to use all his senses to be successful. He counted the horses and adult males. He counted the tips, but suddenly, a big tall Indian came directly from a nearby tipi walking straight towards him. Had he seen him, he wondered. Josh froze.

Mila Hanska stopped ten yards from the stream and began urinating on a bush. He was already thinking about the white girl, and could not wait to take her again tonight. He enjoyed the teenage boy as well, so tonight he thought he might take them both on at the same time. He smiled at his evil thoughts, shook his penis, and scanned the hill across the river out of habit, and then turned, and walked back to his tipi.

Josh followed the big Indian with his eyes as he walked back to his tipi. When he reached his campfire, Josh could tell a smaller Indian was on the far side of this big guy. The big Indian moved to his left. Suddenly, Josh's mouth fell open, and then he smiled. He had found Yuma. He watched the boy work about the fire feeding the white children. He knew they had to be slaves. Yuma rapidly ate the whole time he was working. He noticed the boys were mostly naked, and the girl barely clothed, and realized they probably had not been in captivity very long.

He shuddered as he saw the big Indian pull her top garment off and began suckling and kissing her breasts right in front of the boys by the fire. Yuma did his best not to notice. The Indian spoke and Yuma immediately led the older boy over to him. The boy fell to his knees as Yuma released his master's loincloth. The boy immediately took him in his mouth. After a few minutes, the big Indian led the boy and the girl into his tipi for more sex. Yuma remained with the smaller boy outside, finishing their meal and stowing away the leftover food in rawhide bags he tied onto cords hanging from a pole to keep the animals away from their food.

Josh thought about Yuma's instant response to every word this big guy spoke, and he immediately knew Yuma responded just like new slaves did after they arrived at the plantation and received their first beating for looking directly into the eyes of a white man. He felt so ashamed of how his ancestors had treated their slaves. He suddenly flinched when he heard the girl yelp.

He spotted the man's horse off to the right grazing alone. He would remember what his horse looked like. He hoped he got the chance to kill the big Indian who kept children captive while abusing them. He thought the evening was done when suddenly the naked Indian came from the tipi and yelled something to Yuma. Yuma answered, and instantly the man slapped him hard across the face. Josh had to control himself from charging across the stream and killing Yuma's master that preyed on children. His day would come, thought Josh. His day would come soon.

TWENTY

They moved back to their hideout with a slow and meticulous overnight hike, hiding their moccasin tracks where necessary. When they reached the waterfall, they entered the cave jubilantly, and with great relief and excitement.

"We found him, and he is alive," said Zeke as he gave Josh a hug.

Josh replied, "Yes, but it is going to take an amazing plan to get him from the village without being seen. He is with three other children."

The statement caused them all to pause and think. Throughout all their winter planning sessions, they never once anticipated the possibility of needing to rescue other children. Josh finally sighed heavily, "My military training tells me to stick to the objective, grab Yuma, and run like hell."

"Yeah, but I know you," began Zeke, "your military history let you read about heroes, and you're always the hero. If those were our children, or our brothers and sisters, we wouldn't hesitate. However, the fact is their parents are dead, so most likely there is no one that is going to come and rescue them. We have to snatch the children, too."

Josh sighed heavily knowing Zeke was right, but he felt the odds of success just dropped from five in ten to perhaps only two of ten. "That won't be easy. They are new captives, and not as hardened to running for their lives as Yuma will be. He is wearing moccasins while the children's feet are bare and easy to track. Do we have enough deer hide to make some more moccasins?"

Jeremy looked through their supplies. "I can cut six squares of hide with fur outside. All they would have to do is step on the square, and then we could pull the four corners up and tie a piece of rawhide around it to make it stay in place."

"Why fur out?" asked Zeke. "Wouldn't it be more comfortable with the fur on the inside?"

Josh laughed. "I think we should send our son to military school. With the fur on the outside, they would be almost impossible to track."

Jeremy smiled and asked, "Son?"

"I'm sorry. It just slipped out as I was attempting to brag on you. You are our best friend, but almost young enough to be our son. Either way, we are both extremely proud of you," explained Josh. He gave him a hug. "Cut the squares. Zeke and I need to think and develop a strategy."

Josh drew out the village in the sand on the cave floor, and put an X where Yuma's tipi was. "At least it is close to the water. Once we get across, we should high tail it here as quickly as we can."

"We need a diversion," said Zeke recalling his military tactics class. "But I can't think of any."

Josh smiled. "I was thinking the dynamite might come in handy."

"Oh, I see. Boom and the Indians run this way, and we run the other way."

"That would be too easy," laughed Josh. "We need something that will make that big Indian and a lot of his braves leave the village in pursuit of us, but in the wrong direction."

"How are we going to do that?" asked Zeke.

"Let's enlarge the map. If we attack another war party heading to the plains, but this time using our guns, and then we send them home with bullet wounds. If we set off several sticks of dynamite, what would it sound like to the Indians back in the village?"

Zeke smiled. "It would sound like the cavalry is attacking with cannons, which is crazy, but they might fall for it. I wish we had a bugle."

"I think we'll have to be very fast. We'll kill the war party quickly, and send a shot up dead Indian back, insuring they become furious, and gallop down the trail to see what happened. We set fuses for the dynamite. Then we'll sprint to the village, snatch the kids, and run like hell," grinned Josh.

Zeke laughed as well, but then his face fell deep into thought. "No, we would not know if a bigger war party went to investigate, nor would we know if the big Indian left the village. I think we have to split up. Jeremy and I will attack the war party, set the dynamite, and then send one dead man back, and we'll run to join you. Meanwhile, you watch the village, and if most of the Indians leave including the big Indian, then you sneak across, lead the kids to safety, and start this way. We'll meet and help you with the kids. We'll hide in the cave for several days until we feel safe enough to head for home."

"That sounds like a story out of a dime novel, but you're probably right. Let's think on it and get some sleep. I've crawled amongst the bugs for too long."

"You're not sleeping with me until you scrub that mud off your face," teased Zeke.

Josh and Zeke made love on a bare hide near the fire. They no longer worried if Jeremy could hear them, and he did not mind, but did masturbate in sync with Josh's thrusts. He couldn't help but wonder what it felt like to be either the top or the bottom as the boys sure did enjoy doing it. He secretly watched them from time to time. Soon they all turned over exhausted and slept well.

They waited two days while carefully going over every detail as if expecting a grade from an academy professor. Josh decided they should leave before dawn the following morning. He would wait for the lookouts to change for the day shift, and kill the two fresh lookouts on their side of the stream. Meanwhile, Jeremy and Zeke would set up the rope trap once again. They took Josh's Winchester and Sharp buffalo rifle, along with Zeke's Winchester and binoculars, and Jeremy's Winchester and prized Parker shotgun. They strapped on their pistols as well. This time they intended to snare as many as possible in the rope and shoot them all.

Although Jeremy and Zeke needed to reach their target unseen, they could move faster than Josh because they were hiking away from the sleeping tribe. By dawn, Josh was just twenty yards from the first lookout with an arrow strung and ready. He saw the daytime Indian making his way to the lookout post. When the Indians met they spoke a few words before the retiring Indian finally headed down the hill to fall asleep in the village. Josh caught only a word or two from Yuma's teachings. Once out of sight, Josh turned his attention to the Indian just above him that had just begun his shift, and most likely more alert than his tired predecessor.

The man sat down on a rock making it a more difficult shot. Josh sighed, retrieved a nearby stone, and flung it high over the man's head. The man leaped to his feet as the stone crashed through the trees to the ground. Zip! Josh caught him dead center of his back. The man fell over. Josh rushed to him and found him still alive. Afraid he would scream, he snatched his knife, slit the scout's throat, and pushed the body down the hill out of sight. He took the warrior's arrows and broke them over a rock. He broke the bow as well, flung everything over the ridge, and wiped away any tracks he might have made, though wearing his moccasins.

Jeremy and Zeke completed setting up the rope and covered it with sand and leaves. Above the trail, they buried the dynamite sticks under big rocks at the base of some trees. The sound would carry better from the hill, and the damage to the trail would cause more confusion. They made a torch, and laid down two of the new wooden matches Zeke purchased in Denver at the mercantile store on their last visit. If this worked, he felt they would be forever indebted to British chemist John Walker who invented phosphorus tipped wood sticks in 1827. He and Jeremy practiced lighting them the night before in the safety of the cave. They cut fuses long enough to allow them time to light all the sticks and run away as fast as they could.

With no worry from behind, Josh kept his eyes carefully on the lookout to the northwest. Every time the man turned his head away, Josh moved five yards closer. It took almost an hour and Josh prayed a war party had not yet left, as he was not in position to see the camp. Finally, the man turned, Josh sprinted forward, and drew his bow. Zip!

The arrow went through the man's neck and stuck out the other side. Josh cursed as he had almost missed. The man dropped his weapons and tried to stop the blood with his hands. He could not speak or scream. Josh quickly ran to him, stabbed his knife deep into the Indian's heart, twisted it, and yanked it out as the dead man hit the ground with a heavy thud. Around his neck, he wore a cord strung with ears of the white men he had killed. It disgusted Josh, but he rolled the body over the edge of the cliff, destroyed his weapons, and tossed everything to the gorge below.

Josh wasted no time, sprinting down the hill to the stream, and then carefully made his way to the village. As the tribe began to wake up, one by one the slaves brought gourds and buffalo bladder bags to the river for fresh water, and hauled them back to camp. Other people hiked to the woods to relieve themselves. The activity around the water where he remained hidden frightened him. He spotted Yuma as he stoked the fire while arranging the hot coals to cook some breakfast. He and the small boy came to the river for water just twenty yards from him, but he knew better than to wave to him. He had yet to spot the big Indian. He looked up to the sun as it finally broke over the ridge, lighting the tops of the tipis, and began waiting and wishing he had a watch.

Zeke pulled out his pocket watch and realized it was nearly nine. He thought the Indians were a sloppy bunch and should have started a patrol much sooner. He and Jeremy checked their weapons and then settled in for the wait. Josh had reminded them the best possible opportunity would be late afternoon before the night lookouts made it up the hill. They could snatch the kids, and then in the safety of darkness, they could make their way to the cave. Nevertheless, they would have no choice of the time to start the attack, as it all depended on the tribe sending a squad down the trail.

Josh perked up when the Indian leader finally came out of the tipi, and quickly headed for the woods to urinate. Josh remained flat on the ground in some bushes, but studied him carefully. He was at least six feet four inches tall, much taller than any other Indian he had seen. He had several battle scars on his arms. The man returned to the cook fire, where Yuma made flatbread and folded it in half with some hot beef on the inside, an idea that had just come to him that morning. Mila Hanska gave the primitive sloppy sandwich a funny look, took a bite, and then devoured the rest, while putting his hand out for another. Yuma made him three before he stopped to drink some water. He grabbed his weapons, including his bow and arrows, his spear, and large tomahawk. His tomahawk was one of the first in the tribe made of metal instead of a rock. It was like a hatchet blade on one end, and a dull hammer-like head on the other. There were six just like this one among the warriors. Josh knew it could inflict serious gruesome wounds, and shuttered at the thought.

Mila Hanska left Yuma, walked across the camp, and began talking to his men. Soon after, six of the men flung themselves up on their horses, and left the camp. Josh smiled thinking so far so good. Mila spoke to more of his men and sent another six men to the north. "This is good," whispered Josh to no one. "He is dividing his forces for us. How nice," he added sarcastically, as he snatched a worrisome black bug flying around his face, and squeezed until it was dead. Mila gathered the rest of his men, and told them to prepare their weapons. If the squad found a wagon train, they would all attack with great vengeance. He cursed the white men and all who opposed him.

Jeremy spotted the riders, but waited patiently to yank the rope once more with the tied stick in his hands, and the rope wound loosely around a tree. Zeke cocked his rifles, and laid them where he could snatch them up quickly. As they rounded the bend at a gallop, Jeremy snatched the rope and ran around the tree as fast he could. He put his foot on the tree for more leverage and leaned back. The rope knocked the first three riders off their horses, one of which was trampled by the horse behind him. Zeke shot the man in the rear of the pack and closest to the camp.

Josh's ears perked up when the sound of the rifle echoed through the camp. All the Indians stood and turned in the direction of the sound. Jeremy let go of the rope, grabbed his rifle, and immediately fired hitting the next man from the rear. Zeke picked up the next rifle and hit another man in the face, sending him backwards over his horse. The last man quickly tried to turn his horse, but the other horses were in the way.

Jeremy turned back to the fallen warriors. The first one got to his feet, while holding his neck where he had a rope burn. Jeremy shot him in the heart. He ratcheted his Winchester, and took aim at the second Indian, who had caught the rope right across his eyes, and was partially blind. Jeremy never hesitated, hitting him with a headshot next to an eye. He swung his rifle slightly to his right and towards the partially trampled man as he got to his knees, aiming his bow and arrow at Zeke.

Jeremy grabbed his Parker and fired both barrels sending the Indian's blood and brains flying in the air behind him. Zeke grabbed the Sharps rifle as the last man began to retreat and nailed him. They ran down the trail, threw one of the men over a horse, and tied his body so it would not fall off. Then they slapped the horse on the rump sending him galloping back to camp, obviously dead from a bullet wound. Jeremy quickly retrieved their rope, and leaped over the dead Indians, while carefully avoiding leaving any footprints. He and Zeke ran back up the hill and began lighting the fuses, gathered their weapons, and then took off running to the north to catch up with Josh.

Josh heard the shots and knew by the sound which rifle had been used. He was a little alarmed at the sound of the Parker, knowing Jeremy must have needed it quickly to switch from the Winchester to the powerful gun. He smiled when he heard Zeke fire his Sharps rifle. He was still alive, he thought.

Josh turned to watch the commotion and confusion flow across the entire village. Mila Hanska ran back to his tipi, and yelled at Yuma to get the children inside. He quickly tied the flap down tight over the hole securing them inside. He then swung up on his horse and sprinted to the center of camp. He circled his horse calling to his men who grabbed their weapons and mounted their horses, and in less than a minute, the entire group galloped down the trail. They had gone but fifty yards when the dead man on the horse nearly ran into them.

They cut him off the horse and looked at his wounds. He had been shot. Angry, Mila Hanska and his Kaga Ozuye warriors continued galloping towards the sound of the rifles, leaving the dead warrior lying on the trail.

Josh cautiously made his way across the stream. He waited by a tree for two hungry looking dogs to move to the far side of the open area. He did not see any humans. The camp looked deserted, as all the slaves had been pushed inside the tipis. Josh ran to the back of Yuma's tipi, and carved an inverted V in the back of the tent. The children became frightened when they saw the blade of his knife pierce the dried hide.

Yuma's heart nearly stopped when he saw Josh's face come through the new hole, but sprung to his feet and leaped into Josh's arms as he stepped inside. "Hurry and be quiet children. We must get as far away as we can." He handed Yuma the squares of rawhide. "We must bundle their feet to hide their tracks. Put the fur on the outside, and tie them well, so they don't fall off. Do not make a noise or say anything. Do you understand?"

The children all nodded yes. Josh peeked out the tipi to see if the village was clear for their escape. Josh turned and winked at Yuma, who took up the rear as he stepped through the hole in the back of tipi, and made his way through the woods and across the stream. Josh waited until the children made it across and then he took off running south. He stopped and grabbed the little boy's hand. He heard the dynamite go off. It gave him a boost of confidence as he ran on, thinking so far their plan was working.

The horses of the Kaga Ozuye warriors reared up as the booming sound of the dynamite echoed repeatedly through the valley. Mila Hanska could not believe the cavalry brought artillery through the valley. "What kind of army does this?" Then he yelled at his men to continue to follow him, so they galloped down the trail ready to attack.

Jeremy and Zeke ducked down when they heard the warriors coming down the trail, and watched as they counted roughly forty men on horseback. Zeke noted the big man up front, and felt sure it was the Indian Josh had seen beat Yuma. He wished he could fire the Sharps right into the back of the leader's head, but that would give away their position. After the horses passed to the south and out of sight, Zeke and Jeremy quickly began running once more to the north.

Josh struggled to hang on to the kid, but the terrified boy never let go of him. Josh stopped briefly, and wrapped a rag around the little boy's wrists and hands almost binding them. He then flipped the child back over his head, and stuck his head up between the boy's arms. This allowed the boy to hang there as Josh ran. The girl and boy stumbled from time to time, but Yuma helped them up, and they continued their run.

They met Jeremy and Zeke after an hour of running. Zeke took over carrying the little boy as Jeremy led the kids along the ridge. They heard riders coming up the trail across the stream from them. Everybody rapidly found a place to hide from their view. At the sight of the big Indian, the children began to tremble with fear. Josh noted their alarm, so he smiled and winked at them, trying to assure them they would take care of them, and one day soon, he would take care of the Indian.

Mila Hanska and his men crept up the horse trail, slowly anticipating an ambush as they approached the dead bodies of his warriors killed in the initial attack. They saw the rubble from the fallen rocks, as well as the trees now lying across the trail. When they reached the other side, he studied the ground carefully, finding no tracks anywhere. It greatly puzzled him. They must have fired with long rifles and cannons, he thought.

Carefully, he moved farther down the trail towards the plains, looking left and right for shoed horse tracks, and found nothing but the tracks of their own ponies. He rode about two miles before finally pulling up. He did not believe the white man had guns that would fire over two miles. He decided to divide his force, sending half the men down the trail towards the plains to find the anticipated cavalry.

He retreated with the rest of his men towards the village. They never saw Josh, Zeke, Jeremy, and the children as they rode past their hiding places. Josh nodded at Mila Hanska as he led the war party down the trail. Zeke and Jeremy kept their eyes on him until he rode out of sight.

After they passed, Josh stood up and said, "That's only half of them. They've split up."

"The other half must be chasing our ghosts," grinned Zeke.

"Yeah, but they'll start looking for us soon enough."

Jeremy asked, "How long do we wait before heading out?"

"Our horse tracks are too easy to spot. We'll have to leave under the cover of darkness, and if possible, I think we should wait until it rains."

"That could be a while," said Zeke as he pointed at the blue sky through the leaves of the trees.

"Yeah," replied Josh, "but it is almost summer time. Maybe a thunderstorm will come to our aid. We'll spend days and nights standing guard. We'll scout the area watching for their movements. They won't give up easily, but maybe something will distract them, and we can get away. We must be ready to leave the minute it starts raining, and let's pray it rains at night. Come on, time to start running again."

They had been running almost two hours before they finally split up. Josh hid in the woods nearby, and waited to see if they had been followed. After exiting from a thicket, Jeremy cut east, put the children in the stream to avoid any tracks, and then turned upstream towards the waterfall and the cave. Josh waited almost a half hour, but saw no one. He could hear the Indians arguing at the site of the attack by Jeremy and Zeke. He felt confident they had gotten away secretly. Josh sighed with a bit of relief, left his position, and caught up with the group.

As they started up the hilly stream, the exhausted children began to falter. Josh picked up the girl in his arms, and Yuma pulled the teenage boy along. When they made the cave, they quickly deposited the children, and told Yuma to stay with them and remain quiet.

Josh, Zeke, and Jeremy returned to the trail taking limbs and wiping away every footstep from the mud near the stream heading south all the way up to the cave. They did everything in silence while moving quickly. Josh stood guard near the trail, as Jeremy and Zeke returned to the cave behind the waterfall. Jeremy knew the children were cold, so he added wood to build up the fire. Zeke gave the kids some beef jerky to chew on. They sat down on a deer hide and ate, as Zeke and Jeremy wrapped them in hides to keep them warm.

Once satisfied, Zeke turned to Yuma and gave him a big hug. "We missed you."

Tears fell from Yuma's eyes, "I knew you would come. It was the only thing that kept me from killing myself. Mila Hanska was as mean as ever to me. I suspected he would soon be getting rid of me. Thank you, thank you, and thank you," he added as he hugged Zeke once more.

Zeke smiled and introduced him to Jeremy. Josh came in the cave, and set his weapons down as Yuma leaped into his arms. He swung him around and around hugging him tightly. It made the boys proud of their success, but Josh and Zeke worried the worst was yet to come.

TWENTY-ONE

After arriving at the camp, Mila Hanska began barking orders at his men, and screaming at anyone that moved a tad slow. His anger was boiling over, and everyone in the village thought the cavalry could be riding in at any moment. Even if the army brought in a hundred soldiers, they were still more afraid of Mila. He sent men to check on the scouts, hoping they had seen something. He sent a second squad of six men to the north to be sure they were not about to be attacked from another direction. He put a dozen men on guard on the perimeter of the village. He was fuming at the killing of his men, though he felt nothing for them personally. He yanked his horse around in circles before galloping over to his tipi. He pulled his right foot over the horse's head and slid off as it came to a stop. He knelt down and untied the tipi flap. He yelled for Yuma to come out, as he wanted him to put traveling food together.

When Yuma did not respond, he became angry and yelled into the tipi. Hearing nothing, he leaned inside, and an immediately saw the light of the day leaking into his tipi through the two slits in the back. He went over and realized they were cut in the shape of an inverted V.

He fretted more about the V than the fact that his slaves had escaped. At first, he assumed Yuma had carved the V and led the children out. He would capture Yuma again, but this time he would return him to his camp where he planned to torture him over the course of many days. He would make the boy die slowly for the aggravation and damage he had created to his tipi.

He returned to his campfire hunting something to eat. There was no stew, no flat bread, and no hot tea. He sliced off some hanging meat with his knife, and sat down to chew and think about the V. He recalled the story his warrior told him about the last time Yuma was captured. He had been spotted riding with two white men who had killed several of his men. He knew the children had no relatives to come after them, so he quickly surmised one or both of the white men must have come for Yuma and took the children, too.

He took a stick and drew a circle for his village, added a long line for the trail, and put another circle where his men had been attacked and killed. He then made a circle where Yuma had been taken from his tipi. He drew small circles for the location of his scouts. He continued chewing on the meat while studying his drawings carefully.

Two of his men splashed through the stream behind his tipi. He turned to see them running to him. Quickly they began telling him both of the lookout scouts on the other side of the stream had been killed. Mila Hanska turned back to his map in the dirt, and he put X's over the location of the dead scouts. Then he put X's over the attack on the road. Suddenly, it came to him. The attack on the road had been a diversion. The two scouts were killed because they were guarding the way Yuma's rescuers came in.

He yelled at his men to call in his warriors. Minutes later, twenty warriors crossed the stream on horseback, and began scouting the ground looking for tracks. Finding none, he sent a squad of five to the northwest ridge, and two other men to replace the lookouts to protect his village. He felt fairly confident they would flee to the south, as that is where the two white men had been attacked last fall. He scattered his men with orders to find their tracks. They found none.

Rapidly, he moved his men a full hundred yards to the south before stopping again and scouting the ground. They found nothing. The lack of tracks confused Mila, but he was certain they had come this way. They moved farther south along the bank of the stream, and searched all around the area. Mila Hanska suddenly spotted a partial footprint of a moccasin. It looked fresh, and he knew it could not be one of his men. He knew white men don't wear moccasins, so he began to think perhaps another tribe had stolen his slaves. He thought about this for a moment. Arrows killed the first of his men, but bullets killed the second group, and there was also cannon fire. Could a tribe of Indians and soldiers attack his men in harmony? No, he said to no one. They must be Indian scouts, and he would hang them by their balls before sundown, and then peel their skin off and feed it to the dogs while they watched.

Did they steal his slaves? No, he thought. Soldiers could care less about his slaves, and how would they have known he had any? Maybe they were attacked on the trail, Yuma saw that moment as a chance to escape, and he took the children with him. No, he said again, the children were barefoot. Where are their tracks? Very frustrated, he yelled for his men to search more diligently. They moved farther south and for several hours, they combed the mountainside finding nothing.

Josh saw them coming from his hiding place in the brush. He quickly moved back to the cave while scanning the ground to make sure the human and horse tracks had been swept clean in the edge of the river. He slipped behind the falls and as everyone looked up to see him, he put his index finger to his lips indicating for everyone to be quiet.

Zeke whispered, "How many?"

"About fourteen on horseback," he replied. "They are spread from the top of the ridge down to the stream, and their eyes are on the ground looking for our tracks. He probably has the rest of his men searching northwest."

Yuma moved the children farther into the cave and out of sight. Josh whispered, "Jeremy, stay with the horses and try to keep them calm and quiet. Rub their snouts and scratch their ears if you have to, but keep your weapons ready. Zeke, you watch to the left, and I'll do the same to the right. Let's start with our bows in case it is just one or two men. If so, we'll kill them silently, and drag them inside to hide their bodies."

"And if the whole tribe attempts to breach?" asked Zeke knowing the answer.

"We open up with all the firepower we can muster. I'm going to prepare a few sticks of dynamite with short fuses just in case we need to take out a swarm of Indians."

Zeke sighed, "You think that could happen?"

"No, I don't. With the warriors spread out and looking for tracks, probably one or two men will either work their way around this waterfall, or come close to investigate. I suspect they do not know this area of the country very well."

"Why not?" asked Zeke?

"Their village had not been in that location very long. Most likely they were not there for the winter as there was plenty of firewood still available within twenty yards of the campground. The longer they are there, the less firewood. We used the same presumption behind enemy lines during the war. I doubt these men spend much time hunting. I think they prefer the taste of blood by killing settlers and robbing them of food, but there could be a few hunters in the gang. Okay, let's get ready," added Josh.

They stacked their quivers of arrows against the rock wall of the cave alongside their bows, tomahawks, rifles, and pistols, and secured their knives to their belts. They both fingered their second knife hidden in their right boot. Satisfied, they hunkered down so they could see out, hoping any approaching Indian would only glance in, see nothing, and move away. The warriors had no torches, so he felt confident they would not want to go into an unknown cave in the dark.

Yuma put the fire out, and the cave quickly became dark. Josh wished they could produce a ghost to scare the Indians away, but felt that might be impossible as well as ludicrous. He even wished they had a trained bear like the lion he once saw in a cage in Charleston that would let out a huge roar and scare everyone away. The thought made him smile slightly, but it soon disappeared as he began to think about how many people were depending on his decisions. He prayed they would win and then began waiting.

Mila Hanska remained near the stream along the trail to the plains where he stopped his horse and just watched his men intently as they searched the area. They were about several miles from their village and so far, they had found nothing but a partial print, and that was nearly two miles back. He wondered if somehow they had cut east across the stream, avoiding his riders going to check on the cavalry, and then crossed the trail heading due east by going cross country up and over the ridge. Maybe they had horses hidden farther down the trail to the plains and his squads missed them.

He looked back to the east searching the area for any movement but found none. He turned his horse due west and looked up the ridge. He recalled the killing of the two scouts, and wondered if the enemy on the approach to the village killed them or as they ran away from it. He decided if they found nothing more in the next few minutes, he was going to turn his attention to the west and over the ridge.

Cetan Nagin, the shadow hawk, worked his way across the terrain. He was by far the best tracker of the village, but his skills were far stronger in hunting deer, elk, bison, or bear, and not children. His ears picked up the roar of a waterfall so he kept moving towards it. He usually hunted north of the village where the game was more plentiful, and had never seen this waterfall. He slowly crept up to the edge of the crevice created from centuries of water and ice erosion along the stream and above the waterfall. Cautiously, he searched the ground, but found no sign of the Indian slaves he was looking for. He knew the children did not weigh much, but there must be a track somewhere. He froze where he was and looked around him in a circle. His grandfather had taught when he lost the track of an animal to just stop, and hold very still, and eventually, the animal would move, as it wasn't their nature to hold still. They would nibble a leaf, pull a berry off a bush, or snatch some grass from a riverbank. Cetan had often followed his grandfather's tactics, but this time he still found nothing.

He slid down from his horse and tied the reins to a limb. He climbed down the bank as silently as possible, scanned the riverbed with his eyes, and found nothing moving. He slowly reached into the water and brought a handful of the cool water to his face, while never allowing his eyes to stop scanning the area. His moved left and right hoping to find something out of place. He stood back up with his tomahawk in his right arm ready to swing. He began moving downstream towards the waterfall. The stream went wide at the crest, and then gently slid over the wall, cascading hard to the rocks below. He saw the clear pool created by the falling water and noted how beautiful it was. He walked around the shoreline, climbed down the side of the waterfall, and walked over to the edge of the pool, still searching the ground for tracks.

Suddenly, he heard the unmistakable sound of a rattlesnake. He froze, while slowly allowing his eyes to scan the area. The snake was on the bank sunning his skin on a warm rock. The rattler in his tail began shaking rapidly, warning him. Cetan stepped into the water, and gave the snake a wide berth as he went around the reptile and moved downstream. He moved back to shore and around the waterfall watching for snakes and the tracks of the children and those who helped them.

Josh nodded at Zeke as they could see the warrior through the water, though he appeared blurry while looking through the water cascading over the falls. They each threaded their bows and waited while remaining hidden from view. Cetan Nagin noted the water fell almost three feet from the back of the wall and wondered if he could cross the stream under the waterfall. He took a few more steps forward and realized he could do just that. He took another cautious step forward. Josh pulled his bowstring back, exhaled, and kissed the string to prepare to fire.

Cetan Nagin suddenly heard a long whistle. He turned his head until he heard it again. He turned back to the waterfall for a long second before turning and walking down stream on the muddy bank. Josh relaxed his bow.

Mila Hanska whistled the sound of a hawk to call his men as he turned his horse and began climbing the mountain to the western ridge. His men joined in line behind him. Cetan Nagin climbed the bank, returned to his horse, and swung up. He gave one last glance at the waterfall, and then turned his horse north to join the rest of the warriors.

Mila Hanska motioned for Cetan Nagin to pull up alongside him. "See anything?"

Cetan Nagin shook his head no. "Where do you think they went?"

"They could have double backed east to fool us by staying in the stream, and crossing over while we were investigating the attack. On the other hand, they could have killed our scouts and headed northwest over the ridge. It would have been a tough climb on foot, but they might have horses hidden on the other side, and already outrun us. I'm going to take the men, go over the top of the ridge, and look for tracks on the downward side. When we get to the top of the ridge, I want you to tie your horse off about twenty long steps down the far side and out of sight, then quietly hike back in here, and find a spot to settle down and wait."

Cetan Nagin scratched his head, "You think they are still here?"

"I'm not sure, but I just have a feeling they knew they could not outrun us, so they've hunkered down and hiding from us."

"How long do I wait?"

"Come home tomorrow morning if you don't see anything. Whistle the call of the hawk if you hear or see something. Be careful, these guys have already killed almost twenty of our men. I don't know if they are a tribe, or some strange white men. They are like a white ghost, but the blood they spill is bright red. They will pay dearly for their actions."

Cetan Nagin nodded his agreement and continued the climb to the ridge.

The former Civil War captain limped his way up and down the streets of Denver asking storeowners if they knew anything about three mountain men. He went to the barbershop, the livery stable, a restaurant, the saloon, until finally he came into the mercantile. Ed Leary spotted the rough looking man from the ladder where he was stacking can goods on the top shelf. He especially noted the CSA letters on the dirty band around his hat. He knew at once they were probably the renegade soldiers who had been robbing the settlers around the area.

Ed quickly stepped down the ladder and slipped to the back of the store as the captain looked into the glass countertop at the brand new shiny pistols. Ed caught his wife by the arm just as she started to the front of the store to help the customer. He whispered in her ear, "Go get the sheriff. That man is one of those renegade soldiers. Go out the back way."

She immediately felt frightened, but rushed out the back door, cut down the alley, and then back out to the main street. When she got to the sheriff's office, she found the place empty. She returned to the street, frantically turning left and right trying to spot him.

Ed fingered his derringer in his right pocket, and slowly walked up to the front of the store, "Good afternoon sir, may I help you?"

"This is a fine selection of pistols," said the captain almost too politely.

"I'd be happy to show you one."

"No, that's okay. I just need a little information. I'm looking for three mountain men, very handy with their weapons, and they have the ability to shoot a bow and arrow."

Ed chuckled, "I don't know anyone that can do that except for a few Indians around town. Mountain men died out when the fashions in Europe changed, and no one wanted any more beaver pelts. Silk hats are the style now."

The captain smiled slyly, but suddenly reached across the counter, grabbed Ed by his shirt and yanked him closer. "If I wanted a history lesson, I would have gone to the school at the end of the street. Now I think you're lying to me. Who are these men?"

The color fell away from Ed's face, and he swallowed hard, "I don't know…"

"Excuse me, sir," began the sheriff as he stepped into the shop with his rifle cocked and pointing at the captain. "You're assaulting one of my finest citizens. I'd appreciate it if you would let him go."

The captain looked back over his left shoulder while catching sight of the barrel of the rifle. He slowly let go of Ed who quickly stepped back. "I'm sorry. I didn't mean to scare you. My mistake," he added as he turned to the door.

"Keep your hands up where I can see them, and I believe it is time for you to leave our friendly town. We don't much like strangers who upset our folks. If you come back, you'll end up in my jail." The sheriff moved to his left and away from the door, but he never let his eyes leave the hands of the captain.

"I understand. I'll just head to my horse and ride out. Thank you for your help," he added with a great deal of sarcasm.

The sheriff turned as the captain went through the door, limped across the street, climbed into the saddle, and rode slowly out of town. The sheriff put his rifle down as he slowly eased the striking hammer down to a safe position.

Ruth came running into the store. "Ed, are you all right?"

"Yes, dear, I'm fine. Thanks Sheriff. I think he was planning to beat the pulp out of me."

"You're probably right. What did he want?"

"He was asking about three mountain men who could shoot bows and arrows."

"Bows and arrows? I've never heard of such a dumb thing. Why would they use bows when every white man I know has at least two guns?" he asked.

"I know, I thought it was weird too. Did you see the CSA on his hat band?" asked Ed wiping the sweat from his brow with his handkerchief.

"Yep, another Confederate soldier with no home to go to. Once they get a taste for blood, they just keep doing it. Somebody is going to have to shoot that man to stop him one day. Some of the settlers say there is a gang of these men robbing the farms. I spoke to a lieutenant who told me he had reports of them killing and robbing wagon trains as well. They try to kill everyone so there are no witnesses, but a few children have managed to hide and survive. His men have been on the lookout for them, hoping to catch them in act. I'd better head to my office. I'll see you later."

"Thanks again, Sheriff," replied Ed.

Once he was out of earshot, Ruth spoke up, "Who do you think they were looking for?"

"I suspect Josh, Zeke, and Jeremy. They're the only three mountain men I know, but I would have said two men and a boy."

"Why would they want them?" asked Ruth.

"I don't have any idea at all. I certainly hope the murderers don't come back here, but if they do, you slip out again just as you did that time, and I'll stall them."

Cetan Nagin crept carefully back up to the ridge as the rest of the riders continued down the hill and out of sight. He had tied his horse to a tree well below the ridge. He hoped his mount remained quiet. He found a spot behind a large boulder to hide and wait. He was tired as he had just returned from three days of hunting for an elk to the north, feeling frustrated that it was taking longer and longer to find good kills. He missed hunting with his father, and could close his eyes and still see his grandfather teaching him how to shoot a bow, and how to track an animal. Like his father, he had become the best hunter of the village, and one the tribe could count on to bring home food.

Cetan had been banished from his home tribe four years ago after falling in love with the squaw belonging to his best friend. He had a choice of staying and fighting his friend to the death, or leaving forever. He was not afraid to stay and fight, but he could not kill his friend, so he left in shame and wandered for half a year before joining Kaga Ozuye tribe. He wasn't always happy with the leadership of Mila Hanska, but he did like being part of a tribe again. He had a new squaw and a baby, and was as happy as he could be while still remembering the loss of his family.

Josh and Zeke kept their vigil until nightfall. Slowly, Josh crept out of the cave, worked his way down the stream, and then up the bank scanning the area for any sight of the Indians. He found none, and returned to tell Zeke, the coast was clear. He also told him a large group of black clouds was rolling in from the west. They should eat a good meal, pack up all their stuff, and prepare to move out if it started raining.

Yuma made loincloths from one of Zeke's old shirts for the two white boys and retied all their temporary moccasins. He also made a more modest shirt for the girl. After restarting the fire from the hot ashes, he helped prepare a hot stew, which everyone enjoyed. Josh crept back outside to carefully scout to the south to be sure the coast was clear in case the rains came as he hoped.

Zeke asked, "How long are you going to be gone?"

Josh read his eyes and saw the worry lines in his brow. "I know they are close, but I have to be sure they are gone before we reveal where we have been hiding. We won't have a second chance to hide once we come out in the open. I'll be back in ten minutes," he added with a wink.

Zeke nodded he understood and went about packing their gear. Just as Josh stepped out of the cave, Zeke looked at his pocket watch. He rarely felt a feeling of danger, but he did now. He just sensed something was wrong, but he had no clue what. After he finished packing their horses, he told everyone to stay quiet and ready. He reminded them if the Indians were gone, and the rains came, they would move out in a hurry to the south.

"Jeremy grab your bow and your shotgun, and come with me," said Zeke.

Jeremy asked, "What's wrong?"

"I hope nothing," replied Zeke, "but I have a very uneasy feeling."

Josh worked his way carefully down the stream, leaving no tracks for anyone to find, and felt thankful it wasn't winter, as the water would be near freezing. He climbed up the bank by stepping only on rocks and through a stand of high grass. He would move a little, and then freeze, allowing his ears and eyes to absorb the possibility of any movement. The forest somehow seemed different to him, so he held still longer than usual. In seconds, he realized the animals had fallen silent. He heard not a single bird, frog, or even a cricket. Even the flies and aggravating gnats seem to have left the area. The hair began to rise on his neck. He stared straight ahead. He held his bow ready, not wishing to use his loud rifle or pistol, but he would have no time to pull the string back and turn.

Cetan Nagin noted the movement near the bank of the stream, and crept very slowly onto the back of a huge stump upended in a big windstorm last winter. In his right hand was his favorite battle weapon, a prized metal blade tomahawk. In his left hand, he carried his bow that he slowly set down, so he could use his free hand to steady his climb onto the fallen tree. He froze when he noted Josh's blond hair rising through the grass. He dropped his eyes momentarily while readjusting his grip on his weapon. This was his best chance, he thought. He reared back and down like a panther about to spring through the air to attack his prey.

Josh's nose smelled the Indian just a split second before his peripheral vision noted the movement. He brought his bow up, but not to shoot—to defend himself.

Cetan Nagin flew through the air from his uphill perch like a panther. While descending, he yanked his right hand back, and began swinging it with all the force he could muster directly at the blond head of Josh. He intended to split the skull of this white man like a melon. At the last second before impact, he let out a terrifying guttural scream. The quiet birds suddenly flew, as Josh stopped the tomahawk just an inch from his scalp by gripping his bow in both hands, and ramming it up to meet the handle of the tomahawk.

Josh saw the sharp glistening blade up close, closer than he wished, but with the momentum of the dive, Cetan Nagin went over his head, and together, they tumbled down the hill to the stream. They went over each other several times, with Josh determined to keep the tomahawk from killing him. At the bottom, they broke apart, with the Indian still holding on to his tomahawk, and Josh realizing he had lost his bow in the fall.

Anyone could have panicked at this point but not Josh. He pulled his smaller tomahawk with the rock head from his waist belt, and they began circling, preparing for attack. Suddenly, the Indian stepped back, and let out a loud whistle much like the sound of the hawk. Cetan wished to let Mila know he had found a white man.

Jeremy heard the whistle and at first thought it was Josh, but Zeke pulled him back as they crept from behind the waterfall. "That wasn't Josh," he whispered as they held their bows ready to fire.

Mila Hanska rose up on his horse when he heard the call of the hawk. He knew it came from Cetan Nagin. He and his men were down near the bottom of mountain, and growing weary from staring at the ground, searching for tracks in the sand and finding none. Quickly, he let out a war whoop, and called to his men, who were scattered along an animal trail. They all began to gallop their horses back up the steep hill to the ridge as quickly as they could.

Mila Hanska ducked under the dead limbs of fallen trees that were the result of an early ice storm in the fall. One of his men was not far behind him, and he called to him to hurry along. Mila Hanska kicked his horse hard to force him up the precipitous terrain. He did not see the spooked mountain lion they had missed when going down the ridge, but the frighten lion leaped across a boulder, and sailed directly at him.

His horse had seen the lion, and suddenly bolted forward. The lion missed his target, catching the bare back skin of Mila Hanska with his left paw leaving deep clawed marks that quickly turned red as the blood flowed. The lion could not stop his momentum, dug his rear paws into the hindquarters of Mila's horse, and leaped onto the man behind the chief. The lion instinctively bit the man right in the neck, and together, they tumbled off his horse as it reared and then began falling off the trail out of control.

Mila Hanska winched at the pain from the claw marks, looked back and noted the lion on top of his man, but called to his men to hurry up the hill, leaving the whimpering wounded Indian in the mighty mouth of the lion as he chomped down breaking the bones in the poor man's neck, and crushing his windpipe. Rapidly, his claws ripped the bare chest of the Indian as if made of paper. The lion's mouth, neck, chest and paws were all covered in bright red blood. The man fell limp and surely dead. The lion began dragging his prey down the mountainside, as the man's heart slowed and finally stopped.

TWENTY-TWO

Mila Hanska hated the fact that when he came over the ridge he was farther away from Cetan Nagin than the rest of his tribe. He let out a whoop, and kicked his exhausted horse harshly. White foam dripped from the horse's neck as he responded with a few quick steps, but the terrain was difficult making even a trot impossible. This frustrated Mila Hanska immensely, as he took great pride in leading an attack not following it.

There were men just a hundred yards away doing their best to push their horses through the brush and fallen trees from the ice storm. The forest looked like God had dropped the trees from at least ten miles up. Slowly, the Indians had to weave back and forth as they quickly made their way towards the enemy.

Josh knew he needed to silence the tall Indian as quickly as possible, as he most likely alerted the rest of the warriors. He swung quickly, as the man finished his animal call. Cetan Nagin fended of the blow with the back of his axe, and countered with a quick overhead swipe. Josh rapidly twisted his body, as he spun around to his left, barely escaping being chopped in the back. However, Josh did not stop his movement, but continued to spin, while bringing his right hand up for another blow. His right arm was momentarily out of the Indian's view, and the Indian reacted too late. Josh hit him hard at the shoulder of the warrior's left arm, damaging the muscle. The man screamed out at the pain. If Josh had possessed the metal tomahawk of his enemy with the glistening sharp axe, the fight would have been over.

Unfortunately, for Josh, he brought his tomahawk back too slowly, and the Indian reacted to the pain by throwing a sideward slash towards Josh's head. The pain of his wound caused him to swing slightly upward as Josh ducked. The blade took Josh's hat off, but left his exposed head unharmed.

Josh came up with his knee driving it deep into the man's groin. The man lost the strength of his legs and arms as the pain in his genitals raced with violent signals through his nerves to his brain. He tried to swing the axe again, but Josh came up rapidly with his tomahawk breaking the man's right arm just a bit up from the wrist. The hunter's prized axe fell away.

Josh fell back as the man grabbed his arm, and then reached for his knife with his left hand. The Indian took a deep breath to push the pain away. Suddenly, he charged Josh with a head butt so hard into his chest that Josh let go of his tomahawk, as he tumbled backward. Josh managed to bring his left hand up to grab the wrist of the left arm that held the knife, eighty percent of his strength had left him, but the heart of a warrior pumped inside his chest. He gritted his teeth and pushed downward with all his might. He tried to apply his right arm, but the pain of the broken bone caused him to turn nearly white with throbs of pain.

This was a mistake as it left him no arms to defend himself. From the moment Josh tumbled and lost his weapon, he began reaching for his knife in the sheath on his belt. Now as he lay on his back with the stone sharpen blade of the big Indian's knife ready to take his life away, he wasted no time by quickly bringing his own knife up and thrusting it into the top of the man's stomach. He pushed it in as deep as he could, then savagely yanked it left and upward, breaking a rib before stopping the well sharpened blade directly into the man's heart.

The Indian's eyes went wide, blood oozed from his mouth, and the Indian's knife began to shake, as his strength and life left him. Josh easily moved it away from his face. Cetan Nagin eyes suddenly faded and froze. Josh pushed him away and scrambled to his feet. He snatched up his weapons, including the prized metal tomahawk formerly belonging to the attacker, and spotted Zeke and Jeremy trotting towards him.

"Are you all right?" asked Zeke, his arm aching from holding the bow, trying to decide whether to shoot the Indian or not.

"I'll live, but we're in big trouble." Suddenly, they heard Mila let out a war whoop to call his fellow warriors. Josh sighed, "The time for bows and arrows is over. We must grab the guns quickly!"

All three boys took off on a run, no longer trying to hide their tracks, and rushing into the cave. Once inside the cave, they quickly dropped their bows and grabbed their guns. They returned to the stream, and cautiously crept up the bank.

"There they are—coming down from the top," said Josh as he pointed.

Zeke turned to his right. "There are along the ridge. How many warriors are coming?"

"Fourteen maybe fifteen," replied Josh.

"Okay, I'll do the math. That is just five apiece to kill," laughed Zeke.

Josh gave him a look, as if indicating he had lost his mind. "Five? Are you crazy? I'll have to kill half yours for you!"

Jeremy started to laugh, but as the Indians moved quickly down the mountain, his smile fell from his face. Josh noted the change, and winked at him. "Okay, here's the plan. We use our rifles first, then the Parker shotgun, and the pistols. I'll start by using the Sharps. Maybe I can kill a few before they even get close."

Josh loaded a cartridge and took aim at the last Indian he could see. It was the man just in front of Mila Hanska. Boom! Josh hit the man square in the chest, knocking the suddenly limp body backwards and into the face of Mila Hanska's horse. The horse reared violently while desperately trying to get away from the man and the blood, and spilled the chief backwards off his horse. He slid down the hill and before he could get to his feet both horses galloped north as fast as they could through the brush leaving him on foot.

He spun around and rushed to the top of the ridge so he could see where the shot had come from. Just as he made it onto the ridge, Josh fired again. Boom! The shot once again took out the last Indian he could see.

"Why aren't you taking out the closest Indian?" asked Jeremy. "They are almost to us!"

Josh pushed another cartridge in the barrel. "I was saving them for you and Zeke. That's two for me and only three more before I can sit back and watch you and Zeke take out the rest!"

Jeremy was incredulous and disbelieving at how calm Josh remained in spite of the doom they faced. He looked at Zeke who shrugged and smiled. "Time to go to work. Make your shots count and don't rush. Do it just like we practiced. Exhale slowly, and hit the man dead center of the chest, as that gives us a greater chance of success in case he moves suddenly. Count your shots. Fire!"

The boys fired at the rapidly approaching warriors. The warriors seem to care little for their lives as they charged. Thankfully, the rush to climb the steep ridge had worn their horses down. They easily killed the first three. As they got closer, Josh set down the Sharps, and picked up his Winchester. He chambered a shell rapidly and fired.

All three boys had to duck as numerous arrows flew into the dirt near their faces. They quickly spread apart and fired again. Jeremy missed his first target, and the Indian shot an arrow at him. It bounced off a rock and dinged him in the left arm.

"Ow!" he yelped, and fell back.

Zeke spun around, "Are you hit?"

"Yes, in the arm," replied Jeremy, wincing as he looked at the arrow going in one side of arm, and the stone hanging out the back.

Josh yelled at him, "No time to fret. Break off the shaft and pull it through. Tie your bandana around it, then pick up your rifle, and defend your life. Do it now!" he ordered.

Jeremy immediately did as he was told, though he had never heard Josh talk to him like that. Partly because he was angry, and because he was scared, he quickly did as he was told. By the time he tied the bandana around the wound, he knew Josh was right.

The Indians were rapidly dismounting, and running to rocks and trees for cover while firing. Zeke caught another man in the stomach. The man screamed at the pain, but his legs failed him, and he tumbled down the hill. Suddenly, the Indians stopped charging. Mila Hanska had caught up with them. He ordered them to surround the white men and wait for his signal to fire. They began quickly running from tree to tree.

"What are they doing?" asked Zeke.

Josh replied, "If I were them I would circle us. There are still more of them than us. We've got to move to a better spot, as they will charge at any time."

Josh turned around and searched the area. Not far from the waterfall were several boulders, and a few fallen stumps due to the caving in of the riverbank. "Follow me!" he ordered.

They grabbed their weapons and made a run for it. They leaped over and around the debris just as two arrows screeched through the air hitting the stumps with a thud and quiver. They dove for cover, but came back up with their rifles. They were in the center of the rubble and reasonably protected from all sides. The trio turned with their backs to each other forming a loose triangle of firepower.

"Reload! Don't fire wildly. Let them gain their confidence and when they get close, shoot them dead," said Josh solemnly.

"What if they charge at once?" asked Jeremy.

Zeke leaned into Jeremy knowing he was scared. Zeke knew he was scared, too. "We have guns and they don't. The guys with the guns always win." He paused and added, "We're also better looking."

"Let's hope so," replied Josh with a grin, as he patted Jeremy's shoulder.

The Indian strategy instantly changed from charging with bedlam to the role of hunters determined to stalk and kill the white men. Each climbed and crawled until they could see the hiding place of the evil white men near the waterfall. Mila Hanska peered from behind a bush next to a large tree effectively hiding his position. With the waterfall to the west, the stream banks high on the south and north, they could only escape east. He hoped they would try to make a run for it, heading straight to him. They would not make it, he thought. Suddenly, he let out a yell.

The Indians began firing their bows. The boys quickly ducked down behind the rocks as dozens of arrows continued flying in and around them. Zip! Zip! Zip! The boys waited patiently, realizing they were wasting arrows, and half hoped they would run out when Mila Hanska let out a whoop, and they stopped. Using sign language, he motioned for three men on their side of the stream to charge. They crawled to the top of the bank, reared back with their tomahawks, and charged. Mila Hanska cared little for the life of anyone but himself. He let out a whoop for the rest of his men to fire another volley of arrows, knowing the white men would have to fight the three attackers, and probably rise up enough to be shot by the arrows. He also knew his men would probably die as well.

Jeremy saw the three men just as they leaped. "Look out!" he yelled. He brought his rifle up, and fired, killing the first man. Josh and Zeke spun, but did not get a shot off. They brought their rifles up to defend themselves from the tomahawks. The two men landed on top of Josh and Zeke while knocking Jeremy's rifle down. Jeremy struggled to draw his pistol, but had to duck down to avoid the volley of arrows.

Josh did not waste any time. He was in no mood for another Indian fight. He swung the butt of his Winchester hard into the Indian's jaw with a vicious upper cut. He heard the crack of the man's jawbone, which caused such pain that the man reacted to the blow by standing up. One of his warrior's arrows caught him in the throat. Josh pushed him over the log, but took an arrow in his left hand. He leaped back and broke it off, pushed it through, and tied his bandana over it, pulling it tight with his teeth while watching Zeke.

Zeke struggled with his man. He could not get his rifle from the Indian's grip, as he dropped his tomahawk, and tried to yank the gun away from the white man. Reluctantly, Zeke suddenly let go. The man lost his balance with the abrupt release of the gun and started to fall back. Zeke took advantage of that moment of confusion, instantly drew his pistol, shot the man in the face, and snatched his rifle back with the other hand as the man tumbled backwards.

Josh grabbed Zeke, and pulled him down as three arrows zipped right above the heads. One of the arrows took Zeke's hat off, but left his head unarmed. "How many more?" asked Zeke.

Josh thought a second, "Maybe ten, and the guy that beat on Yuma. We'd better get ready for round two."

Mila Hanska used hand signals again. Two men swung up on their horses, and backed away from the bank about forty yards. When the big Indian gave the signal, they gripped their tomahawks with their right hand, held on to the horse's mane with their left, and kicked with all their might. They drove their terrified mounts right for the riverbed, and directly at the three boys.

Josh heard the charge, turned quickly, and grabbed his Sharps. "Grab the Parker!" was all he had time to say as the two horses sailed outward from the bank. Josh managed to pick up the Sharps, load a cartridge, and start spinning around towards the charge in the flash of a few seconds.

214

Suddenly terrified, Jeremy fell back. Zeke picked up the Parker. Josh knew the poor horses had no hope of reaching the other bank safely. It was a desperate leap. The horses and the Indians would most likely come crashing back to earth crushing Zeke, Jeremy, and Josh.

Boom! Josh fired the Sharps right at the left flank of the lead horse, turning it slightly from their position. "Fire!" he yelled at Zeke.

Zeke brought up the Parker, and fired hitting the second horse in the gut with both barrels. The blast nearly cut the entire breast of the horse away, and it fell quickly to the ground just in front of the rocks. Blood and tissue matter went everywhere.

The Indians dove from the dying horses, one of which slammed face first into a rock in the stream and came up bleeding. Josh dropped the Sharp and shot him with his pistol before picking up his Winchester. The other Indian rolled in the shallow water, and came up charging with his tomahawk. Jeremy had gathered his wits about him by shooting him twice before the man fell back into the water.

All three boys fell back to the ground both to hide from more arrows, and to regroup and reload. It had been a staggering display of the enemy's fortitude and determination. Josh knew they would have to kill them all, right down to the last man. "Reload everything as quickly as you can. Get ready. There's about eight to go."

Just as they finished their reload, Mila Hanska ordered all his men to charge at once. The arrows flew for just a minute, and then they dropped their bows, and raised their tomahawks as they charged. It was a desperate suicide charge, but he was counting on at least some of his warriors getting to the white men.

Josh had just pushed the last shell into his rifle when the Indians charged. Using their Winchesters, they fired quickly. They dropped warriors left and right. Jeremy took a hard smack to the stomach from a thrown rock tomahawk that ricocheted off the boulder in front of him. He fell back out of breath. Josh shot the man as he ran towards Jeremy with his knife pulled.

Zeke and Josh had dropped their empty rifles, and pulled out their pistols. They fired until somehow they managed to kill them all. Jeremy was almost in shock, so Josh shook him. "Reload," he ordered, and then looked at Zeke and winked. Zeke sighed, feeling amazed they were still alive, and tried to smile back. Blood dripped from Josh's wounded hand, and oozed from Jeremy's arm, but they had survived.

They remained behind the rocks as the smoke from their guns rose through tree limbs to the sky. Josh did not see Mila Hanska, but the big Indian saw him. He stared at his enemy, vowing his men would be avenged. He would torture them, cut fingers, ears, and toes off, twist his knife in their eyes,

215

peel their skin from their torsos, and finally cut their hearts out and feed the meat to his dogs. It would be a long, slow, and very torturous death for these three white men. He looked around, and abruptly realized he had lost his horse in the battle. He spotted a fallen warrior's horse wandering downstream, ran to him, and rode towards the trail on the other side to assemble the rest of his men.

Josh knew the chief was still alive. Suddenly, he got a glimpse of him riding hard through the forest. He wanted to go after him, but knew the man was smart, and most likely went for the warriors he had sent after the diversion. "We've got to get out of here quickly before they come back with more men. He gave each a congratulatory hug. Let's saddle up and ride."

They rushed back to the cave, quickly redressed their wounds, unpacked more ammunition, and loaded their Indians weapons and supplies. Cautiously, Zeke crept back out to check for more Indians. He stood guard as Jeremy, Josh, and Yuma led the horses out from the cave. They put the little boy with Yuma on the packhorse. The older boy rode behind Zeke, and Jeremy pulled the girl up behind him. Zeke gave him a wink, and Jeremy blushed as she clung tightly to his back.

Josh led them down the stream until they could turn south in the valley. Once there he picked up the pace going as quickly as they could.

Zeke asked, "What about our tracks?"

"No need. They know where we are. We'll try to lose them later, but right now, we need to put as much space between them and us as possible. They'll have to go for reinforcements, and we need to head south to the fort. Let's go!"

They had but an hour of daylight left, and Josh hoped to use every bit of it. He had no plans to stop, as they needed to move all night, but he knew after dark they would be forced to go slower. He looked up to the sky and realized he was about to get his wish. Lighting zipped across the sky followed by a big boom. The horses neighed at the streaks of lighting and the sound of thunder, but when the rains came, they settled down. The rain started slow, but soon became a huge downpour. He hoped it would slow the Indians down as they tried to track them, but on horseback, they would still be easy to follow. He had no idea how an Indian could stay on a rain soaked horse without a saddle, but he in his heart he knew they would.

Earlier that morning, the renegade captain yelled at his men to pack up their camp and get ready to ride. It had taken days until he secured information from a settler about Josh and Zeke. His wife worked at the bank in town, and she had met them many times. He now knew their names, but no one knew exactly where they lived. Thankfully, she had no idea they had bought over a thousand acres of land in the past few years. The best information he had was one to two days journey north of Denver. He had ridden south to meet his men, and robbed a settler homestead for more supplies before turning north. He had only fifteen men now as some had been killed, others wounded badly, and two deserted. He would have hunted down the deserters, but his desire for revenge on the men who shot him with the arrow, and killed several of his men, drove him to only one reprisal goal at a time. He would not rest until the men who had fooled him were dead, and he would make sure they would not die easy.

His men grumbled, as they wanted to rob more settlers and wagon trains, and head south to Mexico. The captain would have none of their complaining. He shut them up by expertly shooting the ear lobe off the man who complained the loudest. No one bothered to whine aloud again.

"Move out. Let's go!" he yelled. "It's time to ride!"

Mila Hanska met the riders he had sent chasing the cavalry on their way back to camp. He asked questions about their search and soon confirmed his suspicion, the firing of the rifles and explosions were all an aberration to divide his warriors and set free his slaves. He quickly told his men how the white men had stolen the slaves, killed his men, and they would ride south. He told them they must revenge the death of their friends, and they must kill all the white men until there are no more left. He yelled at the warriors to mount up and ride. They had never seen him so angry. They responded with war whoops, shaking their weapons in the air.

They crossed the stream with a force of twenty-one men including Mila Hanska. They carried all their weapons: bows and arrows, tomahawks, knives, and even spears. As they turned south, the rain began to fall. In minutes, they were drenched, and miserably wet and cold. They said nothing. They followed Mila Hanska as he quickly led them back to where he had last seen the white men.

It was dark by the time they reached the stream leading from the waterfall. He did not allow his men time to find his dead warriors, as he thought the scene of their deaths might make them fear the white men. He pushed them south rapidly, stopping now and then to search for tracks that were rapidly disappearing as the rain fell to ground. He knew the white men were on horseback, and they would run because that is exactly what he would do.

Jeremy asked, "How far are we going tonight?"

"I hope to find the cave where we left our extra supplies. We'll need more ammo to defend ourselves from the next wave of warriors."

Zeke asked, "How many Indians this time?"

Josh asked as they climbed a hill in the rain, "How many went in search for the cavalry?"

"About twenty," replied Zeke.

"Yuma? Were there any warriors left in the camp?" asked Josh.

"Probably not, maybe the night time scouts—everyone left for battle except the women and children and a few old men. There were scouts protecting the camp, but they are most likely still guarding the village."

"That makes about twenty or so, and the big Indian will lead them." Josh turned back to Yuma on the packhorse. "What is this chief's name?"

Yuma immediately spit, "He ain't no chief. He has no honor. He is a devil and a brutal master. He would have killed me soon because I was getting too old. He kept his slaves young so he could control them with fear and intimidation. He raped me thousands of times. He raped the girl, and even the older boy. He'll come all right, and he won't quit until he kills us, or we kill him." He paused then lowered his voice and said, "His name is Mila Hanska, demon warrior."

The anger in Yuma's voice surprised them, but in his eyes, they could see his tears. Josh knew Yuma would be killed if he was recaptured, and he was not about to let that happen. Josh knew he would have to kill Mila Hanska, and he would not regret doing so.

TWENTY-THREE

They reached the cave by dawn, exhausted, wet and tired. Unfortunately, the rain had stopped. Josh ordered them to quickly repack the extra supplies, with Josh taking some of the dynamite, and loading it in his saddlebags. He and Zeke also filled their saddlebags with all the ammunition they could hold. They all reloaded their weapons, including their bows and arrows. Josh then led Yuma out of the cave, and together, they climbed up a big rock so they could see.

"I need for you to take two horses and continue south. Do you see that ridge?" asked Josh as he pointed southwest.

"Yes, we were attacked there."

"That's right. You'll take the girl and the two boys, and wait for us there. We're going to ambush and kill as many of them as we can, and then we'll ride up and join you. If we are not there by nightfall, then go over the ridge riding west. Do you think you can find our home?"

Yuma nodded affirmatively. "Yes, but I don't want to leave you behind."

"I know, but I can't take a chance on them catching you. We're going to have to fight them eventually, and I'd rather it be here, and not in our valley. You have a bow and arrows, and there are pistols in the saddlebags. Use them if you have to, but try to stay hidden, so if any Indians get past, they will not find you. Walk in the stream when you can, and try to hide your tracks. I'll see you soon."

Yuma hugged him tightly, and Josh leaned in and kissed the top of his head. "Boy, you need a bath," he teased.

Yuma laughed. "I'm looking forward to jumping in the hot springs." He finally smiled, and Josh smiled back at him, giving him a wink of the eye.

They put the oldest boy and his little brother on the packhorse. Thankfully, the older boy had ridden a horse many times on the wagon train journey to the west. Yuma climbed up on Jeremy's horse, and pulled the girl up behind him. Zeke, Jeremy, and Josh shook hands with Yuma and sent them off.

After they were out of sight Jeremy asked, "So which one of you is going to walk back because I'm taking Zeke's horse?"

Josh and Zeke looked at him and laughed. Josh spoke up first, "You're assuming we're still alive to ride back."

"Yeah, I bet those Indians can't wait to scalp your ugly old head," added Zeke.

Jeremy gulped. Josh smiled. "We're kidding. We're smarter, and better looking than any of those Indians. We're immortal," he added sarcastically.

"Now here's the plan. We're going to slow those Indians down a bit. We'll string up another rope across the trail. We'll quickly cut some sharp sticks, and add them to the trail hidden by leaves. Do you see those rocks up there? We're going to put some dynamite under them, and blow them up. They'll come crashing down the hill at a swift pace.

"We're going to silently kill the last men with our bows, then when they are split up and distracted, we're going to use our rifles, and kill half or more. We can't let them capture Yuma. They'll kill him. Neither can we let them have the children."

Zeke laughed. "Yeah, we'd better not let them capture us either."

"We won't. Let's get busy. We don't have much time."

They left their horses safely tied off near the cave. Jeremy took care of the rope, but this time he added three ropes together, so he could pull it at the last minute, but from a safe and far away position. He tied a handle to one end and measured it so he could jerk it back and lock the handle in a fork of a tree and then run up the ridge.

Zeke took the small axe from his saddlebag and began making dozens of sharp sticks. He found a section of the trail where it narrowed between some big trees and boulders. He covered the sticks with leaves and then ran up the ridge.

Josh took several sticks of dynamite to the top of the ridge. He packed them in the dirt beneath the upside of the rocks. These boulders were the size of two wagons, and once they started to roll, there would be nothing that could stop them. When Zeke arrived, he set about making a torch so he could light the dynamite quickly. He then found a position where he could fire his weapons from an advantage on the ridge to the valley below. He left his rifle there, but took his bow and arrows as well as the torch, and went back to the first stick of dynamite to wait.

Josh and Jeremy ran quickly north along the ridge until they were three hundred yards from the rope and sticks. Carefully, Josh scanned the forest until he found several clear channels where they could fire their bows between a few tree trunks, and take out several warriors on the trail. They moved downward until they were within a safe range of success for their arrows. They remained hidden by brush, but they could see the trail to the north at a small clearing. Seconds later, they saw the first of the riders. Josh whistled the sound of a hawk. Zeke lit the torch.

Josh and Jeremy counted twenty-one men including the man they most wanted to kill, Mila Hanska. The Kaga Ozuye warriors looked even fiercer than the first group, because they had added the familiar black and white stripes to their faces. They rode with some speed while watching the trail for tracks, and the familiar metal horseshoes. Every time they saw a hoof track, they let out a yelp.

"I'll take the last man. You get the second from the last," whispered Josh. "I'll go first. You fire as soon as you can, but hit him dead center of the chest. If we're spotted, and they take cover, we'll shoot as many men and horses as we can, and get the hell out of here."

Jeremy nodded, but Josh was already pulling the string back on his bow while carefully sighting his target. Zip! He hit the last man just before he would have made a turn in the trail. Zip! Jeremy hit the next man. Silently, both men fell from their horses into the bushes along the trail. Their horses continued following the warriors down the trail.

"One more time, and then we run south," whispered Josh.

Zip! Josh hit his target. Zip! Jeremy took down his man as well. The warriors were now a little south of them, and looking down the trail and up the ridge, but did not bother to look behind them. Quickly, the boys ran along the ridge. The trail led off to the east, allowing them time to continue ahead of the warriors. Jeremy sprinted downward about fifty feet from the top of the ridge. He snatched up the handle tied to the rope and waited to yank.

Josh knelt down behind his second firing position. Zeke looked down at the short fuses he had prepared in the dynamite. He would have to run from the first to the fifth, and then dive behind a boulder so he would not be injured from the blast, but the timing of the rolling rocks was crucial. He could see both Josh and Jeremy as they waited.

Suddenly, Mila Hanska pulled his hand up stopping his warriors. He studied the ground and found recent tracks of the horses. Excited, he urged his men forward, and they once again began sprinting without noticing the loss of four of their men.

Josh sighted his target with his bow. Zip! He hit the last man. Zip! He hit the next man. They had just fifty yards to the rope, and then the sticks. Jeremy gripped the handle with one hand so he could yank and run quickly around the tree, and then drop the handle in the fork, sprint up the hill to his next position, and out-of-the-way of the anticipated rolling rocks.

With just forty yards to go, Josh deliberately hit the rear flank of the last horse. The horse suddenly shrieked out at the pain and reared, spilling his rider. The frightened horses in front of him suddenly broke into a gallop. Jeremy yanked the rope as hard as he could, spun around the tree to pull it tight, and dropped the handle in the fork just as the first man hit the rope with his throat at full gallop. The taut rope flipped him backwards into Milo

Hanska, knocking him from his horse as well. Jeremy never looked back, but ran quickly up the hill.

Zip! Josh hit another Indian. Zip! He killed again. Jeremy grabbed his bow, and began firing as well. They wanted to use their bows to hide their location for as long as possible.

Two more Indians went down after hitting the rope, but the next one saw the rope, pulled his knife, and cut it. Milo Hanska got to his feet, and began running after his horse. His men passed him quickly, and suddenly, the first horses hit the sharp sticks, reared up at the pain, and horses and riders began falling all over the trail. Two of men were impaled on the sticks, and then run over by the panicked horses.

Zeke took a breath, and ran along the ridge dragging the torch so it lit each stick of dynamite in succession. Boom! Boom! Boom! Boom! Boom! Zeke heard and felt the first explosion as he dove behind a large boulder. Josh glanced back as memories of war cannons echoed through his head.

Josh and Jeremy watched as the big rocks began rolling down the hill. They were a bit slow at first, and Josh feared they might be too slow, but they doubled their speed with each roll.

The nearest Indian leaped off his horse, and fell into the bushes to hide from what he thought were cannons. Mila Hanska could not catch his horse, but dove behind the trunk of a large oak tree. Suddenly, they started hearing the thrashing of something crashing down the mountainside. It reminded him of a big grizzly charging through the woods to protect her cubs. Terrified, the Indians were afraid to move. For some this was a fatal mistake.

As the rocks whizzed past them, Jeremy and Josh once again began firing their arrows. Zeke ran down the ridge, and knelt down beside Jeremy with his rifle.

The rocks began rapidly rolling across the trail. Each rock took out several Indians. Heads were crushed and bones were broken. Some lived, but could not walk or shoot a bow. A big boulder just missed Mila Hanska by glancing off the big oak tree. The concussion knocked him backwards as the tree was toppled. As he struggled to his feet, he looked south, and watched helplessly, as his men were crushed. Their screams terrified him, and he ran farther into the forest to avoid the remaining boulders.

Josh felt they had reduced their force by two thirds, but he knew they had to kill them all. They set down their bows and picked up their rifles. Jeremy and Zeke began firing their Winchesters. Josh picked up his Sharps buffalo gun, and easily picked off two more Indians. They also shot the wounded men lying on the ground, injured from the rope, sticks, or rocks. They did so without mercy, as they knew these men never gave compassion to any of the settlers or wagon trains. If one lived, they would continue searching for them forever.

Suddenly, Josh spotted Mila Hanska as the Indian stared up the hill. The Indian began yelling at the survivors to run east into the forest to keep from being shot. Josh sighted him quickly. Boom! Josh fired just as Mila Hanska took a step behind another tree, moving down the ravine to the stream, hiding from the barrage of gunfire. The abrupt movement saved his life, but the screaming spiraling bullet took the top half of his left ear off. Blood spurted into the air, as he dove and rolled down the hill and out of sight. He placed his hand over his throbbing ear, as the blood ran between his fingers, and down the back of his arm. Mila had never heard such a powerful rifle. Though bleeding, he moved rapidly into the forest and out of sight.

Josh cursed, knowing he had not killed him. He also knew the ear wound would hurt like hell. He slightly smiled. He loaded another cartridge, and continued firing at any Indian still moving. By the time they ceased fire, only four warriors survived. Josh hesitated, as he wanted to charge down the hill and kill the rest. However, his scouting experience taught him to attack aggressively, then retreat, and plan another attack to finish them off.

The three men snatched up their weapons, and sprinted to the cave. They reloaded their weapons. Zeke and Jeremy would have to ride the same horse. Josh took the lead, as they quickly rode up the ridge and out of sight.

Yuma heard the explosions and gunfire, hoping his friends survived, and that Mila Hanska had not. He tied off the horses, and took up a guarding position looking down the ridge. He gave the older boy a pistol, and though the boy had never fired one, Yuma hoped he could kill at least one if they were attacked by surprise. He gave knives to the girl and little boy, hoping they would defend themselves.

Mila Hanska stood up after several minutes of silence. His head was ringing as the blood continued oozing down his neck. He could not hear the horses of the white men as they sprinted up the ridge. He quickly tore off part of his shirt, folded it into a pad, and then tore off a long strip of his shirt. He put the pad on his ear, though extremely painful to touch, and then used the longer strip to hold it in place, as he tied it over his head. He then set about gathering up his men.

It shocked him to discover his force had dropped from twenty to just four. He counted bodies and realized at least four others were missing. He called with the sound of a hawk, but heard nothing in reply, hoping some of his men escaped the rolling boulders.

Josh pulled his horse to a halt as he heard the hawk sound. He knew it was Mila Hanska, and he knew the next fight would be far more difficult.

Mila Hanska and his men gathered up scattered weapons. Many of their bows and arrows were broken, but they took good weapons from their dead friends, caught their horses, and swung up to ride. He then made an experienced battle decision. The ambush had been successful because the enemy had time to plan it. Now the white warriors were on the run, and no time to prepare another. It was time to sprint forward and charge them.

He drove his horse up the ridge. Then they searched the area where the rocks had been, but found no boot prints as the boys were still wearing their moccasins. They headed south on the ridge until they found hoof prints. They began tracking the two horses to the south. He thought perhaps there were only two of the white men alive, so they still outnumbered them.

Yuma heard the sound of the horses approaching from the north. He drew back his bow, and held perfectly still and ready to fire. Moments later, he recognized Josh on the lead horse, and immediately relaxed his bow with a big sigh.

"Are you okay?" asked Josh as he rode up to him.

"Yes, we're fine."

"Not more than four or five left," said Josh solemnly, "but they will continue tracking us. We must move on quickly."

Jeremy slid off behind Zeke and returned to his horse. The girl rode with Jeremy, Yuma took the packhorse and the little boy, and the older boy rode behind Josh, giving Zeke's horse a break. The group reloaded their saddlebags by retrieving more ammunition from the packhorse. He led them along the ridge until it moved downward to a valley, and then he turned up a stream, stopping briefly to allow the horses a much-needed drink.

Zeke asked, "Where to?"

Josh sighed, "I don't want to lead them to our home. I think we should head south to the safety of the fort, or even Denver if we have to. What do you think?"

Zeke spoke after a moment of thought. "If we head towards the fort, we might get lucky and pick up an army patrol like the one that helped us with the women and children from the wagon attack. They could take the children to safety."

Josh nodded in agreement and turned southward in the stream. Suddenly, out of nowhere a dozen Indians surrounded them with their bows already pulled!

"Hold still, and don't move," said Josh softly. "Damn." He feared they were done for. With his rifle lying across his thighs, he knew he would be shot with at least three or four arrows before he could raise it and fire.

Yuma suddenly began speaking rapidly to the Indians. He knew they were Crows from the northwest, and normally lived in the Yellowstone river basin of Montana and Wyoming, the old hunting grounds of his family. The Crows were fierce warriors, winning many battles against their neighboring tribes. The Crows initially hated the white men, and demonstrated their hatred vehemently by initially attacking the explorers and mountain men, and later the settlers and wagon trains with a vengeance, but in time they became one of the first tribes to make peace with the white men. Eventually they would allow the railroad to cross their lands. While they never trusted the white man, they no longer killed them.

The leader of the Crows began speaking rapidly back to Yuma. Slowly, they lowered their weapons allowing a long sigh from Josh and Zeke. Yuma told them of his escape from the Kaga Ozuye village. He said there were many Crow women and children in the camp. He said they had killed all but a handful of their warriors. He urged them to ride north to save the women and children in the village. He warned them of the scouts around the camp, but said they could easily overpower them.

The leader nodded and smiled at Josh, Jeremy, and Zeke, as Yuma explained they had killed many of the Kaga Ozuye warriors. He acknowledged they were great warriors and he respected them. The friendly Indians began moving away on foot upstream. Josh led his group south, thankful to still be alive. He hadn't planned on the possibly of running into another tribe. They were lucky they were friendly and he hoped their luck would not run out.

They were about ten miles away from the battle on the ridge when darkness fell. He felt there was a chance they could reach a patrol by morning, but little chance of reaching the fort before the warriors caught up with them. He kept pushing his group, moving all night, though slowed by the shadows.

By daylight, they had followed a stream southeast until it reached the edge of the plains. They allowed their horses a good drink. Now that they were off the ridge, and out of the forest, they began picking up the pace to the south looking for a patrol or the fort.

A few hours later, Mila Hanska followed the stream closely searching the riverbank for the exit of his enemy from the water. When he found it, he smiled, and urged his men along. When they reached the valley, he realized the white men had picked up the pace, as the length of the horse strides had increased. The warriors began giving chase.

TWENTY-FOUR

The former Civil War captain finished his coffee and a dried piece of beef. He was in an ill mood because they had yet to find the three white men who had attacked him. Every morning he massaged his buttock, and tenderly felt the scar from the surgery removing the arrowhead. It still ached, particularly after a long ride, but it gave him reason enough to continue their search.

Within the hour, they broke camp, and began riding north along the ridge searching the valley below for a campfire or the fire from a cabin. They found nothing, but the weary renegades pushed on anyhow.

By late afternoon, exhausted from their long ride, Josh pulled to a stop at the top of a hill. He searched the horizon for movement, just as he had done on the last twenty hills with no luck. This time, he saw the sun reflect off a moving piece of shiny metal.

"Zeke, grab your binoculars, and look that way!" He pointed south.

Zeke snatched them from his saddlebags and brought the field glasses up quickly to his eyes. "Six men, and I believe they are in uniform. I don't see a flag, but I bet they are cavalry soldiers. What should we do?"

Josh hesitated, as he knew Mila Hanska could not be far behind, but he could not wait for the soldiers to ride on by without seeing them. Reluctantly, he drew his pistol and fired into the air. He holstered his gun and said, "All right, we need to ride fast as the Indians are behind us, and the cavalry is ahead. I just gave up our position in hopes of catching the cavalry's attention. We must gallop as fast as we can. Let's go!"

Sergeant Green lifted his hand to halt the squad, and turned towards the sound of the pistol. "Riders coming this way," he told them. "Prepare your weapons."

He lifted his binoculars to his eyes and announced, "There are three white men and some children. I doubt they are going to attack us, but keep a good eye. Let's ride to meet them. Move out," he ordered.

The ex-confederate captain also heard the gunshot as it echoed through the mountains, but as he tried to look in that direction, he could not see through the forest. He waited for a few minutes, but no other shots were fired. He turned back to the north believing someone was hunting.

Mila Hanska also heard the shot. He stopped his men and waited for a second shot that never materialized. It puzzled him, but he continued tracking the white men and children, and soon realized the trail led in the same direction as the gunfire. He rode on while unsure as to why they would give up their position. He wondered if it was another trap.

The sergeant called a halt to his men, and gave them an order to bring up their rifles just in case. At fifty yards, Josh slowed his group to a walk, as they moved closer to the squad. "Howdy," he called while smiling. "Boy, are we glad to see you. I'm Josh Johnson." He pulled his steaming horse to a halt, just across from the sergeant.

"I'm Sergeant Green. What can I help you with?" The sergeant began looking over the group, and realized the children were barely clothed, and one was an Indian.

"The Indian boy is my son," Josh lied, "but the other three white children were captured by the Kaga Ozuye warriors. They killed their parents and the rest of the wagon train, and took them as slaves. They need your help."

"How did you get away from them?"

"Well, several of their men attacked us last fall, and took my son Yuma. We were injured and could not pursue a rescue until late spring. We have been hunting their hidden camp for a long time. It is about sixty miles to the north. We created a diversion, got the children out of the camp, and have been on the run ever since."

The sergeant asked, "They are behind you?"

"Yes, but we have cut their force down from over forty warriors to four or five."

"How in the hell did you do that?"

Josh began explaining their attack methods, and soon the sergeant realized Josh and Zeke were obviously military trained. Josh explained they had military training at the academy before the war. He told the sergeant about their military school and the classes they took.

Becoming exasperated as to how long this explanation was taking, Josh directly asked, "Sir, I hate to rush you, but would you take the children with you back to the fort, send a telegraph to their relatives, and start them on their journey home? We'll turn north and lead the bad guys away from you."

"Well, that's kind of you, but don't you want us to stand and fight them?"

"There would be a chance the children might be hurt. We can handle the warriors. These Indians have black and white war stripes on their face. If you ever see one, shoot first as fast as you can. You won't get a second chance. Nevertheless, remember, not all Indians are bad Indians. We met a group of Crows yesterday, and they are going to the Kaga Ozuye village to rescue the rest of the Indian slaves."

The sergeant nodded, "I know. There are good white men and bad white men. We were looking for a bad bunch of white guys. They are a gang of about fifteen former Civil War soldiers. They have been robbing the settlers and wagon trains more often that the Indians. Stay away from them if you can."

Josh nodded, knowing exactly whom he was talking about. The children climbed down from the horses, and the soldiers pulled them up and behind them. "They're good kids and a bit shell shocked. It will take them a while before they will trust you, but they will. Thank you for your help. We'd better get going. Thanks again."

They waved to the kids as the soldiers turned to leave. After a few yards, they picked up their speed to a gallop, and soon out of sight over a hill.

Jeremy asked, "Do you think they will be okay?"

"Yeah," replied Zeke. "They won't have to eat Josh's biscuits!"

They all laughed, as they turned their horses to the north, and were soon hidden by the forest, as they began climbing to the ridge. Josh felt relieved the children were safe, and also glad the four of them could now ride faster if necessary. As their horses climbed, he began thinking about his predicament. Four or five Indians were trailing them, and perhaps somewhere ahead was the ruthless bunch of former soldiers. He began wishing they had killed them all on their last opportunity. He did not have to say anything to Zeke, as he knew the situation as well.

"Take the trail less traveled," suggested Zeke all of sudden.

"What?"

Zeke smiled. "Those coward soldiers are as lazy as they come. They will stay on the easy trails and find campsites with water. They will make big fires and talk too loud. We need to do the opposite. Head to the high ground, cross the steepest pass, and set a trap for the Indians. After we kill them, we'll turn our attention to the soldiers."

Josh grinned and asked, "When did you get so smart?"

"Well, it didn't rub off from you. It just seems logical to me. I guess those classes at the academy paid off."

Josh laughed. "Let me think this through. For your plan to work, the Indians have to think logically, and so do these lazy soldiers. Hmm…it just might work," he added sarcastically. The boys laughed.

When they reached the top of the ridge, Josh stopped. "Zeke, take your field glasscs, and see if you can see the valley behind us. I'd like to know for sure the Indians are behind us, but I'd bet the farm they are."

Zeke retrieved his glasses, dismounted, climbed on top of a big rock, and began scanning the valley. He scanned left and right, up and down until finally he spotted them. He counted aloud, "One, two, three…four, just four of them."

Jeremy grinned. "That's just one apiece. Why don't we take them out?"

Josh smiled. "Don't get over confident. We had surprise to our advantage last time, plus we knew the terrain. They are seasoned warriors. We'll have to look for a good spot, and ambush the Indians with a deadly attack."

Zeke asked, "Yuma? Are you okay?"

"Hungry. I'm starved," he said with a grin.

Jeremy opened his saddled bag and retrieved some hard bread and jerky. He gave Yuma handfuls, and then gave Josh and Zeke some.

"Boy, I can't wait to get back to our cabin and get a real meal," said Zeke.

"Yeah right, if you keep talking about my cooking you'll be preparing your own meal in the barn," teased Josh. "Let's go," he added as he squeezed his horse along the trail.

TWENTY-FIVE

As they worked their way around some big rocks on the top of the ridge, Zeke suddenly asked, "Do you think we'll ever get to have sex again?"

Josh pulled his horse to the left to maneuver around the next boulder, which afforded him, a quick glance, "Would you be quiet? The children can hear you."

Jeremy and Yuma laughed. "The whole forest can hear," said Jeremy. "We don't care, but I doubt this is a good time. We have a group of mean Indians to our rear, led by Mister Ugly himself, and ahead is probably a large gang of thugs. Uh, what's for supper?" he asked casually while grinning.

They answered in unison, "Beef jerky!"

They all laughed while enjoying a few moments to let the tension off, but there was no doubt their lives could change dramatically over the next few days. Josh fell deep in thought, trying to remember the terrain ahead, and wondering how they were going to pull off the two battles, so they could once again return to their peaceful home.

"I miss the hot springs," said Jeremy.

"I miss it, too," added Yuma.

"Would you shut up? You're making me homesick when I need to be thinking how we're going to survive the next few days," teased Josh.

"It'll be dark soon," added Zeke.

"I think that is when we should take the Indians out. I think we should kill them with our Indian weapons, so we can avoid showing the rough riders where we are. Nothing fancy this time, but we'll have to kill them quickly."

"And the plan is?" asked Zeke.

"Not far from here is a narrow pass leading through the boulders, but just beyond it is tight thicket. I think we'll send Yuma ahead with the horses. Yuma, you tie them off and when you hear my owl sound, I want you to pull your horse's tail."

Yuma asked, "Why do you want me to pull his tail?"

"I hope the horse will neigh loudly, just as the Indians reach the narrow pass. This will cause them to hurry through it. Jeremy, you're a good archer, so you're responsible for taking out the last two men. Shoot the last one, and before he hits the ground, hit the second one. Then come forward to help if needed.

"Yuma, after you make the horse whinny, come towards us with my Winchester rifle in case we need you. Do you remember how to shoot?"

"Yes, I do. I practiced in my dreams. I can do it," he said proudly.

"I'm sure you can. I'm so glad you're back with us."

"Thank you for coming to get me. I would have died soon had you not come."

"You'll be safe now—I promise."

"Zeke, you take the third Indian from the rear, and leave the big guy to me," ordered Josh.

"You sure you can handle him?"

Josh smiled. "I'm sure, but if I need help, go for a chest shot, and if you miss, you must tomahawk him to death. Don't stop swinging until you're sure he is dead. You can do it. I'm counting on you."

An hour later, they reached the spot Josh described. All but Yuma dismounted, removed their Indian weapons, including their knives, tomahawks, as well as their bows and arrows. He suggested a spot for Jeremy on top of a big rock with a smaller rock in front to hide him. Zeke worked his way across the trail and found another rock to climb and a place to hide. Josh knew the big Indian would probably react to Jeremy's first shot, as they would most likely be close together walking their horses on the tough terrain. He and Zeke would have to fire at almost the same instant to be successful. He also doubted the big guy would go down from a single arrow, but he would aim for the heart and hope.

Yuma reluctantly went ahead until he passed the boulders and entered the forest. He found a good place to rest the horses, and quickly tied them off to low tree limbs. He pulled Josh's Winchester out of the leather scabbard, and marveled at the engraving detail on the side of the gun. He walked back down the trail a few steps, and waited for Josh's signal.

The sun soon dropped behind the mountains to the west, while clouds moved in covering the moon. From time to time, the moon would peer between clouds, before once again disappearing. Josh hoped they would be able to see their prey, so they could take careful aim, but there was nothing he could do about it, so he might as well push it from his mind. Instead, he recalled seeing Mila Hanska slap Yuma, and force the older boy to service him on his knees. He made a solemn vow that tonight would be the last time the big bastard would breathe on this earth.

After midnight, Josh began to wonder if they were still on their trail, and hoped they didn't have to wait much longer. Five hours later, he heard one of the Indian's horses down the trail. He quickly signaled the others, and then looked to the east and saw daylight coming. If the Indians did not hurry along, the sun would expose their hiding positions, and none of them had bothered to cover their tracks though they still wore moccasins.

231

They knelt down low to prevent any sighting from down the trail. Josh heard a twig snap just forty yards away. He made his owl whistle softly. Yuma had almost fallen asleep, but quickly leaped up, and began pulling the horse's tail. The horse did not make a sound, but rather turned his head around, and gave Yuma a stubborn look. Yuma pulled harder, but the horse remained silent. Yuma panicked.

Josh wondered what had happened to Yuma, but decided he must have fallen asleep. He picked up a large stick, and was just about to throw it just off the trail to make some noise, when suddenly he heard his horse let out a loud repeated neigh.

Mila Hanska heard the horse and motioned for his men to hurry along. He gripped his bow tightly as he squeezed his horse's thighs to nudge him forward. The horse picked up the pace, but never reached a trot. Jeremy saw them first, dropped down, and threaded his first arrow with his second arrow lying on the rock within reach. He saw the big Indian up front and gulped. Then he saw the second guy, followed by the third. He waited until the third guy passed across from him when he sighted the last Indian and fired. Zip! He hit the man strongly in the chest. The man fell back slightly and then flopped forward on his horse. Jeremy quickly threaded his next shot.

Josh fired, but Mila Hanska turned slightly, and the arrow went in just above and to the left of his heart, but deep into his shoulder. Josh knew it had to hurt badly, and the thought pleased him.

Zip! Zeke fired, but though he aimed for the chest, the arrow actually hit the man's bow, and deflected into the rocks. The man quickly threaded his own bow, and pulled back aiming at the white man. Zeke quickly ducked behind a rock.

Jeremy fired hitting the third man in the back on his right side. The man did not fall. Jeremy reached for another arrow as the man turned and slid off his horse. He dropped his bow, lifted his tomahawk high, and began sprinting up the rocks towards Jeremy.

Mila Hanska quickly dropped down beside his horse on the opposite side of the trail from Josh. He wanted to thread his bow, but his left arm was nearly useless. The pain in his shoulder throbbed harshly. He broke the arrow apart just as it entered his shoulder, and tried to reach around to see if it came all the way through. However, the stone remained deep in his shoulder, leaving his arm limp. He looked down at the blood staining his tattered buckskin shirt. He snatched up his bladed tomahawk and carefully looked over the horse for his attacker. He caught a quick glimpse.

Zip! Josh fired at his head, but creased the top hide of the horse. The horse reared and took off down the trail, leaving Mila Hanska exposed. He dove behind a rock as Josh threaded another arrow.

Jeremy threaded a third arrow. He glanced up, but quickly ducked, as the man threw a good size rock at him. He took a breath and pulled the bow back quickly, as the man prepared to leap on him. The Indian drew back the tomahawk and charged. Jeremy bravely leaped up and fired, catching the man in the eye from just six feet away with such force the arrow went through his brain, and broke out the back of his skull. The man spun and fell like a rag doll tumbling down the rock, breaking the arrow, bouncing across the trail, and rolling down the hillside. Jeremy checked the first Indian he had shot to make sure he was dead as well. He saw no movement and his horse had stopped, but he took no chances and fired another arrow directly into the Indian's back and into his heart. He threaded his bow again.

Zeke cursed at his bad luck, but threaded another arrow and ducked behind the rock. The Indian leaped off his horse, and pulled back his bow ready to fire as soon as he caught sight of Zeke.

Zeke felt it was standoff, so he had to think of something fast. He knew the Indian was probably a better shot with a bow than he was. He took off his hat, and stuck it on a spare arrow. He moved it far to the left of the rock he was hiding behind and slowly let it rise. The Indian saw it and let go his arrow. Zip! Zeke heard the feathers whistle as the arrow flew just over the rock, barely missing his hat.

Bravely, Zeke immediately stood, sighted his bow, and fired a short ten-yard shot directly into the man's heart. He dropped like a stone, while bleeding like a gutted pig. Zeke turned to his right and Jeremy gave him a 'thumbs up' sign. He turned to his left, and spotted the big Indian. He threaded his bow to prepare for a shot. Josh was behind a rock with bow ready to fire. Zeke saw Mila Hanska carefully move from rock to rock coming up the hill after Josh. Before he could do anything, the Indian was out of Zeke's sight.

Yuma had to jump out-of-the-way when an Indian pony galloped down the trail towards him. Once the animal passed, he jumped back on the trail and chambered a shell into the Winchester. He knew the fight had begun.

Zeke motioned for Jeremy to protect the rear in case there were others, while he began going down the rock to find the big Indian to protect Josh.

Josh spotted the Indian once more, but knew he had fallen to the ground, and most likely coming up after him. He kept his bow ready. Zip! He got a glimpse, but it was a fake out by Mila Hanska, as he ducked down and the arrow missed him. The Indian leaped up and charged up the rock towards Josh.

Josh had no time to thread an arrow or grab his tomahawk. He swung his bow with all his strength, and hit the big Indian high on his left wounded shoulder. The bow bounced upward catching Mila's bandage head where Josh had shot part of his ear off. Mila screamed aloud in agony, and Yuma recognized his voice. The pain sent the big man down to one knee, but he quickly recovered. Josh swung again, and hit the bleeding rag over Mila's ear once more. The man screamed again at the pain, as his anger began to boil deep inside him.

Josh pulled his tomahawk from his belt, and crouched down ready to fight the big guy. The Indian knew he was bleeding badly, and would soon lose his strength, so he wasted no time, and leaped at Josh while swinging his sharp axe at Josh's chest. Josh deflected the blow with the head of his recently acquired metal tomahawk sending sparks into the air.

The two men slowly circled each other preparing for another attack. Mila Hanska did not wait long, faking a hard sideswipe, making Josh leap back, and then the Indian charged with a hard downward blow. When Josh stepped back, he tripped on loose stones, then fell back, and slid down the boulder hitting the trail with a hard thud. The fall knocked the breath out of him.

Just as he was about to get to his feet, the Indian dropped to his butt, slid rapidly down the rock, and then leaped right on top of Josh with the blade coming down hard towards Josh's face. Josh brought his tomahawk up to defend the attack, but the Mila's blade cut through the shaft of Josh's tomahawk. Mila Hanska brought the blade back one last time for a skull-crashing blow to Josh. Josh tried to scramble from beneath him, but there wasn't time.

Zeke saw him, and quickly tried to bring his bow up to fire. Jeremy turned as he ran across the top of the rocks, but before he could take aim, the axe began its rapid arc.

Boom! The sound of the Winchester pierced the early morning quiet, sending flocks of sleeping birds into the air. Josh swung his face to the left just as the limp exploded head of the axe fell harmlessly to the ground, mere inches to the right of his ear. Mila Hanska still held the remaining piece of the handle. Slowly he turned to see who had shot his axe, and discovered Yuma holding the smoking barrel of the Winchester. The big Indian smiled and threw the handle at the boy.

Yuma ducked to his left, chambered another bullet, and took aim at Mila Hanska. The big Indian pulled his knife from his sheath on his waist and laughed. "I'm going to carve you into a thousand pieces. I'm going to drink your blood and eat your heart."

Josh rolled several times until he was safely behind a rock. He drew his pistol to fire.

Boom! Yuma had pulled the trigger again. Mila Hanska watched the bullet race from the barrel to his chest in the blink of an eye. The shell hit him in the chest on his right side. He staggered a step, but continued moving forward.

Yuma chambered a third shell and took aim. Boom! He hit Mila Hanska in the stomach. The big Indian dropped the knife, and put his good hand over the wound, desperately trying to keep his blood from pouring onto the ground. He looked up at Yuma and snarled like a grizzly at him.

Boom! Yuma fired again deliberately hitting Mila Hanska in the genitals. The man roared in agony, like a wounded buffalo on the plains. Blood oozed down his chin where he had bit a chunk of his tongue off. He coughed up blood, and yet he still defiantly remained standing.

Boom! Yuma shot him in the heart. Mila Hanska dropped hard to the ground on his back. Josh stood, noting the man's eyes had frozen in place. He was finally dead. Josh turned and spotted Yuma holding the rifle as if waiting for the Indian to trick him and jump to his feet. He walked to Yuma and pulled the rifle from his hands.

"It's over. He's dead. He'll never hurt you again." He hugged Yuma tightly and kissed his hair. "You're safe now and you saved me. He was about to thrash me with that axe."

Jeremy and Zeke came running up to them. Zeke gave Yuma a big hug as well. "That was some shot. You hit the axe handle while it was swinging to attack Josh," said Zeke.

Yuma smiled.

"What?" Josh asked.

Yuma laughed. "I was aiming at the back of his head."

The three boys paused for a second and then laughed heartily, and then Josh asked, "Where were you aiming when you shot him in the right side of chest?"

"I aimed at his heart," grinned Yuma.

"Dang, it's a good thing I hid behind the rock or you would have hit me," teased Josh.

Zeke asked, "Where were you aiming when you hit him in the balls?"

Yuma smiled slyly, "That time I was aiming at his balls."

"And the last shot?" Josh asked.

"I aimed for his heart again. I guess my aim improved with a little practice."

"Thank goodness, or we'd all be wounded!" exclaimed Josh.

They all laughed and hugged young Yuma again.

Josh said, "Okay, enough jubilation. I'm afraid those shots were probably heard for miles. We'd better hurry and get out of here. Yuma, why don't you ride one of the Indian ponies? Jeremy, tie off the packhorse to your saddle horn and let's get moving. They'll be coming for us as quickly as they can." Josh quickly reloaded his Winchester, and then swung up into his saddle.

The captain's ears perked up when he heard the first shot. He stopped his horse, and put his hand up for the rest of the men to stop. He turned his horse around and heard the second shot. "It's from over that ridge." He scanned the terrain from left to right, trying to guess which way they were riding. He also wondered what the men were shooting at. He had not forgotten there were Indians in the area, but he felt his veteran soldiers could easily kill any warriors they came across.

"Bill, take several men, head up to the ridge, and pick up their tracks. Follow them as quickly as you can, and do your best to overtake and kill them all. When you catch them, fire three shots rapidly in the air so we can find you, and I'll take the rest of the men, and head up through that valley to the north. I'll try to cut them off should they escape you. If I get them, I'll fire three shots rapidly in the air so you can head our way. Okay, let's get moving. I'm tired of these bloody mountains, hills, and ridges. My butt's killing me. I'm ready to head for Mexico. Let's find these bastards, slit their throats, and head south. What do you say boys?"

The riders yelled with enthusiasm and then galloped off splitting their group. One group headed west, and the other galloped due north as planned. Together, they were ready to kill anyone in their path.

TWENTY-SIX

"Zeke!" called Josh. "Climb that rock and scan the area with your binoculars. We need to know where the renegades are."

Zeke looked up at the big rock, "Do I look like a mountain goat to you? That rock is almost straight up!"

Josh grinned. "You don't want me to answer that do you?"

Jeremy cut in, "Yes, Zeke, you look like a mountain goat."

Yuma laughed and added, "And you smell like one, too."

They all laughed before Zeke answered, "All right, all right, I can take a hint." He climbed off his horse, retrieved his field glasses from his saddlebags, and lifted the strap over his head so his hands would be free to help with the climb.

"Don't fall on your cute butt," teased Josh.

"I won't, I hope," gulped Zeke. He reached upward until he found a handhold, pulled himself up a few feet, and dug his toes in, reached for another hold, and then pulled himself up again. He did this over and over until he was thirty feet higher than the ridge trail. He knew Josh's hand probably hurt from his wound, and Jeremy was sore from his arm injury, so he didn't complain again. When he reached the top, he stood up, put the glasses to his eyes, and began scanning in a slow circle. He failed to see any movement on his first pass, but on the second he caught sight of a group as they came over a small mountain, and then disappeared in the valley below the ridge they were on. He counted the riders.

"Six riders just came over that ridge heading our way," yelled Zeke.

"Dang, there are more soldiers than that so they must have split up. He is using his war strategy. Scan the surrounding area, and see if you can spot the second group," replied Josh.

He knew without any hesitation they were trying to box them in. The other group would be heading up to their ridge somewhere ahead of them. His mind raced for military solutions to the problem, because he knew he had only one chance to save them and kill the ex-soldiers. He knew those men would be ruthless and kill them all. He looked ahead at the terrain and then called up to Zeke. "What is the land like to our west? Is there a deep pass or gorge?"

Zeke gave up searching to the north and turned west to study the land. He adjusted his lens until he spotted what he knew Josh was thinking about. "Yes there is. It's about five miles. We would have to go down the back side of this ridge, cross the river in the valley, turn upstream, and then branch off to the west."

"Come on down. Let's ride," replied Josh.

Zeke climbed down quickly, put his binoculars in his saddlebag, and tied the leather cord. "It's going to be a rough ride down this ridge, but once we're down we'll be okay."

"We need to hurry, but we'll have to take our time to keep from falling and flipping. We don't want to break the legs of one of our horses. I'll go first, but stay about ten feet back, and follow exactly where I do. Tie your gear down tightly as it is going to be very steep. If we have to, we'll get off and lead out horses down. Yuma, hang on tightly to your horse's mane. Let's go," ordered Josh.

They all saddled up, shortened their reins, and slowly followed Josh as he searched for a spot on the trail to start down. "Break off limbs when you can. I want these riders to find our trail. They are not as experienced as we are, and will mostly likely make a mistake or two going down this mountain. Of course, I'm also planning to set a trap for them."

They all wondered what Josh was thinking, but Zeke already knew what he planned. Several times the soft dirt gave away, causing Josh's horse to slip, but the horse bravely adjusted his footing and continued. Josh had to hold on to the horse tightly with his legs, and push back on the saddle horn with his good hand. He took the reins threaded through his palms and grabbed a good hold of the horse's mane to help him hold on, and to let his horse know he was counting on him. His bandaged hand throbbed, but he held on.

When they could, they broke limbs, and left them hanging downward, averaging a limb about every hundred feet. It took them three hours to reach the river where they stopped and let their horses rest, drink some water, and even feed on the grassy banks. All the horses were drenched in sweat from the effort, but they had succeeded what some would have thought at best fool hearted. To Josh's surprise, even the packhorse and the Indian pony made it. Yuma had to grab good handholds to keep his slender body on top, as his pony did not have a saddle. Josh congratulated Yuma as well as Jeremy as he led the packhorse down the mountain.

Josh asked, "Zeke, how far upstream before we turn west?"

"A few miles, we're going to attack them in the gorge aren't we?" asked Zeke.

"We've got to find a way to cut their numbers down as they have us at least three or four to one. They don't know some of our tricks, so we'll use our Indian weapons and other tactics—especially if we can catch either group by themselves. If they join up before we attack, it will be difficult for us to win."

"We have the advantage," said Zeke with a sly smile.

"How do you figure that?"

"They think we are four men instead of two men, a half a man, and a kid," replied Zeke.

Jeremy spoke up quickly, "I resent that. I've killed my share. I'm a man now."

Yuma laughed. "Jeremy, I don't blame you for resenting being called a kid. I killed Mila Hanska, so I must be the one they are calling half a man!"

The foursome laughed heartily while Jeremy tried to splash some river water at Yuma with his boot. "Okay boys, let's saddle up. We have some work to do," said Josh as he swung up into his saddle.

They turned their horses so they could cross the stream, and went up the bank with no intention of hiding their hoof prints. They followed the stream up the trail, going as fast as they dared, as the trail was little more than a deer path. Josh wished he was hunting wild game instead of bad men, but throughout his life he found himself having to do the opposite of what he wanted to do, so he and Zeke could survive. It was never a choice, but he willingly would do anything to get their peaceful life back again.

Bill's men were following the trail across the top of the ridge and soon found the Indians the foursome killed. It gave his men pause at the total annihilation of the warriors, especially the big Indian. He got down off his horse, and saw the numerous shots into the big Indian, and the remains of an arrow sticking out of his shoulder. Leading his horse, he followed the mix mash of hoof prints, until he found five fresh sets of prints. He thought there were only four, but now wondered if two men had been riding one horse. The new hoof prints were shoeless, so he guessed one was riding an Indian pony. Even so, he thought, they wiped out four Indians without a single death on their part. He began to wonder why in the heck he was chasing them on this ridge when he could be in town chasing a pretty girl around the saloon.

He looked up at his men and knew they were having second thoughts and doubts as well. Reluctantly, he called for them to saddle up. "They can't be far ahead. Keep an eye out and let's ride."

They rode about a hundred yards or so when suddenly the trail led off the ridge and down the steep mountain. He stopped his horse, looked across the land below, and realized the hill went down for as about as far as he could see. His shoulders drooped while thinking, why in the hell are they going down there? He sighed wishing they could turn back, but he didn't feel up to challenging the captain.

He led the men down the embankment though he knew if anyone had a choice, they would have turned around and headed back to town. The third rider went a little too fast. His horse suddenly slipped on the red wet clay. His hooves shot out the down side of the mountain, sending the horse crashing to the ground on his side. The slip happened in the flash of an eye, and when the men heard the crunch of a bone snap, they all cringed. The rider's right leg hit the upper part of the trail just a split second before the full weight of the horse crashed down on top of it, snapping the leg in two. The man screamed out at the pain. The terrified horse struggled to gain his footing, forcing him to roll on the man to try to get his balance, and they heard the man's hip snap as well as most of his ribs. The man passed out at the immense pain, letting go of the reins. The horse got to his feet and then began pushing his way down the trail before Bill could grab his reins and pull him to a halt.

He looked back up the mountain and saw his man down on the ground with his leg twisted in the wrong direction. It was then he noticed the man's lower body also turned at an odd angle to the upper torso. There were bloody rib bones sticking out of his chest. He had never seen any injury like it. "Is he dead?"

One of the men climbed off his horse, knelt down, and tried to shake the man's head to wake him. He felt his neck for pulse, found none, stood, and shook his head. The man was dead. He got back on his horse.

"Okay, keep it slow and steady. Let your horse choose where to step. Move on," he ordered as turned to face the steep decline. They abandoned the fallen man without a second thought, or even the mercy of a proper burial.

About half way down, the last man's saddle began to slip to the downward side. He tried to straighten it, but the horse's back was soaked with sweat. Suddenly, the saddle slipped forward as the horse stepped down and over a rock. The man tumbled over the horse's head causing the saddle to slip on to the horse's neck and slightly trapping his legs. He bucked upward with his front hoofs trying to shake it, causing him to flip sideways down the hill. He tumbled over a few times before the saddle buckles broke, freeing him from his predicament. He got up without breaking a leg and made his own path down the hill. The horseless rider had to walk the rest of the way down, cursing all the way.

"Did you hear something?" asked the captain as he put up his hand to halt his group. They fell silent anticipating a second scream, but heard nothing. "Come on, we'd better hurry up. Be on the alert," he ordered.

The captain's group reached the ridge, and turned south hoping to surround the four men they chased. He felt anxious to kill them, knowing that if this hunt took too much longer, his men would most likely revolt and mutiny. He would kill one or two if he had to make the others stay in line, but from then on he would have to watch his back, lest he found himself ambushed one night by his own men.

It was nearly dark by the time Bill's men could see the river. The horses could smell the water, and began going down the last hundred yards too fast. One of them slipped, but this time the horse rolled down the hill like a giant snowball. The rider tried to leap away, but his boot slipped through the stirrup trapping him. The horse landed on his side and immediately rolled crushing the rider, rolling over again, and crushing the limp body once more, and then as the poor horse rolled yet again he broke his front leg. In agony, the horse crashed down the embankment until he came to a halt against a big oak tree.

The horse made agonizing screams over and over. Bill drew his rifle, took quick aim, and shot the horse in the head. The bullet silenced the horse forever. He put the rifle in the sleeve, and returned to going down the hill while cursing their misfortune.

"Did you hear that shot?" asked the captain of his men.

They nodded affirmatively. The captain studied the trail ahead, and knew his men were most likely coming down the ridge. He looked down the mountainside and studied the terrain. He realized their prey had turned west down the mountain, and his men must have caught up to them and fired. Nevertheless, why no more shots, he wondered? He expected three rounds to alert him, or numerous rounds if in battle.

He looked down the ridge trail, "They must have turned west, and our men are chasing them. If we continue south, we'll miss them. We must go down this mountain to the valley below to rejoin them. Come on, let's go," he ordered.

The men sighed despairingly, but said nothing. This area of the ridge was not as steep where the other boys had gone down, but he worried nonetheless. He took his time with the trail, knowing one slip could kill him and his horse. He also thought about the men he was chasing. He knew they were smarter than most, and wondered if they were former soldiers like himself, experienced mountain men, or perhaps they lived with the Indians for a while, picking up their hunting and mountain skills. He wondered who they were.

He looked out to the west and knew the sun would soon be down. He wanted to hurry to the bottom, but with darkness arriving, he would have to go even slower to keep from terrifying the horses.

He sat back hard in his saddle, and hung on to his saddle horn to keep from rolling forward over the head of his horse. He would make these mystery men pay for assaulting his men. He would torture them for shooting him in the butt with an arrow. He would make them pay with more than their

241

life, if he could find a way to do so. He vowed to kill them as harshly as possible.

Josh heard the shot and guessed it to be back in the valley near the stream. With darkness upon them, he hoped the soldiers would make camp at the stream, thus affording them an opportunity to get ready. His eyes scanned the high ridges along the narrow trail heading to the west.

"I think this might be a good spot," he said to Zeke.

Zeke looked left and right. "There's a big boulder up there. It might come in handy."

"I saw it, too, but I think if the riders are still divided we should attack the first group with bows and arrows. Of course, if they see us, then will fire back with their rifles. The noise of the guns will easily guide the second group to this spot."

Zeke sighed. "So, we have to prepare for two battles at once. The first must be in stealth, but how about the second?"

"You're right, we will take the first group with bows and arrows, but the second we'll start with arrows, but once they return fire, we'll use everything we can at once. You take Yuma to the north ridge. There is more protection there. Although he is good with a bow, when it comes to the second battle, I'm afraid he might be shot. There will be lots of gunfire in the second battle."

"You and Jeremy climbing up there?" asked Zeke as he pointed to the southern ridge.

"Yep. You take some dynamite to put under that big boulder and prepare to light it during the second battle. I'll take some up with Jeremy and me. If we find a boulder we'll do the same, but if not, do you see those big trees leaning towards us?" He waited for Zeke to spot them before continuing. "I'll put a small charge at the base on the upper side, which will cause the tree to snap, and fall hard and fast across the trail. I hope to kill some while trapping the rest."

"What about the rope?" Zeke asked.

"Do we have any left?"

"Just one, but we can still use it. We'll have to go to Denver when this is over to buy more," added Zeke.

"You're right and we'll have to buy more of everything as our supplies are getting low. The problem with one rope is how to pull it to do some good and still get up to the ridge. I don't think it is possible. All four of us need to be up here ready to fire at the second group."

Zeke studied the terrain on his side of the hill and found a small boulder. He then followed his eyes down the hill into the valley until he spotted two trees, which were perfect for the snare. "I think engineering can solve that problem. You leave that to me," he added with a grin.

"What are you up to?"

"You'll see. Let's get the horses down the trail in case we need to escape. We'll take a bag of ammunition along with our bows and extra arrows. Let's do it fast so we can get some shut eye," said Zeke.

"Okay, boss," teased Josh, "whatever you say."

They moved down the trail a hundred yards or so, and found a spot to hide the horses. They tied them to a lead line stretched between two trees, removed their weapons, and split up some of the dynamite. Jeremy and Josh headed up the hill to the south.

Zeke spoke to Yuma while looking up the north hill. "I want you to climb that ridge taking your weapons with you. I'm going back into the valley to tie off the rope, and then I'll throw the loose end up for you to catch. All right, get to it," he added with confidence.

Zeke went back to the two trees and tied the end of the rope to the south tree. He then laid the rope across the trail and covered it with leaves and pine needles. He fed the other end under a low limb on the tree on the other side. He whistled slightly and saw Yuma lean out from the ridge above.

"You ready?" he whispered. Yuma nodded so Zeke flung the rope upward and Yuma caught it with a stick. Zeke watched as the boy pulled the slack out of the rope. "That's enough," he called. "Just hold it there. I'm coming up."

Josh and Jeremy went down the trail pass the point where they hoped to pen in the riders. Josh took a stick of dynamite, carefully cut it in half, and then put a fuse in the end of each. He went to the oak trees he had spotted and forced a stick of dynamite in the ground at the base of each one on the upside of the hill. He stretched the fuse out so lighting it would be easy. Jeremy smiled and looked forward to seeing the big trees explode and fall.

They moved back west on the ridge, found two more trees, and placed charges there as well. Then they moved to the center, and back east about half way, and found a fallen old log to hide behind. Each man laid out their guns to the right and their Indian weapons to the left.

"Jeremy, the first group we must kill as silently as we can, so prepare your arrows so you can pick up the next one, and fire as quickly as you can. You take the front of the group and I'll take the rear. I'm sure Zeke and Yuma will do the same. If they come during the night, it will be difficult to see them, but we'll be looking for them, and they won't know where we are. They aren't used to night travel in the mountains, so I hope they'll camp and wait for morning.

"When the second group comes, I suspect they will be double the size of the first so we'll start with the arrows, but they'll be too many to kill, and we'll be forced to use our guns when they start firing back at us.

"Once you fire your rifle then duck down and move two feet to your right and come up and fire again. Then move left and so on, so they will have to guess where to shoot at. Do not watch your man fall. Shoot, drop, move, and shoot again. It won't be like fighting arrows and tomahawks. We must move much faster to avoid being shot. Do you understand?"

Jeremy gulped, "Yep, I reckon so. Can we win this time?"

"Yep, we can," answered Josh quickly, trying to show how confident he had, but in his heart, he knew the odds were very much against them. "Okay, get ready."

They carefully prepared their weapons and then Josh handed Jeremy several matches. "When I tell you, run west and light the dynamite on those trees. I'll run north. Don't wait for the explosion, but instead run quickly back to this spot."

Jeremy took the matches from him, and put them in the crest of his ears like a man might put a pencil. They leaned back against the log and waited.

Zeke made his way up the ridge and walked to where he expected to find Yuma. The boy handed him the rope after he set his weapons down. Zeke took the rope, found the small boulder he had spotted from his horse, wrapped the rope around it several times, and then tied it off. He took a smaller rock and put it in front of the boulder and then using a stick, he carefully cleared the dirt around the front of the rock. When the rock started to roll forward, he quickly jammed the smaller rock under the front to stop it. "That'll do the trick," he whispered to Yuma. The boy looked at him like he was crazy.

They walked to a boulder and laid out their weapons just as Josh and Jeremy had done. He then buried a dynamite stick under a large boulder and laid a match by it to light the fuse. They sat down and prepared their weapons. Once secured, Zeke made the sound of an owl. Josh replied with the same. They were as ready as they knew how to be.

The hours ticked by and Jeremy suddenly had an idea. "Josh, could we cut a dynamite stick into thirds?"

Josh gave him a puzzled look. "Why would we want to do that?"

"If it was a little smaller, we could strap it to the end of our arrow, light it, and shoot it at the riders."

Josh chuckled. "You're liable to blow both of us up."

Jeremy paused and then replied with a grin, "So we're going to do it, aren't we?"

Josh laughed. "Yep, best idea of the night."

Carefully, they cut another stick in the smaller pieces as planned, added fuses, and then stretched some rawhide and tied it tightly around the end of the arrow.

"How does it feel?" asked Jeremy.

Josh felt the weight of the arrow before answering, "It'll drop faster so we'll have to aim two or three feet higher than the target from this ridge to the trail, but it might just work. At the worst, it will scare the horses into rearing and dumping their men preventing their escape. Once on the ground, we can pick the men off. Let's make about a dozen."

Josh took the first watch, and let Jeremy sleep a while. Jeremy took his turn about midnight and woke Josh about three. Zeke did the same pattern with Yuma. They were rested and ready by dawn.

Josh went east on the ridge while motioning to Zeke to stay quiet. He moved from tree to tree and then settled down where he could watch the trail leading from the river to the gorge. He chewed on some jerky, hoping to stop the growling in his stomach. It was a little more than hour before he heard them, but he waited until he could count them. There were five left in the group trailing them. He turned and made his way back to Jeremy, and quickly signaled the number five to Zeke by holding up his hand and pretending to count his fingers.

TWENTY-SEVEN

Bill watched the trail carefully, and felt relieved this day began on mostly level ground, at least compared to the ridge they came down yesterday. The horses and men ate by the river, and he allowed the horses a good drink before starting their journey after the mountain men. He easily followed their tracks and urged his men on.

He stopped when they turned west, and surveyed the terrain ahead. He saw the high ridge and sighed, hoping they would not have to climb yet another mountain. He hated this land while others thought the Rockies the most scenic in the west. He hated the cold, he hated anything to do with work, and yet here he was working his ass off trying to catch four or five unknown men because the captain said to. He wondered what had he gotten himself into.

His scout took the lead as he could track better than Bill. He waved to his men to follow the line, while he climbed off and took a leak. Once finished, he fell in line second to last. He felt some relief when he realized the trail led to a gorge that went right through the mountain instead of over it. They turned to their left leaving the open valley they had been traveling on all morning, and entered the thicker forest of the mountainside. He searched the ground, and saw the same pattern of five sets of horse tracks.

Jeremy and Zeke knew they had to kill the last men first so no one could escape and warn the rest of the riders. They both took aim and waited from opposite sides of the trail. They each counted off the men. Jeremy raised his bow aiming at Bill. Yuma took aim at the second man while Josh aimed at the first. Zeke had the last man targeted.

Zip! Josh's arrow flew strong and straight, and hit the man hard in the chest and into his heart, and out the backside. He fell in a slump over his saddle horn. Zip! Zeke's arrow was two inches higher on his target. The man took the arrow with a hard thud, then looked up to the ridge, and fell backwards off his horse.

Bill thought he heard something, and turned just as Jeremy fired. Zip! The arrow caught Bill as he was raising his pistol up, and turning his horse. The arrow bounced off his wrist causing his gun to fall to the ground, and deflected deep into his stomach. He took hold of the arrow, but could not pull it out. The pain nearly caused him to fall unconscious to the ground.

Zip! Yuma caught the second man in the back. The arrow came all the way through. The man only had a few seconds to stare at the bloody arrowhead just an inch beyond his heart. He then fell to the ground with a hard thud.

Zip! Josh shot the next man in the back, but the man drew his weapon to fire. Zip! Zeke moved his aim from the last man, and shot the man in the face. The man fell off his horse, and the gun did not fire.

Zip! Jeremy put a second arrow into the last man hitting him in the stomach. Zip! Yuma finished him with a shot to the chest. The man fell to the ground.

Bill painfully dismounted, and tried to walk to the cover of a tree, but he was coughing up blood, and his legs became weak. Zip! Josh fired another shot hitting Bill hard in the chest. He fell to his knees, and collapsed on top of both arrows pushing them all the way through his back.

Jeremy and Josh began running to the crevice where they could quickly descend to the trail. Zeke sent Yuma east to watch for the second group, and then he ran down the ridge to help the others. They loaded the men on their horses so the weight would look the same in case they had a good scout, and tied the bodies to their saddle. They removed their weapons, and hid them in the brush. They led the horses on down the trail about twenty yards, and then slapped their butts hard to make them run away. Jeremy even threw a rock or two at them. The poor horses were glad to get away and ran swiftly.

They covered the blood spilled with loose dirt and leaves, and then quickly ran back up the hillside to prepare for the second group. Josh knew the first group had been too easy, as none of the men appeared to be officers. The leader must be in the second group and therein the danger.

The captain and his men did not realize they were camping just eight miles upstream from the second group. The men followed him south along the edge of the stream until they found the camp of his soldiers. He followed their trail across the river, studying the hoof prints carefully. It bewildered him to find five new prints including a shoeless horse. He had no idea where this new horse and rider came from, or for that matter were there three men or five.

The trail was easy to follow, as his men's horses seem to be riding with purpose. He had followed the trail about a mile until he reached a muddy bog. He studied the hoof prints and noted the five mystery riders went to the left and his men went to the right. It was then he realized two of his men were missing. This puzzled him greatly, but then he remembered the gunshot, and wondered if one of his men had been shot. Thinking about the second missing man, he recalled hearing only one shot that echoed through the hills. He thought perhaps the Indians attacked them, and one of his men got off a single shot before dying.

The thought made him shiver with trepidation and anger. He scanned the trail ahead, and then turned to the mountain to his west, and wondered if they had already climbed up and over the mountain as the entire valley remained still and quiet. He walked his horse threw the bog, while taking the holding strap off his pistol. He sensed something was wrong. As he came around the end of the bog, he saw where the tracks all came together again leading into the forest.

Yuma spotted them, and quickly rushed back to the ridge. Zeke waved across the ridge to warn Josh and Jeremy. Jeremy remained to the west ready to light the dynamite sticks. Josh moved east to light his sticks, and carried his bow and arrows with intentions of killing the last few men as quietly as possible.

Yuma readied his bow while Zeke went to the small boulder. Carefully, he removed the small rock holding it. He kept one hand on it to steady it, and made his way around the back of it. He crouched down to hide.

Josh counted the men the moment he spotted them. His heart sank when he reached nine. He studied the captain and wished he could kill him first, as the rest of the men might panic, but he knew they had to kill them all, as one alive might return with more former soldiers to burn their home, and kill them in return. He knew this attack would be much harder as the soldiers would be firing bullets instead of arrows at them, and they were experienced soldiers.

He waited patiently, knowing the ex-soldiers had to lead their horses around a short stand of brush and briars. At this point, the first rider would not be able to see the last riders. He put a second arrow on the log he hid behind. He drew his bow and began counting the men once again. When he saw the last man start around the trees, he fired. Zip! He caught the man in the throat preventing his ability to yell out.

He snatched up the second arrow. Zip! He shot the man again, hard in the chest slumping him over. The riders passed the first big oak tree. Josh grabbed bow and arrows, struck the match, and lit the fuse in the stick of dynamite attached to a tree.

Josh ran fast as the fuse was short. He knelt down to the light the second fuse when the first dynamite exploded. The tree trunk splintered and the entire tree quickly began falling across the trail. The blast caused him to shake, and he dropped the match. Quickly, he picked it up, struck it, lit the second fuse, and ran.

The horses reacted to the sudden blast by wildly turning in circles before taking off on a run as the tree slammed down across the trail hitting the last two men. It snapped the neck of one man, but the other rolled free though scratched heavily on his face from the limbs. The horses galloped hard down the trail, but the captain pulled his horse to a stop, as he surveyed the ridge.

Zeke yanked the smaller rock from the boulder and it rolled off the ridge. The captain heard it, drew his pistol, and fired as Zeke ran to Yuma. He caught Zeke in the thigh spinning him to the ground.

The boulder fell harshly yanking the rope tight across the trail just in time to catch four of the riders, knocking them from their saddles to the ground. The rope broke the windpipes on two men, leaving them thrashing about the ground until they passed out and died.

Jeremy lit his first tree, ran to the second, and on to the third. Boom! Boom! Boom! The final three trees came down swiftly, and fell across the trail. Josh shot another soldier with his bow. Yuma hit one, too, but by the time Jeremy and Josh reached the log, the remaining men were firing upwards at them. They picked up their rifles and fired in return.

Zeke rolled out of sight of the trail, removed his bandana and tied it over the wound, then crawled to the rock and reached for his Winchester, and began firing on the men. He was afraid to light the buried stick of dynamite because he might not be able to crawl away fast enough.

The men below were caught in the crossfire. Josh and Jeremy took turns shooting, and though it seemed like eternity, one by one, they were killing the riders.

The captain darted across the trail and dove behind a log. He fired a shot at the rock where Zeke hid, sending splinters of rock into Yuma's face. The boy stood up as he rubbed his eyes. The captain took quick aim just as Zeke grabbed the boy's arm, and yanked him down. They both heard the captain's shot whistle over their heads. Zeke crawled to the other side, putting the rock between them and the captain. Zeke then rolled to his back, took a leather cord from his carry pack, and tied it around his leg above the wound to slow the bleeding. He then broke an arrow in two, and used a piece to twist the cord tight slowing the blood flow. He then crawled to a spot where he could resume shooting.

The captain knew there were at least two on the north side, and from the sound of the gunfire, he suspected two more on the southern side. Where was the fifth man, he wondered?

In fifteen minutes, the boys had cut the renegades down to just four men, including the captain, but they were all dug in, and trading shots like the early days of the Civil War across an empty field into picket lines.

"Time to try out your new weapon," said Josh.

Jeremy grinned and put down his rifle, picked up his bow and carefully picked up one of the arrows with the small stick of dynamite attached.

"Try to aim for the rock just below Zeke and Yuma on the valley floor. There are two men hiding below it. I'll be ready to shoot them should they try to leap out of the way."

Josh struck a match and carefully lit the fuse and yelled, "Fire!"

Jeremy rose up, took quick aim, and fired his bow. He aimed high as Josh suggested, but his aim was too high, and the arrow stuck in the ridge wall about ten feet over the heads of the men. They looked up and saw the arrow with sparks at the tip, and wondered what in the hell it was. Boom! The dynamite exploded sending a pile of rubble down on the men. Terrified, they started to run away.

Josh shot the first one in the back, and caught the second in the shoulder spinning him around, and falling out of sight. Josh knew he had not killed the second man, but definitely slowed him down.

Zeke spotted the third man slowly trying to climb the ridge below Josh and Jeremy. He waited patiently for the man to clear the brush, and then shot him in the back. The captain saw him fall and fired once again at Zeke, but smartly Zeke had ducked down after his shot.

Jeremy threaded his bow, Josh lit the fuse, and Jeremy's aim this time was on target. It hit the wall just above the man Josh had shot in the shoulder, and exploded on impact killing the man instantly.

Josh looked over at the rock where Zeke and Yuma were. He spotted Zeke. He signaled one or two left with his fingers. Zeke nodded and ducked down. Josh crawled to a second log and studied the ground below. He saw no movement in the valley below. Where was the captain, he wondered?

Suddenly, he caught a glimpse of the captain as he made his way past the last fallen tree and ran across the trail. Josh brought his Winchester up and fired, but missed as the captain disappeared around a big rock. Josh crawled back to Jeremy.

"There's at least one left, and he has crossed the valley, and could be crawling his way up to Zeke and Yuma."

"What do we do?"

"Take your rifle and watch the ridge on the other side. If you get a shot, take it immediately, and don't you dare hesitate. I'm going to take my Sharps Buffalo Rifle, and move forward a bit, hoping for a clear shot or at the worst drawing his fire so you can nail him. I've also got to warn Zeke."

Josh made the sound of an eagle, but got no reply from Zeke though he had heard it. Yuma heard it, too but Zeke had lost some blood and felt too weak to stand. Josh moved forward to a tree to hide behind.

Boom! Just as he reached the tree, the captain fired his pistol hitting the center of the tree trunk. Boom! Jeremy shot at the captain causing him to dive forward into the brush, but he missed him. The captain quickly rolled and sprinted up the ridge on the north side. Josh ran to the southern ridge, and stopped behind a smaller pine tree.

Boom! Josh heard the bullet zip through the leaves on the ground just pass where he stood. Boom! Jeremy fired catching the captain in the left arm. The captain cursed aloud.

Zeke heard the voice, and turned to bring his rifle up in the direction of the sound. He knew he could not run, so he prepared to shoot his attacker from behind the rock. He whispered to Yuma to run east and hide. The boy grabbed his bow and arrows, and quickly crept away. Josh saw Yuma run, but did not see Zeke. His heart began pumping strong, and he felt his pulse in his temples near his eyes without touching his skin with his fingers. He scanned the forest across the ridge, desperately looking for the captain and any sign of Zeke.

The captain stuffed his handkerchief inside his shirt to slow the bleeding in his upper left arm. He then grabbed his pistol and began making his way up the ridge once again.

Boom! Jeremy got a quick glimpse and fired, but just missed the captain as he dove behind the next big rock.

Zeke heard the bullet, chambered another shell into the Winchester, and brought it up to fire. Josh also chambered a bullet into the Sharps and scanned the ridge. Desperately, he had to find the captain before the captain found Zeke. He knew Zeke could take care of himself, but deep inside, he felt something was wrong.

The captain took a deep breath, rose up just a little, and fired at Josh, hitting the tree over his head, and fired a second shot at Jeremy, just missing his left hand. Then the captain rapidly ran up the ridge.

Boom! Zeke fired when he saw the charging captain lunge for him. Zeke missed him. The captain slugged him hard with his pistol across the face, and yanked the Winchester from his hand.

Josh heard Zeke's Winchester giving him a bit of hope. He searched the ridge, but saw no movement at all. He glanced at Jeremy and felt better, knowing he was okay and aiming his rifle at the rock as well.

The captain grabbed Zeke by the hair and yanked him up to his feet, while moving around to his back, using Zeke's almost limp body as a shield. "Come out with your hands up, or I'll kill this man!" he yelled.

Josh's heart nearly stopped and his knees weakened as he turned his Sharps at the sound. His eyes soon saw the bleeding face of his lover. He also noted the blood on his thigh. Jeremy's eyes watered as he focused on Zeke's bloody face. He knew Josh had the man in his sight. He set his rifle down, picked up his Parker, ran west down the ridge and crossed over. The captain was watching Josh, and missed seeing Jeremy make his move.

251

"I said lay down your guns, or I'll put a bullet in the back of his head!"

Josh glanced back at Jeremy's position and suddenly realized he was gone. Where did he go?

"I am going to count to ten and then I will fire if you don't put down your guns and come out with your hands up. I know there are at least two over there. Where are the others?"

Others, thought Josh. There's only Yuma. He knew better than to give up, as the man would kill Zeke, and then shoot the rest of them. He had to stall for a shot, but the captain was smart, and remained carefully hidden behind Zeke. Josh sighted him down the barrel, but did not find a safe target. He hoped Zeke would move at the last second, giving him a shot at the captain.

The man yelled again as he began the count, "three, four, five… you'd better drop those guns or you are going to see his brains fly all over this ridge. Six, seven, eight…"

Zip! The captain's body shuddered at the sudden impact of the arrow, hitting him in his already wounded left shoulder. Yuma quickly threaded a second arrow. The captain turned and saw the kid just forty feet away and fired. The boy fell backwards.

Before the captain could once again aim his pistol at him, Zeke swung back with his fist as hard as he could, and hit the man just above the groin. The captain groaned and let go of Zeke. It was the moment his partner hoped for.

Boom! Josh fired hitting the right shoulder of the captain that sent him sprawling backwards as the massive shell went all the way through his shoulder taking most of the meat and bone with it. He hit the ground hard, and quickly searched for his pistol, but he had lost it. His right arm was useless, so he used his throbbing left hand and pulled his second pistol from his left holster. He saw Zeke leaning against the rock. He brought the pistol up to fire. He cocked the pistol and put his finger on the trigger.

Boom! Boom! From just ten feet away Jeremy fired both barrels of the Parker shotgun to make sure he didn't miss. The shells took the captain's head clean off, sending it tumbling down the embankment. His torso remained on its feet for a long second before falling forward with a deadly thud and just to the left of Zeke.

Jeremy ran to Zeke and eased him down to the ground. He yelled across the trail, "Josh, hurry! Zeke's been shot. The soldier is dead!" Josh took off on a run heading south, crossed the trail, and began hustling up the other side.

Zeke said, "Jeremy, I can hold the tourniquet tight. Go check on Yuma."

Josh sprinted to Zeke laying his Sharps down beside him. "Are you all right?"

"Let's see," began Zeke sarcastically, "I've been shot in the leg, pistol whipped in the face, and I'm tired of having to eat beef jerky on the run, while I long for a hot cooked meal. I hate to admit it, but I'd love one of your biscuits about now."

Josh smiled. "I see you haven't lost your since of humor, though you might be delirious from the pain and loss of blood."

"If I had any sense, I wouldn't be out here in the woods. Is Yuma okay?"

Jeremy led Yuma back to them, "He'll be okay. The bullet grazed his arm. I put a cloth around it." Yuma smiled at them.

Josh grinned. "I'm glad you're okay, and you, too, Jeremy. I'm glad we're all okay."

"That's relative, as I'm the one on the ground with a bullet in me," said Zeke.

Josh began unbuckling Zeke's pants. Zeke laughed. "Now you want sex? Couldn't you wait until I heal up or something?" The boys laughed.

Josh looked at him, "Shut up and lay back. I need to see the wound, you fool."

Zeke gladly fell limp as Josh pulled his pants and long johns down. He easily saw where the bullet entered his leg. He rolled him slightly over while Zeke moaned and groaned. Josh let out a good sigh.

Zeke asked, "Are you looking at my cute ass again? You've got to behave yourself in front of the children," added Zeke, trying to see what Josh was looking at. Jeremy and Yuma began laughing again.

"No, I wasn't looking at your cute butt, although I admit it is. The bullet went straight through. I'll bandage you up, and we'll get out of here, and go home."

"Sounds good to me," replied Zeke.

Josh carried him down the hill while the boys gathered their weapons. Jeremy crossed the trail and went up the hill on the other side to fetch the weapons he and Josh had to leave behind. Josh insisted they reload just in case they ran into more trouble with bad white men or a wandering group of warriors from another tribe. They drank some water, gathered up all the soldier's weapons, added the extra guns and ammunition to the packhorse, saddled up, and began the long ride home. They had only gone about a mile when they found most of the horses belonging to the former soldiers. While Zeke waited in the saddle, they removed anything marked with the CSA stamp, as well as personal effects, tied the horses one after the other, and the lead horse to Jeremy's packhorse, so they could take them as well. The stringer horses followed easily, and seemed glad to be rid of the soldiers as well. Josh didn't plan to stop for anything, but water for the horses until they could get home. Silently, they began the final ride home.

TWENTY-EIGHT

In the two months since returning home to their cabin in the center of their vast land holdings, they finally quit wearing their pistols around the farm, though they often kept a rifle handy and the usual knife in their boot. The fertile land made up for their shortcomings in preparing the soil a bit late in the season, since they spent most of the spring and part of the summer chasing Indians and rough riders. Not one of them had eaten a single bite of beef jerky since arriving home after chewing it daily on the long posse ride. They were preparing to sit down and enjoy the hot meal that Josh had begun cooking late that afternoon. Yuma and Jeremy set the table while Zeke and Josh pulled pots off the fire. The foursome always worked in a tandem effort for the greater good and appetite of all.

Together, they had made six trips to Denver, pulling three to four packhorses filled with as many supplies as possible. With two boys in the household, they needed linens and blankets, along with clothes, boots, and hats. Josh had run into the lieutenant on his way out of the bank, but when asked if he had seen the renegades lately, he replied no. Jeremy offered to let Yuma stay with him, ironically in Yuma's old room, so they built bunk beds in Jeremy's room like Josh and Zeke had in the academy. Yuma asked them to cut his hair like theirs, but after they got started on Yuma, everyone soon took a turn. The next day they arrived in Denver with fresh new haircuts, as if they were greenhorns from back east.

Zeke and Josh once again sat Jeremy down and asked him if he wanted to stay, or was there a relative he wanted to stay with. Jeremy listened as they explained what their life was like on the farm in the Rockies, and how tough it was in the winter. Jeremy laughed. "You fellows have forgotten, I already spent a winter with you. I know what the winter is like. I love the snow."

Josh grinned. "I meant it can get lonely here sometimes. You might need friends your own age that you can pal with and girls you can flirt with."

Jeremy laughed. "You are my own age plus a few years. You certainly don't act your age, except of course when it comes time to shoot, hunt, and kill. Don't worry about me. I'm fine. I love it here. I dreamed of getting out of the city. As hard as the trail was hunting the Indians and the riders, I loved it. And when it comes time for me to find a girlfriend, I'll go to Denver or meet one of the settler girls at the edge of the plains."

Zeke swallowed and then said, "You have been most accepting of our homosexuality, but we wondered if down deep our affection for each other bothers you."

Jeremy fell silent for a moment before raising his eyes to look into their faces. "I never saw my parents love each other. Oh sure, I saw him hump her from time to time, but never making love. You fellows are amazing. You tease each other constantly, you pick on each other, you push and prod, you throw things playfully at the other, and yet without saying a word to each other, I can see just how much you love and trust each other. I've never met anyone like you. You really love each other," he paused to make sure he had their attention before adding slyly, "almost as much as I love my horse."

They all laughed before Zeke teased him, "If you love your horse so much you can sleep in the barn with him."

"And miss out on Josh's cooking? I don't think so." He paused again while feeling a lump in his throat. "You're now my parents, or my uncles, or maybe my older brothers, and most definitely my best friends. You couldn't run me off here with hot iron poker! I love you. I'll do whatever you say." His voice cracked and his eyes watered. Josh and Zeke immediately hugged him.

Josh spoke first. "Well, I guess that settles it. You can live here as long as you want. This is your new home—our home together. We could build another room on the cabin for Yuma, so you don't have to keep sharing your space."

Jeremy replied, "Yuma is fine where he is, and he is great guy. I thought he was about fourteen, but he's really almost eighteen, so we're very close to the same age. I'd like to learn more about Indians. After what he went through, I think he needs me as a big brother. We'll bunk together this year, and maybe build a room next year if that's okay?"

Zeke patted him on the back. "We are so glad you've joined our family. We love you, too."

One night during dinner, Josh planned to speak to Yuma whose ability to pick up the English language amazed them all. He told them at night while in the village, he would repeat all the English words he knew over and over in his head until he fell asleep. When Mila Hanska was not around, he spoke English to keep his language skills sharp.

Josh said, "Yuma, you have recovered remarkably well from your time with the demon warrior. All three of us are so proud of you and we love you so much. However, it would not be fair to force you stay with us when you might want to rejoin your old tribe and live with your people. Perhaps you miss them and maybe you have relatives who are still alive."

Jeremy tried to break the serious tone he thought might be scaring Yuma. "Yeah, you probably miss running around the village in a loincloth and sitting down on briars to take a crap!"

Yuma laughed and playfully punched Jeremy's shoulder. "I like my white man clothes but they do itch sometimes."

Zeke smiled. "They get better after a few washings, you'll see. The point we're trying to make is we would love for you to stay here, but we would fully understand and support you if you wish to rejoin your tribe. Do you understand?"

Yuma spoke quickly, "I may not understand some of the big words but I sense their meaning. I don't think I have any family left. My father's brothers were killed before he was. My mother was killed when I was captured. I had no sisters or brothers. I'm alone like the white wolf that howls on the mountain.

"I have no desire to go back to my tribe. I've been away too long. They know what Mila Hanska does to his slaves. They would treat me with great shame. I would be an outcast. I would not be allowed to marry, and could be forced from the tribe to wander alone.

"You are my tribe, you are my family, you are the ones I love, and I know you love me back. I want to stay here. I dreamed of being here in this cabin with you every night. I want to live with you, and from now on, live as you live. One day, I might want to search out my people and learn more about them. My early tribal life was hard, but I loved the adventure of it. From hearing Mila Hanska talk, the years of happy hunting grounds for the Indians is over. The white man has changed all that. He would never have changed, but I want to.

"I want to stay—if you'll have me," he added with a lump in his throat.

Josh spoke quickly, "Good, because we love having you here, and we love you with all our hearts. We'll be your family, only you'll have two fathers, and one crazy brother!"

They all laughed as Jeremy made a crazy face to make them laugh some more. Josh said, "Okay, gang, let's get these dishes cleaned up. I have a little reading to do. Perhaps we can head to the hot springs near dark. I sure love these long summer days," added Josh.

Josh had cooked the beef stew, corn, biscuits, and apple pie so the other three washed the dishes and put them away, which was a bit easier after Zeke installed a cast iron sink he had ordered, and installed a new drain and new piping to get the hot spring water to the sink. Josh moved over to the cook fire, sat down in a rocking chair, and unfolded one of the newspapers Ed Leary had saved for him at the mercantile in Denver.

Zeke asked, "What's new in the paper?"

"Well, there is a train route being built north of us that is supposed to go all the way to Sacramento, California. I bet the Indians aren't going to like that. I hope we can't hear it."

"I want to see a train," said Yuma.

"You will, but let's hope we have to ride three days or more to see it. The government has allowed all the Chinese workers who want to immigrate to come to America to help build the railroad. I've never seen a Chinaman."

Zeke grinned. "I have. Many of the ships that docked in our town used Chinese sailors to do their dirty work. They are most often shorter than white men, but fierce when it comes to fighting. They have an unusual but very effective way of fighting. They use their hands and their feet. I'm told they are excellent workers."

Josh smiled and read on. After a few minutes he asked, "Ever heard of Alaska? The United States government bought it from Russia. I wonder what in the hell they plan to do with it. The government has already stolen or acquired the land across the plains to the western coast. According to the map, Canada's land separates Alaska from our continental territories. It gets cold enough here. I can't imagine how cold it gets up there. I get chill bumps just thinking about it.

"It says here that John Wesley Powell, who lost an arm in the Civil War, discovered a grand canyon in southwest Colorado. That might be fun to see. Maybe one day we can take a journey to the north into Canada and look for John and Liz, and another trip to the southwest to see that big canyon. Maybe one day we can see the Pacific Ocean."

Zeke put the dishtowel over the back of a table chair to dry, "Let's go another year. We need to grow as much food as we can, and store it up so we can eat better this winter as well as feed our animals."

Jeremy shot back, "And so we don't have to eat beef jerky all winter!"

Josh laughed. "Maybe, but Zeke has been designing a waterwheel so we can build a mill. You'll soon learn how to eat real grits!"

Zeke laughed. "You'll like them Jeremy. I had some down south in 1865 and…" he pretended to pick his teeth, "I still have some in my teeth. They last forever!"

They all laughed as Josh threw the hastily rolled up newspaper at Zeke.

The horses turned from grazing to watch the four naked humans walk the path to the hot spring as the sun was going down. They wore moccasins on their feet, a towel over their shoulders, and Zeke carried a bottle of wine he bought in the mercantile store.

258

Yuma and Jeremy kicked off their moccasins, and then ran the last six feet and jumped into the pool splashing water up and over the sides. Zeke and Josh laughed as they too made the last leap over the edge into the hot water. They all splashed around for a while before settling down into their favorite soaking spots. Josh took a soft brush to Zeke's back and scrubbed him clean. They swapped around, repeated the gesture, and then tossed the brush to Jeremy who helped scrub Yuma. Yuma scrubbed Jeremy for a little while, and then leaped onto his back, and tried to push Jeremy's head under the water. Jeremy managed to flip him over, and together, they crashed into the water.

Josh and Zeke laughed at the boys, and then settled back into a tight cuddle as they kissed, and then looked up at the summer stars. "This is the most beautiful spot in the whole world," said Zeke.

Josh sighed, "You're right. We had to fight our way here, and this year we had to fight to save Yuma and others in the mountains and plains not far from here. I cannot imagine life being any tougher."

Zeke smiled. "Wait a minute, life was tough for a while, but look how easy we have it now. We're soaking in the hot water we get for free all year long, and now we have two sons to share it with."

"Yeah, but I think we have to keep feeding them," teased Josh.

"Perhaps, but they are also helping us grow better food."

"I know, but the other day I was thinking about the girl and the two boys we rescued from the tribe, you know, the ones that we had to leave with the soldiers. I wonder how they are doing."

Zeke smiled. "It is so weird how you and I think alike. When we were in Denver last week, I went to the telegraph office and fired off a message to the fort. I went back after lunch and got a reply. They were transported back to Jackson, Mississippi to live with their aunt and uncle. They have been there for about three months. I then sent a message to their uncle who works part-time in town, and he replied how grateful he was for saving his niece and nephews. He and his wife have a farm and two kids of their own."

"So they now have five kids to take care of? My goodness, that is a bunch of mouths to feed. Maybe we should send them some money," added Josh.

Zeke smiled slyly, "I knew you would say that. I removed the hidden gold bag in my rifle sleeve, and bought a doll from Ruth. Together, we removed some of the padding from the center of the doll and hid the gold bag inside. She sewed it up so it looked like new. We packed it in a small packing crate with various can goods and then nailed it down tight. Ed shipped it for us. I sent the three kids a telegraph and told them how proud we were of them.

I told them we sent them a box of food and a doll. I told them there was a surprise inside the doll."

"You're crazy to send that gold across the country in the doll. Someone will steal it," said Josh.

Zeke smiled broadly. "I doubt it. We marked the crate 'dried buffalo shit'!"

All of them busted out laughing. "I can't wait for them to open that crate," laughed Zeke.

"I hope they write us back, but more importantly, I hope it will help get their life back on track," said Josh.

Suddenly, the cow mooed repeatedly, and the horses starting running in circles and neighing loudly, and then reared back on their hind legs swinging their front hooves wildly. The younger boys stood up in the pool and saw the cow hustling towards the barn, followed by the chickens and the horses.

They stood there naked with the water draining from their bodies and wondering what in the hell was wrong. Josh and Zeke stood up as well. The moon broke from behind a small cloud shining brightly down on their wet steaming backs. As they looked over at the barn, they suddenly realized they were in the midst of a large shadow.

Slowly, they all turned to see what was making the large shadow. Their mouths fell wide open as they looked up into the face of a large grizzly bear. The bear stood at least eight feet tall and weighed easily over nine hundred pounds. He did not seem to be afraid of the naked boys, but looked at them with great curiosity.

Josh whispered, "Don't move. Hold very still."

Zeke whispered back, "Should I grab the hidden pistol?"

"I don't think a pistol would hurt him," replied Josh. "You tried that last time."

Zeke laughed. "Maybe we should use the pistol to shoot ourselves before he eats us!"

Josh grinned. "I was thinking we should feed him something."

Jeremy spoke up, "Feed him what? We're naked!"

Josh smiled. "I think we should feed him Yuma. He would make a great appetizer."

Yuma gulped. He did not know what an appetizer was, but he hoped Josh was kidding.

"I think we should make a run for the cabin," said Zeke.

Josh agreed, "Okay, I'll count to three, and then we'll all take off running. One, two…"

Josh leaped out of the pool followed by Zeke, and then Yuma and Jeremy began sprinting towards the cabin.

"You cheated," yelled Jeremy.

"Tell it to the bear. He's right behind you!" exclaimed Josh.

Jeremy looked over his shoulder and the bear had dropped to all fours, and must have thought the boys were playing chase. He took off after them in a playful, waddling gallop. Yuma screamed as they reached the porch, and then all four of them ran into the cabin. Josh slammed the door and bolted it shut with the cross board.

The bear came up on the porch and began sniffing under the door. "I see his nose!" yelled Yuma as he nervously backed up to the opposite wall.

The nose disappeared and soon they saw his black snout underneath the crack of a hastily boarded up window. He once again stuck his wet nose in the crack and then retrieved it. He then let out a large growl, as if beckoning the boys to come on out and play. The noise made the dishes rattle in the cupboard. When they didn't respond, he sat down in front of the door and put his head down to wait and rest like an old hound dog.

Josh whispered, "What is he doing now?"

Zeke replied from looking through the cracks in the door. "He's sleeping right in front of the door."

"Sleeping?" asked Jeremy.

"Yeah, he's snoring," replied Zeke with a grin.

"What do we do now?" asked Jeremy.

Josh teased, "I still think we should feed him Yuma! He's the youngest."

They all laughed, but Yuma did not think it was that funny. Yuma announced, "I'm going to bed. You guys can deal with the bear." He turned and made his way to the bedroom. They all laughed at him.

"I guess we'll go to bed, too. Jeremy, you're in charge of the bear," said Zeke as he took Josh's hand and led him to their room. They fell on the bed and began kissing and exploring each other's warm skin—a prelude to their intended lovemaking.

Jeremy looked at the door, looked back at Yuma in his room, and over to Josh and Zeke, and then said loudly, "I'm going to give him one of Josh's biscuits. One bite of those things and he will surely take off running!"

TJ Johnson
November 2008
January 2010 Revised

EPILOGUE

I began the rough draft of this sequel wondering if I could create new story lines from old characters and felt anxious to try. Ideas crept up as I drove across the country, or in my dreams during the night, but finally the time came to punch the keys and bring a new tale of adventure to life.

I was hooked on the story two pages in, and just could not wait to finish it. I finished the rough draft sixty-four days later, but forced myself to put it aside, and complete the editing of **Stranded** and **The Will**. What a joy it was to return to the story in the fall and begin the editing process.

As I made the corrections, new plots began bouncing around my brain for **The War Beyond – Part III.** After I finish the production of **The Raceboys, Gay Grifters**, and editing **A Writer's Fantasy – About His Favorite College Basketball Team and his Favorite Player**, as well as **The Blackfeet Boys,** I'll begin working on new adventures for Josh, Zeke, Jeremy, and Yuma. The story will parallel the arrival of the first Transcontinental Railroad, as it brings the east and west coasts seemingly closer together. Meanwhile, the famous Blackfeet warriors descend from northern Montana in a desperate attempt to save their hunting grounds, they cross paths with a group of Chinamen on the run, and Jeremy's heart is broken. When the town asks for their help, they are forced to use their well-honed hunting and tracking skills. I hope you'll join me on another exciting journey for Josh and Zeke.

TJ Johnson
November 2008

Acknowledgements

I must give high praise to my editing friends, and their amazing patience to put up with my mistakes.

Author TJ Johnson

TJ began writing his stories in the eighties, mostly for fun and for friends. He was still working full-time for someone else and the career took up more time than he wished. In 2005, he began working for himself with hopes of spending more time on his writing. On the computer were several novels not yet produced, so while writing new material, he began searching for outlets for the books he'd completed. His favorite part of writing is the crafting of the rough draft, a period in the process when the words fly from the storage center deep in his brain like a movie stuck on fast-forward. The agonizing part begins with the painstaking restructuring as the editing begins, but it is a joy when the tale is finally finished. TJ often works on three stories at once, each in different stages of production. He does this to keep his creative skills at peak performance, and because he believes fiction is just too much fun!

His new release is **The Raceboys** about a national champion forced to come out as a gay driver. Also available is **The Will** and **Stranded.**

Coming Soon: TJ is currently polishing "**A Writer's Fantasy**" about his favorite college sport basketball, as well as his favorite player. In the story, he plays himself as he writes about the fictional Taylor University's historic basketball program, and the circumstances that led up to meeting their star player. The story tells how they fell in love, and TJ begins writing a book called "A Backstage Pass to Taylor University's Basketball Championship." It is meant to a be a funny, improbable, love story, but as TJ states in the beginning, "It's MY fantasy, and I'll write it anyway I please," which means in the story TJ is thinner, has more hair, and far better looking!

Currently TJ is editing **The Blackfeet Boys** set in the northwest in a time when two young warriors must abandon their home with the most feared and blood thirsty tribe in North America, and search for a safe and isolated world together. Followed by **Gay Grifters:** Chris Connors learns his new friends not only steal your wallet and gold, but also your heart and soul! With little honor among thieves, these young gay men take pleasure in robbing their tricks, while aiming for bigger scores. Will the biggest thief in America give up a life of crime for a lifetime of love? Only the tale will tell.

Fans of the War Series (**The War Apart - Part 1, The War Ahead - Part 2**) will be pleased to know that the research is finished, and the writing has begun on **The War Beyond - Part 3**.

Future works may be on the website where you can register for advance notice of new releases. You might enjoy reading the TJ's blog on the website as well.

Requests for additional information and Inquiries can be obtain from **Hard Title Publishing,** at **Info@ItsFiction.com**

WWW.ItsFiction.Com

Contact TJ Johnson at:

Info@ItsFiction.com

1. I try to answer all my email myself; however please read "Bio & Info" on the website before writing as your question – saving time for all! Many readers ask the same questions repeatedly.

2. Please do not add my email address to any group for jokes, thoughts, prayers, or riddles, etc. I always delete these without reading.

3. I do not open any emails with attachments as these may contain viruses or other nonsense!

4. Please do NOT write suggesting plot lines as I delete these quickly, too. I like to write my own stories. If your plot is good, write it yourself! Do not send your manuscript to me – I am a writer, not a publisher, and I do not have the time.

5. All characters and names are part of my imagination and indicate no one particular. If I like a person's name, I may use the first or the last name but never both at the same time. It is true some of the events in my books are historical in nature but many are not. Choosing which to believe is your job, but this is why fiction is fun.

6. If you do not receive a reply, perhaps "Bio & Info" contain the answer already, or your email address is not functioning correctly.

7. If you have read all the above, I cannot wait to hear from you!